[redacted]
MW01706868

Fires of Solstice

JUDY MAYS

Ellora's Cave
Romantica Publishing

What the critics are saying...

3 Stars ~ *Romantic Times Reviews*

5 Hearts "FIRES OF SOLSTICE is a refreshingly different shape-shifter story. Ms Mays managed to give the werewolf mythology a very interesting new twist. As soon as you start reading you will get completely sucked in to the story and it will keep you captivated till the end. The book is full of suspense and it will keep you on the edge. [...] FIRES OF SOLSTICE is a real keeper for all fans of shape-shifters. You can't do anything wrong with a book by Ms. Mays!" ~ *Love Romance and More Reviews*

"Full of action and adventure *Fires of Solstice* is a wonderfully dramatic addition to Ms. Mays stable. I believe *Fires of Solstice* is a strong stand-alone story. [...] The heat between the pair is enough to keep you warm and toasty but doesn't flame to the same temperatures as Ms. Mays earlier books. [...] You can't help but read on to the thrilling completion of *Fires of Solstice*." ~ *Erotic-Escapades Reviews*

"Never before have I read about a man with more dedication to his mate's happiness even as he's torn between that love and his commitment to his pack." ~ *Two Lips Reviews*

An Ellora's Cave Romantica Publication

www.ellorascave.com

Fires of Solstice

ISBN 9781419957390
ALL RIGHTS RESERVED.
Fires of Solstice Copyright © 2007 Judy Mays
Edited by Mary Altman.
Photography and cover art by Les Byerley.

This book printed in the U.S.A. by Jasmine-Jade Enterprises, LLC.

Electronic book Publication June 2007
Trade paperback Publication March 2008

With the exception of quotes used in reviews, this book may not be reproduced or used in whole or in part by any means existing without written permission from the publisher, Ellora's Cave Publishing, Inc.® 1056 Home Avenue, Akron OH 44310-3502.

Warning: The unauthorized reproduction or distribution of this copyrighted work is illegal. Criminal copyright infringement, including infringement without monetary gain, is investigated by the FBI and is punishable by up to 5 years in federal prison and a fine of $250,000.
(http://www.fbi.gov/ipr/)

This book is a work of fiction and any resemblance to persons, living or dead, or places, events or locales is purely coincidental. The characters are productions of the author's imagination and used fictitiously.

Also by Judy Mays

Celestial Passions: Brianna
Celestial Passions: Sheala
Heat 1: Perfumed Heat
Heat 2: In the Heat of the Night
Heat 3: A Midsummer Night's Heat
Heat 4: Solstice Heat
Nibbles 'n' Bits (*anthology*)
Rednecks 'n' Rock Candy

About the Author

Foxier than a Hollywood starlette! More buxom than a Vegas show girl! Able to undangle participles with a single key stroke!

Look! At the computer!

It's a programer!

It's a computer nerd!

No! It's—Judy Mays!

Yes, Judy Mays—romantica writer extraordinaire who came to Earth with powers and ablilities far beyond those of mortal writers. Judy Mays! Who can write wild, wanton werewolves, assertive, alluring aliens and vexing, vivacious vamps. Who, desguised as a mild-mannered English teacher in a small Pennsylvania high school, fights a never ending battle for Heroic Hunks, Hot Heroines, and Sexy Sensuality!

Judy welcomes comments from readers. You can find her website and email address on her author bio page at www.ellorascave.com.

Tell Us What You Think

We appreciate hearing reader opinions about our books. You can email us at Comments@EllorasCave.com.

FIRES OF SOLSTICE

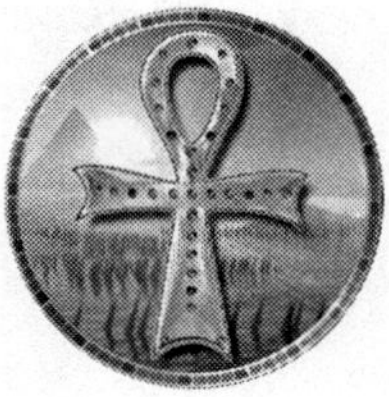

Trademarks Acknowledgement

The author acknowledges the trademarked status and trademark owners of the following wordmarks mentioned in this work of fiction:

Animal Planet: Discovery Communications Inc.

Brillo: Church and Dwight Company Corporation

Heineken: Heineken Brouwerijen

Jell-O: Kraft Foods Holdings, Inc.

Jerry Springer: Universal TV Distribution Holdings LLC LTD

Nike: Nike Inc.

Twilight Zone, The: CBS Broadcasting Inc.

V8: CSC Brands Inc.

Waterford Crystal: Waterford Wedgwood PLC Company

Weather Channel, The: Weather Channel Inc.

Chapter One

"Damn it! Why did James *order* me to come back? My source was ready to crack. Just one more day and I would have had proof of the corruption in the last two major highway contracts!"

Ignoring the shocked glances of her coworkers, Meredythe stomped into the elevator and punched the button for the top floor. After glaring at the blinking numbers, she closed her eyes and inhaled deeply. Leaning her forehead against the cool metal wall, she struggled to control her anger. She had worked so long and so hard on this story, using vacation days and weekends to dig up enough information to warrant an investigation. James had even encouraged her and, up until now, had supported her one hundred and ten percent. Meredythe gritted her teeth and bit off a profanity. James King was her mentor even more than he was her boss. He'd always encouraged her to keep digging and never give up on a story. What had changed?

Biting her lips, she pushed herself away from the wall, clenched her hands into fists and dug her nails into her palms. James had to know something she didn't. Meredythe sucked in another deep breath. She had to calm down.

Her chest rose and fell as she inhaled then exhaled, inhaled, exhaled, inhaled.

She *would* discuss this with James in a rational manner.

One, two, three, four…

He was a fair man. Barging into his office and making demands wouldn't get her anywhere.

Five, six, seven…

She was a professional. She would speak calmly and logically.

Eight, nine, ten.

Squaring her shoulders, Meredythe unclenched her fists and smoothed her skirt.

When the elevator door opened, she tucked some loose curls behind her ear, took one last deep breath and stepped into the opulent reception area. Ignoring her boss's assistant, she headed straight for the door to the inner office.

Unfortunately, her intentions to have a calm conversation lessened with each step as the disappointment she struggled to control roared to life again.

The secretary leaped to her feet. "Ms. Welsh!"

Meredythe stepped past her, shoved the door open and stomped into the room. "What the hell is going on, James?"

"I'm sorry, Mr. King..." began the flustered secretary who'd followed Meredythe into the office.

"Don't worry about it, Mrs. Donovan," the distinguished gray-haired man seated behind the desk answered. "I wanted to see Ms. Welsh anyway. Just don't let—"

Meredythe didn't let him finish. She strode across the room, leaned forward and flattened her hands on his desk. Staring into his face, she mustered as calm a voice as she could. "I really need to talk to you about—"

He nodded. "Me calling you back from Albany."

Silence echoed around the room for a few seconds.

"I have another story I want you to work on."

Meredythe stared at her boss as if he'd grown another head. He never pulled her from one story to put her on another. "Another story? I don't want another story." Closing her eyes, she straightened and swallowed. She had to control her temper! Arguing with James wouldn't get her anywhere. He was just as stubborn as she was.

Her boss's voice was gentle. "Believe me, Meredythe, you won't be losing anything. Go on back to your desk and I'll be down to talk to you in a few minutes."

Someone behind her cleared his throat.

Yanking her eyes open, Meredythe flushed then paled. That wasn't James. Holy shit! There were people over by the bar, hidden from view when she pushed the door open. She'd just barged in on a meeting and started arguing with her boss. He had every right to bust her back to the mailroom for this. Refusing to look around the room, she shifted her weight from one foot to the other and considered her options. At this point, discretion was the better part of valor.

She nodded once. "I'll see you later then."

Pivoting, Meredythe took a single step and plowed into a cotton-covered wall.

The scent of crisp, pine-fresh cologne and warm male enveloped her.

Stumbling, she grabbed on to the bare forearms that had risen to steady her. As her fingers slid through the fine, silky hair covering them, a vortex of heat exploded in her groin and radiated out through her body. Her nipples puckered, her stomach muscles shuddered and her pussy tightened. Gasping, she glanced up…and fell into twin pools of molten silver.

As the room spun around her, Meredythe's world rocked on its axis. Her heart thudded in her chest. A sudden, excruciating stab of pain in her side forced all the air from her lungs and disappeared immediately. Fading visions of fires and wolves flitted through her mind—teasing, tantalizing. Closing her eyes, she sucked in a deep breath. What was happening to her?

She opened her eyes.

The stranger's possessive gray gaze bore into hers, delving into her soul, probing, searching…for what?

Jerking herself free—both from his grasp and his gaze—Meredythe stepped back and glared at him.

Long black hair tumbled over a wide forehead and about broad shoulders, and at least two days' growth of whiskers sprouted from a strong chin and lean cheeks. His nose was crooked and his lips were twisted into a slight smile.

But it was his eyes that compelled Meredythe's attention—dark, stormy gray eyes the color of molten steel. Secrets were hidden in their depths—strange, uncanny secrets that teased her intellect and plucked at her curiosity. Her spine tingled as a jolt of electricity danced up her back. Who was this man? Why did he look at her as if he knew her? She'd never seen him before. Had she?

Gently, he brushed a curl from her cheek.

His voice was a low growl. "Come with me."

Her mouth dropped open. Then, her thoughts roiling, she snapped it shut and wrenched herself free from his mesmerizing gaze. This had to be one of the worst days of her life! First James took her Albany story away. Now some stranger was trying to pick her up, in her boss's office yet!

Gritting her teeth, Meredythe fought down the urge to do what he asked, to leave with him, to discover the passion his eyes promised. The last thing she needed was an arrogant, pain-in-the-ass man and all the complicated baggage that came along with one.

"Come with you? Are you kidding? Bullshit! I don't even know you, and I don't want to. Get lost." Summoning up as much disdain as she could, she continued, "And you need to comb your hair. Better yet, get a haircut and a shave."

Placing both hands against his chest, she shoved him.

It was like trying to move a brick wall.

For a few seconds, the warmth from his wide chest seeped into her palms, traveled along her arms to her torso and filled her entire body.

Her breasts tingled. Moisture pooled between her legs. God help her, she wanted him.

Refusing to accede to her body's demands, she jerked her hands away, sidestepped him and rushed out the door.

Astonished, Bleddyn glanced at the other two men. "What's wrong with her?"

Both James and Rhys struggled to hide grins.

"There's nothing wrong with her," James answered. "This is the twenty-first century and she's an independent woman."

"Independent or not, she's mine." Without another word, Bleddyn leaped through the door after Meredythe.

Still fuming and muttering obscenities under her breath, Meredythe barreled into the break room and slammed the door closed. Pain-in-the-ass men! All they did was screw with her life. God, how she wanted to punch something!

Pushing the tantalizing stranger from her mind, she concentrated on her mentor. All those months spent on that story, gathering leads and information. And what did she have to show for it? Not a thing. She'd always thought James King was a fair man. But now…

He wants to give you another story, interrupted her inner voice. *Maybe it's better.*

Meredythe contemplated that thought for a moment. Then she shook her head. "The Albany story is Pulitzer Prize material," she muttered to the empty room. "It's *my* story."

The desire to punch something grew stronger. Taking a deep breath, she forced herself to relax. She had to control her temper. And brooding certainly wouldn't do her any good. No. She had to formulate a plan to get her story back. She rolled her neck and shoulders, trying to work the kinks out of the knotted muscles. Closing her eyes, she opened her mouth and breathed deeply, then exhaled slowly once, twice, a third time. The knot in her stomach began to relax.

She heard the door open. Too soon for James. Some coworker then.

"Not now. I need to be alone."

"But I want you *now*."

That voice! Damn all fucking men to hell! Spinning around, Meredythe stared at the stranger from her boss's office. His silvery-gray eyes bored into hers. Six feet tall, wickedly lean with muscles clearly defined by his tight, black t-shirt and jeans, he exuded sensuality.

A shiver danced its way up Meredythe's spine and shattered the composure she'd regained as she let her gaze slide down his body. Damn, but he was a hunk. If only he would turn around so she could get a look at his ass. A picture of him standing naked before her flashed in her mind. Her cunt muscles tightened and her nipples tingled. She looked back up into his face.

The corners of his mouth lifted slightly. Amusement appeared in his eyes. "Like what you see?"

Jerking her gaze from his, Meredythe's anger burned higher. How could she find such an arrogant man attractive? She hated arrogant men.

He held out his hand. "Come to me."

Meredythe's eyes widened and heat surged to her face. What was she, a dog? "Bullshit! Just who the hell do you think you are?"

He didn't answer. Instead he kicked the door closed and stalked toward her, his muscles sliding smoothly beneath his clothing.

He moves so effortlessly, like an animal. "What do you want?" she challenged again when he stopped before her.

His eyes bored into hers. "You."

"Me!" she sputtered. This was the last straw. "And just what makes you think—"

Before she could finish, he cupped her face gently but firmly between his hands, nuzzled her mouth with his, then slid his lips over hers.

Shocked, Meredythe froze.

As his spicy scent surrounded her, soft, tender kisses and delicate flicks of his tongue teased her senses. His supple thumbs caressed her cheeks while his strong fingers massaged the sides of her neck. Slanting his head, he pressed his mouth more firmly against hers and tantalized her lips with the tip of his tongue.

Slowly, her body relaxed and she leaned into him.

He growled low in his throat and sucked on her lower lip.

Something inside Meredythe burst free from its cocoon and exploded into flight. Sighing, she opened her mouth, all thoughts of escape melting away.

With that small victory, he seized control. Kisses that had been gentle now seared her lips, drawing forth a hungry, burning response from the depths of her soul. His tongue invaded her mouth, thrusting and swirling against hers in a dance that became more and more sensuous. His mouth conquered, dominated, demanded. A low moan escaped from her throat as she melted against him, palms flat against his chest, and began to drown in the raw, blatant passion of his kiss.

Wrapping one arm around her waist, he laced the fingers of his other hand through her hair and pulled her head even closer.

Teeth clashed against teeth and tongues stabbed and swiped.

Her teeth slid across his lip.

For a second, the metallic taste of blood rolled across Meredythe's tongue, then a bonfire ignited in her soul.

Trapped in a kiss that seemed to drag her soul from her body, she plummeted into a maelstrom of desire.

The tight knot in her stomach exploded with fiery heat that surged through her veins. Moaning deep in her throat, she grasped his soft cotton shirt and tugged at it, trying to rip it away from his body so she could slide her hands across the taut muscles of his chest. As her nerves sizzled, her nipples puckered into tight, aching buds. Hot moisture pooled between her legs and she spread them apart and tried to straddle his thigh.

His groan answered hers as he slid his hands down her back, cupped her behind and pulled her hips against the hard ridge of his erect cock. Then, as he kneaded and massaged her ass with his left hand, he yanked her blouse free from her skirt, slid his right underneath it and cupped her breast.

Ignoring the warning bells clamoring in her head, Meredythe slid her hands up his chest, wrapped her arms around his neck, pushed her breast farther into his hand and sucked his tongue into her mouth.

His harsh whiskers scratching her cheek and chin, he ravaged her mouth with his as he dropped his arm from around her waist.

A low growl rolling in his throat, he squeezed her breast then slid his fingertips down her rib cage, over the waistband of her skirt and along her thigh only to jerk her skirt up to her waist. A hard yank ripped her pantyhose off her stomach. As the flap of nylon sagged, he slipped his hand beneath her silky panties and cupped her moist cunt. Heat branded her ass as he cupped her butt with his other hand to hold her still.

Whimpering, she ground herself against his stroking fingers. Slowly he caressed her clit, swirled his fingers around it, then rubbed again harder.

Gasping, Meredythe pulled her mouth from his, spread her legs farther apart and threw back her head.

"Yes," she hissed. Lord, but his fingers were magic.

"That's it. Open yourself to me."

Immersed in the sensuality he'd wrapped around her, Meredythe simply moaned affirmatively and ground her cunt against his hand. So close… She was so close to coming. Just a few more rubs…

He pinched her clit. His voice was a low growl. "You are mine." Then, as he started to slide a single finger inside her, he leaned forward, slid his tongue and teeth along her jaw to where her neck and shoulder met and nipped her—hard.

That single, sharp pain shattered the sensual haze surrounding her.

Wrenching her eyes open, she froze in his arms. What was she doing? A complete stranger had her clothing half off and his fingers in her cunt. What was wrong with her? No man had ever been able to conquer her sense of self before. This one, though, this stranger…she was putty in his hands. Passionate putty. Deep in her soul, she knew he could make her do anything he wanted. It frightened her more than anything else ever had.

Fear of her passionate reaction to the stranger galvanized Meredythe and provided her with the strength to jerk out of his arms and fall against the table behind her. Gripping the edge to keep from falling, she sucked in great gasps of air. Trembling, eyes wide, she stared at him. He was a complete stranger and she was ready to let him fuck her! What the hell was wrong with her?

Silver eyes glistening with flecks of gold, he smiled ferally, lifted the fingers that had been playing in her pussy to his mouth and sucked on them. Then, nostrils flaring slightly, he slid his fingers from his mouth and held out his hand.

As Meredythe stared at his hand, a moaning sob stuck in her throat. All she had to do was take his hand and give herself over to him to experience passion such as she'd never dreamed existed—passion that would draw her soul from her body and return it altered beyond recognition.

She wrenched her gaze from his hand to his body.

His legs were braced apart and he made no attempt to hide the huge bulge rising in the front of his jeans.

Her gaze flew to his face.

"Come with me! Now!" he commanded in a low voice, his flinty eyes blazing with a passion she'd never dreamed existed, a passion that now terrified her.

Her body swayed forward.

Her mind rebelled.

Gritting her teeth, she swallowed her sob and yanked her skirt down over her thighs. No! She would not give up her *self*. There wasn't a man alive who could be trusted that much.

His terse, arrogant command fanned the flames of her passion—and anger. Gathering her strength, without thought for the consequences, she stiffened her spine and slapped his face hard. As the sharp crack reverberated around the room, his head snapped to the left and his cheek flushed bright crimson under his dark whiskers. While he stood frozen with shock, she scrambled around to the other side of the table.

Eyes now glowing golden, he braced his hands on the table and leaned toward her.

Shivering, she held her ground. "Touch me and I'll scream this building down."

"No you won't," he growled. "You want me as much as I want you. I can smell the desire for sex on you. I tasted your cum. You're slick and wet, ready for me. You want my cock buried in your cunt so far you can't tell where I end and you begin."

Bracing her own hands on her side of the table, she leaned toward him and spat, "How dare you talk to me like that! I don't know who the hell you are, asshole, but I wouldn't fuck you if you were the last man on earth!"

Before he could answer, the door opened and her boss stood there with another man.

"There you are," James' companion said. "We really must be going."

"Not now!" Meredythe's unwanted visitor snarled as he stared at her.

Their noses only inches apart, they stood frozen in place, their gazes locked in a silent battle.

Visions of their hot, straining bodies entwined together appeared in Meredythe's mind and she blinked first, her breath catching in her throat as she stared into his molten gaze.

She swallowed the whimper in her throat and battled down the urge to throw herself into his arms.

He didn't move a muscle.

Meredythe locked her knees together and refused to back away. She would not give him the satisfaction.

"Afraid so, my boy," the dignified stranger calmly interrupted again in a proper British accent.

Snarling, her tormentor raked his gaze up and down her body. "We'll finish this later." Spinning away, he vanished through the doorway.

"When hell freezes over, moron," she snapped at his departing back.

The older man glanced at her boss. "I'll see you later."

James nodded and waved. "Dinner tomorrow then."

Still fuming, Meredythe glared at the open doorway. Who was he? No man had ever made her feel like that. If he hadn't bitten her, she'd have fucked him right here on the table with no thought for the consequences of her actions. Slowly she dropped into a chair. Confused by the passion that the stranger engendered in her, Meredythe struggled with her jumbled thoughts. Why did she feel like she knew him? He was so dark, powerful, dangerous… No, not just dangerous—deadly. More so than any other man she'd ever met. She should be scared to death of him. Why then was she absolutely certain that he would never hurt her?

She shook her head. How could she know that? She'd never seen him before in her life. Had she? That kiss. Her fingers strayed to her lips. No man had ever kissed her like that. It seemed as if he'd wanted to suck her very soul from her body and give her his in return.

"Meredythe?"

Dropping her hand to her lap, she focused on her boss. "Who was he? What was he doing here?"

"I'm here to talk about your investigation," he interrupted as he poured himself a cup of coffee.

With the source of her agitation gone, Meredythe wrestled the dark-haired stranger and the passion she'd shared with him to the back of her mind and concentrated on what her boss had to say. Hope surged. "I'll finish the Albany investigation?"

He shook his head.

"But…"

He sipped his coffee. "How about a story on a serial killer?"

Her eyes widened, then narrowed. "I don't want an exposé on some guy who's been locked up for twenty years. I'm a better reporter than that."

James stretched out his legs and smiled. "I'm not asking you to write one."

"But there haven't been any murders…"

An amused expression appeared on James King's face as he sipped his coffee.

"Well, you know what I mean." Almost completely at ease now, Meredythe was forced to smile herself. This was New York City after all.

Setting his cup on the corner of the table, James rose to his feet, clasped his hands behind his back and began to pace. "I'm asking you to trust me on this. The police don't even realize what's happening yet. Maybe I'm wrong, but all my instincts tell me there's more to these murders than the police suspect."

Murders? Her interest perked. "What murders?"

Stopping in front of the table, he braced his fists on its edges and leaned toward her. "Three years ago, there was a murder in Central Park. Yeah, I know," he said to her skeptical expression, "murders in the park are not uncommon. This one was different. The victim had his throat torn out."

"What did the police—"

"They filed the usual report and assigned a homicide detective, but after they didn't come up with any leads, they shoved the case to the backburner. The victim was a drug dealer. They were glad to get him off the streets."

Meredythe began taking notes. "Go on."

"A year later, there was a similar murder in L.A. Again, the victim was a minor player with a drug cartel."

"That's two."

"Last year, Chicago. Another drug dealer. And six months later the fourth victim was found—a child molester in Boston."

She was scribbling rapidly on a tablet left lying on the table. "Same MO?"

"Throats torn out."

She looked up expectantly.

"Almost six months ago, Philadelphia, a known hit man for the mob."

She tapped the end of the pen against her lips. "So all of the victims were criminals. Are you sure this isn't the work of a vigilante group of some kind?"

"I'm sure."

She leaned back in her chair, fingers steepled under her chin. "What about a crazy vampire cult?" she asked, searching for a bizarre angle.

James shook his head. "Too much blood. From what I understand, they'd want that."

Meredythe locked gazes with her boss. "How can you be sure all the murders are related? How do I know I won't be wasting my time? I mean, why hasn't some cop somewhere been smart enough to see the similarities among the murders?"

He shrugged. "Probably because they're spread so far apart and the victims have all been criminals. Maybe they aren't related, but something—gut instinct—tells me they are. Are you interested?"

A smile twitched at the corners of her lips. "If this turns out to be the work of one man…"

"You could make a real name for yourself," finished King. "A serial killer. A story like this could get you national recognition. Forget Albany, Meredythe. It's not as important as you think it is."

She leaned back. "How can you be so sure? When that story breaks, heads will roll."

"Not when your informant is already in protective custody."

Meredythe bolted upright. "What!"

"Genova decided to come clean. You scared him, Meredythe. The news will be all over television tonight."

Meredythe stared at her boss. Why had she ever doubted him? "I'll take the new story."

"Good," he said, retrieving a data CD. "Here's the basic background information, and I have some files I'll send down tomorrow. Good luck. And don't bother with the subway tonight. Take a cab home, get a receipt and the company will reimburse you for it."

Quickly ducking her head to mask her surprise, Meredythe took the CD from his hand. He'd not only just saved her hours, maybe days, of work but had also given her a break from using the subway. Too many weirdos rode it on Halloween.

James glanced at his watch and added, "Almost five. Why don't you go home early and wait until tomorrow to start?"

She shook her head. "I'd like to familiarize myself with the information on this CD."

He smiled back. "I thought that would be your answer. If I were a few years younger, I'd have taken this story myself. Good luck."

"I won't let you down."

Her boss stared at her and sighed. "I know a few of your coworkers are angry because you were promoted over them, but you were the logical choice. I'll take care of them. This is your time, Meredythe," he answered enigmatically. "You were never the one at fault."

Puzzled, Meredythe followed her boss through the doorway and slipped into her cubicle. Popping the CD into her computer, she began reviewing the information her boss had provided, grateful that James had sent her friend and coworker Alice home. The last thing she needed was the third degree about that arrogant jerk who'd kissed her. As much as she tried to concentrate on her work, her mind kept asking the same questions. Who was he? Why did she feel like she knew him?

Two minutes later, she caught herself staring blankly at her computer, her responses to the black-haired stranger replaying over and over in her mind. Muttering, she shifted in her chair and squeezed her legs together. Just thinking about him had her juices seeping into her panties. His had been the most sensual kiss she'd ever experienced—so hot and hungry. Just the memory had her melting. With a mental shake, she focused her attention on the screen in front of her. "Get your mind back on your work, Meredythe. You'll never see him again anyway."

However, as she stared at the computer, she realized that she wasn't entirely sure whether the idea of never seeing him again was a relief…or a disappointment.

She shook her head. Why was she thinking about that…that *man*? She had a story to do. Shoving the memory to the back of her mind, she concentrated on the information before her. Soon she was completely engrossed with the data from the CD.

* * * * *

Bleddyn slouched in the corner of the limousine and stared out the window. "I certainly made an ass out of myself, didn't I?" he finally muttered. He glanced at Rhys, grimacing at the smile the older man struggled to control. "You don't have to laugh at me."

Rhys' lips twitched. "You were rather…tyrannical."

Bleddyn looked back out the window. "You waited too long to bring us together. She's too independent. How old is she now—twenty-seven?"

Rhys shrugged. "Not so old for this time. Besides, I didn't think I had any other choice. Four times I've tried to bring you together, and every time I failed." He reached over and gripped Bleddyn's shoulder. "We can't wait any longer. You're spending more and more time with the wolves and it's getting harder for you to live as a human. We must succeed. Going feral would be a disaster for you. The bloodlust will eventually become too strong to fight."

Bleddyn shrugged Rhys' hand off. "I'll manage. Are you sure she's safe? Slade is undoubtedly searching for her."

Rhys turned toward the window. "Undoubtedly. He's been obsessed with her ever since he learned she'd kill the bloodlust in you. Allowing her to grow unguarded was a risk, but it worked. He never expected that. I've always guarded her closely and brought her to you when she was sixteen or seventeen."

Bleddyn snorted. "*Tried* to bring her, you mean."

Rhys smiled. "You were together today."

Bleddyn's snarl echoed around the car. "Will she accept me? She's never had a choice before."

"I believe now that's why I've always failed. We can't force her into your arms. If Meredythe won't accept you for yourself, the ceremony would be nothing more than rape. Violence won't save you—love will."

"Yeah, right." Swallowing his irritation. Bleddyn rubbed his chin. "I didn't exactly get off on the right foot with her." Bleddyn's gaze returned to the New York skyline. The full moon appeared and disappeared between the tall buildings. "Damn it, Rhys. I've never treated a woman like that. You said I wouldn't see her today. I wasn't ready for her! Now she'll probably run screaming in terror when she sees me again."

"Don't underestimate her, Bleddyn. She's a very strong woman," his companion answered. "You could try courting her."

Bleddyn snapped his head around. "What? I've never—"

"Had to court any woman, I know. They've always thrown themselves at you. But none of those women mattered. Meredythe does, and she will not docilely submit to your dictates."

Bleddyn snorted. "I need the moon. Why in the devil's name did you arrange this lecture tomorrow night? You don't normally make mistakes like this."

Steepling his fingers, Rhys cleared his throat. Then he said, "I didn't make a mistake. There have been…inquiries. Subtle inquiries about certain murders. Someone is asking questions. Too bad the lecture isn't tonight. With that new medicine Dr. Haverstrom concocted—"

Sardonic laughter interrupted him. "I've learned not to rely on 'medicine'. I was ready to fuck Meredythe right there on the table like some kind of animal, and where would I have been then?" He turned his head away.

"What happened to your lip?"

Bleddyn fingered the scab that had formed. "She must have cut it with her teeth."

"Did she swallow any of your blood?"

Bleddyn glanced back at his mentor. "I wasn't exactly paying attention to what she was swallowing—except for my tongue."

Rhys started to reply then stopped. He stared at the man he'd raised from infancy. Bleddyn never spoke of women so crudely. His bloodlust was getting worse.

Chapter Two

Meredythe glanced at her watch. 8:15. She'd gotten everything from this data CD that she could. Standing, she arched her back. Lifting her arms above her head, she stretched upward, turning and twisting her neck and rolling her shoulders to work out the kinks that had grown there during the time she'd spent hunched over her computer. "I should've listened to Aunt Evie about my posture," she muttered to herself as she popped the CD out, put it in a plastic case, dropped it into her briefcase and turned off the computer. Grabbing her purse, she shrugged into her coat. As she left, she nodded to the woman cleaning the office and rode the elevator to the lobby. With a "Happy Halloween, Ms. Welsh", the doorman hailed a cab when she stepped outside.

Twenty minutes later, she stepped out of the cab into a group of miniature goblins, witches and ghosts. Wishing them all a Happy Halloween, she hurried into her building. As she entered her apartment, she dropped her purse and briefcase on the small table. A nice, long, hot soak in the tub would be perfect.

"Merrooww!"

"I know, Methuselah, I'm late. I'm sorry. I'll have your dinner in a minute. Only two more days and you'll be home. Then you can boss Aunt Evie to your heart's content," she muttered to the large, fluffy, blue-gray cat. Holding her breath, she opened a can of cat food, dumped it into a bowl and set it on the floor. The strong odor of fish wafted upward. "Jeez, Thuse, how can you eat stuff that stinks so much?"

Disappearing into the bathroom, she turned on the hot water and dumped half a bottle of bubble bath into the old-fashioned clawfoot tub. The heady scent of passionflowers swirled through the air with the steam. After a deep breath, she headed into her bedroom and stripped. For a moment, she stared at the ripped pantyhose she'd been wearing. Then, with a curse, she balled them up and tossed them into the trash.

Glancing at her reflection in the mirror, she started then stepped closer. Her cheeks looked like she'd rubbed a Brillo pad against them.

An unshaven face appeared in her mind's eye.

"No! He was an asshole—not worth thinking about!" She shoved his face from her mind.

Mind fixed firmly on the information she'd reviewed, Meredythe strolled naked into the kitchen, pulled a bottle of white wine out of the refrigerator and poured herself a glass. Wrinkling her nose at the taste, she decided to drink it anyway. It had only been in the fridge a week and didn't taste *that* bad.

Carrying her wine back into the bathroom, she turned on the cold water. Methuselah joined her.

Glancing down at the cat, she smiled. "Care to join me? No? Not interested?" she continued when the cat wrinkled his nose and ambled out the door. Sticking her hand in the water, she swished it around a few times. Perfect.

Turning off both faucets, she set her wine on a small table next to the tub, pinned up her hair and climbed in. Leaning back, she rested her head against the rolled edge of the tub and closed her eyes, willing her tense muscles to relax.

The dark-haired, gray-eyed man appeared in her mind's eye again. His kisses had been the most erotic she'd ever experienced. What would his mouth on her nipples feel like?

Both nipples puckered in response.

A shiver danced down her spine.

Water splashed as she slapped it. Damn it! Who was that guy? Why couldn't she forget him?

The man in her mind smiled and beckoned to her. His clothing disappeared and he stood before her naked.

His erect cock bobbed.

She shivered again.

Water swirled around her as Meredythe shifted. Her pussy began to ache.

As her mind began to travel down new, erotic paths, she rubbed a knuckle against her distended nipple then slid both hands down her stomach. She twirled one finger in her pubic hair while another parted the lips of her pussy.

Her clit was hard.

She rubbed it.

"Mmm." Thrusting her hips forward, she arched her back. Cool air teased her nipples as they rose from the warm water. Warm, silky water caressed her arms.

In her mind, she heard him chuckle seductively.

She rubbed harder at the memory of his fingers sliding, swirling and stroking against her. Her cunt muscles contracted. She was so hot, so ready to come. A few more rubs.

The thought of him thrusting his rock-hard cock into her pussy had her shuddering and gasping.

"Ahh."

Water swirled and eddied as waves of pleasure rolled over her.

"Meerroow?"

Water splashed as Meredythe jerked her hand away from her cunt, sat up and tossed a heated glare in the direction of the huge cat that was using the toilet lid as a platform.

He batted at the bubbles in the tub then stared at her with an all-knowing expression.

Meredythe stared back.

An uncanny light flickered in the cat's eyes.

Grabbing the washcloth and soap, she started scrubbing her legs. He was only a cat. What difference did it make if he watched her masturbate?

She glanced at him again.

He was grinning a Cheshire grin.

"Don't look at me like that." She slapped a small splash his way.

Drops of water scattered as Methuselah shook his head then glared at her. *Only a cat. That's what you think, Meredythe*!

Meredythe shook her head. What was that buzzing in her ears?

With an aggravated hiss, Methuselah jumped to the floor and minced out the open door, tail high in the air, displaying wounded dignity as only an indignant cat could.

Meredythe sent another small splash after him then closed her eyes again, forcing her mind away from the dark-haired, gray-eyed stranger, refusing to acknowledge how her body responded to his blatant sexuality. Instead she compelled herself to review everything she'd read in the last two hours. There was a murderer out there, and she was going to find him.

Quickly she swiped the washcloth over her sensitive nipples. The memory of the stranger kneading her breast surfaced.

No! She would not give in to urges caused by him!

"Fuck! I don't even know what his name is. Forget that asshole, girl. Focus, Meredythe! Focus! Murder. Think murder! Blood! Guts!" Dropping the soap into its dish, she wrenched her mind back to the information she'd been studying.

Three years wasn't all that long. Should she look back farther? What about the dates? There was something there. All the murders happened around June 21 or December 21, except for one on March 21. Why? What was so special about those dates? Aunt Evie would know, but she wasn't home. It was

October now. If this guy followed through, there'd be another murder in December. But where?

With a sigh, she fished the plug out of the drain with her toes and rose, water and bubbles sluicing off her. Wrapping herself in a fluffy towel, she headed for the bedroom where she threw on an old sweatshirt and tattered sweatpants. Returning to the living room, she sat down at her computer.

"The longest and shortest nights of the year," she said to the empty room after a few minutes. "Maybe there is some kind of cult involved."

Yawning, she stretched. "I'm too tired to get involved with this now, Thuse," she muttered to the cat that had jumped up onto her lap. "Besides, if I start, I won't stop, and I have to go to work tomorrow." Shutting down the computer, she rose and scooped the cat into her arms. "Come on. Time for bed."

She yawned again as she snuggled under the covers. Methuselah curled next to her. Pulling him into her arms, she said, "What do you think, Thuse—is this a better story than Albany?"

It will change your life forever, Meredythe.

Meredythe shook her head again. Damn buzzing.

The cat stretched out next to her. His nightly lullaby—a deep rumbling purr—soon had her asleep.

Outside, the sky darkened and wisps of clouds stretched their fingers toward the round moon, obscuring its light. Young Halloween trick-or-treaters were back home, tucked safely in their beds, their dreams filled with visions of gorging on the candy they'd collected. Older revelers were still out and about—the parties they were attending would go on to the wee hours of the morning.

In a select few residences, small groups of white-clad worshipers commemorated the old Druid celebration of Samhain.

In Central Park, a wolf howled.

* * * * *

Sitting up, Methuselah stretched and nudged Meredythe with his nose. Mumbling something incomprehensible, she rolled over. After another long stretch, the cat jumped off the bed, trotted across the room, snaked his way under the drapes and leaped onto the windowsill where the radiance of the full, white moon bathed him with luminescent light. Arching, he rubbed himself against the window then jumped back down to the floor. Nosing around the edge of the drapes, he found the cord that would open them and leaped. His claws caught in the soft rope and the drapes parted. Soft moonlight flowed across the bed.

Meredythe mumbled something and rolled away from the moon's silvery light. Jumping back up onto the bed, Methuselah snuggled next to her and began to purr.

Roll over, Meredythe. The moon beckons.

She mumbled again and rolled back over. Eyes narrowing, Methuselah stared intently into her face. His purr became deeper, its cadences dancing in a rich, melodic rhythm.

Meredythe began to dream…

"This is rape," a woman's voice spat.

Head bowed, Meredythe clawed her way toward consciousness. Rape! Where was she?

Smooth but hard wood braced her back and cradled her buttocks. Clearing the fog from her brain, the scents of rain, fresh pine and wood smoke tickled her nose.

Her voice low and intense, the woman spoke again. "Do you honestly believe Bleddyn will agree to the ceremony with her like this?"

Ceremony? What ceremony? Bleddyn? What did a man named *Wolf* have to do with her? Chin resting against her chest, eyes still closed, Meredythe tensed her wrists slightly. They were bound to the arms of the chair in which she sat. God's breath, she was still a prisoner.

The deep thumps of drums reverberated around her, strong and low, in time with her heart. Better to let them think she was still senseless.

Keeping her head bowed, she slowly opened her eyes and peered out from beneath her lashes.

A man and woman, both dressed in white robes, stood in front of her.

Obviously angry, the woman stood before the man, her hands fisted on her hips. "Has she awakened yet?"

The old druid pushed himself erect and shook his head. "Not yet, Eibhlin."

Frowning, the woman glanced over his shoulder at her.

Meredythe forced herself to breathe normally.

"The potion should have worn off by now. How much did you give her?"

The druid's tired voice held a hint of irritation. "Half again as much as the first dose. She's more spirited than you led me to believe."

The woman tsked and turned her attention back to the druid. "Bleddyn will not take her if she's unconscious."

Meredythe bit the inside of her cheek to keep from screaming. Take her! Again she tensed her wrists against her bonds. She had to find a way to escape.

The druid tugged at his beard. "I didn't have a choice," he answered in a tight voice. "She tried to run away at least half a dozen times during the journey."

"By all the gods," Eibhlin snapped, "did you just throw her on the back of your horse and take her away from everything she's ever known?"

He winced. "There was no time. We had to be here on Samhain—before the sun set."

Eibhlin glared at him. "Does she even know why she's here?"

The druid's shoulders tensed at the woman's question. Muttering something under his breath, he turned away and gestured toward the blazing bonfire. The flames rose into the darkness.

Eibhlin crossed her arms over her bosom. "Fire tricks won't change anything. With her like this, the ceremony will be nothing but rape. Do you honestly believe Bleddyn will agree?"

The druid whirled to face her, his voice low, potent. "He has no choice! The seeress's prophecy is clear. Only the blood of the pure, untainted woman who is destined to be his mate will save him. He must take her or succumb to the bloodlust. Just this once, will you not support me?"

Muscles tense, Meredythe waited for the woman's answer.

Eibhlin opened her mouth as if to say something, but then she dropped her eyes and nodded once. "I've always supported you, Rhys, in one way or another. Now is not the time to argue. I only hope she is not completely traumatized. Your spells are set?"

He nodded. "All the paths are guarded. Only those invited are here."

Both turned to face the bonfire. Beyond them, Meredythe spied men and women leaping about it, the tattoos on various limbs bleeding in and out of the shadows.

The druid mumbled a curse under his breath then snarled, "We are so few now, and little if any hope remains. The acolytes and priests of this new god are driving the old religions and beliefs to extinction. Our time grows short and without the moon, all could be lost. What will we do then? How will we save him? Bleddyn needs—"

Before Rhys could finish, wolves howled deep beneath the shadowed trees. From the small clearing the deafening beats of drums and shrill, whistling bleats of pipes answered them. Then a deeper, more powerful howl rolled about the clearing.

Meredythe glanced toward the shadows beneath the trees.

"He comes," Eibhlin said.

The druid grasped her arm. "You must go now. He'll be angry if he sees you here."

Her nostrils flared. "I have as much right to be here as you do."

Rhys shook his head. "He's had enough trouble accepting what he must do. Having to mount the girl before your eyes…"

Meredythe shuddered. This couldn't be happening!

Eibhlin jerked her arm free and nodded once, sharply. "Mind her then. And have him bring her to me when the ceremony is complete. Mayhap I can soothe her shock." Muttering blasphemies under her breath, she pulled her hood back over her hair and disappeared into the shadowy oak grove.

The druid turned back to Meredythe. "Open your eyes. I know you're awake."

Meredythe stiffened but complied. Angry tears spilled down her cold cheeks as she clenched her teeth. She jerked her wrists impotently against her bonds then spat, "I will not do this! You cannot ask this of me!"

The howls of the wolves grew closer and she shuddered. Her anger drained away to be replaced with fear. In a voice barely above a whisper, she pleaded, "Let me go. Please."

Pity momentarily flashing in his eyes, he stepped to her side and patted her shoulder. "Do not fear, child. Your destiny approaches." Then, as an afterthought he added, "He will not harm you."

As the wailing pipes and thundering drums reached a crescendo, the druid turned away from her and raised his oak staff above his head. Tendrils of dark green mistletoe richly swathed in small, white berries dangled along its length. "Behold," he proclaimed in a powerful voice, "he comes."

The drums and pipes ceased abruptly.

Meredythe strained her eyes, trying to see into the shadows beyond the bonfire. The howling of the wolves rose to an earsplitting crescendo and suddenly ceased. Only the hungry roar of the fire punctuated the silence. The pagan worshipers waited tensely, all eyes turned toward the shadowed forest. Even the dark seemed to wait with breathless anticipation. Jerking harder against her silken bonds, she searched deep within herself for the anger that had sustained her thus far. She would not sit meekly and sacrifice her virginity to some man on a druid's altar. She would fight. Besides, if she could become angry enough, she could keep at least some of her fear at bay and not scream with the terror that threatened to overwhelm her.

A sudden movement drew her eyes to the edge of the clearing where black and gray wisps of night swirled and eddied. A single, triumphant howl reverberated around the clearing as the blackness deepened. Gradually, a form materialized.

Meredythe bit down on her bottom lip to still its trembling when a naked man stepped into the dim light. Violent shudders racked her body as he trod toward the dais, skirting the bonfire that now illuminated his features. Stormy gray eyes were locked on her. His cheekbones were high, his chin firm. His lips were drawn into a slim, angry line. His nostrils flared as if to catch her scent. Thick, black tangles cascaded about his broad shoulders and down his back. Muscular arms relaxed at the sides of his broad chest as his long stride carried him across the clearing.

He was the most compelling man she'd ever seen…and he terrified her.

When he stopped before the dais, she pressed herself back against the smooth wood. Jerking more frantically against her bonds, she still raised her chin defiantly as his gaze traveled the length of her body. By the blessed White Lady, she would not cower before him.

Stepping closer, he loomed over her.

She refused to lower her eyes. She would not look there, between his thighs where his cock hung, thick and heavy. Trembling, she spat, "Get away from me, hell spawn."

He recoiled sharply. Then, eyes narrowing, he bent toward her.

Before he could touch her, the old druid stopped him.

"Wait, Bleddyn, your worshipers seek your blessing."

"They do not worship me," the younger man growled, his stormy gray gaze never leaving her. "This is simply an excuse to give their lust free rein without worrying about the consequences. Release her and I'll take her to Eibhlin."

He did not want her! Meredythe released the breath she was holding when the druid grabbed the naked man's arm and pulled him away from her.

But the druid's words did not offer comfort. "I cannot. You must complete the ceremony. There is only one cure for the bloodlust within you. You must take her tonight, under the Samhain moon."

He jerked his arm from the druid's grasp. "And what ancient laws demand an audience, old man? Why torture her like this? Why must I rut upon her like a stud in full view of his master? I am not an animal and she does not deserve this!"

The druid staggered back.

Hope momentarily flared in Meredythe's heart. The man, Bleddyn, was no more eager for this…ceremony than she was.

The druid raised his head to the sky and muttered something incomprehensible under his breath. Slowly he straightened to his full height. In a low yet powerful voice he said, "Only under the light of the full moon, with the pure and untainted blood from your ordained mate, will the demon of lust and carnage be driven from your soul. Tonight is Samhain, a night of power. Those gathered here bring more power."

"Superstitious nonsense!"

"Don't be a fool, young pup," the druid snapped. "Remember who I am."

A mirthless smile played about the younger man's lips. "Who you were."

Meredythe's eyes darted back to the druid. Only the slight widening of the old man's eyes betrayed how deeply that barb had struck. After what seemed an eternity, he acquiesced. He seemed to grow smaller before her eyes.

When he answered, his voice was softer, quieter. "Very well, who I was. But I have never lied to you."

Time seemed to stand still, but then taut muscles relaxed and a full, wolfish grin raced across the younger man's face. "No, old man, you have never lied to me."

Meredythe sagged with relief when he turned away from her and looked out over those who had assembled. Maybe he'd tell them all to go away. Her relief was short-lived. All fell to their knees. More than one woman, though, raised her head and greedily eyed his naked, muscular form.

The scent of lust permeated the air.

From the back of the crowd, a male voice called out, "Take her, Bleddyn. Mount her. Mate. Be free."

Renewed fear stabbed at Meredythe's heart and she intensified her struggles, moaning as a splinter stabbed her wrist, but the silken cords were too tight. Biting her lip until blood dripped into her mouth, she raised her head when the druid stepped back to her side.

"I'm sorry," he murmured, "but they will be satisfied with nothing else. Only this once…"

"Rape," she hissed, her gaze locked on Bleddyn's muscular back and taut buttocks. "This is rape."

The druid simply shook his head. "They are drunk on mead and anticipation. Without sex, they'll rise up against us. Your fate will be even worse then." He lifted his hand and blew a white powder into her face. "Forgive me."

She coughed then stiffened when she inhaled the powder. Almost immediately, the world began to spin around her.

Bleddyn turned back to her as the crowd grew more raucous. She now sat immobile, muscles refusing to obey her.

A soft, incomprehensible oath escaped his lips. He jerked his head at Meredythe. "What have you done?"

"Calmed her," Rhys answered as he wiped his hands on his robe. "The effects are short-lived, but she must cooperate or the crowd—"

"Damn them to all the seven hells."

"Be gentle with her," the old man whispered as he stepped away.

Deep within her mind, Meredythe struggled to regain control of her body. Tears rolled down her cheeks as she ordered her body to fight, but her muscles refused to comply and all she could do was stare at the naked man before her.

For a moment, his chin dropped to his chest, misery evident in his gaze. "Forgive me this night. I'd give anything to take you away from this…travesty," he said in a low voice. "But I must be free of this bloodlust! You are my only hope."

Leaning forward, he wiped the tears from her cheek, sorrow swimming in his soft gray eyes. "Perhaps the drug will make it easier for you. Later, when we're alone, I'll treat you more gently. I won't mount you again until you know me better."

Releasing Meredythe from her bonds, he lifted her into his arms and cradled her close to his chest. Stepping to the sheepskin-covered altar before the bonfire, he gently laid her down. Glancing about at the worshipers who drew closer, he growled audibly at the lust blatantly evident on their faces.

A woman off to the left bared her breasts.

Internally, Meredythe shuddered though her body remained perfectly still.

Bleddyn ground his teeth and growled, "Damn them all!"

The wolves howled anew.

Turning his attention back to her, he brushed some stray curls from her face. She stared into his eyes, begging silently. He blinked quickly, but not before she saw his tears.

"I'm sorry. Please forgive me," he whispered. Then his hands moved on her body.

Silent screams echoed though Meredythe's mind when he carefully slipped the shift from her shoulders and bared her chest. Cool air swept over her and her nipples puckered. Ever so gently, he traced the dark mole resembling the head of a howling wolf high on her left breast.

Ignoring the lust-filled crowd gathered about him, he pulled her shift down her hips and legs, his gaze halting at V of her thighs. Meredythe's eyes widened when his shaft surged and jerked. Impotently, she willed her arms and legs to respond, to flee the violation to come.

Then the pregnant moon finally burst free of her cloudy prison and luminous white light bathed the clearing. The man at her side threw back his head to absorb her gentle light. Cords of muscle in his neck strained as he howled his triumph.

The wolves answered.

He slid his fingers between her thighs—testing, teasing, seeking a response.

Meredythe's scream echoed only in her mind.

Again the thunder of drums reverberated about the clearing.

Closing her eyes, Meredythe retreated deep into her subconscious, desperately trying to hide from what was to come. Locked away within herself, she would be safe, would feel nothing.

His supple fingers, however, became more and more insistent. She moaned low in her throat, his skilled caresses inexorably drawing her back to consciousness. Her body arched into his hand and she opened her eyes.

The ripe moon framed his powerful form as he bent over her. His stormy gray eyes stared deeply into hers. "Don't fight me. Please," he pleaded. "Just this once. Then I will take you away from here."

Sluggishly, she recoiled. "No!"

"Yes," he growled in a low voice. "We must."

She tried to struggle but her limbs refused to obey. The drug still controlled her.

Effortlessly, he locked his hands around her waist and turned her over. Leaping onto the altar, he knelt behind her, spreading her legs with a muscular thigh, the crisp hairs tickling and teasing the tender skin of her inner thighs.

The soft wool beneath her teased her nipples into aching points. He caressed and cupped her ass, massaging and spreading each cheek. He slid his thumbs down between her thighs until he found the nub hidden in the soft folds of flesh. She moaned again when he pinched it. Her nipples tightened even more as shafts of tingling heat raced into her groin.

Meredythe buried her face in the sheepskins and sobbed. Why did her body welcome his touch when what he was doing was against all the laws of men and gods?

"Forgive me," he growled as he positioned her hips. His hard cock brushed against the inside of her thigh. He slid it between her moist lips, guided the head into the opening of her quim and gathered himself for his first thrust.

Pfltttttt.

Pfltttttt. Pflttttt.

Arrows fell like rain around them.

Meredythe's scream of pain echoed around the clearing when one arrow embedded itself deeply between her ribs. Blood spurted, its sweet smell filling her nostrils. The howls of the wolves changed from triumph to rage as she collapsed onto the altar.

Racked with pain, Meredythe stared through her tears at the bloody chaos that now surrounded them. The old druid was shouting and waving his arms wildly as more arrows arced through the sky. A burly, black-robed priest holding a huge cross before him led other mounted, sword-waving men toward them.

"Kill them," he screamed as his men attacked, slashing and stabbing anyone who moved. "In the name of our great and all-powerful God, kill the devil worshipers. Sacrilege and blasphemy!"

Blood gushed. Both men and women screamed as they were cut down.

"The girl. Save the girl," the priest bellowed as he watched the slaughter with a malicious, toothy grin.

An unearthly howl split the night to be answered by others deep in the shadows under the trees. Scores of wolves poured into the clearing, ripping and tearing at human flesh.

A fire burning in her side, Meredythe cried out as Bleddyn cradled her in his arms and rolled from the altar. Closing her eyes, she rested her head against his shoulder. Darkness beckoned—a darkness that promised freedom from the horror of the last few days. She sighed. Yes. That's what she wanted. No horror. No pain. She floated toward the gentle darkness.

But his voice—Bleddyn's—refused to release her.

"No. Please, Meredythe, you must live. Don't leave me. I need you."

Struggling back through the pain, she forced her eyes open. Turbulent gray eyes filled with hopelessness and longing stared down at her. The silvery light of the moon bathed the two of them, filling her with a sense of peace and comfort. The gossamer form of a white-robed woman appeared behind him.

"Take me with you," she begged.

The woman's eyes met hers and she smiled. In that moment, Meredythe understood. Her life marched with Bleddyn's. She was his only hope, and he would never hurt her. With the last of her strength, she lifted her hand and cupped his cheek.

"Bleddyn. Wolf…"

"Give her to me," Rhys commanded from beside him. "You cannot win this battle. Go with the wolves."

Bleddyn's head snapped up, rage leaping in his eyes. Another unearthly howl split the air, this time one of loss and revenge. "I will not leave her!"

On the other side of the altar, the priest's horse reared as its rider jerked back on the reins.

"Sacrilege! Spawn of Satan, you die now!"

Rising, Bleddyn quickly laid Meredythe in the druid's arms. Her protest died on her lips. She was too weak to utter it. She blinked as her sight became blurred. Bleddyn faced the priest, hate and the promise of death emanating from him.

The broad-shouldered priest stared at her, his triumphant gaze now one of horror. "What have you done to her?"

"Your men shot her, priest of the peaceful god," the druid stated sarcastically. "Be gone from here. You know not whom you face."

The priest threw back his head and laughed loud and long. Throwing back his black cowl, he glared back at them. "You know not whom *you* face," he answered demonically. The top of the cross he carried was pointed. He lowered it and positioned it like a lance.

Ignoring the boast, the druid nodded his head and a ball of burning light shot toward the priest's skittish horse. The gelding screamed and began to buck.

"Run, fool," he snarled at Bleddyn. "You have no chance here today."

Bleddyn hesitated, glancing once more at Meredythe, blinking the tears from his eyes.

"Go! I have her. She's not dead yet, and many futures lie before us."

One last time, Bleddyn caressed her cheek. "I will find you, no matter when you are."

With a snarl and another heartrending howl, he leaped away, tearing at the priest's men with hands and teeth. A few strides away from the fire, the wolves enfolded him in a blanket of snapping teeth and ripping jaws. None were able to stand before them. Again, a swirling black and gray mist surrounded Bleddyn as he shifted. Only wolves disappeared into the darkness of the forest.

Body now numb, Meredythe closed her eyes. Bleddyn would find her, no matter when. Unconsciousness beckoned, but the voices of those around her continued to echo through her mind.

"Abomination! Devil! Werewolf!" exploded from the throats of the soldiers.

"You're a fool," said the priest. "The wolf may have escaped, but the girl is mine."

"What do you want with her?"

"She is innocent of the blasphemy that occurred here. Her soul can be saved. There's a nunnery close by."

Meredythe moaned and fought to stay conscious. The priest was lying. She could hear it in his voice. She didn't dare go with him. She struggled to talk. Instead she coughed, warm blood trickling from her lips.

"She'll die before you get her there."

"She will not!"

With the last of her strength, Meredythe forced her eyes open. The priest stared at her with vicious hunger.

"*Tanau*!" the druid barked, and the bonfire exploded behind them. Clasping Meredythe tightly, he stepped back into the conflagration, his voice deep with command. "*Difannu*!"

From the forest, a single, anguished howl followed them into the fires.

Screaming, Meredythe wrenched her eyes open and bolted from her bed. Her knee banged against a small table, rocking it onto two legs. Both the lamp and alarm clock clattered to the floor. Scrambling across the moonlit room on her hands and knees to the overstuffed chair sitting in the corner, she grabbed a baseball bat lying next to it and pulled herself onto wobbly legs. Bat clenched tightly in her fists as she shook uncontrollably, she sucked in gasps of air as her gaze darted from first one corner of the room to another.

"Merrooww?"

Her knees buckled and she collapsed onto the floor, the bat thunking beside her.

"Methuselah?"

He leaped from the bed and crawled into her lap. His deep purr rumbling, he began kneading her thigh with his paws.

Still shaking, Meredythe pulled him into her arms and hugged him tightly.

He snuggled close and purred more loudly.

After blinking her eyes dry, she set him on the floor and pushed herself to unsteady feet. She carefully picked up the fallen clock and lamp and put them where they belonged. Four staggering steps had her back on her bed.

Shuddering, Meredythe clasped a pillow to her chest. "A nightmare. I was dreaming. My God, Thuse, it was seemed so real! I could smell the wood burning, the ropes hurt my wrists and that arrow…"

She gasped with remembered pain. She could still feel the fiery tearing of the arrow as it embedded itself deeply in her side. Eyes widening, she dropped the pillow and lifted her sweatshirt. Her trembling fingers brushed the scar on her rib cage.

"I fell against a broken gate, Thuse! I got this scar when I fell against a broken gate when I was only four. Aunt Evelyn told me so. It was only a dream! It wasn't real!"

The cat jumped up beside her and rubbed his head against her knee. Then he stretched out against her thigh and began to purr deep in his throat.

Almost immediately, her tense muscles began to relax. Her eyelids drooped.

That's enough for tonight, Meredythe. Go back to sleep.

Slumping against the pillows, she yawned, her thoughts drifting to the man in her dream—Bleddyn, the naked man who looked exactly like the stranger from James King's office. She moaned as her memory replayed his caresses, his firm hands kneading her breasts, his skilled fingers plucking her nipples, his hard cock probing between her thighs.

Jerking herself upright, she flung the pillow across the room. What the hell was she doing reliving a dream where a man tried to rape her?

Methuselah's butted his head against her thigh. His purr became louder as it wrapped itself more deeply around her subconscious.

Sighing, Meredythe blinked. She settled back against her pillows. The gray-eyed, black-haired man faded from her mind.

"God, Thuse, what a night," she muttered.

After tossing and turning a few minutes, she snuggled into the middle of the bed. Her breathing deepened.

Methuselah tucked his paws against his chest and smiled his Cheshire smile. Meredythe's past would soon become her present.

Chapter Three

The scantily clad young woman shuddered as an eerie mist drifted above silent ponds and swirled around ghostly statues and wraithlike shapes flitted amongst shadow-laden trees while more tangible figures staggered along the gentle paths illuminated by the pregnant moon. More than a few of Halloween's mortal revelers sought new adventures in Central Park. Others with darker intent sought satisfaction in other ways.

"Come on, bitch," snarled the heavyset man as he jerked her along behind him.

She wrenched her wrist free of his bruising grasp. "Quit talkin' to me like that, Reggie."

"I'll talk to you however I wanna, Sal," he answered, shoving her ahead of him. "Now get your fat ass moving. There's plenty of drunks wanderin' 'round the park lookin' for a hot piece of ass. And you owe me extra for those freebies you're givin' out."

Plump buttocks sliding beneath her tight skirt, the garishly dressed young woman stomped over the uneven path—as much as she was able to stomp in bright orange stiletto heels.

Lousy son of a bitch, she swore to herself as she moved deeper into the park. *I'm goin' back to Tennessee as soon as I have enough money for a bus ticket. Cousin Reggie can find somebody else to whore for him.*

Ten minutes later, the dark surroundings finally got the better of her anger. Disoriented by the eerie mist eddying through the trees, unsure of her location, she halted abruptly.

Nervously glancing at the shadows under the trees, she spun around at the sound of a low growl. The bushes rustled.

"Who's there?" she demanded, her voice quavering as the clouds parted and luminescent moonbeams danced with wisps of dark mist.

More rustling.

A man appeared—a naked, black-haired man with stormy gray eyes.

Her eyes widened. "What're you doin' runnin' around the park naked?"

"Looking for you," he growled as he moved closer.

Dropping her stare to the thick cock jutting from the dark nest at the juncture of his thighs, she licked her lips. "You want a piece, mister?" She looked up to his face.

His grin was wolfish as he held out his hands, palms up, and shrugged his shoulders. "I don't have any money on me."

Her gaze traveled back down his body. Shivering, she smiled and licked her lips again. He didn't have any money? Hell, she was willing to pay *him*. "Won't cost you nothing."

Sticks cracked and bushes rustled again as Reggie barreled into the small clearing. Shoving the dark-haired man out of his way, he stomped to Sally and grabbed her arm. "I knew you was cheatin' me, bitch, givin' it away for free."

She jerked back, trying to wrench her arm free. "You were gonna watch? You creep."

He tightened his grip. "Watchin' my investment. And you owe me more money, you stupid slut. How many other assholes did you fuck without makin' 'em pay?"

Raising his other hand, he slapped her hard, grinning demonically as she struggled to break free.

"No, Reggie, don't hit me again. Please. I'm sorry. I didn't mean—"

"You ain't worth the money I sent to get you here, whore," he shouted, backhanding her brutally. He released her arm.

Her ankle turned and she lost her balance.

Reggie balled his hand into a fist.

As Sally fell to her hands and knees, a vicious snarl ripped through the small clearing and a large, dark shape exploded from the bushes to their left. In one long leap, it landed on the man, its sharp, gleaming teeth snapping at Reggie's fleshy throat as he futilely beat at his assailant.

Sally's scream melded with his.

Then, just as quickly, his terrified screaming stopped.

Sally shrieked again.

An immense black wolf, neck hairs bristling, stood over Reggie's body, blood dripping from white fangs. Licking his gore-flecked jowls, it eyed her speculatively.

Eyes rolling back, Sally melted to the ground.

As the full moon embraced him with her luminous glow, the wolf lifted his head and howled long and triumphantly.

After one last glance at the bodies lying before him, the wolf sprang away and disappeared into the deep shadows beneath the trees.

Minutes later, a shadowy, human-shaped figure slipped out of the park.

* * * * *

When Bleddyn pushed the door open, Rhys turned away from the window. Setting the full brandy snifter on the table, he locked his gaze on the younger man. "Where have you been?"

Bleddyn threw himself down on the sofa and stared into the roaring fire. "Out."

"Where?"

"I'm not a child."

Rhys clasped his hands tightly behind his back. "There's blood on your jaw."

Bleddyn rubbed his chin then stared at the brown flecks on his fingers.

The older man began to pace. "Damn it. You were supposed to take the medicine. You agreed not to kill again."

Bleddyn shook his head, trying to clear the fog from his brain. His brow wrinkled as he searched his fuzzy memory. Kill? He killed someone? Masculine screams jogged his memory. "There was a man. He was beating a woman."

Rhys raked his fingers through his hair. "What have you done?"

Bleddyn shifted as his memory cleared. Fuck! He *had* killed again. "He was a pimp—a mean one."

"And the woman?"

Anger rose. Hurt a woman? Never! "I didn't hurt her."

Relaxing visibly, Rhys stopped in front of Bleddyn. "I'm sorry. I should know better. When you weren't here, I thought… After that meeting with Meredythe…"

Shoving himself out of his chair, Bleddyn kicked a footrest out of his way as he stomped to the sideboard to pour himself a brandy. "The urge was too strong. I had to get out."

"Surely, with the medicine, you could wait—"

Snarling, the younger man pivoted to face Rhys. "For what? For Meredythe to welcome me into her bed? That Goddamn medicine doesn't work. It shot my self-control to hell. It took me a couple of centuries to reach the point where I could pretty much control the compulsion, the urge for blood or sex. That medicine completely eliminated it. I had *no* control. None! I was *compelled*. The damn bloodlust was in control."

Rhys' shoulders drooped. "So you got what you wanted."

Briefly, a sated smiled slipped onto Bleddyn's mouth and he felt the demon that inhabited his soul look out through his eyes. "Not what I wanted, but it will suffice."

"Damn it..."

"Don't start again, old man," Bleddyn snarled over his shoulder as he hurled the crystal brandy snifter into the fire where it shattered into a thousand sparkling pieces.

Flames shot up the chimney when the alcohol flared.

"I am what I am. I've accepted it. It's about time you do too. You have never understood the overwhelming urge—the lust—for the hunt and the kill. To have my victim's throat between my jaws, to feel the terror pumping through his veins with his blood. When that pimp started beating her, I had to kill. The bloodlust demanded it. I couldn't control the craving for fresh blood once I heard her screams and smelled her fear."

Bleddyn braced his hands against the mantel and stared into the dancing flames.

He heard Rhys step forward and tensed. The last thing he wanted was pity.

Rhys cleared his throat and started to speak. "Bleddyn..." He didn't finish his sentence.

Instead silence roared through the room.

Finally he said, "The woman saw you kill him, didn't she?"

Bleddyn rolled his shoulders. Shoving himself away from the fireplace, he turned, filled another snifter and gulped the rich, red liquid. "The woman saw a wolf."

"There aren't that many wolves running around New York's Central Park," Rhys commented dryly.

Bleddyn swallowed more brandy. "She probably doesn't know the difference—probably thought I was some kind of big dog."

"You have to leave the city. Go back to the estate."

Nostrils flaring, Bleddyn's head snapped up. "What about the lecture? You set it up. And I'm not leaving without Meredythe."

"You can't stay now!" Rhys raked his fingers through his hair again. "Not after this last death."

Bleddyn poured more brandy. "I thought that was the plan. Get Meredythe interested in the story and she'd come to me herself."

"She will," Rhys cajoled, "but so will at least half a dozen other reporters if they start putting two and two together. A little digging and they'll discover Dr. Bleddyn Glyndwr, noted authority on wolves, was in each city where and when one of these murders took place. The inferior reporters will come to you because you're an expert. The good ones will want to know what you had to do with the deaths."

"Then you better make sure nobody except Meredythe finds out." Setting his empty glass on a table, Bleddyn disappeared into his bedroom.

Once inside he stripped and stepped into the shower, braced his hands against the tiles, bowed his head and let the pulsating hot water relax the tension in his shoulders. How he hated this lust to kill. Would he ever be free?

A picture of Meredythe appeared in his mind's eye. Absolutely fearless, she'd thrown her flaming curls over her shoulder and arched her delicate auburn eyebrows at his comments. Then she'd shot blue daggers with her eyes, daring him. How could he resist kissing her? She was so beautiful, more beautiful than he remembered. And her lips... He groaned, remembering their taste.

His cock stirred.

Gathering his will—he would not give in to lust again tonight—he forced himself to relax.

His cock stilled.

Opening his eyes, he pushed himself away from the wall and turned his face into the spray. A smile twitched at the corner of his lips. After his kiss, she'd had the audacity to slap him. And she hadn't backed down, hadn't cowered in fear as so many others had.

Gods, how he needed her.

* * * * *

"Do you know what you do to me? Do you have any idea how stimulating, how arousing it is for me to see you like this, laid out before me like a gourmet meal? Your nipples are hard and pointed, begging for my mouth. Your stomach is smooth, perfect for licking and kissing. Your legs…gods, Meredythe, but your legs are beautiful. So perfectly toned. Do you have any idea how I long to have them wrapped around my waist while I bury my cock in your cunt?"

He dragged the tips of his fingers down her rib cage to her stomach. "You're wet, Meredythe. I can smell your pussy, and it smells so sweet my mouth is watering. I'm going to taste you tonight. I'm going to lay myself between your legs and suck the sweetness from your cunt until you can't stand it anymore and scream for me to bury my cock inside you."

Moaning, Meredythe shivered as he caressed her navel. Just the thought of his mouth between her legs had more juices flowing. Why had she fought him when she'd first met him? How did she manage to walk away from him?

"You want me and we both know it," he continued. "That day in your boss's office, your body cried out for mine and you fled rather than give in to it. Then, when I found you, you finally listened to your body. Your nipples practically pushed themselves out of your shirt to get to my mouth and your cunt dripped with cum. You wanted my cock buried deep."

His hands were magic and she couldn't deny his words. "Yes, oh yes. I want you. I want your cock inside me."

His chuckle was arrogant. "I'll bury it deep, I promise. But first, I've dreamed of getting my mouth on your breasts."

Bending over, he sucked her nipple into his mouth, twirled his tongue around it, then nipped it.

Moaning, Meredythe arched her breast farther into his mouth. "Oh gods, yes. More. I want more."

His fingers slid between the slick folds of her cunt. "You're so wet, love," he murmured against her breast. "So wet and wild." He lifted his fingers to his nose and inhaled.

Meredythe's breath caught in her throat. His eyes seemed more golden than silver now, and his face was tight with controlled passion.

"You smell like woman and sex and passion. I want you."

Then he licked his fingers.

Meredythe shuddered. Gods, what was he doing to her?

He slid his hand back between her thighs and pinched and rubbed her swollen clit. Her hips bucked against his hand. He bit down lightly on her nipple.

He rubbed harder. "Come for me, love. Come for me." He slipped a finger inside her.

"Ahh!"

Heat radiated outward from her cunt as Meredythe flew apart. Once she was able to focus, she stared into his now-golden eyes.

A bonfire erupted behind him. Slowly, his form melted then reformed, and a huge black wolf stared down at her.

Once again Meredythe exploded out of a dream, filled with fear.

"Merrooww?"

Pulling the cat into her arms, she sat in her dark bedroom and held him close until his rumbling purr calmed her frayed nerves. "Shit, Thuse, what's happening to me? Why am I having these dreams? How can I let one jerk affect me so much even if he has a body to die for?"

Methuselah rubbed his head against her chin then squirmed until she released him. As usual, he stretched out beside her and purred.

Raking her hair back off her face, Meredythe stared into the darkness. Another dream. Just another dream. She squeezed her legs together and shivered as fresh desire danced in her cunt. No, not a dream—another nightmare, and no nightmare was going to drive her from her bed, not even one with a dream lover who made her come in her sleep.

* * * * *

Early the next morning, Meredythe was driven from a restless sleep plagued by visions of wolves and fires when Methuselah batted her nose.

She cracked her eyes open and glared first at him then at the clock. Six a.m.

Methuselah meowed once commandingly, jumped off the bed and looked back over his shoulder.

"All right, all right, I'm coming." She sat up, yawned, stretched and swung her legs over the side of the bed. Groaning, she pushed herself to her feet.

Stumbling across her bedroom, she knuckled sleep from her eyes and followed the cat's insistent meows into the kitchen. Dumping some dry cat food into a bowl, she shoved it under his nose. "There. Now quit complaining."

Then the phone jangled.

Muttering a curse when her groping hand knocked the receiver from its cradle, she scrambled under the table after it on her hands and knees. After another curse—she'd bumped her head on the edge of the table—she sat in the middle of the floor and lifted it to her ear.

"Hello?"

Silence as she listened.

"James? What?"

Meredythe held the phone away from her ear, stared at it, then listened into it again. "What did you say?"

Her eyes widened. "Another murder? In the park? Are you sure it's the same—" Her entire body tensed. "I'm on my way."

Thoughts whirling, Meredythe scrambled to her feet and hurried back to her bedroom, stripping off her sweats as she went. Once there, she pulled on a t-shirt and a pair of jeans and dragged her brush through her hair. Not giving a thought to makeup, she shoved her feet into a pair of running shoes and pulled a black blazer from her closet.

Hustling into the living room, she grabbed her tape recorder from the bottom desk drawer and shoved it into a backpack. Dumping her purse on the sofa, she grabbed her wallet, her press ID, a tablet and a couple of pens and shoved those into the backpack too. After a quick stroke for Methuselah, she grabbed her keys. She was out the door less than fifteen minutes after her boss called.

"Elevator's too slow," she muttered and scrambled down the four flights of stairs to the street. Luck was with her. She was able to hail a passing cab immediately. As she settled into the seat, her mind whirled with the information she'd read yesterday.

* * * * *

"What a mess," the homicide detective grunted to the uniformed officer as he shoved another piece of gum in his mouth. "Make sure you don't touch nothing. The forensic guys will be here soon."

A siren blared in the distance.

The younger officer shuddered. "I wouldn't touch it with a ten-foot pole, Sarge. What do you think happened?"

The whining siren drew closer.

Ignoring his own order, the sergeant nudged the body with his toe. "Bastard had his throat torn out. By all the footprints, I'd say it was a pretty big dog."

Flashing lights cut through the gray fog that cocooned the small clearing.

"'Bout time," the detective muttered.

The siren stopped screaming as a van with "NYPD Forensics" on the side appeared on the wide pathway and halted. Two men emerged. The first began taking pictures. After he finished with the body, the second man knelt next to it.

"Shit, what a mess."

The first man looked up. "How many pictures you want, Kim?"

"Everything within a hundred-foot radius. Make sure you get pictures under those trees over there too."

"Got it," the photographer answered as he disappeared into the bushes.

The overweight detective pushed himself closer. "Whaddaya think, Doc?"

Busy gathering evidence, the younger man never looked up. "I'll let you know after I examine all the evidence."

"Asshole snob," the sergeant muttered a bit too loudly, shifting his weight from one foot to the other as he watched the other man poking around the dead man's body.

"You said there was a witness? I'd like to talk to her," the younger man stated as he examined the ragged neck wound.

"What for?"

The young scientist sighed. Sergeant Hooper was a real pain in the ass. "There was obviously some kind of dog involved. Maybe the witness can tell us what kind."

"Witness is a whore. The only thing she knows about dogs is doggy style," the sergeant said with a loud guffaw, obviously pleased at his own joke. "Somebody used his fist on her. Probably the owner of the dog. Besides, she's not here. Ambulance already took her to the hospital. You guys shoulda got here quicker."

Neither noticed Meredythe until she was straining against the yellow police tape. "Kim? Kim Takimo? Is that you?"

"Back off, lady, you can't come in here," the sergeant blustered, but his eyes were glued to what he could see of her braless chest behind the open flaps of her blazer.

Pulling out her ID, she flashed it in his face. "I'm a reporter. I have every right to be here."

"Says who?" he sneered, his eyes darting from her chest, to her ID, to her face and back to her breasts. Her nipples were trying to see what was going on too.

"Never mind, Sergeant," Kim interrupted. "I'll take full responsibility."

"Any evidence goes missing, it's your ass, Doc." Then, swearing under his breath, the sergeant stomped away.

Turning to the young patrolman, Kim glanced at his nametag and said, "Keep the joggers from coming down that path, Officer Poole. Call for backup if you think you need it." Then he sauntered over to Meredythe.

As the young policeman hurried away, Meredythe muttered, "What a freaking asshole that sergeant is."

Grinning, Kim said, "You're right about that, Meredythe. How have you been?"

A wide smile appeared on her face as she turned her attention to the young man in front of her. "Just fine. How are Terri and the new baby?"

The young man's grin widened. "They're both doing great. Jason even sleeps through the night now."

"That makes Terri's life easier." Glancing toward at the gory body, Meredythe eyed the corpse, mentally shuddering at the brutality of the crime, thankful she had a strong stomach. "What happened?"

He looked back toward the body. "This guy had his throat torn out by some kind of dog. I'll know more once I can get my samples to the lab. Why are you interested?"

Leaning against the police tape, she pulled a small camera out of her bag and snapped some pictures. "Let's just say there might be an angle to the case."

"Not talking, huh?" he teased with a grin. "You reporters…"

She grinned back. "Ha! Like you forensic guys are real forthcoming. If you'd given me just a little hint about old man Stockard…"

"I can't jeopardize a case. And why do you have to keep dragging up that one? It was two years ago."

Shifting, she leaned closer and snapped another picture.

"Where's your photographer?"

She snorted. "Somebody should show up pretty soon. I just like my own stuff on top of what they can give me. Different angles and perspectives can give me clues. And if you'd have told me how Stockard was murdered…"

"You know I couldn't do that. Not revealing how the victim died is what caught the murderer."

"I'd have waited."

Turning to face Meredythe, Kim cocked an eyebrow. "Bullshit."

She grinned back and slid her camera back into her bag. "Anything you can tell me about the case?"

With a good-natured groan, Kim turned back to the body. Meredythe shifted from foot to foot as he used tweezers to lift something she couldn't see from the ground.

"Hey, Doc," the homicide detective yelled. "Where'd Poole go? I need to ask him some more questions about hooker."

Meredythe's ears pricked. "Hooker? There was a witness?"

Kim sighed. "A prostitute. Someone beat her up. She's at the hospital now."

A tablet and pen appeared in her hands as if by magic. "How bad was she hurt? Is she a suspect? Which hospital and what's her name?"

He shrugged. "Sorry, Meredythe, can't tell you. She's a witness in an ongoing homicide investigation."

"I bet they took her to the closest one," she mumbled. The tablet and pen disappeared in her purse. "Thanks, Kim. I owe you one."

"You owe me five, but who's counting?" he answered with a grin as he rose. "Why don't you get out of here before someone smarter than Hooper shows up and tosses you out on your ass?"

Chuckling, Merry blew him a kiss. Then she hurried across the grass and disappeared down the path.

* * * * *

Muttering curses under her breath, Meredythe stalked from one end of the counter to the other. "Listen, all I want to do is talk to the woman who was brought in from Central Park this morning."

"You're not a doctor and you're not family. Go sit over there. You can talk to her later—if she comes out," answered the formidable nurse, hands on her ample hips.

"Nurse should have been a drill sergeant," Meredythe muttered as she flopped down in a chair. Flipping through one magazine after another, her gaze jerked from the slow-moving clock hands to the emergency room exit and back to the clock again. Patience. A good reporter had patience. Everything comes to those who wait.

Finally, after an hour and a half of fidgeting and flipping through every dog-eared magazine in the waiting room, Meredythe heard the inner door swoosh open. A battered young woman walked out, followed closely by a frowning police officer. Fishing in her bag for a couple sticks of gum, Meredythe quickly shoved both of them in her mouth and began chewing furiously until she had them at the perfect consistency for snapping. Loosening her hair from its ponytail, she shook the fiery curls over her back and shoulders, slipped out of her blazer and threw it over her arm.

Rising, she fixed a brazen expression on her face. Adding an exaggerated sway to her hips, she sauntered toward them.

"It would be best if you came to the station with me," the young officer demanded as he grabbed the battered woman's arm.

She wrenched her arm free. "No. I already told you what I saw. I wanna go home."

"Hey, whaddaya think you're doin'?" Meredythe demanded with a loud crack of her gum. "She don't hafta go nowhere with you unless you arrest her. Did you arrest her?"

"Who are you?" the officer snapped, his gaze immediately dropping to nipples pebbled against her t-shirt.

"I'm her friend, that's who. An' she can go home if she wants to." Meredythe's unbound breasts swayed as she locked arms with the other woman and guided her toward the exit.

The officer's eyes were now locked on her swaying ass. "We need her at the station."

Meredythe pushed the door open. "Then you hafta arrest her. She ain't done nothing wrong."

The door slid shut behind them.

"Thanks," the battered woman said after they were half a block away.

"You're welcome."

"Who are you?"

Meredythe pulled her companion into a coffee shop. "Come on, I'll buy you a cup of coffee."

After hesitating, she slid into a seat at the small table. "You ain't a working girl, are you?"

Meredythe smiled. "Not the same kind you are, no. I'm a reporter." Holding out her hand she said, "Meredythe Welsh."

The young prostitute stared at Meredythe's hand a moment then gingerly clasped it. "Sally Forbes. Why'd you help me, Ms. Welsh?"

"Call me Meredythe," she said as they sat at a table and she signaled the waiter. "Coffee, black, and some Danish. What would you like, Sally?"

"Uh, the same," she mumbled self-consciously. The entire right side of her face was bruised and both eyes were black. Her lip was split and she was still dressed in her "working clothes"—a too-short orange skirt and low-cut black blouse. The garters holding her black fishnet stockings in place were plainly visible.

The waiter leered.

"Wipe that smirk off your face and get our coffee," Meredythe snapped after she glanced up.

"Why should I? My boss don't want prostitutes here, especially beat-up prostitutes."

She slapped her ID onto the table. "Then your boss is going to have a feature story about just how bad the service is."

After the waiter flushed, mumbled an apology and hurried away, she turned back to her companion and said, "I'd like to know what happened in the park."

Paling under her bruises, Sally started to rise.

Meredythe slid a twenty-dollar bill on the table. "All I want is a little information, and I promise you'll never see me again."

Swallowing nervously, Sally grabbed the bill and glanced around. Settling back into her seat, she asked, "What do you want to know?"

Meredythe waited until after the waiter set their coffee and a plate of pastries before them. Another icy glare from her had him hurrying away.

"How old are you, Sally?" she asked, setting her small tape recorder on the table.

"Nineteen," the other woman answered nervously. "What's that for?"

"I want to make sure my story's accurate."

Sally shifted uneasily in her seat. "What kind of reporter are you? Is this gonna be on television?"

"No, I work for a newspaper. Can you tell me what happened? Please?" she coaxed gently, selecting a pastry from the plate and taking a bite. Sugar powdered her lips.

Sally's stomach growled. "Oh. Well, I was in the park, you know, working," she answered, licking her lips as she eyed the pastries. "Reggie said there'd be a lot of horny guys there an' they'd get inta doin' it in the woods, what with it bein' Halloween and all."

Meredythe licked the sugar from her fingers. "Go ahead, have one. Who's Reggie?"

Sally grabbed a pastry and bit into it. "He's, ah, was my cousin," she mumbled as she chewed. "He brung me here to work for him."

"Is he the one who died?"

"Yeah, that big, black dog kilt him."

Meredythe sipped her coffee as Sally finished her first pastry and grabbed another.

A big, black dog. Interesting. For an instant, the wolf from Meredythe's dream appeared in her mind. Ruthlessly, she ripped the memory apart and returned her attention to her companion. "Do you remember anything else about the dog?

Was it wearing a collar? Did it have any distinguishing marks?"

She sucked sugar off her fingers. "Distinguishing marks?"

Meredythe rested her elbows on the table and cupped her coffee cup in both hands. "You know, white patches."

Sally shook her head. "Naw. It was all black and I didn't see no collar, but it was pretty dark." Then her face brightened. "I could see that it had really thick fur. It didn't look like any of the huntin' dogs my dad used ta raise. It kinda looked like one of them sled dogs. Yeah, that's it, a sled dog."

"What about the guy who hit you? Was he the dog's owner?"

She shook her head. "No, Reggie hit me on accounta I was gonna give a freebie to a john."

Meredythe cocked an eyebrow. The dog was protecting Sally? No way. "What exactly happened last night?"

The young prostitute licked the last of the sugar from her fingers and locked gazes with Meredythe. "Well, first this guy walks outta the bushes naked, an', well—he looked so good I told him I'd do him for free. That's when Reggie jumps outta the bushes and starts slappin' me around for givin' it away. Then that black dog came outta nowhere an' kilt Reggie. He jus' tore his throat out. I thought I was gonna be next. That's when I fainted."

Her pimp watched! Meredythe shuddered mentally. "Did you see the dog's owner?"

"I didn't see nobody 'cept that naked guy. An' he was gone before the dog came. Do you think there's wild dogs runnin' around the park?"

Setting her now-empty cup on the table, Meredythe frowned and nibbled her fingernail. A dog appearing out of nowhere and rescuing a prostitute from a beating by her pimp? It didn't add up. "What did the man look like?"

"What man?"

"The one who came out of the bushes?"

"Oh, him." After a gulp of coffee, Sally smiled whimsically. "Well, he was kinda tall but not real tall—six feet maybe. An' what a body, all muscle! Wide shoulders, nice chest, great abs. An' his dick—"

"Er, what about his facial features?"

"He was handsome, I think. It was kinda dark so I couldn't see him too good. An' he had lotsa dark hair. It was real long and curly. An' his chest was covered with hair too. An' his eyes were gray. I remember 'cause the moon came out, an' they looked like silver."

Unbidden, the picture of a dark-haired, gray-eyed man leaped into Meredythe's mind. She slapped it away. What a ridiculous thought! Thousands of dark-haired, gray-eyed men lived in New York.

"Do you remember anything else? Did he have any tattoos or anything?"

Sally shook her head and eyed the last pastry.

Meredythe smiled warmly. "Go ahead. You can have it. Who found you?"

Sally grabbed the Danish. "Some homeless guy tripped over me."

"Do you remember what he looked like? Was he the same man as earlier?'

"No way. The john smelled…woodsy. Yeah, like at home in the pine trees after it rained. The guy who tripped over me was old and stank worse than rotten eggs. The smell's what woke me up 'cause he was bendin' over me. Then he saw Reggie lyin' there with blood all over him and kinda screamed a little and then he ran away quicker 'en you can say jack shit. I started screamin' all over again an' a cop heard me. He's the one who called the ambulance. He was a nice guy, for a cop."

Woodsy? Again a pair of silvery-gray eyes appeared in her mind. Cursing mentally, Meredythe pulled her attention back to the young prostitute. "What was the homeless man wearing? What did he look like?"

Sally shrugged. "I don't know. He was dirty an' he stank. He made me gag so I closed my eyes. But I think he was wearin' a long brown coat."

Frowning, Meredythe scrutinized the young woman who was now licking the last crumbs from her fingers, puzzling over all she had learned. *A naked man comes out of the bushes and they agree to have sex for free. Then her pimp appears and starts beating Sally because she's giving out freebees. A big black dog appears out of nowhere and rips the pimp's throat out. Sally faints but comes to when a smelly homeless man bends over her. What's going on? Is this the serial killer's work? Does he or she use a dog to murder his victims?*

Meredythe grabbed a pencil and tablet. She had to check if there were dog prints at the other murder sites. Or was this some Halloween thing? Or was there a rabid dog loose in the park?

As Meredythe scribbled away, lost in her thoughts, Sally rose. "Thanks for the coffee, but I gotta get home now."

Meredythe shook free of her musings. "What? Hey, come back here. I have more questions." She shoved her tape recorder, tablet and pencil into her pocket and rose to follow Sally, but the waiter grabbed her arm.

"Wait a minute, lady. You gotta pay the bill."

"Shit!" she snapped, digging into her backpack for her wallet. Shoving a couple of bills into his hand, she muttered, "Keep the change." She slipped past him and hurried out the door. Craning her neck, she pushed past pedestrians. When she reached the corner, the light changed and traffic surged. Across the street, a woman in a short orange skirt hurried down to the subway.

"Damn it!"

A well-dressed, silver-haired woman hmphed and stared down her nose at Meredythe as she hurried by.

Defeated, Meredythe turned and walked back the way she had come. The other pedestrians ignored her as she talked to herself. "I probably got everything she knows anyway. I need to see Kim again. He knows more—if I can get him to tell me about it."

Reaching into her bag, she pulled out her cell phone and punched in a number. "Alice? I'll be late getting to the office today. I'm chasing a lead on the story Mr. King gave me. If you need me for anything, page me. I'll check in later and let you know what I'm doing." Severing the connection, she dropped the phone back in her backpack and hailed a cab.

* * * * *

As the black limousine glided quietly through New York City's morning traffic in the direction of Columbia University, Dr. Bleddyn Glyndwr sat comfortably ensconced in the plush seat silently perusing the marked columns in the small stack of newspapers piled next to him. His lips twitched every now and then at unexpected wit. When he finished, he looked up into his companion's amused stare. "I never knew Meredythe had a sense of humor."

"You never had the chance to know her at all. This time…"

With a weary sigh, Bleddyn laid his head back and closed his eyes. "Don't start lecturing me again, Rhys. I've agreed. I need to get to know her first—and let her get to know me."

"Then make sure you control that damnable temper."

A ghost of a smile appeared on Bleddyn's lips as he remembered a stinging slap. "Who's going to tell Meredythe to control hers?"

Chapter Four

Frowning first at the body on one table and then the photographs in his hand, Jon Bowers glanced up at his partner. "What do you think?"

Kim probed the jagged gash on the corpse's throat. "He definitely died from the wound in his throat."

Lifting a magnifying glass, Jon held it over a photograph. "Judging from all the footprints, it was a feckin' big dog. These prints have close to a five-inch width and five-and-a-half-inch length. Heavy too. I can see marks from the cracks and lines on the pads."

Kim glanced over his shoulder. "Any way to find out what kind of dog it was?"

Jon shrugged. "Maybe. I have a friend who trains all kinds of dogs for movies. He might be able to tell me."

Kim started to gather his notes. "The lab should be able to give us more information once they analyze those hairs we found stuck to the guy's hands. What's the priority on the case, anyway?"

"Unless we get another dead guy with his throat ripped out, not as high as it should be. The double homicide from two nights ago still has main priority. State representative's grandson is more important than a pimp. This guy has no family here except the cousin he was pimping for. Before she was taken to the hospital, she told the officers at the scene she didn't care what happened to the body."

Gathering up the photographs, Jon shoved them into a manila envelope then looked at his wristwatch. "Look, it's after eleven now. Let's break for lunch. My buddy Frank is at Columbia University for some kind of show or lecture or something so I'll head over there and show him the photographs. If he doesn't know what kind of dog belongs to this paw print, there might be somebody else there who does. I'll see you when I get back."

"I'll walk out with you," Kim said as he wheeled the body back to refrigeration then shrugged out of his lab coat. "I'm meeting my wife for lunch."

They were barely out the door into the abnormally warm November sunshine when Kim spied Meredythe hurrying up the sidewalk. "Oh shit." Grabbing Jon's arms, he pulled him into a crowd of people.

Meredythe saw Kim try to duck out of sight. Waving her arm, she called, "Kim. Kim, wait a minute."

"How does she get around so fast?" he muttered. "Watch yourself with her, Jon. She could get blood out of a stone."

Jon's head was swinging back and forth. "Who?"

Before Kim could answer, Meredythe was before them. Not giving her a chance to speak, he said, "Meredythe, this is my partner, Jon Bowers. Jon, Meredythe Welsh, a very stubborn reporter."

She stuck her tongue out at Kim as she held out her hand to Jon. "Pleased to meet you." Since most of her attention was fixed on Kim, she didn't see the slow smile that spread across Jon's face.

Kim did. Meredythe was a beautiful woman, and his fertile imagination sprouted the seeds of an idea. She and Jon would make the perfect couple. And it would get her off *his* back.

"I'm pleased to meet you, Ms. Welsh," Jon said as he shook her hand.

"Likewise," she answered absentmindedly. Her attention was on the shorter man. "Kim, I have a couple of questions I want—"

Hands on his hips, her friend scowled. "Come on, Meredythe. Give me a break. I'm meeting Terri for lunch. Can't you come back later?"

"Maybe I can help you, Ms. Welsh," Jon interjected hopefully.

Meredythe hadn't really paid much attention to Kim's partner when he was introduced. When she turned her full attention to him, her gaze traveled from his head to his feet. Not bad. Not bad at all. Much nicer to pump a good-looking man for information than a homely one.

Jon Bowers was over six feet tall, blond-haired and blue-eyed with two of the most adorable dimples she'd ever seen, and the wire-rimmed glasses he pushed back up his nose added to his appeal. He looked scholarly sexy. She really didn't have the time or inclination to get involved with any man, but that didn't mean she didn't like looking. And Jon Bowers was *very* nice to look at.

She smiled broadly and said, "Call me Meredythe."

Kim grinned at the rapt expression on his partner's face. "Better be careful, Jon. She'll drain every drop of blood from your body if she thinks it will get her a story. You two can duke it out. I'm going to lunch." Then he disappeared into a waiting cab.

Jon shifted the manila envelope he carried under his arm and hailed another cab. "What can I help you with?"

Meredythe paused. Kim she knew she could trust, but this guy? So what if he was good-looking? "Maybe I should wait until Kim's not so busy."

He smiled. "So which forensics' reports from unsolved crimes do you want to see?"

Her eyes narrowing, Meredythe simply stared at him. Good looks and brains. She'd have to be careful with this one. "Who says I want to see any reports?"

"You're a reporter and Kim's in forensics," he continued. "Why else would you need him? Solved crimes are public record. You're looking for something else."

Meredythe pursed her lips, then smiled. "Did anybody ever tell you you're too smart for your own good?"

His smile became a grin. "Only my mother."

She grinned back. "How about joining me for lunch? We can talk."

He smiled ruefully and shook his head. "Wish I could, but I have to see a man about a dog."

Her pulse quickened. "It's about that murder in the park this morning, right? You're going to find out what kind of dog killed that guy."

Startled, he stared at her. "Kim's right about you, isn't he?"

With a chuckle she nodded. "Don't you ever forget it. Mind if I tag along? I'll still buy you lunch."

As she talked with Kim's partner, Meredythe shifted her body slightly and combed her fingers through her hair. The movement of her arms pulled her blazer away from her braless chest. Widening her eyes slightly, she gave her upper lip a quick lick, once again mentally congratulating herself for taking that class on body language and then schooling herself to have the courage to follow through on what she learned. As she had intended, Jon Bowers didn't have a chance.

She smiled mentally as he dragged his eyes away from her mouth. He swallowed. "Umm. Sure, why not," he answered with a shrug and opened the door of the waiting cab. "If you know about the prints, it won't hurt if you know what kind of dog it was. I'm headed out to Columbia University. I have a friend there who might be able to help me."

She slid into the cab and waited until he joined her and gave the cabdriver the address, then asked, "Do you have any ideas?"

He tightened his hold on the manila envelope. "All we know for sure is that it's a large dog."

"How large?" she asked, eyeing the envelope he held. She'd love to see what was inside.

"Judging by how deep the paw prints are, I'd say he weighed well over a hundred pounds."

Meredythe's eyebrow rose. "He?"

He grinned at her. "With mammals, the male of the species is usually larger and more aggressive than the female. While it's possible that this dog could be female, it probably isn't."

She looked out the window to hide her momentary distress. "I guess it doesn't really matter. Either way, the man's dead."

He admired her profile. "What did you want to find out from Kim?"

Her glare had him raising his hands, palms forward. "Hey, you want information from me. It's only fair that you share."

Biting her lower lip, she stared at her companion. Could she trust him? What did she know about this guy anyway? Sure, he worked with Kim, but then she worked with Harry and he was a scumball. Oh well, what the hell. She wouldn't tell him everything. "You know the dead man was a pimp?" After his nod, she continued. "Well, one of his girls, the one involved, saw the dog. She said it was big, black and had a lot of fur, like a sled dog."

Bowers smiled and nodded. "That narrows it down. Sled dogs are strong. One could easily kill a man. We found some black hairs stuck to his hands too."

She'd love to get her hands on one of those hairs. "Do you think it was some kind of weird accident? What about the dog being scared and thinking it was defending itself? Or is someone training a dog to kill?"

Grimacing, he shifted on the seat and shrugged. "I don't know, but there aren't too many options. A dog will protect its master, but that wasn't the case here. Nor have there been any reports of rabies or dogs running wild in the park. I checked."

Fixing her gaze on the back of the driver's head, Meredythe pondered everything she'd learned so far. Why would a dog protect someone, kill for someone it didn't know, then disappear? It just didn't make sense. "This is really weird," she mumbled.

"What?"

Meredythe gathered her scattered thoughts and turned her attention back to her companion. "Nothing. How long have you known Kim?"

"We started working together last year. What about you?"

"About six years now. His wife was my roommate until she met Kim. Left me high and dry without a roommate our junior year."

"And you've been making him pay for it ever since, haven't you?"

Meredythe grinned. "Don't you forget it."

* * * * *

Jon held the back door open for Meredythe. "My friend will be back here somewhere. There's some big shot giving a lecture and Frank was supposed to bring a couple of his dogs for props."

Meredythe's eyebrows rose. "Props? What is it, a dog and pony show?"

Before he could answer, a security guard challenged their presence. Meredythe pulled her press ID from her purse and held it up. "We're here to cover the lecture."

After a cursory glance, the guard shrugged and stepped out of the way. "Just don't get too close to those cages. Some of those animals are mean."

Meredythe threw an inquiring glance at Jon, but he just shrugged and led her deeper into the building. Soon another man crossed their path.

Jon stepped past Meredythe and called, "Frank, hey, Frank."

The short man stopped. "Jon? Is that you?" he asked with a wide grin as he stuck his hand out. "What the hell are you doing here? Somebody find a dead body somewhere on campus?"

Jon grinned back and shook hands. "Not today, but I do have some questions about a case and decided to come to an expert."

After the handshake, Frank turned his attention to Meredythe. "And who do we have here? Hello, lovely lady. Don't tell me you're with this sorry excuse for a man. How could you possibly be interested in a guy who cuts up dead people for a living?"

Meredythe rolled her eyes at his speculative stare. Another flirt. Couldn't men keep their minds out of their pants?

"Meredythe Welsh, Frank Messner. She's here for the same information I am, Frank, so stop flirting," Jon said before she could comment. "Can you tell us what kind of dog made these footprints?"

Meredythe craned her neck to get a look at the photos when Jon handed Frank the pictures.

After a quick glance, Frank started and perused the photos more carefully. Finally he said, "These aren't dog prints, Jon."

Meredythe frowned and bit her lip, mind whirling. "But those have to be dog prints. What else could they be?"

"Wolf or wolf-dog."

Meredythe's mind leaped back to her dream of the night before. Wolf?

Jon's skeptical voice pulled her from her memories. "A wolf? In Central Park? No way."

"Wolf-dog then. Here, look." Frank held the photo up for both of them to see. "Paw prints are too big for a dog. See the spread and the length? Those prints are almost six inches long. This is one hell of a big animal. What do you need to know for and what does Central Park have to do with it?"

Jon directed a level stare at his friend. "Whatever made those tracks killed a man in the park last night."

All hints of flirtation were gone from Frank's voice as he said, "The Bronx Zoo has some Mexican gray wolves, but they certainly weren't out for a walk in the park. And wolves won't bother nobody if nobody bothers them. No, not a wolf." He handed the photos back to Jon. "Damn bastards and their dog fights. It must be a mix. A hybrid isn't afraid of man. Fuck, but there are assholes out there who think crossbreeding wolves and dogs is a good thing."

Meredythe got her tape recorder out. "Did you say something about dog fights? Aren't they against the law?"

"She's a reporter," Jon said to Frank's questioning stare.

"Yeah, but that doesn't mean they don't happen. They're becoming a real problem. As long as there are guys who think it's macho to own a dangerous dog that can tear some other guy's dog to pieces, we'll have problems. Now folks are thinking it's cool to own a wolf hybrid."

Meredythe shifted her tape recorder and cursed under her breath when her tape ran out. Grabbing a tablet from her purse, she started writing. "Are there a lot of these hybrids around? Are they dangerous?"

Frank stared at them a moment then said, "Come with me and I'll show you." He led the way down the hall to a closed door. Before unlocking it, he said, "No quick moves. They're all in kennels, but I don't want them upset."

A low, threatening growl greeted them as Frank opened the door. "Damn," he muttered in a low voice. "I knew I should have left Hammer at home."

Three kennels were placed in different corners of the room. He ignored the low growl from the farthest cage. "These are what you get when you crossbreed wolves and dogs. Sweetie here is half wolf and half Collie and pretty easygoing," he said, indicating a mostly white wolf-dog in the closest kennel. "She was a family pet until she attacked the garbage man. The family's kids were in the yard and she thought he presented a threat."

Jon stopped just inside the door, but Meredythe followed Frank right up to the kennel. She bent closer when the wolf-dog wagged her tail. "But there are dogs that will do that. How can you blame her?"

Frank smiled briefly. "She tore a six-inch gash along the guy's leg. She's lucky she wasn't put down."

Meredythe squatted to get a better look inside the kennel.

Still in the doorway, Jon shifted from one foot to the other. "Meredythe, maybe you shouldn't get too close."

She ignored him. "Why wasn't she put down?"

Frank grinned at Jon then turned his attention back to Meredythe. "The family really pushed to save her. They had home movies of Sweetie playing with the kids. That and the guy she bit owned a couple of German Shepherds, so he sort of understood why she attacked him."

"How did you get her?"

"I have a license to keep and train exotic animals and have picked up a couple of wolf-dogs over the years. Now the police call me if they aren't sure what to do with the animal. I figured I could train them to use in movies."

"So you train them all?" Meredythe asked, leaning closer to the kennel. Sweetie woofed and wagged her tail.

"Sometimes. Sweetie here is a real pleasure to work with. She seems to like you. Would you like to meet her?"

A broad smile on her face, Meredythe looked up. "Can I?"

He smiled back at her. "I wouldn't offer if I didn't think it would be safe."

"Wait a minute, Frank," Jon interjected. "Are you sure this is a good idea?"

Frank winked over his shoulder. "Anything the little lady wants."

Jon took one nervous step into the room. "Meredythe, I don't know about this."

She rose and stepped back from the kennel. "Relax, Jon. If Frank says she's safe, she is. He wouldn't risk his professional reputation."

Throwing a smirk over his shoulder, Frank opened Sweetie's kennel and snapped a leash on her collar. "Come on, girl. Got someone here to meet you."

Tail wagging, tongue lolling out, Sweetie leaped out of her kennel and pushed her head under his hand.

"Sit."

Sweetie obeyed.

"Just hold out your hand and let her get to know you."

Jon took another step into the room. "Meredythe!"

She waved him off. "Oh, be quiet. She's not a wild animal. She won't hurt me."

Holding out her hand, Meredythe moved forward slowly. Sweetie stretched out her nose and sniffed. Rising to her feet, she licked Meredythe's hand and wagged her tail.

Stepping closer, Meredythe ran her hand over Sweetie's fur. Closing her eyes, she concentrated on the soft, wiry texture of the wolf-dog's fur. Unbidden, a pair of muscular forearms covered with springy black hairs appeared in her memory. A pair of gray eyes gazed into hers.

The wolf-dog sighed and leaned against her leg.

Meredythe opened her eyes and smiled at Frank. "She's beautiful."

"Yes she is," agreed Frank. "If all hybrids were like her, we wouldn't have any more problems with them than we do regular dogs."

Meredythe pointed to the wolf-dog in the second kennel. "What about that one?"

"This is Jocko. Come on, Sweetie, back in you go." After he returned Sweetie to her kennel, Frank opened the second one and snapped a leash on the black male. He came out of the kennel with a low growl.

Jon swallowed and stepped back toward the door. "Jesus, Frank."

"Don't worry, Jon," he said with a chuckle. "Jocko's a gentleman. He was just warning you to stay out of his personal space."

"He's not dangerous?" Meredythe asked. She was dying to pet Jocko as she did Sweetie, but she wouldn't do so without an invitation. Silvery-gray eyes appeared in her mind. The wolf-dog, Jocko, stared at her and woofed. Frank's voice brought her back to the present.

"Jocko is half wolf, half Husky. His previous master made the mistake of bringing him along when he moved back from Alaska. Jocko couldn't handle the culture shock."

"Didn't you say that prostitute saw a black dog attack her pimp?" Jon asked from the doorway.

Meredythe glanced back over her shoulder and then looked at Frank. "Jocko didn't get out last night, did he, Frank?"

"No!" he answered emphatically as he put Jocko back in his kennel. "Last night Jocko and the others were in New Jersey."

Ruthlessly squashing her musings, Meredythe made a note on her pad. She was a reporter, damn it. She didn't have time for daydreaming. She looked up at Frank. He was probably telling the truth, but it wouldn't hurt to double-check. She looked at the last kennel. "Who's the last one?"

"That's Hammer," Frank answered with a sad sigh as he latched Jocko's kennel and stepped toward the last kennel. A low growl erupted into a full snarl. Frank stopped where he was. "He won't be coming out to meet you."

Waves of grief and despair so strong she almost gagged on them rolled out of the kennel and poured over Meredythe. A sharp pain pierced her mind.

Save me.

As quickly as it had manifested, the pain subsided. She blinked and shook her head slightly. What was wrong with her? First she couldn't stop dreaming about a jerk with black hair and gray eyes no matter how hard she tried. Now she was hearing voices.

Quick glances at both men told her they hadn't noticed. They stood talking as if nothing had happened. What was going on? Without moving any closer, Meredythe knelt and peered into the kennel. "How dangerous is he?"

Frank grimaced and said, "Very. He's a wolf and a Mastiff cross whose owners used him to fight. The only reason he's still alive is because I got to him before the police did."

Meredythe's heart ached. No living thing should feel the way this poor animal did. She leaned over farther, squinting. All she saw was a dark brown blur. "Has he ever attacked a human?"

"If he did, I'd put him down myself," Frank answered. "He was used to fight other dogs."

Fear joined the misery emanating from the kennel.

Meredythe swallowed the sudden lump in her throat.

Jon scowled. "What the hell did you bring him for if he's so dangerous?"

"He's the whole point of this lecture. The doc wanted to show everybody just how dangerous wolf-dog hybrids could be."

Rising, Meredythe took a deep breath and started writing. She had to get a hold of herself before she collapsed in a puddle of tears. "The doc?"

"Doctor Bleddyn Glyndwr," Frank explained and led the way back out into the hall. Meredythe's battered emotions began to relax when the door closed. "He's an expert on wolves and knows as much about wolf hybrids as anybody in the country. I've worked with him before. He's giving a lecture today. That's why I'm here."

Meredythe looked up from her notepad. "So if I wanted to know anything about wolves or wolf hybrids, then this Dr. Glyndwr is the man to see?"

Frank nodded. "That's right. I'd be happy to introduce you."

She smiled. "Thanks. I have a few questions I'd like to ask him."

Frank led them from the room, carefully locking the door behind him. "Sure thing."

Meredythe scribbled a few more things on her pad. "Is that door always locked? Could anybody else get in and get one of them out of a kennel without you knowing about it? What about where you keep them at home? Are they always locked up? Does anyone else have access to them?" Frank was probably telling the truth, but she had to ask anyway.

"Look, Ms. Welsh, none of my animals got out last night and killed that guy. If you won't take my word for it, I'll be happy to show you a footprint from each of them. None of them have feet big enough to leave a track that large." With those exasperated words, he turned abruptly and stomped down the hall.

Jon stared after his friend then looked at Meredythe. "Never question Frank's word about his animals. Makes him pretty mad."

"Obviously."

Only a quick blink of her eyes betrayed her regret at Frank's pique. It had taken her almost a year and some very long lectures from James after she lost a couple of stories, but eventually she learned not to let it show how much it hurt when people were distressed or angered by questions. She didn't want to hurt anyone's feelings, but if she didn't ask the questions, someone else would. That didn't mean she liked it.

Taking her arm, Jon pulled her after his friend. "Come on. I think Frank went this way. You really know how to make friends, don't you?"

She looked away and blinked again. "Asking questions is my job, Jon. Making friends isn't."

* * * * *

"In conclusion," Bleddyn said to his rapt audience, "crossbreeding wolves and domestic dogs is more than irresponsible. It's dangerous."

After half an hour of questions, he cordially excused himself, declining the invitation to the cocktail party that had been organized in his honor—much to the chagrin of the department chair's wife. Bleddyn snorted to himself. The last thing he wanted was a bored university wife trying to lure him into her bed.

Rhys led the way behind the stage. "This way. We can avoid the crowd if we go out the back. The car's waiting."

Bleddyn led him in the opposite direction. "I want to check the animals and see Frank first. He's probably going to have to send Hammer to the estate."

Rhys glanced at his companion. "Bad?"

"Hammer won't trust any human, not even Frank. If I could only get my hands on the bastards who abused him..."

Turning a corner too quickly, he literally ran into Meredythe and the man who was with her. The man bounced off the wall and fell to his knees. She slipped and also would have fallen if Bleddyn hadn't reached out and grabbed her before she could tumble to the ground.

Grateful for the support, Meredythe pushed her hair back out of her face. "Thanks. Sorry, I wasn't watching where I was going." When he didn't release her, she said, "I'm okay. You can let go of me now." Then she looked up into his face. It was the jerk from her boss's office. He'd shaved since yesterday and his hair was pulled back into a ponytail that emphasized his finely chiseled features. He was also wearing a very well cut, very expensive suit. But his eyes were the same—the same probing, smoky gray that bore into the depths of her soul.

What the hell was he doing here?

"You!"

A sexy smile slipped onto his lips. "Hello."

Meredythe tried to wrench her arms free, struggling against him and the strange feelings suddenly surging through her body. "Let me go!" She looked into his eyes and lost herself in the passion mirrored in them.

Bleddyn reacted without thinking. Meredythe was here, in his arms, and she had stopped struggling. He tightened his grip ever so slightly and pulled her closer. Lowering his head, his lips sought hers.

A shocked gasp escaped her, but she didn't fight him. Instead, she shuddered slightly and flattened her hands against his chest.

A growl began low in Bleddyn's throat. His woman. His.

Someone grabbed his wrist and tugged. "Hey, buddy. What do you think you're doing? Don't you understand English? She told you to let her go."

Caught in the mesmerizing gray mist of his eyes, Meredythe leaned closer. But her bemusement and uncertainty were replaced by shock when the passion in his eyes changed, became more dangerous, more feral.

Was that a snarl?

At her side, Jon stumbled back. "Who is this guy, Meredythe?"

Meredythe blinked. What was she doing? She wrenched herself free and stepped back. She was tempted to slap him like she had in her office, but remembering his reaction from yesterday, she decided against it. She chose a verbal assault instead. "Who the hell do you think you are, you…you…*cretin*? I don't know you and I don't want to know you. Come on, Jon. Let's get out of here."

Again it was Rhys' hand on his arm that kept Bleddyn from following her.

Fury burned in Bleddyn's eyes. "She's with another man."

"Calm yourself," his friend soothed. "She's with men every day. It doesn't mean anything. You heard Jim. She doesn't even date. All she's interested in is her career. I'm sure he's just a colleague."

Slowly the tense muscles under Rhys' hand relaxed. Bleddyn unclenched his fists, but the scowl didn't leave his face. "If he's taken her to his bed…"

Rhys shook his head. "You're as much hers as she is yours. No one else will take your place. She won't sleep with another man even if she doesn't understand why."

Turning abruptly, Bleddyn stalked away. He still had to see Frank about Hammer. Besides, if he went after Meredythe now, he just might do something he'd regret.

* * * * *

Meredythe stepped off the elevator grumbling about men and their macho attitudes. Jon Bowers had been entirely too inquisitive about the guy at Columbia. Like she couldn't take care of herself! As if it was any of Jon Bowers' business anyhow! Who the hell did Jon think *he* was?

Her friend Alice laughed. "You don't even have a steady guy and you complain more about men than any other woman I know."

Meredythe dropped her bag on a chair. "Well, they can be such pains in the ass."

Alice grinned. "How was lunch? Was he cute?"

Gray eyes appeared in Meredythe's mind. Cute? The guy was drop-dead gorgeous. "Was who cute?"

"The guy you had lunch with, Kim's partner?"

Another man's face appeared in her mind. "Who? Oh yeah, Jon. How did you know—"

"Kim called and asked if you were back yet," Alice answered with a grin. "He mentioned you were probably having lunch with his partner. So is he cute?"

Closing her eyes, Meredythe sighed and turned. She wouldn't get any work done if she didn't answer Alice. Planting her hands on her hips, she said, "Around six-two, blond hair, blue eyes and dimples to die for. And very intelligent. And he offered to pay for lunch. And he cuts dead people open for a living. Anything else?"

Alice smirked. "That will do for now. By the way, somebody sent you roses."

"Roses? Who?"

Alice stared at her in mock amazement. "Do you think I read the card?"

The corners of Meredythe's mouth twitched as she walked toward her desk. "Envelope sealed?"

Alice followed her to her cubicle. "Well, aren't you going to open the card?"

Meredythe stared at the vase of two dozen blood-red roses sitting on the corner of her desk.

"They came in that vase," interjected Alice as she set the bag next to the desk. "That's real Waterford crystal. Whoever this guy is, he has great taste."

Meredythe reached for the white envelope that was so obvious against the crimson background. Opening it, she pulled out the card.

I apologize for my actions yesterday. Please forgive me.

Alice was behind her, standing on tiptoe trying to see over her shoulder. "Who are they from?"

Meredythe shoved the card back into the envelope and stuck it in her pocket. "There's no signature."

Alice clapped her hands together. "Ooh! A secret admirer. How romantic! And lunch with another guy. Your love life is definitely on the upswing."

"Listen, Alice, I have work to do. I'll talk to you later, okay?"

"But—"

"Alice..."

Muttering under her breath, Alice disappeared around the partition and headed toward her own desk. One day Merry was going to fall for some guy—hard. She only hoped she'd be there to see it.

Meredythe's blood warmed as she stared at the roses. There was only one man who'd done anything yesterday that required an apology. And any feelings of remorse hadn't stopped him from acting just as highhanded today. Slowly she reached out and stroked soft petals. Who was he? And why couldn't she stop thinking about him?

"Next time I talk to James, I have to find out his name."

Chapter Five

Methuselah turned his attention from the moon to Meredythe's bed. Sighing in her sleep, she rolled over. Jumping from the windowsill onto her bed, he sidled against her and nudged her shoulder.

She muttered something incomprehensible and rolled away from him.

That's it, turn over. There are more memories for you.

Rolling over, Meredythe turned her face toward the moon…and began to dream.

Incessant clanging from the church bells shattered the peace of the small town, wailing and lamentations rising above their clamor. A frenzied crowd pulled a house to the ground while flames licked the foundations of another.

"Damn it, Rhys," Bleddyn snarled as they shoved their way through the terrified crowd. "You said she'd be safe here."

The older man began to walk faster, past one family group after another, all hastily loading their meager possessions onto carts. A small mob scrambled around and between them, screaming about the end of the world.

Rhys put his hand out and grabbed a brown-clad monk hurrying in the opposite direction. "Brother, what has happened?"

Grimacing, the cleric shrugged his hand off. "Leave me be. I have no time." Then his shoulders sagged. "There are too many. I can't care for all of them. My brothers have all succumbed."

Grabbing two handfuls of brown robe, Bleddyn jerked the obviously exhausted man close. "Succumbed? Who? How did they die?"

The tired man crossed himself. "The Black Death. May God in all His wisdom have mercy on us."

Paralyzing fear sapped the strength from Bleddyn's muscles and he released the monk, who staggered away. He was soon lost in the crowd. After a moment of frozen silence, Bleddyn jerked his eyes to Rhys. "Meredythe!" Then he began to run.

"Bleddyn, wait," Rhys called after him, but the swirling crowd had already swallowed him.

Snarling, Bleddyn shoved another wailing person from his path and rounded a corner. Flames licked the house at the end of the street. Meredythe lived with a family in the one next to it. A huge figure stepped into the street and blocked his path.

"Out of my way, fool," he growled.

"You're the fool, young wolf," the huge man answered.

Bleddyn stopped and peered into the man's face. Recognition stabbed his brain. His blood boiled and the beast in his soul howled with rage. Snarling, he bared his teeth. "Slade! What do you want?"

A toothy grin spread across the huge man's face. "The same thing you do, but neither of us shall have her now."

The urge to transform and attack surged and swelled. Bleddyn swore silently to himself and wrestled with the devil in his soul. Slowly, desperately, he fought then conquered it. Muscles locked rigidly into place, he glared at Slade. "What are you talking about?"

The big man shrugged. "She's dying. The plague has claimed her."

Every muscle and nerve in Bleddyn's body shrieked with denial. "You lie."

Slade gestured to a small cart that almost blocked the alley behind him. "See for yourself."

Pushing past the other man, Bleddyn stepped to the cart and pulled away the blankets. Meredythe huddled on bloodstained sacking, her eyes closed. A weak cough added more blood to that on her chin and chest.

Climbing into the cart, he gently lifted her into his arms. "Meredythe, Meredythe, can you hear me?"

Slowly, as though with great effort, she opened her eyes. When they finally focused on his face, she smiled weakly. "Are you an angel? Have you come to take me to heaven?"

With a sob, heedless of the blood, he pulled her against his heart. "No, you can't die. I won't let you."

"Give her to me and she won't," Rhys commanded.

Slade stood behind the older man, his arms crossed across his chest, a haughty smile on his face. "Yes, fool. Give her to the old man so he can save her for me. I can wait a few more years."

Hate leaping from his eyes, Bleddyn lifted his head and glared at his enemy. "You will never have her."

The large man threw back his head and laughed. Once he regained control of himself, he taunted, "You don't have the strength to defeat me, wolf."

Sliding out of the cart, he placed Meredythe in Rhys' arms and, unmindful of the crimson blood covering his chest, he stepped toward Slade, his teeth bared in a feral grin. Flexing his huge arms, Slade stepped forward.

"Hold, fools," Rhys commanded. "Think what you're about and where you are."

Both men halted as the clamor of the frenzied crowd intruded. Smoke from burning buildings now swirled about them. People shoved past them, disappearing into the darkness of the alley, seeking escape from the crowds and flames behind them.

With a low growl, Slade turned his attention to Rhys. "You're right…this time, old man." His gaze locked with Bleddyn's. "We'll meet again, wolf. Then I'll kill you and the girl will be mine." Turning, he melted into the crowd.

Bleddyn stared after him. "Why? He had her. Why did he give her to us?"

Rhys shifted Meredythe in his arms. Her head lolled against his shoulder. "She'll never live until the next full moon. He can't save her but hopes I can."

Bleddyn reached out and caressed her cheek. She coughed and more blood spurted from her lips. "She's getting weaker. Can you save her?"

"Even I cannot cure the plague," Rhys answered resignedly as she coughed up more blood. "I must take her into the flames."

Bleddyn closed his eyes and bowed his head. "More waiting."

"Fate has decreed it so, my son," Rhys answered gently. "Go now. I'll find you when she is born again."

Turning, Rhys disappeared into the thick smoke pouring through the alley. Bleddyn turned away. Melding with the crowd, he soon slipped through the gaping gates and strode toward the nearby forest. There, at its edge, black and gray mists merged.

Rhys faced the conflagration before him.

Meredythe struggled weakly in his arms. "Am I dead? Am I in hell?"

Rhys looked down and smiled. "No, Meredythe. For you the fire offers sanctuary. You will be able to rest and get well again.

"*Tanau*!" he barked, and the flames roared toward the sky. Then he stepped into the inferno.

Minutes later, those who trudged along the road to the edge of the forest crossed themselves as a mournful howl rolled out from beneath the dark trees.

Wrenching her eyes open, Meredythe stared at her ceiling and shivered. What in the world was going on? Why was she having these crazy dreams?

Turning onto her side, she propped herself up on her elbow and punched her pillow.

"Meeoow?"

She glanced at him.

Methuselah was lying in a beam of moonlight, paws tucked into his fluffy chest, smiling a Cheshire smile.

"What are you laughing at, you…you…cat? I bet you don't even get nightmares." Flipping back to her other side, Meredythe turned her back on him. As soon as she closed her eyes, *he* appeared—thick dark hair, smoky gray eyes, sexy grin. Gritting her teeth, she flopped over again. Damn him. No wonder she was having nightmares. Between researching murders where guys had their throats torn out and being harassed by a guy who just happened to have the same color hair and eyes as the john the prostitute described, no wonder she couldn't sleep.

Rising on her elbow, she punched her pillow and flipped it over. "When did it get so hot in here?" The silky nightgown she wore was plastered to her body.

She was hot.

She was sweaty.

She was horny.

"Oh shit."

Meredythe flopped onto her stomach. "I am *not* horny. It's just hot. I don't give a damn about any man!"

She rolled over onto her back and closed her eyes. Sleep. She needed to get to sleep.

She pulled her damp nightgown away from her breasts. Her nipples ached.

She shifted restlessly.

Moisture seeped between her legs.

Her clit ached.

She flopped onto her stomach again. "Okay, I'm horny."

She rolled back over. Closing her eyes, she pulled her nightgown up to her waist. "Okay. Just a quickie."

Meredythe slid her fingers over her abdomen, nudged the crotch of her silk panties aside and brushed her aching clit.

"Ahh. Yess."

She thrust her hips upward as her fingers seemed to take on a life of their own—swirling, dipping, rubbing. Her nipples tightened more and bolts of tingling pain seemed to burst from the tips. Moisture drenched her fingers as pressure built.

She arched her back.

A familiar face appeared in her mind. Black hair, gray eyes, hard body.

She slipped her fingers in and out of her cunt and pinched and rubbed her clit. Body slick with sweat, she let her free hand drift up her rib cage underneath her nightgown to knead her breast then pinch her nipple. Tender pain surged straight to her groin. "Ahh!" She pumped her hips against her fingers.

In her mind, the dark-haired stranger smiled. His gaze urged her on.

When her orgasm finally exploded, tears trickled down her cheeks.

"Ahh." Pleasure rolled over her as her internal muscles shuddered and rolled.

Slowly her muscles relaxed, her breathing slowed and the final shiver danced down her spine. She opened her eyes and sighed.

Even with her eyes open, *he* continued to smile at her.

A warm weight snuggled against her side and Methuselah's purr began to vibrate against her. After a long sigh, Meredythe relaxed and her tense muscles unwound. Her eyelids drooped. Soon she slept deeply.

* * * * *

A cold wind whistled through the alley, but Bleddyn didn't feel its bite. When a car passed by, he stepped farther back into the shadows, but his gaze remained on the dark window of the fourth-floor apartment across the street. The sounds of footsteps and laughter approached and he melted deeper into the darkness, remaining deathly quiet as a couple passed only a few feet in front of him. They were too engrossed in each other to notice him, which was just as well. The sight of a naked man hiding in the alley would undoubtedly have them calling the police.

Once they were gone, Bleddyn eased forward, his eyes searching. Earlier, Meredythe had appeared at her window and he'd barely been able to subdue the sudden urge to go to her and make her his. Thankfully, she'd disappeared and he'd been able to bring his longing for her under control. Closing his eyes, he again returned to Jim King's office yesterday when she'd stomped in, her eyes flashing with blue flames, her thick auburn hair curling riotously around her shoulders. He felt his body stir as he remembered the kiss they exchanged later, the kiss she'd answered with passion as deep and wild as his own. Shuddering, he took a deep breath and opened his eyes. He needed her—now. The moon was full. He stepped forward.

An icy blast hurtled down the alley and enveloped him in its coils. His head jerked up and he spun around. The wind changed, but he remained still, nostrils flared as he searched for the elusive scent that had just challenged his senses.

Slade was in the city.

Black and gray mist swirled and a large black wolf loped back through the alley. Keeping to the shadows, he headed back uptown. After half an hour at a steady pace, he reached another dark alley. Again mist swirled. Reaching into a box waiting in the alley, Bleddyn retrieved his clothing. After he was dressed, he stepped out onto the street. His hotel was only two blocks away. He had to let Rhys know Slade was back.

The sound of glass smashing farther back in the alley reached his ears, but he ignored it. Slade was far more important than whoever was back there.

In the alley, the drunk who'd just witnessed Bleddyn's transformation curled into a fetal position and grabbed his half-empty bottle.

* * * * *

Bleddyn slammed the door closed. "Slade's here."

Rhys put down the newspaper he was reading and looked up at his worried companion. "We leave for the estate tomorrow as planned."

Bleddyn's eyes narrowed. "Did you hear what I said? *Slade* is here."

"I know. He arrived on an afternoon flight from Paris."

Bleddyn grasped the back of the sofa so hard his fingers left deep furrows in the material. "You know he's here? Why didn't you tell me?"

Rhys sighed tiredly and laid down his paper. "It was only a matter of time before he showed up. Once we came together here, he was sure to follow. You know we rarely see each other unless Meredythe is involved."

Bleddyn's fingers gouged holes in the sofa. "Exactly. We have to get her. We can't leave her unprotected."

Rhys waved his hand. "Slade doesn't know where she is. And tomorrow, when we leave, he will follow us, believing we are going to her. There are simply too many people in New York City for him to waste time searching for her. Besides, he'd never believe that we'd leave her alone. Remember, he believes she's probably no more than sixteen or seventeen. We've never waited this long before."

Snarling, Bleddyn began to pace. "I don't like it. Too much can go wrong with this scheme you and King devised."

"Trust me. Meredythe is safe. And in a week or so, if that long, she'll be coming to Dr. Bleddyn Glyndwr for information."

Bleddyn stopped pacing and stared into the flames burning in the hearth. "Slade will follow us too."

Rhys nodded. "Yes, he will. But when I leave the estate, he'll follow me. Winterbourne has been your home for the last ten years, and your remaining there won't raise his suspicions. I've visited you from time to time. Slade will assume I was visiting again. And I've always been the one to make periodic visits to Meredythe when she was growing up. He'll follow me, hoping I'm doing so again. I'll lead him to one of our decoys. There's one just across the border in Canada."

Bleddyn turned his head. "Which one?"

"The eight-year-old. Slade will let her be once he sees her. She's still too young for his purpose."

"I still don't like to leave Meredythe here alone."

Rhys sighed. "She won't be alone. I've asked Damian to keep an eye on her, protect her if necessary. He's agreed."

Bleddyn's body tensed. "Damian! But he's—"

"One of the best friends you have. One of the few friends you have. He owes you his life. Surely you don't think he'd hurt her."

Bleddyn shook his head. "No. He won't hurt her. It's just, he's so damn…compelling. One look into his eyes and women can't resist him. I've seen him in action."

Rhys' tense shoulders relaxed and he chuckled. "He's only guarding her, Bleddyn. She'll never meet him."

Bleddyn turned his attention back to the flames. "I hope you know what you're doing, Rhys."

*****

Meredythe stared at her computer screen, her mind not on the words displayed there but on the dream she'd had the night before, one that had unsettled her so much she hadn't been able to stay sleeping. Instead, she'd gotten up at four a.m. and had been sitting in front of the computer ever since.

Shivering, she jerked her concentration back to her computer screen. She was just working too hard. That's why she was having crazy dreams.

Methuselah jumped up onto her lap and pushed his head under her hand.

Smiling, she gathered him into her arms, refocusing on the text before her. "There were dog prints at three of the murder sites, but two of the victims were found on concrete. So there could have been a dog there. It wouldn't have been able to leave tracks on concrete."

She continued to stroke Methuselah. "The dog tracks at one of the murder sites are attributed to the seeing eye dog of the blind man who found the body. At least, that's what the police report says."

Pursing her lips, she shifted her gaze to the manila envelopes stacked on her couch. "I wonder..."

Rising, she dropped the cat on the sofa, picked up the folders James King had sent her and carried them to her kitchen table. There, she pulled the photographs from each and spread them out on the table. "This is the print from the murder here. Now let's see if any of the others match."

Slowly, she sorted through the photos until she had them all lined up. Straightening, she looked at the cat that sat in the chair next to her. "I'm sure not an expert, Thuse, but those tracks all look the same to me." She bent closer. "See this large crack to the left of the pad? That same crack is in every picture. And look at this photo, the one with the prints from the blind guy's dog. They're not all the same. There are two different sets of tracks here. And this print has that same crack in it.

Thuse, the same dog was at every one of these murders. His owner committed all of them." Picking the cat up, she danced around her kitchen. "I did it. I've established a connection. James is right. There is a serial killer out there."

Setting the cat on a kitchen chair, she gathered up the photos and slipped them into a new envelope. Then, stopping only long enough lean over the roses and breathe deeply, she headed for the shower. She had to be at work in an hour.

* * * * *

As Meredythe typed another query into her computer, her phone rang.

Muttering to herself, she grabbed it, propped it between her ear and shoulder and continued typing.

"Hello?"

"Meredythe, it's Jon—Jon Bowers."

She stared at her computer.

"Meredythe?"

"Hello, Jon. How are you?"

"Great, great."

Silence from the other end. He cleared his throat. Then more silence.

Meredythe fidgeted with a pencil. "What can I do for you?" she finally asked when he didn't say anything.

"Ah, well." She could picture him crooking his finger under his shirt collar to loosen it. "Would you like to go to dinner with me? Tonight?"

Meredythe held the phone out and stared at it. Dinner? A date? Her? With Jon Bowers? A mental picture of the tall, blond-haired man appeared before her. Well, his dimples were really cute. She pressed a key on the computer. And maybe he had some new information about the murder.

"Meredythe, are you there?"

"Ah, yeah, Jon, I'm still here." She frowned at the words that appeared on her screen. *Damn, another dead end.* "Ah, sure, dinner sounds good. What time?"

His sigh of relief was audible on her end of the line. "Great. I'll pick you up at seven o'clock."

Hunching her shoulder, she tilted her head and wedged the phone against her ear as she typed another question. "How about I meet you?"

There was no hesitation on his part. "Sure, okay. Do you like Italian?"

She stared at the computer screen and typed in another question. "Ah—sure. Who doesn't?"

"How about Pellegrino's in Little Italy?"

"Fine," she said somewhat absentmindedly as she continued typing. "I'll meet you there at seven."

His voice was eager. "Great, I'll see you there."

She hung up her phone and cursed at her computer screen. Again, nothing. Every question she'd researched this morning was a dead end. Shoving her chair back, she rose and stretched. Dropping her arms, she settled back onto her feet and opened her eyes. Maybe if she organized what information she had, it might jumpstart her brain.

Sitting back down, she pulled up files and printed them out. Then she spread them out on her desk. When Alice walked around the edge of the partition an hour later, she was completely engrossed in her research.

Her friend nudged her shoulder. "You want me to order you some lunch?"

Meredythe never looked up. "Tuna fish on wheat with lettuce and tomato."

Alice grimaced. "Don't you ever get tired of tuna fish on wheat with lettuce and tomato?"

"No."

Alice stepped over to a chair. "You dropped one."

Meredythe looked up. "What?"

She retrieved a sheet of paper from beneath a chair. "You dropped this one."

"Thanks, which one is it?"

Alice cocked her head and looked at her boss. "It's the one about werewolves."

Meredythe frowned and snatched the paper from her friend. "Werewolves? Where did this come from?"

"Don't ask me. I only work here," Alice answered with a shrug. "I'll be back with your lunch when it gets here."

Meredythe continued to read the paper in her hand. "Yeah, sure." She didn't hear Alice leave. Werewolves? There were people who believed they were werewolves? Looking up, she pursed her lips and stared at the wall. Could someone with a wolf or wolf hybrid be acting out some kind of fantasy? Dropping the paper on the table, she returned to her computer. Soon she had reams of information about werewolves, and it was fascinating reading. When Alice brought her lunch, she thanked her absentmindedly. Her friend smiled fondly and placed the sandwich next to Meredythe's elbow and left. After the first bite of her sandwich, another thought occurred and she rose and shuffled through the papers on her table.

"I was right. Twelve murders in the last eight years—every one of them on a date important to the ancient Celtic calendar. Ostara, Spring Equinox, March 21. Beltane, April 30. Litha, Summer Solstice, June 21. Mabon, Autumn Equinox, September 21. And last night's murder, Samhain, Oct. 31. This keeps getting weirder and weirder," she muttered to herself.

Dropping all the papers on the table, she flopped into her chair and stared into space. "Aunt Evie will be able to help me. I guess having an aunt who's Wiccan has finally become an asset."

She went back to her lunch. As she chewed, her mind leaped from one seemingly outrageous idea to another. As the afternoon wore on, her common sense asserted itself.

Reshuffling all of her printouts and notes, she soon had three separate piles on the desk.

She had her back turned when she heard a step. "Not now, Alice. I'm still busy."

"It's five o'clock, Meredythe," answered James King. "I told Alice to go home."

Blinking, she straightened up and spun around. "I didn't realize it was you."

Her boss chuckled. "Engrossed in your work again. Someone could set off a bomb outside and you wouldn't hear it."

She grinned.

"How's the story coming?" he asked before she had a chance to say anything.

She turned back to the table. "There have been twelve murders in the last eight years that have identical MOs, three of them here in New York. Frankly, I'm surprised no one has put any of them together yet."

James stepped closer to her desk. "Really?"

She nodded. "Yes, and all of them occurred on days that are important to the ancient Celtic calendar. In my opinion, there's some kind of cult involved. And those photos of dog prints you gave me—they're wolf or wolf hybrid prints."

He grinned. "I knew I could count on you, Meredythe. What next?"

Glancing at her watch, she said, "Next I go home and get ready for my date." Since she was shoving papers into folders, she didn't see the shock on his face.

He stiffened. "Date?"

She chuckled. "Yeah, Jon Bowers—the forensics guy handling this latest murder—asked me out. I want to see if he's learned anything new."

Since her back was still turned, she didn't see the relief that leaped onto her boss's face. "Yes, well then, enjoy yourself. I'll see you tomorrow."

Sliding the files into her briefcase, she turned and smiled. "Tomorrow's Saturday, and I promised Aunt Evie I'd be over. Besides, I have to take Methuselah home. I'll see you Monday."

He inclined his head. "Monday, then. Enjoy your weekend." Then he smiled. "If I know you, you'll spend most of it working."

She grinned back as she slipped her coat on. Slinging her purse over her shoulder, she grabbed her briefcase. "I promise not to work too hard, boss."

He stood aside for her to precede him as he chuckled. "See that you don't. I want you bright-eyed and bushy-tailed on Monday morning." He escorted her to the elevator. "Tell your aunt I said hello."

"I will. Goodnight."

"Goodnight, Meredythe," he answered as the elevator doors slid shut.

* * * * *

Jon held the chair. "Have you ever been here before?"

Meredythe smiled at the waiter who held out a menu and shook her head. "A couple of times. Their ravioli platter is wonderful."

Jon grinned up at the waiter. "That's what we'll have then. Italian dressing on the salad?" After her nod, he asked, "Wine?"

She shook her head. "Not tonight, thanks. Just water with a slice of lemon."

Jon looked up at the waiter. "I'll have a Heineken."

"So how's the investigation going?" she asked after the waiter left.

Jon grinned ruefully. "Kim said you wouldn't waste any time."

She grinned back. "I am who I am. Have you learned anything new?"

The waiter returned with their drinks and Jon thanked him. After sipping his beer, he said, "No. Four more bodies have been brought to the morgue since then. One of them is a city councilman. So the murder in the park has been shoved on a backburner."

Meredythe scowled into her water glass. "And that's probably where it will stay unless there's another one." Of course, if she wrote a story about the two that came before this one, the public would be clamoring for the police to find the murderer. But it was still too soon. Someone else could find the murderer before she did.

Jon's waving hand caught her attention. "Earth to Meredythe. Are you still with me?"

"Sorry." She set her glass down. "Ah, did you get anything back on the hair samples you sent to the lab?"

He shook his head. "You don't forget anything, do you?"

"No," she answered with a grin, "I don't."

The waiter placed their salads on the table.

He poured more beer in his glass. "The samples were contaminated."

She reached for her fork. "What do you mean?"

"The DNA reading came back as wolf and human. Since there's no way that's possible, somebody screwed up," he answered and took another sip of his beer.

The hand holding her fork froze halfway to her mouth. Salad dressing dripped onto the tablecloth. Wolf and human! The information about werewolves leaped into her mind.

Jon waved his hand in front of her face again. "Meredythe, are you okay?"

She shook her head. "What?"

"You look like you've just seen a ghost."

She set her fork on the edge of her plate and reached for her water. After a quick sip, she picked up her fork again. "It was nothing. I just felt a tickle in my throat."

Jon dug into his salad.

Meredythe picked at hers. "How...how did the sample get contaminated?"

Jon shrugged. "Who knows? A tiny scrap of skin, a microscopic drop of blood. All we know is the DNA didn't match the guy who was killed. My bet is one of the technicians made a mistake and won't admit to it."

The thoughts whirling in Meredythe's brain slowed. After a bite of salad, she said, "You're probably right. I guess you don't have any hair samples left."

Jon grinned. "We do. This time I'm going to check it myself as soon as I get some time. But that's enough about work. The work week's over. There have got to be other, more interesting things to talk about."

She didn't fail to notice the slight blush on his cheeks or the way he pushed his glasses back up onto the bridge of his nose. The waiter set their meals in front of them, and Meredythe forced herself to relax. Jon was really a nice guy, and she was hungry. She could take a couple hours off. "So, how did you get interested in cutting dead people open?"

Time passed quickly. Jon was a charming and witty companion. As they left the restaurant, he threw his arm around her shoulders. She didn't shrug it off. Laughing at another of his seemingly endless stories about working in a morgue, she allowed him to steer her down the sidewalk.

The November evening was warm. It was a nice night for a walk.

As the laughing couple brushed past him, Slade turned and followed them with his gaze. The woman had wavy red hair, but she had to be past twenty-five. Besides, neither the wolf nor the druid would ever allow another man to be so familiar with the wolf's woman. Pulling a cell phone from his pocket, he punched in a number.

"They've left the city," said the voice on the other end, "heading north."

"They're heading for Bleddyn's estate, then," he muttered.

He tossed one more look toward the redheaded woman walking away from him. Something about her…

He shrugged and turned away. There were thousands of redheaded women in New York City. Throwing his arm into the air, he hailed a cab, slid in and gave the address of his hotel.

As the cab merged with the other traffic, a tall man dressed completely in black stepped from the shadows. The light from a streetlamp flashed off dark eyes in a pale face as he turned and followed Meredythe. He'd promised Rhys that he'd keep an eye on her.

Chapter Six

Splotches of bright November sun speckled the driveway as Meredythe eased her car to a stop underneath the almost leafless oak trees.

His bushy tail lashing back and forth, Methuselah braced his forefeet on the dashboard. "Merrooww."

Her fingers stirred the fur on his head. "Glad to be home, aren't you, Thuse? Me too. The one bad thing about living in the city is not having you and Aunt Evie with me."

The front door slammed open and a sprightly, gray-haired woman dressed in a bright orange sweater and brown skirt flitted across the porch and down the steps. Stopping halfway to the car, she set her hands on her hips and scolded, "It's about time you're finally home. What took you so long?"

As soon as Meredythe opened the car door, Methuselah leaped out and sprang across the lawn. Evelyn Woods bent, scooped the cat into her arms and cuddled him against her chest.

Grinning, Meredythe got out of the car and followed at a more sedate pace. "Sorry, Aunt Evie," she said after giving her aunt a quick peck on the cheek. "I overslept and traffic this morning was horrible. Seems like everybody was trying to get out of the city. Oh, and James says hello."

Her aunt beamed. "Such a nice man, James King. I'm so glad you work for him."

The gray cat squirmed in her arms. "Merrooww?"

She hugged him once more. "Of course I'll put you down now, dear. Off you go."

With a quick flick of his tail, Methuselah disappeared around the corner of the house.

Smiling, Meredythe shook her head. Aunt Evie would never believe that her cat didn't understand every word she said.

Evelyn tucked her arm through her niece's. "Come along, dear. I have pies in the oven."

Meredythe patted her aunt's hand then shrugged free. "I'll be right in. I have to get Thuse's things from the car."

"I'll put on water for tea and we'll have a nice chat." Looking over her niece's shoulder, Evelyn waved and called, "Good morning, Mr. Hoffnagle."

Meredythe grimaced as the neighbor's tirade about daughters of hell, blasphemy, abominations walking the earth and not suffering witches to live shot fanatically across the street.

"Why are you so nice to him, Aunt Evie, when he's so mean to you?"

Her aunt patted her arm. "He can't help the way he was raised, dear. Besides, the nicer I am to him, the more frustrated he gets. Now get Methuselah's things. The water will be ready for tea in a jiffy."

A door across the street boomed shut. Evelyn waved at the closed door then turned and walked into her own house.

Meredythe chuckled as she hurried back to the car and grabbed the two bags that held the cat toys, two cans and a half-empty box of cat food, and a spare litter box. Shoving the car door shut with her hip, she lifted the load in her arms and headed toward her aunt's house.

Her lips twitched. Like every other house on the block, the flowerbeds at the front of the house had been cleaned and mulched for the winter. The fallen leaves from the oak trees were all raked up and bagged. The house was even freshly painted—at least the Wiccan good luck symbols were.

As she paused next to the brightly painted sign advertising tarot card readings, a feeling of peace enveloped her. Then, stepping on the first of fifteen rune stones that trailed through Evelyn's front yard to her porch, Meredythe silently recited the mantras for each charm. When she reached the porch, she brushed each of the six wind chimes for luck. First, the silvery crescent moons. The second had multicolored eggs. Third, the copper Egyptian ankhs. After those, the golden suns. Next, the black-and-white chime with three male and three female symbols. And finally, her favorite, the wind chime composed of rich, red phalluses. Instead of the delicate music of the other five chimes, this one's music was much deeper and more powerful. When she caressed it, the deep bongs followed her into the house.

After closing the bright blue door firmly, she walked across the foyer's round, multicolored carpet that was woven into a perfect pentacle. Once in the living room, she dropped the bags and her coat onto the purple sofa, stepped around the stuffed ocelot crouching under her aunt's prize rainforest fern and pushed through the beaded curtain that divided the living room and kitchen. Closing her eyes, she breathed deeply. Gods, but it was great to be home.

Opening her eyes, she stepped into the spacious kitchen and said, "I see you got a new sign advertising your tarot readings."

Her aunt beamed as she opened the oven. The smell of cinnamon, nutmeg and apples wafted toward her. "It's so much nicer than the other one, isn't it? The blue and silver swirls are such a nice touch."

Meredythe reached around her aunt and grabbed the whistling kettle from the stove. "Well, I'm glad you've cut back your readings to Monday and Wednesday. You had too many strange people running about the house."

A wide grin appeared on Evelyn's face. "Now isn't that funny. That's exactly what most of my neighbors say about my friends."

Chuckling, Meredythe lifted the tea canister down from its shelf. "What flavor are we having today?"

"Chamomile and rose hips. And get another cup. My new neighbor is coming over to meet you."

Meredythe reached up into the cupboard. "You have a new neighbor? And she comes for tea? You mean there's finally someone in this neighborhood who's not afraid of you?"

Making a face over her shoulder, Evelyn set the third pie on the counter. "Meredythe! My neighbors like me. At least, most of them do. Just because they won't come into the house… Anyway, Mary Francis is a wonderful woman. I want you to be nice to her. And none of those nosy reporter questions. She and I have a lot in common."

"How nice of you to say so, Evelyn," said the woman in the black-and-white habit who walked in the back door without knocking. Methuselah and a calico cat followed on her heels.

Tea leaves spilled onto the counter as Meredythe completely missed the pot. She blinked twice. "You—you're a…"

"Nun. How did you guess?" Blue eyes twinkling, the woman continued, "Did I forget to wash the word *nun* off my forehead again this morning?" Shaking her head in mock frustration, she continued, "No matter how often I ask *Him*—quite nicely, I might add—not to put it there, *He* just seems to think I need the reminder."

Meredythe's mouth dropped open. A nun? Here? In her aunt's house?

"Close your mouth, dear," Evelyn said as she removed her oven mitts. "You look rather undignified. Didn't I tell you the church purchased the house next door after the cloister across town burned down?"

Meredythe snapped her mouth shut. After swallowing, she began, "But my aunt is…"

Sister Mary Francis nudged Meredythe away from the counter and wiped up the tea Meredythe had spilled. Then she poured hot water into the teapot. "A witch, or at least thinks she is. Yes, I know. And I find her to be quite fascinating. It will be quite a coup if I can convert her."

Meredythe's eyes bugged out and both older women laughed.

"What did I tell you, Mary Francis? She takes everything so seriously."

Meredythe sank into a chair. "I think I've stepped into the Twilight Zone or something." The calico cat jumped into her lap and began to purr.

Sister Mary Francis set a steaming cup before her. "Here, dear. This will help calm your nerves. Oh, and that's Jezebel."

The teacup stopped halfway to Meredythe's mouth. "You named your cat Jezebel?" *A nun named her cat Jezebel*?

"Believe me, she's earned the name," Mary Francis said with a defeated sigh. "She looks upon every male she sees as a potential conquest. And he doesn't even have to be a cat. You should see what she does to the neighborhood dogs. And men! I don't even like to think about it. Drink up, dear, you look like you could use it."

"I could use something a lot stronger," Meredythe mumbled into her cup before she gulped the tea.

Her aunt placed a slice of hot apple pie before her. "Tell me how this tastes. I tried a new recipe."

Taking a deep breath to bring some order to the chaotic thoughts swirling through her brain, Meredythe simply nodded. Maybe something to eat would help her regain her composure. She couldn't remember the last time she'd been this flustered.

Wrong, murmured her insidious conscious. *You were more flustered when* he *kissed you.*

Firmly shoving *that* particular thought into a locked compartment in her mind, she set her cup down and picked up her fork. With both older women looking on, she dug into the pie. A wide smile appeared as the combination of flavors danced with her taste buds. "Mmm. I didn't think you could make a better apple pie than you already did, but I was wrong. What did you add?"

Clasping her hands in front of her bosom, Evelyn said, "Maybe someday I'll tell you, dear, but right now it's a secret."

Meredythe laughed. "Keep your secrets, Aunt Evie. We both know I'm not much of a baker. Now how was your trip to Tucson?" She scooped up another chunk of pie.

Sister Mary Francis cut two more slices and joined them.

After thanking her, Evelyn said, "It was just wonderful. I met the most fascinating Navajo medicine woman. And she gave me a fabulous recipe for lemon sage chicken. Next time you come for dinner, I'll make it for you."

As they ate, Evelyn continued to relate anecdotes from her trip. Finally, Sister Mary Francis rose. Meredythe glanced at her watch—barely half an hour had passed.

The nun reached across the table and held out her hand. "It was so nice to meet you, Meredythe. What with all your aunt has told me, I felt like I knew you before we met. But I simply must be going. If I don't help Father Paul organize the rummage sale, we'll end up selling the hymnals."

Meredythe grasped her hand firmly. "It was nice meeting you too, Sister."

"Call me Mary Francis, dear. Don't bother to get up, Evelyn. I'll see you tomorrow. Come along, Jezebel."

Evelyn poured herself another cup of tea as her guest headed for the back door. "Goodbye, Mary Francis. I'll talk to you tomorrow."

As Meredythe watched, Jezebel rubbed her cheek against Methuselah and then followed her mistress out door, her tail cocked in the air.

Meredythe chuckled. Thuse definitely had a besotted expression on his face. "Wow! Her name really fits."

Evelyn sighed. "Every cat in the neighborhood makes its way into Mary Francis' yard at least once a day. And so do the dogs if they get loose! And not a single one tries to chase her! Jezebel drives them all to distraction."

With a grin, Meredythe reached over and stroked Thuse's head. "A nun with a cat named Jezebel. What's the world coming to?"

He sneezed then yawned at her. *If only you knew, Meredythe.* With a flick of his tail, he strolled out of the kitchen.

When Evelyn would have risen, Meredythe gently clasped her wrist. "Aunt Evie, I need some information."

Curiosity colored her aunt's features as she settled back down. "What is it, dear?"

Meredythe threaded her fingers together and propped her elbows on the table. "The ancient Celts…did they offer human sacrifices on their important holidays?"

Her aunt frowned and leaned back. "Why do you want to know?"

Rising, Meredythe meandered over to the sink where she rinsed out her cup. "This story I'm working on now—a serial killer. All of the murders occurred on the same dates as old Celtic holidays."

Evelyn pursed her lips and drummed her fingers. "It's been so long…" she murmured, mostly to herself. Then, glancing up at her niece, she continued, "Sometimes, if conditions were dire enough, a person would volunteer to sacrifice himself or herself for the good of the people. And then, there were times that enemies… But on every important holiday? Definitely not."

Leaning her hips back against the sink, Meredythe gripped the edges of the counter and muttered, "Well, there goes that theory. I'm sorry, Aunt Evie. I know Celts really weren't into human sacrifice, not like people seem to think. It's just that I've been racking my brain and typing until my fingers cramp, but I can't come up with anything else."

Evelyn rose and carried the two other teacups on the table to the sink. "What exactly are you looking for?"

"A clue as to who's responsible for the murders I'm researching."

"What do you know so far?" she asked as she rinsed them out.

Meredythe frowned and crossed her arms over her chest. "There have been twelve murders in the last eight years—three in New York, the rest in cities across the country. Every victim has had his throat torn out, and the murders that happened on dirt had wolf or wolf-dog tracks around the bodies."

Evelyn's hand went to her throat. "On my. How dreadful. And you said all the murders happened on Celtic holidays?"

Meredythe counted them off on her fingers. "Yule, Ostara, Litha, Mabon and Samhain."

"Are you sure?" Evelyn tapped her lips with a finger. "And there were wolf tracks at all the sites? In all the different cities?"

"Around the bodies not on concrete."

"Well, then," her aunt said with a frown, "you need to find out who is able to travel around the country with wolves without raising suspicion. Circuses maybe?"

Meredythe grinned and threw her arms around her aunt. "Circuses, of course. I knew I could count on you, Aunt Evie. You've always had the answers whenever I needed them."

"And I'm always here whenever you need me, dear," her aunt replied as she returned Meredythe's hug. "Now I suppose you're going to leave right away."

Meredythe flushed. "I know I just got here, but..."

"You want to go work on your story. Go on, dear. You know where to find me."

"I promise I'll come for dinner next week. What night?" she said impulsively.

Evelyn's smile was fond. "I'm busy with appointments for tarot readings all next week and I'm dining with Mary Francis the following Tuesday. Better make it a week from Thursday."

Another hug. "A week from this coming Thursday. It's a date, Aunt Evie. I promise. I'll be here with rings on my fingers and bells on my toes."

Evelyn laughed. "Mind what you say, dear. I might hold you to it. It's been quite a while since we danced naked in the moonlight."

Meredythe laughed with her. "Wouldn't old Mr. Hoffnagle just love that?" After one last hug, she hurried into the living room and shrugged into her coat.

Her aunt followed her out onto the porch. "Drive carefully, dear. I'll see you Thursday night."

After blowing her aunt a kiss, Meredythe slid into her car. As she backed out of the driveway, her brain was spinning with names of circuses.

* * * * *

"Is she gone?"

Evelyn closed the door firmly behind her. "Yes. James was right. She couldn't wait to get back to work on her 'story'."

Mary Francis set the tray she was carrying onto the coffee table and sat down on the purple sofa.

Jezebel jumped up and settled next to her.

Lifting a cup, Mary Francis sipped. "I made us some more tea. There's a definite nip in the air today."

Sighing, Evelyn settled into an overstuffed chair covered with a multicolored afghan. "It's a wonder you don't slosh when you walk with as much tea as you drink."

Her friend chuckled and scratched underneath her wimple. "Ugh, why didn't Rhys pick an order that would ease up on its dress code?"

Evelyn snorted. "And how was he supposed to know what nuns would be wearing now all those centuries ago? Besides, you were the one who insisted on joining in the first place."

Shrugging, Mary Francis continued to sip her tea. "We couldn't just let them take over, you know. Someone had to infiltrate their church and see what their religion is all about."

Grasping a cup of tea, Evelyn frowned. "Morgana was supposed to—"

Jezebel hissed.

Her cup clattered on her saucer when Mary Francis set it down. "Morgana was a traitor, interested only in herself, not the good of her people."

A low growl rolled through Jezebel's throat.

"Are you sure she's dead?"

Mary Francis nodded. "No one could have survived that fire."

Jezebel's low growl became a snarl.

Sighing, Mary Francis stroked the angry cat from the top of her head to the tip of her tail. "I'm sorry, dear. None of us thought her curse would last after her death, but at least you're still alive."

"Morgana always *was* good with curses," Evelyn mumbled into her cup.

*****

"Damn it! Why can't I find anything?" Meredythe swore at her computer as she slapped her palms on the desk. She'd been searching over a week and every potential lead had fizzled out.

"Problems?" James King stopped before her desk, an amused smile on his face.

Meredythe wrinkled her nose at her boss and said, "I can't seem to get anywhere. Do you know not a single circus has an act with wolves? Can you believe it? I was sure I'd get a good lead by checking out circuses."

Her boss sat down. "Wolves seem too dignified to lower themselves to the casual entertainment of humans—to me anyway."

She turned her attention back to her computer. "Yeah well, I'm not personally acquainted with any so I couldn't say for sure. I really need to consult an expert on wolves. Maybe he or she can give me some insight into their behavior and whether or not they could be trained to kill. That guy who spoke at Columbia University, what was his name?" Shoving her chair back, she rose, went to her desk and began shuffling though her notes. "Here it is. Dr. Bleddyn Glyndwr."

James chuckled then said, "You pronounced his name wrong, Meredythe. His name is Welsh. The *dd*'s are pronounced like a *th*, the *y* like an *i*, and the *wr* is pronounced like an *oor*. So his name is pronounced *Blethin Glindoor*."

Meredythe stared at her notes. Interesting. Her ancestors had been Welsh too. But then, with a surname like Welsh, that was pretty obvious. "I wonder where he lives. I wish I could have gotten there quickly enough to meet him, but he was already gone by the time I got to the auditorium." She returned to her computer, her fingers flying over the keys.

James King sat silently, another small smile on his lips. The more she found out for herself the better.

She held up a sheet of paper. "Here it is. He has his own website. What do you know? He lives in upstate New York—Winterbourne to be exact. What a break. James, I'll be out of the office for a few days."

He nodded and rose. "When will you leave?"

She frowned. "It's already Tuesday. I'd like to leave today, but I promised Aunt Evie I'd be there for dinner Thursday and I'm not going to stand her up again. I guess I'll leave from her house Friday morning."

Jim clasped his hands behind his back. "How do you know this Dr. Glyndwr will be there? Are you going to call ahead?"

Frowning, she tapped her lips with a finger. Then she shook her head. "No. Whoever committed the murders travels with a wolf or wolves. Maybe this is the guy we're looking for. I don't want to warn him that I'm coming. If he's off lecturing, I'll just nose around town and see what I can find out about him."

Her boss frowned. "You will be careful."

Meredythe grinned. "I'm always careful, boss. You know that."

He smiled wryly. "That's why I've had to bail you out of jail three times."

"Stop worrying."

After he left, she returned to her computer. Five minutes later, she had a motel reservation. Grimacing, she wished she hadn't promised to meet Jon for dinner later. Well, she could always call and cancel. She glanced at her watch. Four o'clock. She stared at the blank screen then shrugged. At the moment, she was at an impasse, having exhausted every lead except this Dr. Glyndwr. Why not have dinner with Jon again? He was fun.

Switching off her computer, she put her files into her briefcase and shrugged into her coat. After slinging her purse over her shoulder, she grabbed her briefcase.

Stopping in front of her friend's desk, she said, "I'm going home early, Alice. I'll be back in tomorrow and the next day, but then I'll be heading upstate for a couple of days."

"Sure thing. Oh, and enjoy your second date."

Mumbling under her breath about nosy friends, she stomped out of the office.

* * * * *

The new moon was high in the sky when they got to the door of her apartment building. Meredythe turned to Jon, a warm smile on her face. "I had a wonderful time. Thanks for inviting me."

He smiled down at her. "I had a great time too."

Silence stretched between them. Jon shifted his weight to his other foot. "Ah…"

"I guess I better go in now," she interjected before he could hint that she should invite him in. "I'll let you know when I get back. Next time is my treat."

She smiled mentally at the obvious relief on his face. He must have been expecting her to dump him. Poor guy had probably been a real geek in high school. And even if he was good-looking now, how many women wanted to go out with a guy who dissected dead people?

"I'm looking forward to it," he said. "Do you think you'll be back next week?"

She shrugged. "I don't know. I should be, but you never know. Once, I spent three weeks in little town gathering information for a story."

When he stepped closer and laced his fingers through hers, she swallowed. When he bent down to kiss her, she didn't draw back. His kiss was gentle yet searching.

With a sigh, she answered.

When he finally lifted his head, she smiled. He lifted her hand to his lips. "Remember to call me as soon as you get back."

"I will."

He stepped away but waited until she disappeared into her building. By the time she reached her apartment and hurried to her front window, he was gone. She lowered the blind, surprised at her thoughts. Jon was really a nice guy, and she liked him. Maybe there could be a future for the two of them. She closed her eyes.

Then why was it the kiss she kept remembering came from a man with gray eyes rather than blue?

Across the street, a shadow slid out of the alley. Damian shook his head. Rhys was not going to like this report.

* * * * *

Meredythe stuck another file in her briefcase. "Okay, Alice, I'm leaving now. I'll call when I get settled in my motel."

Alice looked up from her computer. "Do you have everything? You have your laptop, don't you? I don't think Mr. King will be too happy if you charge another one to your business account because you left yours at the office."

She stuck her tongue out. "If you had put it in my briefcase like I asked you to, I wouldn't have forgotten it."

Alice grinned. "You're the hotshot reporter. You should have checked to make sure it was there."

Meredythe shuffled through her briefcase once more. "Where's the Chicago file?"

Alice stepped to her side. "Isn't it in there? I remember handing it to you yesterday morning, and you put it in your briefcase."

Meredythe stopped shuffling papers and looked up at the clock—4:50. "Oh shit. I left it at home."

Alice shrugged. "Stop and get it on the way. You're driving in that direction anyway."

She snapped her briefcase shut. Stopping at her place wasn't *too* far out of her way. "I guess I could. I'd like to have it."

"Well, then, that's your answer. I'll call your aunt and let her know you're running late."

Meredythe headed for the door. "Thanks, Alice. I appreciate it."

"Sure thing. Good luck. And be careful. The weather report is forecasting an early snowstorm."

* * * * *

"Shit, not another one!" Damned if she hadn't hit every red light between the building where she worked and the one where she lived. Turning onto her street, Meredythe glanced up toward her apartment.

Light shone out the front window.

Frowning, Meredythe slowed and rolled down the window. She hadn't left any lights on this morning.

Words as sharp as daggers stabbed into her mind. *Do not stop. Flee.*

Her head snapped up and she looked around. "What the…"

Fool! Run! Now!

An icy breeze blasted her, and a tall man clothed entirely in black strode out of the alley toward her. Her eyes leaped to his pale face. His black eyes burned like coals, and his white-fanged grin had icy shudders racing up and down her spine.

Get out of here, now! Then…forget.

She stomped her foot onto the gas. Her car sped down the block and turned the corner.

Damian waited until her car disappeared. He looked up her lighted window at the huge silhouette outlined there. Then he melted back into the shadows.

In Meredythe's apartment, Slade swept his arm across a table, shattering glass objects against the wall. Grabbing the TV, he heaved it across the room. He'd heard the car speed away. She'd eluded him again.

* * * * *

Snow was falling gently when Meredythe pulled into her aunt's driveway, muttering to herself because she'd somehow forgotten to stop at her apartment and pick up the Chicago file even though she planned on going there directly from her office. Oh well, she'd just have to do without it. Grabbing the wine on the front seat, she slid out of the car.

Evelyn met her at the front door. "I'm so glad you're here. I was beginning to worry. I have Methuselah's things all ready."

Meredythe froze in the doorway as her aunt looped a large shopping bag over her arm. "Thuse's things? Ready? I'm here for dinner, remember? Lemon sage chicken?"

Her aunt bustled about the living room shoving toys into another shopping bag. "I know, dear, and I'm very sorry, but I've a sudden change of plans. You remember Lady Sara, my friend from England? She sent me a ticket so I could come and spend Yule at Stonehenge." She stopped in the middle of the floor and clapped her hands together. "Imagine, Yule at Stonehenge. Can you think of anything better? I wish you could come with me."

Meredythe stood in the open doorway, snowflakes brushing past her to settle on the foyer floor. "But, Aunt Evelyn. I'm going upstate tomorrow. I can't take care of Thuse. And it's barely the middle of November. Yule isn't until December 21."

Evelyn handed her another shopping bag. "I know that. But Sara wants me to come now. And of course you can take Methuselah. Just leave him in your motel room. I'm sending enough toys to keep him occupied. And leave the TV on. He loves Animal Planet or better yet, Jerry Springer."

Meredythe dropped the other bag. "Aunt Evie, I don't even know if the motel allows pets."

Evelyn waved her hand in the air. "They'll never even know he's there. Now you better get going. The snow is coming down faster. I'm all packed too, and my taxi will be here in ten minutes." Turning, she looked up the staircase. "Methuuuuuuselah. Come along, dear. Meredythe is waiting for you."

Meredythe shifted the wine to her other hand. "You're leaving tonight?"

Instead of coming down the stairs, the cat sauntered out of the kitchen and Evelyn lifted him into her arms. "Yes. I know it's rather short notice, but I simply can't turn this invitation down. You understand, don't you, dear?"

Closing her eyes, Meredythe sighed with defeat. Goodness knows she wouldn't change a single thing about her aunt, especially her spontaneity. "Okay, Aunt Evie. I'll take Thuse with me. You have a good time at Stonehenge."

The squirming cat between them, Evelyn hugged her exuberantly. "Thank you, dear. I'll make it up to you, I promise. And I'll bring you a t-shirt."

"I know you will. Enjoy yourself."

Laughing, Evelyn pushed her cat into Meredythe's arms and glanced at her watch. "Oh my. I must get my suitcases downstairs. Good luck, dear. I hope you find the information you're looking for." She looped the shopping bags over Meredythe's arms, gave her a little shove and shut the door behind her.

For a moment, Meredythe stared at the closed door. She had a shopping bag covered with Christmas trees looped over her left arm and another with big orange balls looped over her right. A bottle of wine was tucked into her left armpit and Methuselah was rubbing his chin against the stem as he balanced himself against her arms in her already overburdened grasp. A gust of wind scattered snowflakes and rang wind chimes as she looked down into his smug face. Shaking her head at the vagaries of life, she said, "Well, Thuse, you ready for a road trip upstate?"

Joyful tinklings and deep bongs followed them off the porch and down the path of rune stones to her car.

* * * * *

"Are they gone?"

Evelyn let the curtain fall and turned. "Yes, Rhys. She just pulled out. You know, I don't like the look of this weather. The snow's coming down harder."

The old druid joined her at the window and smiled. "The weather never has been one of my fortes, Evelyn. We'll just have to trust the Goddess that she gets there."

The back door slammed. Sister Mary Francis pushed the beaded curtain aside and joined them. "Are they off then?"

Jezebel sauntered over to Rhys, sat at his feet and meowed.

With a smile, he lifted her into his arms. "Hello, Jezebel. You haven't changed at all, have you?" A loud purr filled the room as he stroked her.

Mary Francis sighed. "Honestly, Rhys. Must you encourage her?"

There was a sharp knock at the door and they all froze. "You didn't forget to give her something, did you, Evie?" Mary Francis asked as she backed toward the kitchen.

"No, I didn't," Evelyn answered as she peered out from between the closed curtains again. "Oh, it's just Damian." Opening the door, she said, "Come in, Damian. You must be freezing out there."

"The cold doesn't have much of an effect on me," he said with a slight smile. "Rhys is here, isn't he?" He started when he saw the room's other inhabitants.

The cat hissed loudly and sprang from Rhys' arms to the sofa where she arched her back, fluffed her tail, spat and growled repeatedly.

Damian's lips twitched. "Hello, Mary Francis. I guess your cat is still angry with me."

Mary Francis glared at him. "And can you blame her? You wanted to drink her blood."

"Now, Mary Francis," Rhys cajoled.

A stern look on her face, the nun rounded on the old druid. "Don't start, Rhys. I don't know why you trust him. There is no such thing as a reformed vampire."

Evelyn grabbed Damian's arm and pulled him farther into the room. "That's enough, Mary Francis. This is my house and I'll invite Beelzebub himself if I'm so inclined. Damian, you're paler than you should be. When was the last time you, ah…ate?"

Damian swayed slightly then smiled at his hostess. "Too long, I'm afraid, but I had to find Rhys. Slade was in Meredythe's apartment, waiting for her."

Even Jezebel froze at that comment.

Mary Francis shuddered and crossed herself. "Thank God she came here straight from work."

Damian shook his head as he leaned against Evelyn. "She didn't, but I managed to convince her not to go into her apartment."

"And we all know how you managed to do that, don't we?" Mary Francis muttered.

His toothy grin had Jezebel hissing and spitting again. "I didn't have much choice."

When he swayed again, Evelyn shoved him toward her kitchen. "You come with me. I have a raw steak in the refrigerator. That will hold you over until you can get…something."

He allowed her to guide him toward the kitchen. "Thank you, Evelyn. You're a queen among women."

Once Damian was out of sight, Jezebel quit hissing. Mary Francis lifted her into her arms. "What now, Rhys? Slade obviously didn't take the bait."

Rhys braced his hands on the back of the sofa. "We wait. Slade isn't going anywhere in this snowstorm. Once Meredythe is at the estate, she'll be safe. Not even Slade is stupid enough to attack Bleddyn on his home ground."

* * * * *

"Damn!" Meredythe cursed as the tires spun for the third time. She stepped on the gas again. The tires spun faster, but the car only slid deeper into the ditch at the side of the road. Gusts of wind buffeted the shuddering automobile on all four sides while snow and ice pellets bounced off the windshield. Grabbing her purse, she fished around and pulled out her cell phone. "Shit! No service. Damn these mountains! I'm going to have to walk." She pushed the door open and stepped out into the swirling snow.

"You wait here, Thuse," she said to the cat's inquiring meow. "I can see a light at the top of this hill, so there must be a house up there. I'll walk up and see if I can get us some help." She shivered as snow slapped her face. "Damn, but I wish I had a hat."

Closing the car door firmly, she left Methuselah curled up on the front seat. Shoving her hands into her pockets as deeply as she could, she hunched her shoulders against the biting wind—thankful it was at her back rather than in her face—and started climbing toward the flickering light. Slipping and sliding, she struggled up the hill, falling to her hands and knees repeatedly.

More than once she stopped to shake her numb hands—hands that spent more time in the snow bracing her falls and pushing her now-wet hair out of her face than they did in her semi-warm coat pockets. Tears had frozen on her cheeks when she finally skidded to a stop at the top of the hill, raised her head and looked straight into the most hideous face she'd ever seen.

The howling wind blew her shriek away. Shaking from more than the cold, she yanked her hair out of her face and grasped the cold stone to keep from falling. "Damn it, Meredythe, it's only a statue of a gargoyle. Get a hold of yourself."

Squinting toward the light, she could see the vague, dark outline of a house through the blowing snow. With a tooth-rattling shiver, she stepped away from the meager shelter of the gargoyle and plowed through the knee-high snow toward the house. By the time she reached the door, she was soaking wet and shivering uncontrollably. Sighing with relief, she leaned against the doorbell.

A few minutes later, she slapped her numb hand against it again. Damn it! Somebody had to be home to help her.

She'd just raised her fist to pound when the door opened, dim light and precious heat pouring out. She didn't notice either. Instead she gaped at the black-haired, gray-eyed man who stood before her.

He smiled, stared deeply into her eyes and said, "Hello, Meredythe."

Chapter Seven

An icy gust of wind shoved snow down the neck of Meredythe's coat and into the foyer of the house. She didn't notice. The man in front of her demanded all of her attention. Of all the people in world, how did she manage to end up at *his* house? Another freezing blast of wind enveloped her and she shivered. Her teeth began to chatter.

He grasped her arm. "Damn it, Meredythe, get in here before you freeze to death."

She ignored the shivers that racked her body when another blast of wind caressed her bare neck, and she wrenched her arm free. "I will not. I just need directions. How far to the town of Winterbourne?"

An amused look appeared on his handsome face and he folded his arms across his chest. "You already passed it."

She shoved her freezing hands into her pockets, trying to ignore the icy water running down her back. Sheer force of will stopped her shivering. "It's not snowing so hard that I wouldn't have recognized houses when I went by them."

Neither his stance nor his expression changed. The cold blasts of wind seemed to have no effect on him even though snow was swirling around his legs. "You took a wrong turn and ended up in my private drive. You should have stayed to the left instead of veering right."

"Fine. As long as I know where I'm going, I'll leave." Spinning away from him, she took a step and went down on one knee when her foot slid out from under her. Before she was completely down, he was at her side and offered his hand. She ignored it and pushed herself to her feet.

"Damn it, Meredythe, your car's stuck in a drift or a ditch, isn't it? How do you propose to get to town?"

Her back to him, Meredythe gulped as still another icy blast forced her breath back down her throat. After a deep breath, she clenched her teeth and said, "I'll walk if I have to."

He placed his hand on her arm again. "Please, if you try to walk to town, you'll get lost in the storm."

She took a step away from him, but the wind shoved her back. He reached out, and this time she accepted his steadying hand.

"Damn, damn, damn," she muttered, mostly to herself. "The least I could have done was ended up on Dr. Glyndwr's doorstep."

Behind her, he cleared his throat. "Yes, well…"

Meredythe closed her eyes and dropped her chin to her chest. How could she be so stupid? Why hadn't she realized who he was when she ran into him the day of the lecture? This couldn't be happening to her. "You're him, aren't you? Dr. Bleddyn Glyndwr?"

Snow was piling up on the doorstep and blowing into the hallway. His hand remained on her arm. "Yes, I am. Please, come in. You'll end up sick if you stay out here."

Shivering, she turned to face him. *Stop being stupid*, she told herself. *He's right. You'll end up dead if you try to walk anywhere in this blizzard.* "Okay, I'll come in, but only until it stops snowing. I have a motel reservation."

"Fine," Bleddyn agreed. Once he had her inside, he'd find a way to make her stay. And according to the latest weather report, that wouldn't be too hard. "Anything you say. Just come in and let me close the door."

She stepped forward then stopped. The wind blew her hair over her face and she was forced to use both hands to get it out of her eyes and mouth. Spitting the last curl free, she said, "Oh, I can't, at least not yet. Thuse is in the car. I have to go get him."

Bleddyn cocked an eyebrow. "Thuse?"

She shivered so hard a tear trickled down her cheek. "My cat—I mean, my aunt's cat."

At first, Bleddyn simply stared at her. Then he sputtered, "A cat? You brought a *cat*? *Here*?"

She flushed and her eyes narrowed. She braced her hand against the doorway as a gust of wind tried to push her inside. "I wasn't planning on stopping *here* first. If it weren't for this stupid snowstorm, you wouldn't even know I was anywhere near Winterbourne." She pushed herself away and took a step backward.

Like hell I wouldn't. Bleddyn caught her arm. Damned if she wasn't going to go back out into that storm to get the blasted cat. "Wait. I'll get your cat. You're already soaked. There's a fire in the study. Come in and get warm."

She stiffened. "You promise you'll get him?"

An exasperated sigh escaped Bleddyn. "I said I would, but not until you come in by the fire."

Meredythe allowed him to pull her into the house and close the door. "This way," he said as he led her away from the dimly lighted foyer and into a dark hallway. *God, this place is creepy,* she thought, trying to see through the shadows lining the walls. Didn't he believe in using electricity?

He looked over his shoulder. "Sorry it's so dark, but the power's out. I've got a generator running, but I use as little electricity as possible when it's on." He stopped and pulled a door open. Light and toasty warmth poured out. With a deep sigh of satisfaction, she stepped into the warm room.

He plowed into her back and had to steady her to keep her from falling when she stopped abruptly. Another shiver racked Meredythe's body, but this one had nothing to do with the cold. She swallowed nervously.

A large gray wolf looked up as they entered the room and rose slowly from her place by the fire. Settling on her haunches, she ran her tongue around her jaw.

Meredythe swallowed again. "That—that's a wolf."

He chuckled and slid past her. Stopping next to the wolf, he turned back to Meredythe. "Her name is Keri."

Meredythe stood absolutely still. Melting snow dripped off her coat to the floor. "You live with a wolf?"

He smiled and his hand strayed to Keri's head. "She won't bite you, I promise. Come, I'll introduce you."

Meredythe edged forward, her mind whirling. *She kind of looks like that wolf-dog Sweetie, all white and silver. I guess this guy knows what he's talking about. He is an expert.* Another thought leaped to the forefront of her mind. *He's got this wolf. Maybe he has a black one too. Maybe he's the guy I'm looking for. He was in New York when the last murder occurred.*

She shivered. If Dr. Glyndwr was the murderer, she could be in real danger here. However, she didn't fit the profile of all the other murder victims. Besides, there was no way he'd murder her in his own home, was there? And James knew she was here. So did Aunt Evie. Meredythe looked from the wolf to Dr. Glyndwr. His eyes met hers calmly. What was it about him? She...she trusted him. Deep, deep down, she was absolutely sure he would never hurt her. Why?

A slight smile twitched on his lips. All she could see in his eyes was concern, amusement...and a challenge. She glanced down at the wolf, Keri. Her tail thumped against the floor. Okay, what did she have to lose?

Your hand? she thought.

She flexed her stiff, cold fingers and unbuttoned her coat.

He gestured to her left. "Just drape it over the back of that chair."

After dropping her coat, she pushed a wet curl out of her face and edged forward, stopping about a foot away from the wolf. She sighed as the heat from the roaring fire reached out and enveloped her. She didn't care if the wolf did eat her. At least she'd be warm.

Her host chuckled. "Hold out your hand and let her sniff it."

"I know the routine," she said more sharply than she intended as she reached toward the wolf. "Frank Messner introduced me to Sweetie."

The wolf sniffed her hand. Then she nudged it with her nose and slid her head underneath. Meredythe started. Then she smiled and slid her hand down the wolf's head and neck. "Her fur is so smooth!"

Her host grinned. "She likes you. Now sit down and get warm." Striding across the room, he pulled open the door of a liquor cabinet and grabbed a bottle of brandy. Pouring a healthy portion into a glass, he returned to the fire and placed it in her hand. "Drink it all. It will help warm you up."

The wolf curled up before the fire as Meredythe settled into a chair and swallowed some brandy. She coughed as it burned its way down to her stomach. Warmth flowed outward as the brandy took effect.

Her host disappeared out the door only to reappear minutes later carrying a gray bundle. "You've got to get out those wet clothes, at least the jeans, or you'll get sick."

Meredythe glanced down. Her jeans were wet to her thighs and her Nikes were soaked. "I'll change while you get Thuse." She raised her hand to hide a yawn.

Bleddyn smiled. She'd been so astonished when he opened the door and then so obstinate about accepting his help, he'd thought he'd have to physically restrain her from going back out into the blizzard. Now, though, she looked ready to fall asleep.

Her head nodded. She jerked it up and took another sip of brandy. Then she glared at him. "Don't stand there staring at me. Go get Thuse."

Placing his hand over his heart, he bowed. "As you command, my lady."

Chuckling at the shocked expression on her face, he left the room. Making his way through the dark house with a sure step, he soon reached the kitchen. Grabbing a flashlight, he stepped out into the mudroom and pulled on a pair of boots. Then he shrugged into a heavy parka and checked the pockets for his gloves. Turning on the flashlight, he stepped out into the swirling snow.

"Damn wind is howling louder than the wolves," he muttered when he finally reached Meredythe's car after struggling through snowdrifts for fifteen minutes. "A cat. What possessed her to bring a cat? Damn thing probably won't even come to me once it gets my scent. It's apt to bolt as soon as I open the door. How will I explain that to her?" Frowning, he pushed his way through the deepening snow to the passenger side of the car. He'd have to dig through a four-foot drift to get into the driver's side. Luckily, this side was more protected. After a few tugs, the door opened.

"Okay, cat, where are you?" he grumbled as he shined the flashlight into the car. A pair of green eyes glowed back at him.

It's about time you got here.

As the words echoed in his mind, Bleddyn stumbled back. What in all the seven hells was Meredythe doing with a Familiar?

The cat minced his way across the seat, wrinkling his nose when snow blew in on him. *How do you think we kept her hidden all these years?*

Bleddyn leaned forward and braced his hand against the car. "Rhys knows?"

If a cat were able to snort with disgust, it would have. *Are you really as stupid as you seem? How have you managed to stay alive all these years?*

Bleddyn muttered an obscenity under his breath. "Okay, Rhys knows."

The cat sat on the seat and curled his tail around his feet. *Well, at least you display some intelligence. Meredythe's overnight bag is in the backseat. The rest of her luggage is in the trunk, but we can wait until tomorrow for you to get that. You'll need to bring the two shopping bags though.*

Dumfounded, Bleddyn simply stared. A cat was giving him orders.

Don't just stand there. The storm is getting worse.

Jerking his hands away from the car, he glared at the cat. "If you expect me to carry all of that, you have to walk."

The cat craned his neck and stared into the swirling snow. *Okay, only the bag with my food. And I'll ride your shoulder.* He flexed his claws for emphasis.

Muttering obscenities concerning both Methuselah's and Rhys' ancestry, Bleddyn pushed past the cat and leaned over the seat. Grabbing the shopping bag covered with Christmas trees, he checked inside. Cat food. When he reached over and jerked Meredythe's overnight bag toward him, the bottle of wine fell on the floor. He flashed his light on the label then reached down, grabbed it and shoved it into the bag with the cat food.

Pushing himself back out of the car, he slung Meredythe's bag over his right shoulder and grabbed the shopping bag with his left hand. He already held the flashlight in his right. Glaring at Methuselah, he asked, "Are you coming?"

The cat yawned. *Turn around and I'll jump onto your back. I'll be able to use Merry's bag for support.*

Muttering to himself, Bleddyn turned. He grunted when the cat landed on his back. Damn thing weighed more than he expected.

I'm ready. Make sure you shut the car door. There's enough snow inside already.

Bleddyn complied with a growled curse. "If anybody sees me carrying you, I'll never live it down."

He dug his front claws deeper into Bleddyn's parka. *There's no one here to see you except wolves.*

Bleddyn snorted. "Like I said, if anybody sees me…"

The snow fell faster and more heavily as Bleddyn made his way back up the hill. After numerous slips and slides and even more numerous curses, he reached the front of the house and headed for the door. No way was he carrying a cat any farther than he had to.

When he reached the steps, Methuselah jumped from his back. *Thank you.*

Bleddyn's brow lifted. Courtesy from a cat. Who'd have believed it?

Urged on by insistent meows, Bleddyn stamped as much snow off his boots as he could, then opened the door. Methuselah snaked between his legs and disappeared into the dark hallway.

"Damn cat," Bleddyn muttered as he dropped the shopping bag by the door where it could stay for all he cared. Setting the overnight bag on the floor, he shrugged out of his coat and hung it over the back of a chair. Then he sat down and removed his boots. Rising, he grabbed the bag and padded silently back to his study in stocking feet. The slightly open door told him the cat had found his mistress.

Pushing the door open farther, Bleddyn's gaze went immediately to Meredythe. She was curled up in a chair she'd pulled closer to the fire, asleep. Her empty glass lay atop her wet shoes and socks where it must have dropped after she fell asleep. Her rich, auburn hair was mostly dry and curled riotously about her. Her breasts rose and fell softly, her nipples clearly outlined by her wet sweater.

Wet! Bleddyn dropped her bag and hurried to her side. "You little fool. You'll catch pneumonia."

Without a second thought, he peeled off the sweater and bra. His eyes were drawn to the mole shaped like a wolf head high on her left breast. Carefully, he traced it. Yes, she was definitely the one. His gaze drifted down her breast to her rosy nipple and his finger followed. Already pebbled in the cool air, it tightened more as he stroked his thumb over it.

The shadow in his soul pushed against his willpower.

Heat shot to his groin and his cock hardened. How would her nipples taste? Sweet? Spicy?

His mouth began to water.

Gritting his teeth, he shook his head. No. She was sleeping. He would not, could not take advantage of her.

Jaws clenched against the urge to suck her nipples into his mouth, Bleddyn pulled the sweatshirt he'd brought earlier over her head then took a deep breath. With her tantalizing breasts covered, he could think again, be sure of his control. Then he glanced down at her wet jeans.

Fuck. Just the thought of her naked from the waist down had the blood in his cock throbbing in time with his heart. But there was no one else here and she couldn't stay in those wet clothes.

Quickly as he could, Bleddyn unfastened her jeans and pulled them off her icy legs. Momentarily distracted by how cold her thighs were, he massaged heat back into them.

Mumbling something incoherent, she rubbed her cheek against the soft leather of the chair's back but didn't awaken.

Once her thighs were warm again, Bleddyn allowed his gaze to slide to the dark juncture of her thighs. His breath caught in his throat and his nostrils flared. The tiny wisp of pink satin did little to hide the neatly trimmed fiery curls from his hungry gaze or mask her sweet, musky scent from his sensitive nose.

He slid his hands up her thighs and slipped his thumbs under her thong's slender straps. They would tear so easily. Sliding his cock deep into her cunt would be just as easy.

His control slipped more.

Again, he inhaled deeply.

Her tantalizing scent surrounded him.

His throbbing cock strained against his jeans.

The darkness in his soul awoke completely and howled, *Mine*!

Bleddyn slid his fingers under her panties toward her cunt.

Shifting, she opened her thighs.

A soft moan reached his ears.

His fingers reached the soft curls of her cunt.

Bleddyn reached for the zipper of his jeans with his other hand.

Take her! *Spread her thighs and mount her*! howled the entity in his soul.

Have you ever seen anything more pathetic and bedraggled than a cat that's been out in a blizzard? asked a dry voice in his mind.

Bleddyn snapped his attention away from Meredythe and locked gazes with the wolf stretched before the fire.

The cat sat next to her, furiously grooming himself.

The cat stopped licking long enough to glare at the wolf. *Shut up, Keri.*

Concentrating on their voices, Bleddyn sucked in a deep breath, breathing through his mouth to lessen the temptation of Meredythe's heady scent. "You two know each other?"

The wolf yawned then licked her lips. *Finish dressing Meredythe, Bleddyn, before she catches a chill.*

Squashing the snarling darkness that wanted him to roll her over, mount her and plunge his aching cock into her cunt over and over, Bleddyn focused his attention on Meredythe's face as he pulled her panties off and slipped the sweatpants up over her legs and hips. Then he slid her feet into thick, woolen socks.

Rising, he exhaled slowly. Thanks to Keri and the damn cat, he'd managed to strip the clothing off Meredythe and dress her in some of his sweats without the dark entity that inhabited his soul seizing command of his body. He shook his head. Without them, he wouldn't have been able to control himself. And the last thing he wanted to do was drive her away.

Now, however, he was firmly in control of himself again. Looking down at Meredythe, he smiled. She reminded him of a contented wolf pup the way she was curled on the chair. Bending, he lifted her into his arms.

The heads of both the cat and wolf snapped up.

He grinned at them. "I'm putting her to bed—alone. If it makes you both feel better, I'll sleep down here with you."

Readjusting his burden so that her head rested against his shoulder, Bleddyn strode out the door. He walked unerringly through the dark hallway then up the steps. Once he was on the second floor, he turned right and shouldered open the third door he came to. He didn't need a light as he carried Meredythe to the bed and laid her down. It was his room. Quickly, before the urge to strip her naked and make passionate love to her overcame his good intentions, he jerked the blankets down, settled her on the bed and pulled the blankets up to her chin. Then, with as little noise as possible, he put more logs on the fire in the fireplace. Once it was burning merrily, he returned to stand by the bed.

The soft glow of the fire reflecting off glass added an ethereal quality to her beauty. The memory of her rose-tipped breasts and the fiery curls between her thighs appeared in his mind. Her sultry scent teased his nostrils. Bending over, he caressed her cheek.

Mumbling something unintelligible, she rolled over.

After a quick kiss on her forehead, Bleddyn stalked stiffly back across the room and through the door. Once outside, he closed it firmly, leaned back against it and spread his legs, shifting against the uncomfortable tightness of his aching erection imprisoned in his tight jeans. He might be able to control his lust, but he couldn't control his cock. And the full moon was still some time away. How in the world would he survive with a constant hard-on?

Cock aching, Bleddyn stomped down the staircase and returned to the library. Both Keri's and Methuselah's heads snapped up when he slammed the door open.

"Out!"

The cat hissed and the wolf growled. Neither, however, balked at his command.

Bleddyn sucked in a deep breath as he closed the door firmly behind him. The last thing he needed was those two commenting on his condition. Flopping down into the chair where Meredythe had so lately slept, he stretched out his legs and opened his jeans. His cock leaped out, straining upward, jerking as it sought Meredythe's hot cunt.

As her scent surrounded him, Bleddyn grasped his cock and began pumping it slowly and steadily. Closing his eyes, he leaped into a fantasy where he was half reclining on the bed next to Meredythe and slid his fingers through her silky curls until he reached her wet pussy. There, he rubbed her hard, little clit a few times, then slid first one then a second finger into her and pumped them. Bending his head, he captured her mouth with his in a long, tongue-twisting kiss, then nibbled his way down her neck and across her collarbone to suck on a cinnamon-colored nipple as she arched her breast into his mouth.

In the chair, Bleddyn groaned and spread his legs farther apart as he imagined himself burying his cock deep inside her, her cunt muscles grabbing and sucking him. He groaned. Her cunt would be hot and wet and tight, he just knew it. His balls drew up and began to burn.

As his cum erupted high into the air, Bleddyn clutched arm of the chair with his left hand. Slowly, he released his cock and stared at his shaking hand. Christ, but he couldn't remember the last time he'd come that hard and long.

* * * * *

Meredythe snuggled deeper beneath the covers. She was deliciously warm and didn't want to wake up. A log on the fire cracked, and she opened her eyes. The clock on the nightstand displayed red numbers—7:15. Pushing herself up into a sitting position, she raised her arms and stretched. Then she remembered. Her eyes flew around the room, but she was alone…almost.

"Merrooww."

Her gaze dropped to Methuselah and she pulled him into her arms. "What have we gotten ourselves into, Thuse?"

She lifted her eyes from the cat and gasped. The wall before her was made entirely of glass! A chunk of snow meandered its slow way down one of the panes. She looked up and gasped again. Half of the roof was glass too! My God, she'd slept in a picture window. Dropping the cat, she rolled out of the bed and looked around more carefully.

The king-sized bed was centered immediately underneath the glass portion of the roof facing the glass wall. Slowly, she walked to the huge window and gazed out onto a winter wonderland. Snow still fell heavily. There was no way she'd be able to leave today.

"Damn," she muttered and turned around. Methuselah was curled up on the bottom of the bed, watching her. "I guess we'll just have to make the best of it."

She gave him a quick stroke as she passed the bed. A large sofa was pushed against the head of the bed facing the fireplace. A dresser and chest of drawers sat against opposite walls. There were three doors. She opened the first to reveal a walk-in closet, filled with men's clothing. The second, a spacious bathroom. Meredythe sighed gratefully as she stepped inside. She needed to use the facilities.

After washing her hands, she grabbed the brush that was lying on the sink and began to struggle with her tangled hair. When she walked back into the bedroom, the third door opened and Bleddyn Glyndwr sauntered in.

"Good morning."

She stepped back but continued to brush her hair. She could be just as nonchalant as he could. "Don't you know how to knock?" Then she grimaced as the brush encountered a particularly stubborn snarl.

"I did. You didn't hear me." His eyes followed her hands and he shoved his fists into his pockets. "I'd be happy to brush your hair for you."

She stepped back. "No! I mean, I can manage myself. What are you doing here anyway?"

He looked as eager as a puppy who'd just found a new best friend. "It's my room."

Meredythe was not impressed. She didn't want a new best friend. "I figured that out when I saw your clothes in the closet. Why did you put me here, and," she continued in a harder voice, "where did you sleep?"

"This is the only room that had a bed already made. And I slept on the couch in the study. I have a crick in my neck to prove it. Just ask your cat."

Methuselah sneezed. *She doesn't know, idiot.*

"Oh yeah, like he could answer me. What kind of fool do you take me for?" Still brushing her hair, Meredythe forced herself to stay calm, trying to act nonchalant, like being in a strange man's bedroom was an everyday occurrence. No way would she allow him to fluster her.

Grudgingly, she admitted to herself that he probably was telling the truth about where he slept. Dark stubble covered his chin and he still wore the sweater and jeans he'd been wearing last night. His long hair was loose on his shoulders and looked almost as tangled as hers. She closed her eyes. He was without a doubt the sexiest man she'd ever seen.

When she opened her eyes again, he was smiling tenderly. "I've never considered you a fool, Meredythe."

She jerked the brush through her hair one last time. "How do you know who I am?"

Breaking eye contact, he stepped toward her. "James King told us."

She stepped back. "Us?"

She muttered under her breath as he walked toward her. But he passed her and knelt before the fireplace. After jabbing the burning embers with the poker, he placed two more logs on the fire. Only after he rose and faced her did he answer. "Rhys and me."

The older man's face appeared in her memory. "Oh yeah, the old guy who was in James' office with you."

He nodded and took a step toward her. The dark whiskers softened his chin. And those eyes… Those smoky gray eyes.

She grasped the brush tighter. *Get a hold of yourself, girl.* "Why are you stalking me?"

He stiffened. She did not doubt the surprise that appeared on his face. "Stalking you? I'm not stalking you."

Meredythe shifted uneasily. Nobody could pretend to be that amazed. Was she wrong about him? "You could have fooled me. You were the one who barged into *my* break room."

He ran his hand through his hair.

Meredythe crossed her arms over her chest and tapped her foot.

He sighed. "I apologized for that. I'll apologize again. I'm sorry. I wasn't myself that day. I certainly didn't intend to anger—or frighten—you."

Meredythe sniffed, but she did relax a little. "I wasn't frightened," she lied. "What about Columbia University?"

Placing his hands on his hips, he cocked his head and stated, "I was scheduled to deliver a lecture. I had no idea you'd be there."

Everything he said sounded so reasonable. Then her eyes narrowed. "What about Jon?"

"Who?"

The confusion on his face appeared to be genuine, but her reporter's instincts leaped. Was that a slight stiffening she noticed? Was he tense? Uneasy? "The blond-haired man who was with me."

A bored expression appeared on his face and her eyes narrowed. He was definitely hiding something. "Oh, him. What about him?"

Her chin lifted. "You threatened him."

He crossed his arm over his chest. "I did not."

She stepped forward. "Yes, you did. I heard you."

He snorted. "I didn't say a word."

"You snarled at him."

"Snarled? I *snarled*?" A slight smile twitched at the corners of his mouth. "I think you're imagining things."

She took another step. "I did not imagine it. You snarled at him."

He uncrossed his arms and slid his hands into his back pockets. His sweater stretched tautly across his chest. "Why?"

Meredythe stared at how the soft wool clung and took another step forward. "Why what?"

He removed his hands from his pockets and pushed his sleeves up. His voice dropped, became huskier. "Why would I snarl at someone?"

Meredythe's eyes shifted to the black hairs on his forearms as he crossed them again. She remembered grasping his arms before and how soft those hairs were. Was the hair on the rest of his body as soft? His chest? His groin? A picture of a thick cock rising from a nest of dark curls exploded into her mind and her mouth began to water. How would he taste?

He cleared his throat.

Mentally shaking her thoughts free of the new erotic path they sought, she shrugged. "I don't know." Her eyes rose to his. They looked as soft as morning mist. Again she conquered her rebellious thoughts. She jerked her gaze from his to the fire. "But I'm going to find out."

Reaching out, he lifted a curl from her breast and tucked it behind her ear. "You're free to discover any secrets I have."

Her eyes flew back to his. How had she gotten so close? She'd been standing half a room away and he had never moved! Those wonderful gray eyes. She licked her lips. *My God, he's going to kiss me again.*

Instead he stepped away. "And you're the one who showed up on my doorstep last night."

She blinked and tried to gather her scattered thoughts. "What?"

Bleddyn clasped his hands behind his back as her blue eyes darkened to sapphire. If she kept looking at him like that, he was going to kiss her breathless. And if he did that, they'd both end up writhing naked on the floor. He couldn't give in to the temptation, not now. The full moon was only a short time away. If he wanted to finally fulfill the prophecy that would drive the devil from his soul, he had to wait until then. He'd waited centuries for Meredythe. He could wait a few weeks more. He *would* wait. "You showed up on my doorstep last night. Are you sure you're not stalking me?"

She reacted as he expected. The innocent desire in her eyes instantly changed to anger.

"Me? Stalking you! Are you nuts?"

He backed away and turned to the door. "If you say so. I brought your overnight case along when I got your cat. I thought you'd like a change of clothing. It's sitting by the door.

I'm going to go back to your car and see if I can get the rest of your luggage now that it's daylight."

She shook her head. "Thank you. But you don't have to bother with the rest of my things. I'll be leaving once the storm is over."

He smiled back over his shoulder when he reached the door. "Have you looked outside? It's still snowing and, according to the Weather Channel, it's not going to stop before tonight at the earliest. Even then it could take days for us to get out. The entire Northeast is having two to three or more feet of snow dumped on it."

Her mouth fell open and she hurried to the other side of the room, to the huge glass wall. "You're kidding, aren't you? I can't stay here. I have to—"

He turned to face her once more. "What? Get to your motel? Why? You were coming to Winterbourne for something. Why can't you do it here? Unlike most of the rest of town, thanks to my generator, I have electricity and the phone lines are still up."

She spun around, the clenching and unclenching of her hands betraying her uncertainty and panic. "But I can't stay here."

Bleddyn watched her, a trace of sadness brushing his mind. Why was she afraid? He would never hurt her. "Why not? It's not like you have a choice."

Methuselah jumped off the bed and began to wind his way back and forth between her legs. Looking up, he meowed.

Meredythe bent down and gathered him into her arms. As she cuddled the cat against her chest, he could see her tense muscles relax. Methuselah's contented purr seemed to ease her frayed nerves. After a deep sigh, she said, "You're right, Dr. Glyndwr. I'm sorry if I seem ungrateful, but I'm used to controlling my own life. I didn't expect to be stranded by a snowstorm."

Bleddyn stared at Meredythe. The swirling snow on the other side of the huge window behind her emphasized the copper, auburn and burgundy strands in her hair. The blue-gray color of the cat in her arms accented the sapphire of her eyes. Her embarrassed flush brought delicate color to her cheeks. When she began to gnaw on her bottom lip, his eyes dropped to her mouth. How would he be able to wait to take her to bed?

Tearing his eyes away from her mouth, he concentrated on the swirling snow behind her. "There are clean towels in the bathroom if you want to take a shower. It's going to take me a while to get to your car and dig it out. I'll take Keri with me. There's fresh coffee in the kitchen."

"Dr. Glyndwr," she said softly as he turned away and grasped the doorknob.

He glanced back over his shoulder.

She smiled tentatively. "Thank you for your hospitality. I do appreciate it—really."

"Call me Bleddyn," he said then walked out the door, pulling it closed behind him.

Meredythe dropped Methuselah from her arms and turned to look out into the storm. This room was at the back of the house, so she couldn't see her car. But then with the swirling snow she couldn't see anything but snow-covered mounds anyway. Sighing, she pivoted and walked across the room for her overnight case. A long, hot shower would feel great. Then a cup of coffee. And she had to call James and let him know she had arrived safely.

Once she was in the bathroom, she stripped off the thick socks and baggy sweatpants, then pulled off the sweatshirt and dropped it to the floor. The she stiffened and stared wide-eyed into the mirror. She was completely naked. "I didn't change my clothes last night," she said to her reflection. "That means…"

Even though she was alone, her face, neck and the tops of her breasts flushed crimson. Bleddyn Glyndwr had stripped off her wet clothes—all of them. He'd seen her naked. He'd touched her.

That last thought brought the kiss they'd shared in the break room to mind. She stared into the mirror, mesmerized by the woman who stared back at her—a woman she didn't recognize. Her skin was flushed. Her lips were parted and her breath came in short gasps. Her breasts felt and looked fuller, and her nipples had hardened into aching pebbles. A shiver raced up her spine as a soft ache spread outward from her groin. She moaned. If just the thought of his kiss did this to her, what would happen when he kissed her again?

She spun away from the mirror and turned on the water. As soon as she had the temperature adjusted, she stepped in and let the hot water sluice over her, her mind fixated on the fact that she knew it wasn't *if* Bleddyn would kiss her again but *when*.

And, heaven help her, she was looking forward to it.

She screamed with frustration. "Damn it, why do you have to be so sexy! I'm here for a story, not a man."

Only the sound of rushing water answered her.

Meredythe slammed her fist into the wall then winced at the pain engulfing her hand. Damn him.

Closing her eyes, she leaned her head against the shower stall. As she'd known it would, his smiling face appeared in her mind—his smiling face and naked body.

"Oh hell." Dropping the washcloth, she sank to her knees and slipped her fingers between her legs. She'd never get her mind back on her story without some relief. A quick fantasy would take care of that.

A stab of heat raced straight to her nipples, and they tightened into hard buds. Leaning her head back, Meredythe slid her fingers between her lips and touched her swollen clit. Shivering as waves of pleasure raced through her body, she opened her eyes, her gaze focusing on the showerhead. Her fingers stopped moving when she realized it was removable.

Rising, she pulled the showerhead from its mount and directed the pulsating bursts of water from one nipple to the other. Both tightened as spikes of heat radiated outward and downward through her stomach and into her groin. Cupping her left breast, she kneaded and squeezed. Her nipples tightened even more.

Moaning, Meredythe sank to the floor, slid onto her behind and leaned back against the wall. Bending her knees, she braced her feet on the floor and opened her legs wide. When she reached down to brace her left hand on the floor, her hand bumped the bottle of body wash. Grabbing it, she turned it upside down and squeezed it all over her breasts, stomach and pubic hair. Its spicy scent—his scent—permeated the hot, humid air of the shower. Slowly, she began to rub the foam into her body. Then, with a picture of Bleddyn's silvery gaze foremost in her mind, she directed the pulsating water directly against her swollen clit. Oh yes!

"Ahh!"

As her clit vibrated, her back arched and she had to brace her free hand against the floor to keep her balance. What started as a whimper evolved into a full-bodied moan as she held the showerhead closer to her throbbing clit. Her hips jerked forward and she slid to her back. Switching the showerhead to her left hand, she slid the fingers of her right between her legs and began to rub.

"Bleddyn! Oh yes! Oh yes! Oh yes!"

The showerhead thunked to the floor as the orgasm ripped through Meredythe. Warm water ricocheted off the wall onto her shuddering body as waves of pleasure rolled outward from her groin. Palms braced flat against the floor, she clenched her internal muscles and experienced a second, milder orgasm.

Slowly, her shuddering decreased until she finally lay still. Panting, she pushed herself first into a sitting position, then to her feet. She leaned against the wall to steady herself. Eventually her breathing steadied. Using both hands, she replaced the showerhead, hanging on to the fixture until her legs could support her, and let the warm water sluice down her body.

Raising her head, she closed her eyes against the pulsating water. In her mind, a naked Bleddyn smiled at her, his cock thrusting straight out from his body, his wolfish grin all-knowing. Once again Meredythe slapped her hand against the shower wall. Damn him, the bastard. The mind-blowing orgasm she'd just experienced hadn't done a bit of good. She still wanted him.

Chapter Eight

When Bleddyn finally nudged the back door open with his hip, rock and roll was blaring from the radio. As the aroma of frying bacon surrounded him, his gaze leaped to Meredythe. Standing with her back to him, she was whisking eggs in a large bowl. Her fiery hair was pulled back into a braid that reached to her waist. A baggy blue sweater covered her torso to the top of her thighs. However, when she raised her hand and opened a cupboard door, the soft wool rose high enough for him to admire her tight jeans as her ass dipped and shimmied while she sang along with the music.

A picture of her bent over the back of a sofa, her legs spread and her naked ass thrust into the air leaped to his mind. His fingers itched to stroke and fondle. His cock stirred.

He concentrated on the scent of the bacon. "It smells wonderful," he shouted over the music as he dropped the two suitcases on the floor and set her briefcase next to them. "I'm not much of a cook myself."

Bowl and whisk in hand, she whirled.

Bleddyn hung his parka over the back of a chair, sat down and began to pull off his boots. "Sorry. I didn't mean to startle you." With a smile, he nodded toward the suitcases. "How long were you planning on visiting me? You have enough clothing for two months."

Setting the bowl back on the counter, she reached over to the radio and turned the volume down. Then she dropped a gob of butter in a frying pan and set it on a hot burner. "I believe in being prepared. Sometimes fieldwork takes longer than I anticipate."

Bleddyn grunted then dropped his second boot on the floor. "And just what was the 'fieldwork' that brought you to me?"

Eyes wary, she glanced over her shoulder and watched him place his boots in the mudroom and grab a mop. "How do you know I was coming to see you?"

He grinned at the surprise that appeared on her face when he mopped up the melted snow he'd brought into the kitchen, sure she hadn't expected to see him clean up his own mess. "You mentioned it last night. Something about wishing you were stranded on Dr. Glyndwr's doorstep."

Exasperation replaced her surprise. Bleddyn turned and put the mop back outside the door, opening it wider for Keri to come in. Obviously Meredythe didn't like surprises.

After dumping the eggs into the now-hot frying pan, she turned back to him. "You're an expert on wolves. I have questions I want to have answered."

Crossing his arms over his chest, he leaned back against the refrigerator, his expression completely open. "Sure. I'll tell you anything you want to know."

Her smile brightened the room. "Great," she began. "What would happen—"

Smoke began to rise behind her.

Bleddyn shifted his feet. "Meredythe?"

Her frown betrayed her annoyance at his interruption. "What?"

He grinned as the odor of burning bacon reached her. "The bacon. It's burning."

"Damn!" Spinning, she grabbed the skillet and dropped it just as quickly. The handle was too hot.

Chuckling, Bleddyn pushed away from the refrigerator and joined her at the stove. "Here, let me do that. I'll salvage what I can. You better watch the eggs."

"Eggs!"

Shifting to give him room, she sighed with relief as she stirred the eggs. They, at least, hadn't burned.

Wrapping the handle in a towel, Bleddyn lifted the pan and carried it to the sink. "Only a few pieces are burned."

A low whine came from the other side of the kitchen and Keri licked her jowls.

Bleddyn didn't even look at her as he picked the unburned bacon out of the pan. "No, you may not have it. You're watching your weight, remember?"

After a low growl in his direction, the wolf disappeared in the direction of the study.

Meredythe glanced toward Bleddyn. "How did she understand you?"

He placed the last of the bacon on a plate. "Dogs learn the word 'no' fairly quickly, and wolves are smarter."

After one more quick stir, she divided the eggs onto two plates, placing the larger portion on his. "They are?"

Bleddyn smiled at the seemingly innocent inflection of her words. She was fishing for information. Well, he'd give her some.

The toast popped up. "To a certain extent. And, like any animal—including humans—some are smarter than others. There's jam in the refrigerator. Would you like orange juice or a cup of coffee?"

She set the plates on the table and opened the silverware drawer. "Coffee. No cream—I drink it black."

"So do I," he murmured.

Meredythe poked her other hand with the fork she was lifting out of the drawer. His husky tone nudged all of her defenses awake.

When she glanced his way, he was sitting at the table buttering a slice of toast. "Thank you for making breakfast. I usually make do with toast and coffee."

Without breaking eye contact, she slid into the seat across the table and shrugged. "It's the least I can do. You've been very kind. Not everyone would have spent almost two hours digging my car out of a snowbank just to get my luggage."

His eyes were soft and his smile was tender. "Anything for you, Meredythe."

She simply stared. Why did he look at her and talk to her like she was his long-lost love? She didn't even know the man. She glanced down at her plate then looked up again. He was shoveling food into his mouth like he hadn't eaten in a week.

Glancing up, he swallowed and said, "Finish your breakfast and I'll introduce you to my wolves."

She tried to hold her eagerness in check. At last she was getting somewhere. "You have more than just Keri?"

"Besides Keri, there are six here now," he answered between bites.

Meredythe's mind began to sort through all the information she'd gathered. Maybe one of them was black. "Where do you keep them?"

"I have two hundred acres of woodlands and meadows enclosed with a fifteen-foot fence. They roam free inside."

She swallowed a piece of bacon. "They roam free? Have any of them ever gotten out?"

He started on his second piece of toast. "Only once, and I found him on my front porch. I have two men who patrol the fence on a weekly basis to check for breaks. I'll have to go out and check it today. They won't be able to get here."

She swallowed another bite. "What happened to that wolf who got out?"

"He died three months later in his sleep in front of the fireplace. He was an old wolf."

Keri wasn't the only wolf he let sleep in his house? "How long ago was that? Did you have Keri then too? What color was he? How did you know he wouldn't attack you?"

His gaze locked with hers as he sipped his coffee. "Five years ago. He was gray. Keri's been with me since I've lived here, and wolves don't attack people. They'd rather run away. There's not one documented case of an unprovoked wolf attack on record. Those few wolves that did attack humans were rabid or protecting themselves or their cubs."

Meredythe dropped her gaze and pretended to concentrate on her food. If wolves never attacked people unless they were provoked, what was the explanation for the murder in Central Park? According to Sally, that wolf appeared out of nowhere. Maybe it wasn't a wolf. Maybe it was a hybrid. But Frank had seemed so sure when he said the prints came from a wolf. This story would definitely require closer investigation.

She stabbed a piece of bacon. Could Dr. Glyndwr be involved? She glanced up and then quickly dropped her eyes back to her plate. He'd been the perfect host so far and seemed to be cooperating. But then she hadn't asked him any really tough questions yet.

Leaning back in his chair, Bleddyn pushed his empty plate away and sipped his coffee. Her face was so easy to read. His statement about no unprovoked wolf attacks had her mind whirling. He wondered how long it would take for her to admit exactly why she was here. James King hadn't given him all the details when he called the day after she decided to come to Winterbourne.

Laying her fork on her now-empty plate, Meredythe rose and carried it to the sink, mentally compartmentalizing her newest information. She better slow down before she let something slip. Bleddyn Glyndwr impressed her as being pretty intelligent, and she didn't want him becoming suspicious of her motives. "I'm glad to see you have a dishwasher."

He finished his coffee and rose with her. "I'm even worse at cleaning up after myself than I am at cooking." At her raised eyebrows, he continued, "I have a housekeeper come in once a week. I had the dishwasher installed when she told me she didn't want to find a week's worth of dishes sitting in the sink."

Her back to him, Meredythe grinned. "Just how big is your house? I couldn't see much last night."

He stepped closer. "Forty-eight rooms."

The silverware she was rinsing clattered into the sink. "Forty-eight? What do you do with all of them?"

"Nothing. I only use three or four, not counting the kitchen. The entire west wing is closed off. And I've never used either tower."

She spun around. He was right behind her. "Either tower? This place has towers? Like a castle?"

He nodded and reached around her to put his own plate in the sink. His chest brushed against her breasts. Then he stepped away and returned to the table. Picking up the butter dish, he returned it to the refrigerator. "It looks a lot like one. The original owner was the youngest son of an English duke and modeled this place after his home in England. The family pretty much died out and the last descendent sold the estate to me. It met my requirements for forest and open land perfectly."

She set the frying pan with burned bacon in the other half of the double sink to soak. "This will be easier to clean later. Why did you locate here in New York State? Why not out west somewhere?"

He brought his coffee cup to the sink and handed it to her. "Westerners are less tolerant. There aren't any large cattle or sheep operations around here—just dairy farms, and the cows are mostly kept indoors.

She rinsed it and put it in the dishwasher. "So the residents of Winterbourne aren't bothered by your wolves?"

"They were leery at first, but they've accepted me. It's amazing what a few judicious donations to the local high school and community library will do. Are you ready?"

He shifted sideways and leaned against the counter. Turning her head, Meredythe realized that he was only inches away. Cocking her head, she looked up and fell into his misty gaze. Her eyes dropped to his lips.

"For what?"

When her tongue flicked out of her mouth and moistened her top lip, Bleddyn pushed himself away from the counter and retreated to the back door. "To meet my wolves, what else? I think there's a pair of boots out back that will fit you. I have a couple of extra parkas out there too."

Meredythe blinked and remembered where she was. A shiver raced up her spine. Why did he keep having this effect on her? "What? Oh yeah, the wolves."

He glanced back over his shoulder. "Are you coming?"

Taking a deep breath, she nodded. She was going to get to the bottom of these murders come hell or high water, no matter how sexy her number one suspect was.

The cold air had a sharp bite and fat flakes of snow still floated from the sky as Meredythe followed her host down a path he must have shoveled earlier.

"I have to feed Hammer first," he explained as he opened the door to a large shed that had kennel runs extending from the other three sides.

Cold hands fisted in her coat pockets, she followed him in. "Hammer? The wolf-dog Frank Messner had at Columbia University?"

"The same one." Bleddyn dumped some dry dog food into a bowl then mixed a can of wet with it. The low growl that was emanating from a dark corner erupted into a full-fledged snarl when he opened the door to the kennel run. He set the bowl on the floor and set a fresh bowl of water next to it. The snarling and growling didn't stop until they left the shed.

Once he'd latched the door, Bleddyn sighed. His chin fell down against his chest. Meredythe's hand on him arm brought his attention back to her. The sorrow and regret on his face startled her.

"Dr. Glyndwr…Bleddyn?"

He patted her hand. "Don't mind me. I'm just not used to defeat. I've had Hammer for a bit now and haven't made any progress with him. He still snarls whenever I get close. If I could get my hands on the bastards who did this to him…" With a quick smile he tucked her hand under his arm. "But you're not here to hear me complain about my failures. The wolves are this way, probably in the cave I built."

She grabbed his arm with her other hand when her foot slipped as they struggled through knee- to thigh-deep snow. "You built a cave?"

He stopped until she caught her balance, then led her forward. "Chicken wire, plaster of Paris, some cement and a little gray paint. It doesn't look half bad now that the trees I planted around it have grown."

Stopping in front of a gate, he removed the glove from his hand and dug the key for the lock out of his pocket. A quick flick of his wrist had the lock and chain off. Swinging the gate open, he glanced her way, a mischievous smile on his lips. "Want to come in?"

Eagerness mixed with fear. She looked around cautiously. "Are you sure it's safe?"

Again he trained those misty gray eyes on her. "You'll always be safe with me, Meredythe. I give you my word."

That icy shiver sauntered up her back again. *But just how good is your word?* "Maybe just inside the gate."

His grin was contagious, and she answered him with one of her own as he led her inside the enclosure and fastened the gate firmly behind them. She halted after three steps. His chuckle wafted back over his shoulder as he headed for a locked shed. "They aren't here yet, and I could use some help."

After a quick look around, she forged through the knee-high snow after him. If his wolves did appear suddenly, there was no way she could run fast enough to get away, but she might be able to get inside that shed. "Why do you need my help?"

"I can't carry six dishes of food at one time."

"Oh. What are you feeding them?"

He started dumping food into the six dishes sitting on a shelf. "Dog chow."

She blinked. "I thought wolves ate meat."

"They do," he answered as he handed her two dishes of food. Then he placed another one in the crook of her arm. "Can you manage three of them?" After her nod, he continued, "But a couple times a week, I give them commercial dog food. They seem to enjoy the change."

He gathered up the other three dishes and led her out of the shed and across an open area toward a pine tree. "The snow's not as deep here," he said by way of explanation.

After setting his dishes down, he took two from Meredythe. "Just set that one down at your feet and back up a little." Then he pursed his lips and whistled. A couple of yelps emerged from some nearby pine trees. Then four wolves exploded from the undergrowth and headed straight for them.

Stumbling back, Meredythe lost her balance and landed on her butt. Before she could struggle back to her feet, a mouth full of teeth appeared before her eyes. She snapped her eyes closed and raised her hands to ward off the attacking wolf.

She swallowed a scream. *Oh my God, I'm going to die.*

A sloppy tongue swiped across her face. She opened one eye slowly, then the other. A gray wolf sat before her, staring intently. Chuckling, Bleddyn stepped into her field of vision and squatted next to the wolf. "This is Spring. She's the friendliest one."

"This is friendly? What's she like unfriendly?" The wolf's tongue lolled out. Meredythe shuddered at the sight of sharp teeth at eye level. Tugging her eyes away from the wolf, she concentrated on Bleddyn.

He extended his hand. She grabbed it and he pulled her to her feet. When she saw the five wolves that sat behind him, she stepped closer to his side.

Bleddyn smiled to himself and slipped his arm around her. Her eyes locked on the wolves and she snuggled closer.

"As I said, you've already met Spring. The three sitting together are, from right to left, Storm, Snow and Honey. The mostly white female off to their left is Breeze and the large male is One-Eye. Breeze and One-Eye are the parents of the other four. Last winter I had two wolves here. Come spring, my population had tripled."

Meredythe frowned mentally as the wolves scattered to their dishes and began to eat hungrily. No black wolves. She eyed the pups warily. "You mean they aren't even full-grown yet? They look awful big to me."

He chuckled and planted a quick kiss on her nose. "They're eight months old. I think you'll be more comfortable outside the gate. I want to examine them and make sure they're all healthy, then I'll be out."

"They won't chase me?" she asked dubiously.

His grin was not comforting. "Not if you don't want to play."

She blanched. "Play! With them?"

Another kiss on her nose and a quick squeeze from the arm around her waist. "Go on. I'll be out in about fifteen minutes."

Meredythe backed away slowly. Bleddyn sat down in the snow. The wolves ignored her and, except for the one-eyed male who remained aloof, gathered around him.

Once she was outside the gate, Meredythe began to breathe again. Her host remained seated, the wolves milling about him, sometimes eating, sometimes staring at him, sometimes licking his face or rubbing their bodies against his. Meredythe leaned against the fence and stared. She had never seen anything like it in her life.

Eventually Bleddyn rose and walked over to the largest male. He stared at him for a few minutes then gathered up the now-empty dishes. Stacking them together, he headed for the gate, the four younger wolves jumping around him.

He waved them away. "Go play somewhere else."

Tongues lolling out in what could only be wolf laughter, the four of them sprang away and began chasing each other around. They disappeared into the undergrowth. Their mother rose, and after a quick swipe of her tongue on the large male's muzzle, she followed her rambunctious children. The male rose and followed them.

Meredythe continued to stare at the spot where they'd disappeared until Bleddyn joined her outside the enclosure. After securely locking the gate, he asked, "What do you think of them?"

"I-I've never seen anything like it. They're so beautiful. Aren't you afraid of them? What if one of them bit you?"

He grinned a wolfish grin. "I'd bite back."

Nonplussed, Meredythe simply stared. He leaned over and kissed her nose again. "I have to go check the fence, and that will take most of the day. Why don't you go on back inside? I'm sure you have work to do. There's a computer in my bedroom if you want to use it. I refilled the generator, so you don't have to worry about the power going off."

He was already walking away.

"Bleddyn?"

He turned. "Yes?"

She shoved her hands deep into the pockets of the parka she was wearing and swallowed. "Why—why do you keep kissing my nose?"

She had no trouble recognizing the passion that leaped into his eyes. "Because if I kissed you anywhere else, I wouldn't be able to stop."

Spinning away, he forged his way to a garage and opened the door. In a minute or two, she heard a low roar and a snowmobile appeared. After a jaunty wave, he headed into the woods.

* * * * *

Bleddyn rode the snowmobile along the fence for about a mile, then guided it beneath the low-hanging limbs of a hemlock tree. Once underneath, he cut the engine, dismounted and stripped off his clothing. Black and gray mist danced with the still lightly falling snow and a large black wolf leaped from beneath the tree. He'd be able to travel much more quickly this way. Then he could go home to Meredythe.

* * * * *

A large snowflake landed on Meredythe's nose. *He wouldn't stop kissing her*? Shaking herself free of her musings, she returned to the house, leaving the boots and parka where she had gotten them. Once inside the kitchen, she quickly cleaned the skillet. Picking up the burned bacon, she headed toward the trash can. Pursing her lips, she stopped then wrapped it in a paper towel. She just might have a use for this later.

Slinging her briefcase over her shoulder, she grabbed her suitcases and headed for the staircase. Once she was upstairs, she opened the first door on her right. The room was dark, but she found the light switch easily enough. A large, unmade double bed stood in the center of the room. Odds and ends of furniture were pushed against the walls. Bleddyn hadn't been lying when he said his bedroom was the only one fit to use. Well, she'd take care of that right now. No way was she sleeping in his bed another night.

Staring at the bed, the memory of the kiss he'd given her in the break room leaped to her mind. Ruthlessly, she squashed it.

Striding across the room, she pulled open the heavy drapes. Weak light filtered in as she looked down over the hill that led to the front of the house. The path Bleddyn had made to get to her car was filling up again. Meredythe looked up. Heavy gray clouds still blanketed the sky, and a steady snow still fell. With a sigh, she turned her back to the window. If she wanted to sleep in this room tonight, she had a lot of work to do.

"Meow?" Methuselah minced his way across the room, his tail curled into a question mark.

"Thuse, you've come to keep me company," she said as she lifted him and cuddled him against her chest. His rumbling purr rolled around the room when she set him on the bed and stroked him.

Smiling, she wondered if Bleddyn would purr if she petted him. Her eyes widened as she stared at her reflection in the mirror across the room. She had to stop thinking about *him*. Besides, he didn't look like the purring type.

"Get a hold of yourself, girl," she muttered. "You're here for a story, nothing else." Her lips twitched. "No matter how sexy your host is."

Methuselah's sneeze jerked her mind back to the project at hand. She wrinkled her nose. "There *is* a lot of dust in here, Thuse. I'll bet this place hasn't been cleaned in months, and I, for one, don't plan to spend the entire night sneezing."

* * * * *

The snow had finally stopped by the time Bleddyn returned.

Keri met him at the garage.

"What are you doing out here? I thought you wanted to stay inside next to a warm fire."

Keri sat down and curled her tail around her toes. *Meredythe has been sitting in front of Hammer's kennel for the last two hours trying to get him to come out.*

Bleddyn cocked to his head to the side. "Why?"

She sees it as a challenge.

"And she told you all this? Somehow, I can't see her sitting down and having a conversation with a wolf. At least not yet."

She told Methuselah.

"She talks to the cat? I thought she didn't know he was a Familiar."

Keri sighed. *You can be quite obtuse at times, Bleddyn. Humans talk to animals all the time. You really need to spend more time with them.*

His grin was wolfish. "I plan to."

She ran her tongue over her teeth. *Don't jump to any foregone conclusions, Bleddyn. Meredythe spent most of the day cleaning the front bedroom. She intends to sleep there tonight.*

That wiped the grin from Bleddyn's face. "I told her I'd sleep on the couch."

No, you told Methuselah and me you'd sleep on the couch.

Muttering under his breath, he turned and trudged toward Hammer's kennel. The sight that greeted him stopped him in his tracks. Hammer stood in his outside run a few paces from the safety of his kennel, chewing on something yet growling at the same time. Meredythe sat in the snow on the other side of the fence.

Glancing his way, she said, "He's so beautiful."

Bleddyn glanced at the wolf-dog again, doubting that anyone had ever referred to him as being beautiful. He was heavier than a wolf, his Mastiff ancestry obvious in his blocky, muscular body and square snout. His fur was also shorter than a wolf's, a muddy brown color, or so Bleddyn had thought. Meredythe's comment had him looking more closely. In the dying winter light, he could see the wolf-dog's coat was a kaleidoscope of brown shades ranging from almost black to streaks of honey brown. In his own way, he was beautiful.

Squatting beside Meredythe, he asked, "How did you get him to come out?"

She was still watching the growling dog. "The burned bacon. I guess he was sick of dog chow."

"And he came right out for you?"

She smiled and shook her head. Keri sat down beside her and Meredythe reached out to stroke her fur. "He came out about ten minutes ago. I just sat here and waited for him. I got the idea from you."

"Me?"

"The way you sat on the ground and talked to your wolves. I figured it wouldn't hurt to try. So I tossed the bacon over the fence, sat down and started to talk. I was discussing the importance of Shakespeare's *Hamlet* on modern literature when he finally came out."

Bleddyn's chuckle caused the wolf-dog to snarl.

Meredythe propped her chin on her fist. "I'll bet he's afraid of men. That's why you haven't made any progress with him."

Bleddyn rocked back on his heels and looked from Meredythe to Hammer. "You may be right. His owners beat him."

"And his name isn't Hammer."

Bleddyn's head snapped up. "How do you know that?"

"I decided it was a terrible name, and I told him so."

Keri's head rose a fraction of an inch. *Shadow. His name is Shadow.*

Meredythe continued, "Shadow. That would be a good name for him. What do you think, Bleddyn?"

Her eyes were locked on the wolf-dog that now sat quietly staring at her, so she didn't see the speculation on Bleddyn's face. "How did you decide on that name?"

A happy smile on her face, she glanced at Bleddyn. "It just popped into my head. And I won't take *no* for an answer. His name is Shadow."

With a small woof, Shadow rose and disappeared back into his kennel.

Bleddyn rose and held out his gloved hand.

Meredythe placed her hand in his, and he pulled her to his feet.

"You're an amazing woman, Meredythe."

With a saucy smile, she turned and headed back toward the house. "I know" drifted back over her shoulder.

Chapter Nine

"You could have had my room again," Bleddyn said as he escorted Meredythe up the staircase that night.

She sighed. He was being such a gentleman, rising when she entered the room, getting up and opening doors for her, insisting on escorting her up the stairs to her room. A girl could get used to attention like this.

Smiling, she shook her head. "Your hospitality is enough. I'm not going chase you out of your own bed."

She didn't see the mischievous smile that appeared on his face. "It's big enough to share," he said when they reached the hallway at the top of the stairs.

Her nostrils flared as she jerked to a halt, but before she could answer, he held up his hands, palms forward, and added, "I'm only teasing."

She directed a level stare at him as he continued, "You'll have to share my bathroom though. Your room is part of the master suite. The door next to the closet leads to the bathroom."

She shook her head. "I don't want to be a bother. Surely a house this big has another bathroom."

He grinned. "I think there are seven, but the water's turned off in all of them. The pipes have to be replaced."

Methuselah meowed from the top of the staircase. She glanced down and smiled at him. "Don't be so impatient, Thuse." Her eyes met Bleddyn's smoky gray orbs. "It's past his bedtime."

Bleddyn muttered something about cats under his breath, cupped her elbow and guided her down the hall.

She smiled and said, "Isn't it amazing how well Thuse and Keri get along? I can't believe it. He hates dogs."

Bleddyn stopped before the room she had chosen earlier that day. "Keri's a wolf. They have much better manners than dogs."

Smiling, she turned to face him. He stepped closer and she backed away only to be brought up short by the door. His spicy pine scent enveloped her. She swallowed. "It stopped snowing."

He lifted his hand and twisted one of her fiery curls around his finger. "Yes, it has."

Her eyes followed his fingers. "Do you think I'll be able to get into town tomorrow?"

"Why would you want to do that?" His voice had dropped. It was huskier. His fingertip brushed her cheek.

The doorknob dug into the small of her back. "I-I have a motel reservation."

His head dipped. The dark stubble of his whiskers shadowed his face. "Cancel it. You came to Winterbourne to see me. Here I am, and you have my undivided attention. Why leave?"

Her nipples pebbled as a finger trailed down her jaw and neck.

She closed her eyes and shivered. "I… Um…"

The slight pressure of Methuselah's sleek body against her calf muscles calmed her nerves as the cat wound in and out of her legs. Any uncertainty she had about staying disappeared when his rumbling purr reached her ears.

Opening her eyes, she stared into Bleddyn's face. Something…there was something about him. She tilted her head back and closed her eyes again. She could no more deny his request than she could stop breathing. "Yes. I'll stay."

He stroked her bottom lip with his thumb and the soft caress had her entire body tingling. Heat pooled in her groin.

Her nipples pebbled into tiny stabs of pleasure-pain. She shivered and tensed for his kiss. A sigh escaped as she closed her eyes.

He cupped her cheek and stroked her bottom lip with his thumb again.

Meredythe sighed heavily and leaned forward.

The low growl that rolled up and down the hallway caused her eyelids to jerk open. Was there a wolf in the hallway?

Instead, her gaze locked with Bleddyn's. His slid his hand over her cheek and gripped her neck, his thumb now caressing her jaw. Passion danced in his eyes, passion and hunger and something dark, something…evil? His hand tightened on her neck.

Gasping, Meredythe pulled back.

A shadow flickered through his eyes, but he immediately dropped his hand and stepped back. "Good. I'll see you in the morning. Sleep well."

As Meredythe watched, Bleddyn melted into the shadows.

Blinking rapidly, she shook here head. Her eyes had to be playing tricks on her. After a deep breath and small shiver, Meredythe reached behind her, grabbed the doorknob and shoved the door open, practically falling into the room. She switched on the light and waited impatiently while Methuselah sauntered in. Then she closed the door behind her—firmly.

Her spine tingled again and she took another deep breath as she steadied herself, her back flat against the door. Bleddyn Glyndwr. What was he doing to her? What was he, some kind of magician? Another scintillating shiver racked her body as she pushed herself away from the door.

Grabbing a suitcase, she heaved it onto the bed, opened it and pulled out a nightgown—a long, warm, flannel nightgown that buttoned all the way up to her neck. Then she turned toward the bathroom door. A nice, hot shower would help calm her nerves.

Just as she reached the door to the bathroom, she heard the shower start. Muttering an obscenity that would have shocked her Aunt Evie, she leaned her head against the door and swallowed. Involuntarily, a picture of Bleddyn, water streaming down his nude body, appeared in her mind. Wide chest, slim hips, muscular arms and legs. And there, at the juncture of his thighs…

Was his cock long, slender, thick? Was it straight or slightly bent?

Swallowing she groaned and thudded her forehead against the closed door—twice. Damn! How would she ever get any work done with him distracting her?

Turning back toward the bed, she stripped her sweater over her head and tossed it on the floor. Jerking her suitcase off the bed, she let it thunk to the floor. Then she stripped off the rest of her clothing and pulled the nightgown over her head. Muttering more obscenities under her breath, she climbed up onto the high bed and burrowed under the quilts. Damn Bleddyn Glyndwr. Why did he have to be so freaking sexy? After tossing and turning a while, she pushed her hand under the blankets, yanked her nightgown up to her waist and slid her fingers between her thighs. She was wet and slippery, and her distended clit was hard and aching.

Spreading her legs, she closed her eyes and rubbed her clit.

A sharp gasp escaped her throat as her hips rose.

Meredythe shivered as her aching nipples pebbled. Damn, but she was horny. He'd done this to her—Bleddyn Glyndwr. She should be thinking about a murderer, not her sexy host.

Another stab of desire knifed through her pussy.

The hell with the murderer! She needed relief—now! She rubbed her clit harder and imagined how Bleddyn's hard cock would feel sliding into her.

Oh yes, she hummed to herself. His hands would cup her breasts and he'd rub his callused fingers against her nipples. Then he'd slide one down her stomach like he had that day at work and slide first one finger then a second into her aching pussy.

But his fingers wouldn't be enough, and she'd let him know it. No, she'd need his cock buried deep inside her to satisfy the ache she felt. She'd need his cock thrust in then pulled out and thrust in and pulled out over and over.

Oh yes, just…like…that!

"Ahh…"

Meredythe's fantasy had barely begun when a strong orgasm ripped through her. Relief flooded her body, but Meredythe wasn't completely happy. She'd been too primed, too ready. She wanted a long, drawn-out lovemaking session, even if it was only with herself.

"I should have had a couple glasses of wine," she muttered to herself.

Flopping over, she stared into the darkness for a few minutes. Then, shoving her host's sexy body into a corner of her mind, she shut and locked the door on it and turned her thoughts to her reason for being here—to find information that would lead her to a murderer.

Curled next to her, his rumbling purr vibrating against her side, Methuselah rubbed his head against her arm.

Soon Meredythe was asleep.

* * * * *

Bleddyn braced his hands against the wall of the shower stall and let the ice-cold water sluice down his taut, aching body. It didn't work. His cock was just as hard and aching as when he'd fled Meredythe. Almost, he'd accepted her unspoken invitation when she lifted her head away from the door, lifted her lips toward his. He groaned again as his cock jerked. His hand strayed downward, but he curled it into a fist and smashed it against the marble tiles. Two of them shattered and crumbled to the floor.

He ignored them, trying to will his cock into submission.

It didn't work. Not even the pain in his knuckles dulled the ache in his groin.

"Damn. Bloody, bloody damn."

Pulling a vision of Meredythe's naked thighs into his mind, he fisted his cock and began to pump.

In his mind, he spread her thighs and slid his fingers through her silky curls until he reached her wet cunt. After rubbing her clit a few times—her moans got louder—he slipped his finger into her hot, wet slit.

She gasped and tightened her internal muscles around his fingers to suck them deeper.

He pulled his finger out and rubbed her hard, little clit a few more times, slid two fingers into her and pumped them. Bending his head, he captured her mouth with his in a long, tongue-twisting kiss, then nibbled his way down her neck and across her collarbone to suck on a distended nipple as she arched her breast into his mouth.

Still fisting his cock—up down, up down—Bleddyn imagined Meredythe pushing his head away from her breasts, down her flat belly to her wet cunt.

In the shower, Bleddyn shuddered. Just imagining sliding his tongue into Meredythe and sucking her hot, sweet juices into his mouth had his balls aching even more.

In his hand, his cock became harder.

Panting, he imagined lifting his head, shifting his body onto hers and burying his cock deep inside her as her cunt muscles grabbed and sucked his cock. Her pussy would be hot and wet and tight, he just knew it.

Hips thrusting, Bleddyn fisted his cock more tightly as the burning in his balls roared upward. Hot cum erupted and spurted high against the wall of the shower. Gasping, he braced his forearm against the wall and leaned his head against it. In seconds, though, the ice-cold needles of water bouncing off his back roused him. Turning on the hot water, he leaned back and let the now-comfortable shower sluice down over him. After sucking in a deep breath, he smiled. If fantasy sex with Meredythe could make him this weak in the knees, what would the real thing do to him?

As long as Meredythe was in his house but not in his bed, he'd ache for her. Besides, he didn't want temporary relief. He wanted to bury himself deep inside her hot, tight body and explode while they drowned in mutual passion.

He shivered as the water continued to rain down. Six days. The full moon was in six days. He could make it. He'd waited over a thousand years for Meredythe. He could wait six more days.

*****

"You're so beautiful," he murmured against her neck. She turned her head to give him easier access and he sucked on the pulse throbbing there. Reaching down, he lifted her nightgown and pulled it over her head. When he buried his head between her breasts, she moaned and arched against him. Turning his head, he nuzzled her breast, his tongue slowly outlining her areola. When he sucked her nipple into his mouth, she gasped and stroked the sleek muscles of his naked back.

"Easy, love, slowly. I want to make this good for you." His hand slid down her stomach.

"Bleddyn, please," she moaned and arched against his hand when his fingers slid between her legs.

She moaned and thrust against his hand.

"Meredythe?" The voice seemed to come from a million miles away.

"Umm?" She arched again. His fingers were pure magic.

"Meredythe, are you all right?" Was his tone worried?

She opened her eyes. Bleddyn leaned over her, a concerned expression on his face. She lifted her hand and caressed his cheek. Then, she lifted her head toward his, her lips parting. Her kiss was tentative, butterfly soft. His lips were warm and firm, his kiss gentle.

Then she realized she was awake.

Her eyes opened wide as she pushed away from him, a squeak escaping her open mouth. When he sat down on the edge bed and braced his hand on the other side of her hips, she shoved herself back so hard, her head thwacked against headboard.

Bright sparkles exploding before her eyes, she grabbed the blankets and jerked them up to her chin. "What are you doing here?"

Leaning closer, he brushed a curl away from her mouth and tucked it behind her ear. "I heard your cat meowing and scratching at the door. When I opened it to let him out, you moaned. I thought you might be ill, so I came to investigate."

She closed her eyes and shook her head slightly, struggling to bring her clamoring senses under control. "I'm fine. I was just dreaming."

His smoky gaze bored into hers. "Dreaming? A nightmare, perhaps?"

Bright flecks of gold floated in his gray eyes. Funny, she hadn't noticed them before. The blankets she had clutched so tightly slipped to her waist.

"Yes, that's right. It was a nightmare."

His fingers played with the top button of her nightgown. "Want to talk about it?"

The back of his hand brushed against an aching nipple. The electrical jolt shot straight to her groin. The sudden, aching stab also cleared the sensual haze seeping into her body.

She planted both hands on his chest and pushed him away. "No!"

As he sat up, a smile twitched at the corners of his mouth. "Are you sure?"

She crossed her arms across her rebellious breasts. "Yes, of course. Um… I'd like to get up—take a shower."

He rose and smiled down at her. "Would you me to scrub your back? I'd be more than happy to."

Her body shivered in anticipation, but her mind was in firm control. "No!"

Hands on hips, he cocked his head. His gaze traveled from her face to her chest. "You're sure?"

Beneath her crossed arms, her nipples tightened even more. "Yes!"

The promise of passion disappeared from his face and his smile became achingly tender. "Then I'll go make breakfast."

Her heart seemed to quiver in her chest as she cocked an eyebrow. "I thought you didn't cook."

"I don't. I have discovered that I am a tolerable baker, however. How do blueberry muffins sound?"

The expression on his face was so open and innocent she relaxed. Her smile became more natural.

"Fine. Anything. I'll see you in a little bit."

"Enjoy your shower." Pivoting, he strode across her bedroom and out the door, closing the door firmly.

Pulling her legs up, Meredythe crossed them, planted her elbows on her knees, dropped her chin into her cupped hands and stared at the closed door. Who was Bleddyn Glyndwr? Why did she find him so compelling? True, he had to be one of the most fascinating men she had ever met, but he was also one of the most vexing. Why in the world had she ever agreed to stay here? She snorted and glanced at her reflection in the dresser mirror.

Her reflection stared back, expression clearly saying, *That's because he's sexier than any man you've ever met. Face it, Merry—you have the hots for him.*

Her chin snapped up. "Now wait one damn minute, Meredythe Welsh." She stabbed a finger at her reflection. "You're here because you wanted to see what you could find out about wolves and these murders. That's why you agreed to stay here instead of going to the motel. And it will be a lot easier to find out what Dr. Bleddyn Glyndwr is hiding if you stay here in his house rather than in a motel. And he *is* hiding something. You know it and I know it. All you have to do, girl, is get him to trust you, to feel comfortable with you."

She shook a finger at her reflection. "But you are not going to seduce him. You're not like Heather. You have never slept with any man to get information for a story, and you're not going to start now. No, you will stay friendly yet professional the whole time you're here. You will be pleasant, but you will not encourage him. Business, girl—you're here on business only. No sleeping with informants."

Sitting up, she threw off the blankets and slid off the bed. She'd find out what Dr. Bleddyn Glyndwr was hiding if it was the last thing she did. So what if he was the sexiest man she'd ever met? That didn't matter in the least.

* * * * *

Mouthwatering odors were wafting around the kitchen when Meredythe joined Bleddyn approximately forty-five minutes later. A pan of muffins sat on top of the stove and he was just pulling a second pan from the oven.

"They smell wonderful." She paused and breathed deeply. "I thought you said you couldn't cook. Aunt Evie would be impressed."

"These are my one claim to culinary fame." Straightening, he set the second pan beside the first then tossed his oven mitts on the counter. "Aunt Evie?"

Meredythe shoved her hands into her back pockets. "My Aunt Evelyn. She raised me after my parents died in a car accident."

"I'm sorry." He looked and sounded sincere.

She shrugged. "That's okay. I was only a year old so I don't remember anything about them. How about you? Do you have a family? Brothers? Sisters? Parents?"

He grabbed the first muffin pan and turned it over. The muffins tumbled onto a plate. "I'm an only child. And I never knew my father."

She stepped to the counter and grabbed a coffee mug off a hook. "Your mother?"

For the barest second, he stilled. "My mother… I see her…periodically."

Meredythe's back was turned so he couldn't see the smile she allowed herself. He was hedging. What was it about his mother that he didn't want to talk about?

Frenzied, angry barking and howling interrupted her before she could speak again. A muffin rolled to the floor as Bleddyn dropped the second pan and headed for the door. "That's Ham— Shadow. Something's wrong."

Meredythe followed close on his heels. Grabbing a parka, she jerked it on, slid her stocking feet into a pair of boots and slammed through the outside door. Cursing, she shaded her eyes from the sun's glare. Bleddyn was already standing in front of Shadow's kennel, his fingers laced through the wire, talking to the wolf-dog in vain.

She stopped next to him and shouldered him out of the way. "Shadow," she said in a no-nonsense tone to the wolf-dog that paced along the far side of his fence, growling and snarling ferociously, "calm down. What's wrong? No one is going to hurt you. We won't let any strange man do anything to you."

Bleddyn stepped back and watched as she alternately commanded, cajoled and finally convinced Shadow to calm down and relax.

"That's good. Now that's better, isn't it—listening to me instead of barking until your throat hurts." She glanced quickly over her shoulder. "Bleddyn, leave me alone with him for a while." She turned all her attention back to the wolf-dog. "See, Shadow, I told you everything was okay. No one here is going to hurt you. I won't allow it."

From the corner of his eye, Bleddyn saw a familiar figure disappear around the corner of the house. He placed his hands on Meredythe's shoulders and leaned forward. "I'll leave Shadow in your hands. He likes you." *So do I.* His lips brushed her cheek and his hands caressed their way down her arms. Even through the parka, he knew they raised goose bumps. Then he stepped away.

Meredythe sensed rather than saw him leave, her complete attention again on the unhappy wolf-dog. "No one will take you away from me, Shadow, I promise."

* * * * *

Bleddyn pushed open the door of the east tower and ascended the stairs, entering the unlocked door at the top. Warmth rushed down the cold stairwell until he closed the door again. "I thought you were more subtle with your arrivals," he said to the old man who was poking at the fire.

Rhys looked over his shoulder. "Sorry. I didn't think I'd appear so close to Hammer's kennel. Are you sure you'll be able to save him?"

Flopping into one of the old leather chairs placed in front of the hearth, Bleddyn grinned. "I can't. He won't have anything to do with me. But Meredythe can. By the way, his mother was a wolf and named him Shadow."

Rhys stopped poking the fire and sat down in the other chair. Two cups of steaming tea appeared on the table beside him. "Meredythe? She's working with him? Why? What have you told her?"

Bleddyn shook his head at the offered tea. He'd already had plenty of coffee. "I haven't told her anything. She just plopped herself down in front of Shadow's kennel yesterday and kept talking until she wore him down."

Rhys' eyebrow rose marginally. "She discovered his name?"

A fond smile appeared on Bleddyn's lips. "She said Hammer was a terrible name for him, and Shadow would be much better. She thinks the name just popped into her head."

Rhys pursed his lips. "She's changing already, before the ceremony. Amazing. You haven't…"

Bleddyn rubbed the back of his neck. "Taken her to bed? No. I never knew I had this much willpower."

Rhys leaned over and patted his knee. "The moon is waxing. Not much longer."

Bleddyn rose and smiled wryly. "Believe me, I'm counting the days." Staring into the fire, he asked, "What about Slade? Were you able to lead him to Canada?"

"I know he followed me. Where he is now, I can't be sure. I didn't try to find him, afraid he'd follow me back here."

"You're staying then?"

Rhys sipped his tea. "I think it best, in case he decides to come back here."

Bleddyn sighed with resignation. "I should have killed him when I had the chance."

Rhys shook his head. "You couldn't. Your honor would never allow it."

Bleddyn turned and grimaced. "That's a rather archaic term for the twenty-first century."

Rhys' entire face crinkled with amusement. "Then why haven't you taken Meredythe to your bed yet?"

The younger man snorted. "I'm not taking any chances. The seeress said full moon, so I'll wait."

Still smiling, Rhys said, "You're reading it too literally, Bleddyn. If she's willing now, the ceremony might be easier for her."

Bleddyn clenched his teeth. "I don't plan on having an audience this time, Rhys."

"Still, under the influence of the moon, you'll be more…savage."

Bleddyn rose. Hands clasped behind his back, he began pacing the room. "I know what I'm doing."

Rhys shrugged. "If you say so."

Bleddyn stopped before Rhys. "Will you be joining us in the main house?"

"No, I'll stay here and leave you two alone. Leave you to your courting, so to speak. Now if I were you," he added with a grin, "I'd get back to the kitchen. Keri always had a sweet tooth."

* * * * *

When Meredythe eventually returned to the kitchen, Bleddyn held a chair out for her and poured her a cup of coffee. The he set a plate full of muffins in front of her. "I managed to get back here before Keri ate more than two of them. How's Shadow?"

Cupping the hot mug in both of her hands, she gulped some coffee and sighed as its warmth began to seep into every crevice of her body. "He's calmed down. I fed him. I hope you don't mind." She reached for a muffin.

"Not at all. I'm glad he's so taken with you. Would you like some butter?" he asked as he sat down in the chair opposite hers.

"No, I like them just like this." She took a bite and sighed as sugar and blueberry—and was that really cinnamon?—exploded in her mouth. Closing her eyes, she tilted her head back and sighed.

His eyes locked on the pulse in her throat, Bleddyn swallowed thickly.

Eyes still closed, Meredythe bit into the muffin again. She chewed slowly and swallowed. Then she licked the crumbs off her lips—slowly.

"Umm."

Lust pounding through his veins, Bleddyn abruptly shoved himself away from the table, his chair scraping along the floor then tipping precariously on two legs. In seconds he was at her side, fists clenched on his thighs as he struggled with himself. More than anything he wanted to drag her into his arms and carry her to his bed. After a short but fierce struggle, he conquered his lust.

Meredythe opened her eyes and stopped breathing.

His eyes were soft and compelling. Dampened passion simmered in them.

"Thank you," he murmured.

She drew a shaky breath. "For what?"

Leaning closer, his eyes on her lips, he said, "Shadow. You've broken through his wall of fear. We'll be able to save him now."

Bracing his left hand on the table, he reached over and cupped the back of her head with his right. Eyes never leaving hers, he lowered his mouth to hers. He kept his eyes open and watched her expression as he nibbled her lips.

After her initial start of surprise, she relaxed and her mouth softened under his. His lips teased, titillated, tempted. He kept a tight rein on his lust when she relaxed with a sigh, closed her eyes and leaned into him. Her lips moved against his, tentatively at first, then with more confidence. Her hands rose and rested lightly on his chest, her fingers grasping onto his shirt.

When her tongue touched his lips, Bleddyn groaned, tore himself free and fled to the door. "I'm going to feed the wolves. Then I'm going to pull your car out of that ditch. I have a tractor. I'll put the car in my garage then. There's plenty of room for it. Send Keri if you need anything." Then he was gone.

Meredythe shivered and took a deep breath. Compared to the first kiss he taken from her in the break room, this one was so much more…selfless.

Get a hold of yourself, Meredythe. It was just a kiss. A simple kiss. Rising, she refilled her coffee mug. Then she grabbed the plate of muffins and headed toward the staircase. If he was going to pull her car out, she had at least a couple uninterrupted hours to work. Maybe she could find something interesting on his computer.

Keri raised her head and followed her out of the kitchen, her eyes locked on the muffins. Meredythe smiled down at her. Then she snorted, remembering the last thing Bleddyn had said. Send Keri if she needed anything.

Meredythe shook her head. Yeah, like a wolf could understand what she said and then manage to tell Bleddyn.

* * * * *

Slade stood before the neat white house with the green Wiccan symbols painted on the siding. He flinched at the charms, but they didn't deter him as he walked up the steps and rang the doorbell. He waited impatiently, cringing every time one of the chimes tinkled, shuddering when the phalluses bonged, cursing impotently when no one answered the door.

He'd just raised his fist to pound on the door when it was jerked open by a small, disheveled, gray-haired woman with a dazed expression. She blinked a few times then plastered a wide smile on her face.

"Good morning. I'm so sorry it took me so long to answer the door, but I'm brewing a new love potion and I couldn't leave it. I'm Evelyn Woods," she continued, sticking out her hand. "What can I do for you?"

Slade's smile was more of a grimace, but he engulfed her small hand in his huge paw and shook it as gently as he could. If she thought she was a witch and could brew love potions...well, she was obviously half mad. But she was the only lead to the girl he had.

"I'm here to see Meredythe Welsh. I...I went to college with her. Since I was in town, I thought I'd look her up."

The old woman's smile became brighter as she tugged his hand gently and pulled him through the door. "You're one of Meredythe's old college friends? How wonderful! I'm her Aunt Evie. Please come in, come in. Do you like pumpkin pie? I just baked two yesterday and I'll just bet it's the best pumpkin pie you've ever eaten."

"Ah, no thank you, Mrs. Woods. I'd just like to see Meredythe." He tried to get his hand back, but somehow the old woman steered him into her kitchen and had him sitting at the table with a piece of pie in front of him before he knew what happened.

The old woman positively beamed. "You must call me Aunt Evie. All of Meredythe's friends call me Aunt Evie. I'm sorry, but she's not home right now."

He ignored the pie. "When will she be home?" he asked eagerly. This foolish old woman would hand the girl to him without even knowing what she was doing.

At that moment, the back door creaked and a cat minced her way across the floor then jumped up onto the kitchen counter. Slade swallowed nervously as he stared into her green eyes. A cat! He shuddered internally and unconsciously stroked the scars on the back of his left hand. How he hated cats.

"Do you always let your cat on your kitchen counter?" he choked out.

The old woman started and looked at the cat as if she hadn't noticed her before. "Jezebel. What are you doing here? Mary Francis will be in a tizzy if she can't find you." She turned back to Slade. "I'm sorry, but Jezebel isn't mine." Then she brightened. "But I do have a cat." Turning, she scuttled over to the back staircase and called, "Methuselah? Methuuuuuuuselah? Where are you, dear? There's a man here who would like to meet you."

Slade clamped his mouth shut on the explosion of anger rolling through his throat. Not another cat! Damn this idiotic old woman.

Jaws clenched, he clutched the edge of the table, shifted in his chair and growled, "No, Mrs. Woods, please. Could you just tell me when Meredythe will be home?"

The back door slammed and a scratchy voice flowed into the room. "Evelyn, have you seen Jezebel? She's gotten out again."

All the blood drained from Slade's face when the nun walked into the kitchen. His chair clattered to the floor as he catapulted out of it. "I really have to leave, Mrs. Woods. I just remembered an appointment. I'll come back to see Meredythe another time."

"Evie," the nun continued in her scratchy voice, "didn't you tell me Meredythe went to Chicago?"

The aunt's hands fluttered about her face and chest like butterfly wings. Slade's eyes followed their movements. The scents of cinnamon, nutmeg and ginger drifted toward him and seemed to settle around his shoulders, confusing his senses.

"Goodness me," the old woman murmured. "How can I be so forgetful? Meredythe said she'd be gone for at least three weeks, maybe more. She's a reporter, you know. A very good one, and she's working on a new story. If you'd like to leave your number…"

Slade raised his hands palms forward and backed away from the two women. "No, no. If I'm still in the city in three weeks, maybe I'll stop back."

"Well, I'm glad you stopped by. It's always nice to meet Meredythe's friends," the old woman continued as she marched across the kitchen and tucked her hand under his arm.

As he tried to bolt from the room, she jerked him to a halt. How could such a small bird of a woman be so strong?

Slade shook his head, trying to clear his senses. The old woman's voice seemed to come from a hundred miles away.

"Wait, you didn't get a chance to eat your pie. I could wrap it up for you to take along."

He wiped his face with his hand and shook his head emphatically. "That won't be necessary. Please, I can't be late for my other appointment."

She guided him toward the front door. "Well, then. I won't be the cause of you losing business or something like that. Thank you for coming. Please come back again. Meredythe's *friends* are always welcome."

Before he could answer, he was on the front porch and the door was closed tightly behind him. A sudden gust of wind had all the wind chimes jangling discordantly. He cringed, practically ran from the porch and disappeared down the block. As he hurried away, a thought popped into his mind. Chicago. That's what the file he found in her apartment was labeled. At least he knew where she was. He'd be there by tomorrow.

Inside, Mary Francis turned to her friend. "That was a masterful performance, Evie. You have the addlepated old lady act perfected."

Evelyn chuckled. "I thought he was going to wet his pants when Jezebel walked in. And when he saw you! He must have a horribly guilty conscious if a nun shakes him up that much."

Mary Francis smiled. "Do you think he took the bait?"

Evelyn nodded. "His mind was completely open as I wove the spell. He'll go to Chicago to find her. She and Bleddyn will be safe now—for a while anyway."

Chapter Ten

Methuselah pushed open the door to Rhys' tower and sauntered in.

"I expected you earlier," the old druid said.

Meredythe stayed up later than I expected mulling over the information she's gathered.

"Has she figured out anything about Bleddyn?"

Methuselah jumped into an overstuffed chair and sat, his tail curled around his paws. *No, the idea of werewolves is still too unbelievable for her to consider.*

Rhys sighed and sipped some tea. "I don't know whether that's good or bad. Ah well, all things progress in their own time. Is she asleep now?"

Yes.

Rhys set his tea on the table. "Good. Shall we proceed? She has more memories to experience."

* * * * *

"Let me go!"

A jagged nail scraped the tender skin of her upper arm, but the viselike fingers wrapped around Meredythe didn't loosen. She dragged her feet, digging soggy furrows in the muddy soil as her captors wrenched her forward. Even though she twisted this way and that, she was unable to avoid the clumps of mud and rotted vegetables pelting her already bruised body.

The frenzied crowd surrounding her surged closer. A gap-toothed woman grabbed a handful of tangled hair, yanked her head back and slapped her. Bright specks of light zigzagged before her eyes. When the men holding her arms jerked her forward, long strands of red remained in her tormenter's fist.

"Burn her! Burn the witch!"

Meredythe struggled harder, the fear she thought she had under control beginning to assert itself. Her voice trembled. "I'm not a witch! Please. You must believe me. I've done nothing but help you."

Ignoring her, the two men dragged her toward the huge pyre that had been built in the field next to the village church. When her frantic pleas garnered no pity from the hysterical crowd, she called down curses.

The crowd ignored the first and didn't fear the second. Their new cleric had promised God would protect them.

One of her burly captors, the village blacksmith by trade, shoved her up the ladder laid against the tower of logs and brush. Once on top, he pushed her against the pole wedged in the center of the pyre, jerked her hands above her head and tied them to the iron ring dangling from the top of the pole. When she started to curse him, he shoved a filthy rag in her mouth. Then he descended the ladder, pulling it away when he reached the bottom.

"Daughter of Satan, now you'll burn," a scraggly haired woman screamed. "You'll burn in hell for spelling me boy. He'd be alive if not for you."

A gangly farmer flourished a stout club. "She cast a spell on me cows, she did, and soured all the milk and spoiled the butter."

"Witch!" spat a buxom lass, the village beauty, her face screwed into a mask of hatred. "She spelled Hob baker's son away from me, she did. When she's dead, he'll love me again."

"She conjured the rains, she did," another farmer yelled as he shook his fist. "Me crops rotted in the field. What will I feed me babes come winter?"

Meredythe blinked, trying to conquer the tears flooding her eyes. She would not let these people see her fear. She blinked and glanced skyward. A low moan escaped through her gag and she lowered her watery gaze. She stared at the blurry, roiling mass of humanity. Hate rolled up the pyre and surrounded her.

Three men climbed onto a scaffold that had been built before the pyre, just high enough that they stood above the crowd. The local squire stepped forward and raised his hands to quiet the crowd.

"We are a peaceful village, a law-abiding village," he began. "We seek only to tend our farms, raise our children and live in peace. We wish harm on no man or woman. But we will defend what is ours."

Shouts of agreement rolled from the crowd.

The corpulent squire nodded sagely. "For years, the old woman, Edyth of Deepwood dwelt amongst us. We opened our hearts and hearths to her. Little did we know that we gave shelter to one of Satan's snakes. But God has delivered us from that daughter of hell. Reverend Thormachton came among us and revealed the evil we nourished in our bosom."

The black-robed cleric bowed and accepted the accolades of the crowd.

When the cheers died away, the squire continued, "No more will the witch cast her demon spells. She is dead, killed by the brave blacksmith Ham."

More cheers erupted, this time for the brawny man who blushed and ducked his head.

Again the squire raised his hands for quiet. "What's more, his heroic efforts also brought into our hands the witch's evil acolyte."

He turned and pointed to the struggling girl. "She will be punished for her blasphemy."

The crowd surged closer, screaming their approval.

The squire raised his hands and the crowd quieted. "But we are not ignorant, unlearned people here in our small village. We do not simply accuse, judge without justification, convict without evidence. No man shall say we broke the law. We follow the law. This witch burns by writ of law, the Law of Witchcraft set down by our good Queen Elizabeth."

He motioned the village minister forward. The black-robed man held up a sheet of parchment and read, "BE it enacted by the King our Sovraigne Lorde the Lordes Spirituall and Temporall and the Comons in this p'sent Parliment assembled, and by the authoritie of the same, That the Statute made in the fifte yeere of the Raigne of our late Sov'aigne Ladie of the most famous and happy memorie Queene Elizabeth, intituled An Acte againste Conjurations Inchantments and witchcraftes, be from the Feaste of St. Michaell the Archangell nexte cominge, for and concerninge all Offences to be comitted after the same Feaste, utterlie repealed."

Meredythe tugged at the ropes binding her wrists. There had to be a way to escape!

The minister droned on.

"AND for the better restrayning of saide Offenses, and more severe punishinge the same, be it further enacted by the authoritie aforesaide, That if any pson or persons after the saide Feaste of Saint Michaell the Archangell next comeing, shall use practise or exercsise any Invocation or Conjuration of any evill and spirit, or shall consult covenant with entertaine employ feede or rewarde any evill and wicked Spirit to or for any intent or pupose..."

Meredythe choked behind her gag as she labored to draw air into her lungs. How could this have happened? All she wanted to do was help people. She was no witch. Edyth hadn't been a witch either, just an old woman who understood herbs and how to use them to ease suffering. Again, she jerked her arms against the bindings that held them over her head, futilely. Then, slowly, the silence penetrated her thoughts. The cleric was looking up at her.

"Meredythe, once of Wales, you have been tried and convicted of witchcraft, your guilt proven to the satisfaction of all here assembled. Not twice, but three times the old woman Edyth was proven to be a witch and you her evil acolyte. Confess now. Repent your sins and receive the grace of God to save your immortal soul."

She shook her head. No words could get past the gag.

"Burn her," screamed a woman in the crowd. "Burn her now."

The rest of the crowd took up the chant. "Burn her. Burn the witch."

The minister looked to the squire. He in turn looked at the third man on the scaffold, the man wearing a black hood.

"So be it," the squire said. "By writ of law."

All three men descended from the scaffold. Once on the ground, the executioner grabbed a burning torch and shoved it in and out among the kindling mounded around the bottom of the pyre. The dry wood caught fire quickly.

As smoke entered her lungs, Meredythe's eyes widened in panic. The flames that were rapidly consuming the dry wood mesmerized her as they crawled closer and closer. Smoke billowed and wrapped itself around her. Her eyes began watering in earnest and she tried to cough through her gag. The heat was becoming unbearable. Her skin began to blister. Only the ropes binding her to the pole kept her from collapsing into a shuddering heap.

The two men pulled their horses to a halt and stared at the smoke billowing skyward from the village.

"What's happening?"

Rhys frowned. "It's market day, Bleddyn. Perhaps they're celebrating something…a wedding?"

Before Rhys could say more, the roar of a crowd drifted to them. Frowning, he turned his attention back to the village. "I don't like this." He urged his horse down the hill. Bleddyn followed close behind.

The few streets of the small village were empty as they galloped toward the church. Once he reached the edge of the meadow, Rhys cursed and forced his mount through the mob, laying his whip freely on heads and shoulders. Bleddyn's more powerful stallion followed, his great, snapping teeth clearing his way.

"Hold!" the minister demanded as he stepped fearlessly before the horses.

"You ignorant fools," Rhys bellowed as he guided his horse around the black-garbed scarecrow of a man and pulled his mount to a sliding stop before the now-roaring bonfire. Sliding from his mount, he threw his arms into the air and barked out a single word. "*Tanau*!"

Flames blazed from his fingertips, rolled down his arms and engulfed him. Striding forward, he climbed the burning pyre until he reached Meredythe's side. After a quick slash of his hand, her arms fell free from their bindings. Gathering her into his arms, he shouted another command. "*Difannu*!" As the fire roared toward the sky, the old man and the girl disappeared.

Wisps of burnt ash and still-burning embers floated down amongst the crowd. More than one person stood gaping as the pyre disintegrated. Slowly, every eye turned to Bleddyn. What had happened was beyond their comprehension. Accusing an old woman and young girl of witchcraft was one thing. To see it so blatantly displayed was another. Who were these men? What were they?

Bleddyn sat absolutely still on his restive stallion, glaring at the crowd. The squire stepped forward and opened his mouth to speak. One swift glance from Bleddyn and he stumbled back, the acrid odor of urine seeping through the crowd as his bladder failed.

The cleric was not so easily cowed. Holding his cross before him as a shield, he strode forward. "Warlock! Devil's spawn. Get you gone from here."

Bleddyn lifted his foot from his stirrup, planted it in the middle of the cleric's chest and shoved him down into the mud.

"Do not goad me, fool," he snarled, "or you will be dead before the sun sets."

Frightened murmurs began to eddy around the outskirts of the crowd. Women clutched children to their breasts and began to weep. Surely the devil himself was among them.

Grabbing the reins of Rhys' horse, Bleddyn wheeled his mount and galloped back the way he had come. None of the village's frightened inhabitants noticed the tears trickling down his cheeks. Once again, he had failed her. Again he must wait.

The next morning, after a fretful night that had most of the men nervously guarding their homes, Meredythe's would-be executioners discovered every ox belonging to the village was dead, its throat torn out. In the nights that followed, the sheep died, as did the cows and many of the pigs. The squire's prize breeding rams were found lying in their own entrails. None of the village's inhabitants ever saw anything, no matter how diligent they were. There were no clues…except one set of wolf prints that disappeared into the forest. Wolf prints in a place that hadn't seen a live wolf in a hundred years. By midwinter, the village was abandoned.

* * * * *

The wind blustered and whistled among Chicago's tall buildings. Fists clenched at his sides, Slade stared out at the swirling snow. How was he supposed to find the girl in a snowstorm? Cursing impotently, he wrenched the drapes closed. After taking a couple of deep breaths, he reached for the phone and growled his request. If he couldn't hunt, he might as well eat.

* * * * *

Meredythe sighed and stared at the computer screen. Every site she'd searched had been a dead end. What's more, every time she tried to ask Bleddyn questions, something—Methuselah, Shadow or Bleddyn himself—distracted her. And she never even realized she'd been sidetracked until hours later. The last five days had revealed nothing. "Damn! Why can't I find anything? I'm a better reporter than this."

Slapping her palm on the desk, she jerked her eyes away from the screen. Her gaze drifted around the room, finally reaching the fire burning merrily in the grate. She shuddered. Last night's dream had been a nightmare. Burning at the stake. The dream had been so vivid, she'd been able to smell her flesh burning.

"Forget it, Meredythe," she muttered out loud. "It was just a dream. Get your mind back on your work."

Pushing away from the computer, she rose, stretched her arms above her head, rolled her shoulders then wandered to the huge glass wall. Movement in the wolf enclosure caught her eye and she smiled. Crossing her arms over her chest, she cocked a hip and leaned against the glass. Bleddyn was there, with his wolves, playing. He'd get up and run and the four younger wolves would tackle him. Then he'd wrestle with them. At least she thought they were wrestling. All those snapping teeth. She straightened. Did he just bite one of them back? Meredythe blinked. She had to be imagining things.

Most of the snow from the snowstorm that had stranded her here at Winterbourne had melted. Some remained in shaded places, but for the most part, it was gone. She frowned. The snow was gone and the road was open. Why was she still here?

Stretched out on his back, Methuselah lolled on the bed, his forepaws curled over his chest. Meredythe's thoughts had him gyrating to his feet. He jumped to the floor, trotted across the room and butted his head against her shin.

"Meerrooww?" *Pick me up, Meredythe.*

He rubbed against her legs.

"Thuse, did you have a nice nap?" she asked as she lifted him and cradled him in her arms. "Dreaming about catching more mice?"

His deep purr embraced her.

A memory surfaced and Meredythe giggled when Bleddyn's appalled expression appeared in her mind's eye. She didn't think any man could be so horrorstruck by a dead rodent. But the look on his face when Thuse had laid that mouse so proudly at his feet had been priceless.

She cuddled the cat closer as his rumbling purr filled the room. Meredythe closed her eyes and rubbed her cheek against his soft fur. When she opened them, the question of why she remained in Winterbourne had disappeared from her mind.

The cat squirmed and she let him drop to the floor. Turning away from the window, she meandered back across the room and shuffled through the papers she had strewn across the sofa in Bleddyn's bedroom. A single sheet fluttered to the floor.

Methuselah meowed from where he now perched on the edge of the bed. *Pick it up, Meredythe.*

She reached for the paper and glanced at it. Werewolves.

She frowned. Where were those notes she'd taken?

Returning to the computer, she shuffled through a pile of CDs and popped one in. She pursed her lips as she read the words on the screen.

"The word *werewolf* is a combination of the old Saxon words '*wer*', man, and '*wolf*'—man wolf. '*Wer*' is related to the Latin '*vir*', the root word of virile."

A darkly masculine face tugged at her consciousness and a smile tickled her lips. *Virile, huh*?

She shook her head and her mind swatted the picture away as she continued to concentrate on the computer screen.

"'*Lycanthrope*' and '*lycanthropy*' come from the Greek, '*lykos*', wolf, and '*anthropos*', human being—wolfman. Lycanthropy is also used in medical terminology to refer to the delusion that one has changed or can change into a wolf."

She sat up straighter. "A delusion?"

Her fingers flew across the keys.

An hour later, she leaned back and stared at the screen.

"Werewolves," she murmured to herself. "That's it." All those people who had been murdered with a wolf or wolf-dog involved. Somebody who thought he was a werewolf was responsible for all of the murders.

She shuddered and looked at the cat. "My God, Thuse. The serial killer is some guy who thinks he's a werewolf!"

Methuselah curled his paws under his chest and smiled a cat smile.

* * * * *

Once he reached the back porch, Bleddyn shucked off his muddy sweater, dropped his boots and sauntered into the kitchen. If Meredythe weren't here, he'd strip down to his skin. As it was, he'd be sure to have mud dropping from his jeans all the way to the bathroom.

He rolled his shoulders to get rid of the kinks then plodded from the kitchen to the hallway. He was cold, tired and he wanted a shower. Stopping by the open door of the den, he looked in. Keri was sleeping in front of the fire, but

Meredythe was nowhere to be seen. That meant she was working on the computer—in his bedroom.

"You want more than a shower," he muttered to himself as he climbed the stairs. "You want Meredythe."

When he reached the top of the steps, he paused, his werewolf-enhanced hearing immediately noting the tapping sounds coming from behind the closed door. He groaned. She was there, only a few feet away from his bed. How was he going to make it to the bathroom?

He paused before the door and leaned his forehead against it as erotic fantasies became vivid pictures. To have Meredythe wrapped in his arms, their bodies straining against each other…

Blood flooded his cock.

Beads of sweat burst onto his forehead and rolled into his eyes. His hands trembled. Would it really matter if he waited until the moon was full? Could he make love to her now? Would it matter?

Taking a deep breath, he grasped the doorknob, pushed the door open and stepped into the room. Meredythe's head snapped up. A rosy blush covered her cheeks as her breath quickened. Her excited scent wrapped itself around him. His body tightened.

"Meredythe…"

Her voice was eager. "Werewolves."

Bleddyn felt as if he'd been dunked in cold water. "What?"

His cock went limp.

She erupted out of her chair and leaped toward him.

"Werewolves, Bleddyn. There are people who think they're werewolves! They can be anywhere, maybe even right here in Winterbourne. Can you believe it? That's the answer. I just know it is."

Throwing her arms around his waist, she plastered her body against his and hugged him exuberantly.

Bleddyn fisted his hands.

"Here? Are you sure?"

"Well, probably not here in Winterbourne," she answered into his chest as she squeezed him again. "That doesn't matter. What matters is that there are people who want to be werewolves, people who think they *are* werewolves. Can you believe it?"

She pulled her cheek from his chest and looked up…and seemed to lose herself in the soft mist of his gaze.

Her arms were still wrapped around his waist. Bleddyn shifted, aligning her body with his, bringing the pressure of her hips where he most wanted it.

"And why is this important?" he murmured against her hair.

Her fingers swirled against his back. Her breasts were crushed against his bare chest. And her pelvis was flat against his. Desire returned.

"Meredythe?" He fought to keep his arms at his sides.

Her smile was soft. "Hmm?"

"Werewolves?"

The hard pressure at the juncture of her thighs brought Meredythe back to herself. "Oh!" She dropped her arms and stepped back. What was she doing? He was practically naked.

"I'm sorry. I was… You came in and…"

He brushed her cheek with his knuckles. "Don't apologize, Meredythe. You can hug me any time you want."

Heat surged up her neck to her cheeks. Struggling to regain her composure, she blurted, "There are people who think they're werewolves."

His lips twitched. "I know."

That comment diverted her attention from his naked chest. "You do? Why didn't you tell me?"

His smile was amused. "I didn't know you were interested. You told me you were here to interview me about my wolves. You never mentioned werewolves."

Now she flushed for another reason. She hadn't told him about the murders. "Yes, well, I am interested."

He stepped back and crossed his arms over his chest. "Why?"

She gnawed on her lower lip. Her heart told her he wasn't guilty. He wasn't the murderer. He couldn't be. He was too...gentle. But he did have wolves. "Oh. I—ah—just sort of came across the information."

Leaning back against the edge of the open door, he cocked his head to one side and struggled to concentrate. His groin ached. If he had kissed her, she wouldn't have denied him. He could smell her arousal all the way across the room. "Do you expect me to believe a reporter of your caliber just 'comes across' information?"

She lifted her chin and their gazes locked.

She put the computer between them. "I was getting bored and followed a new thread."

He smiled. "Bored? Did you miss me?"

Her chin rose. "How could I miss you when you were just outside? And why would I miss you to begin with?"

Grinning broadly, he answered, "My scintillating conversation?"

She laughed outright. Hands on her hips, she said, "I don't think I've ever met a man like you, Bleddyn Glyndwr."

A dark fire leaped in his eyes. "No, you haven't."

Mesmerized by the passion in his eyes, Meredythe shivered. If she didn't get out of here...

"I'm going to go talk to Shadow now. I haven't been down to see him today yet."

Bleddyn remained still, his gaze locked with hers. Then he nodded. "He's anxious for your company." He turned toward the bathroom then stopped. "Meredythe?"

She was still standing, watching him. "Yes?"

"I have to make a trip into town—to the grocery store. Would you like to go along? Winterbourne has a fairly decent restaurant. We could get a bite to eat without having to worry about doing the dishes."

Her mind raced. He hadn't told her everything he knew about werewolves, she just knew it. She might learn something. The fact that Bleddyn was so devastatingly attractive had nothing to do with her agreeing to go to dinner. "Yes, I'd like that."

"Great. I'll be ready in about half an hour, so make sure you feed Shadow."

"I'll do that now."

After he disappeared into the bathroom, Meredythe turned off the computer, gathered up her papers and CDs and shoved them into her briefcase.

Dinner with Bleddyn. Her mind began to wander down erotic paths. The dark, curly hairs on his chest were as soft as they looked. A picture of the thin line of dark hair that disappeared beneath the waistband of his jeans appeared in her mind. A shiver slid down her back.

She stared at the closed door of the bathroom. Just how did Bleddyn look naked? Did his butt really look as good as it did in those tight jeans he wore? And his cock... She took a step toward the door.

The sharp pain in her leg dissolved her fantasy.

"Ouch! Methuselah, how often have I told you not to use me as your scratching post?"

"Meerrooww," the cat answered and weaved back and forth through her legs.

She glanced at the closed bathroom door once more and shivered. After a quick stroke from Methuselah's head to the tip of his tail, she said, "I'm going out to see Shadow now."

Methuselah yawned and rolled over onto his back. *Finally. I didn't think she was ever going to pay attention to that lead about werewolves.*

* * * * *

"It's a small town—barely eight thousand people when you count the outlying areas," Bleddyn said as he maneuvered his truck into a parking spot at Winterbourne's only grocery store.

"Pretty quiet, I'll bet," Meredythe answered as she looked around.

Bleddyn's grin flashed. "Better for wolves that way. Not as many people to bother them."

Releasing her seat belt, Meredythe opened her door and jumped out. "I can see your point."

Bleddyn walked around to her side of the truck. Tucking her arm under his, he led her into the grocery store. Thirty minutes later, he wheeled the cart back out to the truck and deposited their purchases in the back. "We can leave the truck here. The restaurant is only a few blocks away."

Meredythe looked up and down the street. "Aren't you afraid someone will steal everything?"

"No. Winterbourne is a quiet town, remember."

"It's quiet towns like this that have the most skeletons buried in its closets," she snorted as she slid her arm under his and nudged him forward. "Come on, I'm hungry."

Chuckling, Bleddyn lengthened his stride so he could keep up with her.

Meredythe closed her eyes and took a deep breath of fresh air. A cold breeze ruffled her hair and she shivered. Even though a warm front had come through and melted most of the snow, late November in upper New York State was still cool and brisk.

Though it was after six o'clock, many of the shops on Main Street were still open, their owners outside stringing garland or Christmas lights or both around their doors and windows. Every one of them wished Bleddyn and her a good evening.

Meredythe smiled. Small-town America, where everybody knew everybody else. How she loved it! Someday, when she'd accomplished everything she wanted to in journalism, she'd retire to a town like this and write…something.

As they strolled toward the restaurant, Bleddyn stopped numerous times to introduce her to various townspeople. Henry Hamilton owned a drugstore that still had a soda fountain. Agnes Carson had a dress shop with one of the loveliest wedding gowns she had ever seen in the window. Then there was Sally Marsden's Miscellany Shoppe where, Sally told her, she could find just about anything she could imagine. Just glancing in the window told Meredythe it was the kind of shop Aunt Evelyn would love. She made up her mind to go browse soon.

"The restaurant is in the middle of the next block," Bleddyn said as they stopped at the curb.

"If we ever get there," Meredythe teased as they crossed the street. "Is there anyone in this town you don't know?"

Bleddyn grinned, but before he could answer, they were interrupted again.

"Bleddyn, good evening."

Bleddyn nodded. "Hello, Richard. How are you? Anything exciting happen in town today?"

"Mrs. Thompson's cat got stuck up her sycamore tree," the older man answered with a grin. "And Billy and Bobby Norwood were caught stuffing eggs into old lady Brenner's mailbox again. You know, the usual." His gaze shifted to Meredythe. "And who's this pretty lady?"

"Meredythe Welsh, meet Richard Fletcher, owner and publisher of *The Winterbourne Chronicle*. Meredythe's a reporter from New York."

The portly man's handshake was robust. "A reporter! With you, Bleddyn? What's the world coming to?" he said with a wide grin. "You should be honored, young lady. Bleddyn Glyndwr has allowed exactly one other reporter to interview him in the years he's been here—me. You are certainly in select company. How did you manage to get your foot in the door?"

After he left go of her hand, Meredythe shook it, opened and closed it, then shook her fingers again to restore the circulation. "The blizzard sort of blew me in. He either had to let me in or let me freeze. How did you manage to get an interview, Mr. Fletcher?"

"Call me Richard. It wasn't hard. I just drove up to the house and refused to leave until he talked to me."

"He sat in the driveway for five hours," interrupted Bleddyn. "I think he'd have stayed all night."

Fletcher nodded. "I would have. Kept the doors locked tight too. That wolf he lets run loose sat under a tree and stared at me all day. Wouldn't let me out of my truck."

Meredythe chuckled. "Keri was a lot nicer to me."

"You're a lot prettier than I am, Ms. Welsh."

"Meredythe, please, and Keri's a female," she bantered back.

Fletcher's laughter rolled down the street. "Smart girl you've got there, Bleddyn. Better be careful. She might discover all your secrets."

Meredythe laughed with them, but…

Did she detect a note of warning in Richard Fletcher's voice?

"I don't have any secrets to hide, Richard, you know that," Bleddyn answered with a wink. "Now if you'll excuse us, I promised Meredythe a meal at the Winterbourne House."

"Why didn't you say so? Just get the special, whatever it is. You won't be disappointed," Fletcher said. "Goodnight, Meredythe. Enjoy your stay in Winterbourne. You won't find another town quite like ours anywhere else."

"Goodnight. It was nice meeting you."

With a jaunty wave, Fletcher slid into the blue pickup truck parked at the curb and drove away.

"Quite a character, isn't he?" Meredythe asked.

Bleddyn gently grasped her elbow and guided her down the street. "Very much so, but a good friend, nonetheless. Here we are."

They stopped in front of a red brick building with a simple wooden sign reading *Winterbourne Public House and Restaurant*. Bleddyn pushed the door open then stepped back for Meredythe to precede him.

Gentle warmth rolled out the door, embracing Meredythe and pulling her forward into the softly lighted foyer. Through a door on at her left, she could see a long mahogany bar where a handful of patrons chatted convivially. A burst of laughter lured her to the doorway. Glancing to the back of the room, she noted the small group of men chuckling around a dartboard. The tall, gray-haired bartender strolled down the length of the bar and leaned against it.

"Good evening, miss. Can I help you?"

Before she could answer, the woodsy cologne Bleddyn favored enveloped her. He slipped her coat from her shoulders and said, "She's with me, Zach."

The bartender's grin was affable. "Evening, Bleddyn, what can I get for you?"

"Nothing tonight. We're here for dinner."

"Then you'll want the special."

"I'll take your word for it."

A buxom blonde bustled down the length of the taproom toward them. "Hello, Bleddyn. Two for dinner?"

"Meredythe, I'd like you to meet Penny O'Calahan, chef extraordinaire of the Winterbourne House."

Penny's Irish accent was unmistakable. "Go on now, Bleddyn Glyndwr. You'll be turning my head with all that blarney."

The bartender's voice rolled across the bar. "Her head is swelled enough already. I have to live with the woman, you know."

Smiling, Meredythe asked, "Have you been in America long?"

"Ten years ago, himself at the bar talked me into moving here to manage his restaurant. I wasn't here more than five months and himself forced me to marry him."

"Forced! Ha! More the other way around, woman."

Fisting her hands on her hips, Penny snapped. "Don't you be telling people I plied you with the drink until you were agreeing to marry me, Zachary O'Calahan, or you'll be sleeping in your bar tonight."

Grumbling and laughter drifted across the bar, but Penny's order went unchallenged by her husband.

"He's a good man, Zachary is," she stated as she led Meredythe and Bleddyn into the dining room, "but he needs reminding of his place now and again." She glanced over her shoulder at Meredythe. "Men are like children. They need structure and discipline. Don't be forgetting that," she said with a meaningful glance at Bleddyn.

Bleddyn chuckled as they followed Penny. "We'll have two of tonight's specials. Do you want anything to drink, Meredythe?"

"What's the special?" she asked as she slid into the booth.

"Shepherd's pie," Penny answered.

"Then I'll have a beer. Whatever you have on tap."

Bleddyn seated himself across the booth. "Make that two."

"Aye, two drafts." With a warm smile, Penny bustled off and returned almost immediately with their drinks. "I'll have your dinners out in a jiffy."

Glancing around, Meredythe sipped her beer. Penny had seated them in a fairly secluded booth away from the other diners. The large potted shrub sitting just behind them also sheltered them from curious glances.

Leaning back against the high back of the booth, she smiled and said, "So, Bleddyn, what do you know about werewolves?"

Chapter Eleven

Bleddyn glanced around the room. The low hum of conversation from other diners drifted toward them but didn't intrude. More people than he'd expected were here, but Penny had seated them in a secluded booth. When the waitress delivered their two mugs of beer, he nodded his thanks. Lifting his, he sipped slowly.

Meredythe sat perfectly still, her eyes locked on his.

"Well?" she asked.

"Lycanthropy."

"What?"

"The scientific name for believing oneself to be a werewolf."

She frowned. "I know that. I want to know how much you know about it. You are the expert on wolves."

After another quick glance around the dining room, he set his glass down. No one was paying attention to them. "I've studied the phenomena off and on over the years."

Her fingertips rolled a drumbeat on the hard oak table.

"And?"

Ignoring the other diners, he focused on Meredythe. She sat across from him, eyes sparkling with interest. Lifting her beer, she sipped then placed the mug back on the table. White foam smothered her upper lip. When her tongue swiped her lip clean, his cock jerked. Erotic images of what that tongue could do to his body flashed behind his eyes.

"Bleddyn?" Her tone was impatient.

Shoving his fantasies into a dark corner of his mind, he reached for his beer. "Most lycanthropy can be attributed to schizophrenia or other mental diseases."

Locking both hands around her glass, Meredythe leaned forward, her breasts brushing the top of the table.

"I read that. What about the ones who aren't mentally ill but still believe they're werewolves?"

Bleddyn pulled his eyes away from the nipples that pushed against her soft sweater and sipped his beer. After a couple of quick swallows, he said, "Lycanthropy is not really my field of expertise. I'm interested in real wolves, not people suffering from delusions."

She pursed her lips and started to draw circles in the condensation on her mug, her thoughts obvious. Bleddyn swallowed more beer. He knew she was frustrated with his answers. He hadn't told her anything she hadn't or couldn't find out for herself. And she didn't believe him. She wanted to know how much he really knew. He was an expert on wolves. Werewolves should be a kind of sideline.

"Bleddyn Glyndwr knows more about werewolves than any other man in the country," rasped a hoarse voice.

Beer sloshed from Meredythe's mug when it slipped from her fingers and thumped to the table. Silence eddied away from their table as conversations halted and the other diners turned their attention to the gaunt man who hovered at the end of the booth as if to block their escape.

Meredythe leaned closer, only to jerk back as tears welled in her eyes. The foul odor oozing from him chased her as far back into the corner of the booth as she could get. Gagging from his stench, her hands automatically dug into her purse for her pen and notebook. She glanced up. The man was staring intently at Bleddyn.

Scraggly salt-and-pepper whiskers shadowed the lean hollows of his cheeks while stringy clumps of gray hair hung limply about his face and shoulders. An old suit of indiscriminate brown hung from his lanky body. Both hands were fisted and shaking, as if he were struggling to keep them at his sides. From his eyes glowed the light of fanaticism.

Shivering, Meredythe grabbed her beer and gulped. Twice she'd interviewed people frantic for a cause. One had ended up committing suicide and the other had murdered her family. She'd arrived at the scene before the bodies had been covered. The lifeless eyes of a little blonde-headed girl flashed through her mind.

Bleddyn's low voice pulled her back from the horror of that particular day. "Meredythe?"

Once he had her attention, he said, "Excuse me a minute while I take care of this."

When he pushed himself out of the booth, the other man was forced to step back. Meredythe let go of the breath she was holding. Still, she had to breathe through her mouth. She gripped her pen and waited. Bleddyn had placed himself squarely in front of the other man, blocking Meredythe's view. How could the stench not bother him?

"I told you to stay away from me, Anderson," he said in a low voice as she recorded their conversation.

Meredythe turned in her seat and leaned to the side, trying to see around Bleddyn.

"Master," the older man hissed back, his tone feral, "you could rule the world. You have only to take and all will be yours. I live to serve you, as do others."

Rule the world. Bleddyn? She wrote faster.

Bleddyn crossed his arms over his chest. "You're a mad fool, Anderson. I'm a doctor of zoology whose expertise is the study of wolves, nothing more."

The other man's gaze shifted around Bleddyn to Meredythe then back to Bleddyn. He nodded with what seemed to be approval. "You have chosen your mate. Good. We will worship her as queen."

Meredythe's pen scratched a zigzag line to the bottom of the tablet as she jerked her head up. His mate? Her gaze snapped from the old man to Bleddyn's back. She blinked once, shook her head, then blinked again. Was the room getting darker? Or was Anderson's disgusting smell affecting her vision?

Bleddyn stood, body stiff, hands clenched at his sides. Since his sleeves were pushed up, she could see the muscles tensed, veins bulging in his forearms. A misty aura seemed to surround him. Where did it come from? She blinked again. That guy's stench was really beginning to affect her vision.

She shifted her gaze back to Anderson. A feral light blazed in his eyes as he eagerly licked his lips. His body was taut. He seemed to be waiting for something. What?

Her gaze returned to Bleddyn's back. If only she could see his face!

Bleddyn closed his eyes, struggling to control his temper. Anderson had seen Meredythe, referred to her as his mate. The old man was crazy, crazy enough to try something. If he so much as touched her…

Visions of Anderson restraining Meredythe raced through his mind and his control began to slip. Silver and black mist appeared before his eyes. His vision became unfocused. The primitive beast in his soul roared.

Crush! Maim! Kill! My woman, my mate. Mine!

A dark mist began to form.

"I told you to stay out of my restaurant, Morton Anderson!" Penny O'Calahan snapped. She jerked to a halt when she got close enough for his noxious odor to envelop her. "Jesus, Mary and Joseph," she gagged as she crossed herself. "You're smelling like someone three weeks dead and buried. "You'll be chasing all my customers away. Get out! Zachary, call the sheriff."

"I'm already here, Penny," said a bulky, broad-shouldered man dressed in gray. "I was hoping to get some supper. Rose has her book club tonight, you know," he added with a grin.

"Just be smelling him, Hank," she snapped through the apron she held up to her nose and mouth. "He's ruining my business, he is."

"This is a public restaurant," the lanky man snarled. "I have as much right to be here as anyone else."

"Not smelling like the grave, you don't," Penny snapped. "You've no right to be coming in and harassing my customers about full moons and werewolves and Dr. Bleddyn. If anybody'd be asking me, you should be locked up in a madhouse. It's where you belong, what with your howling at the moon once a month and all."

Taking a deep breath, the sheriff stepped closer to Anderson and grabbed his arm. "Do you want to lodge a complaint, Penny?"

"I certainly do."

"Sorry, Anderson. You have to go."

The older man swung his glare to Bleddyn. "Put these humans in their place, Master. How can you allow them to treat me like this?"

Slowly Bleddyn unclenched his fists and forced himself to relax. His vision cleared. Thank God for Penny. If she hadn't come in…

The beast was getting stronger. The full moon was too close for him to lose control of his temper. But just the thought of Anderson getting his hands on Meredythe…

Bleddyn shuddered mentally and fought back another surge of darkness. After taking a deep breath, he said, "He's getting worse, Hank. I can't come into town without being harassed."

The sheriff nodded. "Stop in my office tomorrow and swear out a complaint. I'll take care of everything."

Anderson tried to tug free. Glaring at Bleddyn, he snarled, "Fool. You could have everything. The full moon offers you power. Do not deny her." He turned his maniacal gaze to Meredythe. "Demand that he accept his destiny. He will make you a queen among women. Tomorrow, bring him to me. During the ceremony, all will be revealed."

The sheriff hauled Anderson across the dining room. "Come on. Stop bothering these people."

"Do not deny your heritage, Bleddyn Glyndwr. Destiny awaits you," he howled as the sheriff dragged him through the door.

"Humph!" Penny snorted, waving her apron to clear the stench. "It's time he was locked away, what with his raving and all. It's a wonder he hasn't murdered somebody in their bed yet."

Bleddyn forced a grin onto his face. "Now, Penny."

"Don't you be now Pennying me, Bleddyn Glyndwr. The man's a menace and you know it. And your meals are on the house tonight. I'll not be taking your money, so don't be trying to sweet-talk me."

Spinning on her heel, she bustled into the kitchen.

Meredythe stared at him, her pen poised. "What was that all about?"

Bleddyn slid back into the booth, picked up his beer and chugged it down. Raising his hand, he signaled for the waitress. "Another beer and a glass of water, please. Would you like another drink, Meredythe?"

"No, I'm fine. Who was that," she repeated, "and what was he ranting about?"

Bleddyn grimaced. Why did Anderson have to be in town tonight? "That was Morton Anderson. He thinks he's a werewolf."

Meredythe leaned forward. "Really? What did he mean about you accepting your destiny?" She flipped to a clean page in her tablet.

Bleddyn cursed to himself. If he'd have known Anderson was in town, he'd never have brought Meredythe with him. A quick glance across the table confirmed his fears. She was entirely too curious about the old fool. Normally Anderson wasn't a danger. All he had to do was avoid the fool. But Meredythe's eyes were sparkling and he could practically see the wheels turning in her mind. If he didn't answer her questions to her satisfaction, she'd go looking for Anderson. And if the old man got his hands on her, who knew what he'd do. Bleddyn focused his gaze on Meredythe's face. Her pen was poised, ready to write. Well, he could always tell the truth…sort of. Her reaction would be interesting.

Taking a deep breath, he said, "I'm a werewolf."

The disgusted glance she shot his way told him how much she believed him. Well, he'd tried to tell the truth.

"Now stop your fooling, Bleddyn Glyndwr," scolded Penny as she set their dinners and an aromatic candle on the table. "Don't be scaring the girl with that fool's delusions."

"If Anderson had any sense," Bleddyn mumbled into his beer mug, "he'd be afraid of Meredythe."

Meredythe stared at the older woman. "Delusions?"

Bleddyn grinned. "Anderson is convinced that since I have wolves, I must be a werewolf."

She picked up her pen. "You're kidding."

"No, he's not," interrupted Penny. "That crazy old man has been chasing after Bleddyn for the last year and a half. Ever since Anderson moved to Winterbourne and bought the old Van Hocken place, he's been badgering Bleddyn to come out to the farm on the night of the full moon to take part in his heathen ceremonies."

"Damn it, woman, quit your gossiping and get back to your kitchen," her husband bellowed from the bar.

"Don't you be telling me what to do, you sorry excuse for a bartender! You've three thirsty men sitting with empty glasses at the other end," she snapped back. But she did disappear back into her kitchen.

Bleddyn lifted his fork. "They're quite a pair."

Meredythe was not distracted.

"This Morton Anderson really thinks he's a werewolf? What kind of ceremony is he talking about?"

Bleddyn concentrated on his food. "I've never gone to one, so I haven't got the faintest idea."

She looked up from her tablet. "You aren't even curious?"

He glanced up. "And lend credence to his delusions that I'm a werewolf?"

Meredythe furrowed her brow. Bleddyn had a point there. This man, Anderson, obviously had mental problems of some kind. She scooped some food onto her fork and shoved it into her mouth, contemplating what she'd learned about Morton Anderson as she chewed. He owned a farm. He could have all kinds of animals there.

"Does he have a wolf?"

Bleddyn stopped eating. "I certainly hope not! Who knows what he'd do to it."

Meredythe jabbed a chunk of meat with her fork. Morton Anderson didn't seem like the kind of guy who was especially kind to animals. And Bleddyn would never allow any wolf, or a wolf-dog, to be hurt—not if he could help it. That was one thing she was sure of. He'd steal the animal if that would be the only way to get it away safely.

She chewed slowly. But what if Anderson had a wolf or wolf-dog and Bleddyn didn't know it? Anderson could be her killer—or maybe one of a group. Penny said he held ceremonies on the nights when there was a full moon.

"Does he travel a lot?"

Bleddyn buttered a roll. "Who?"

"Anderson."

He shrugged. "How should I know? I stay as far away from the man as I can."

Meredythe scooped another forkful of food into her mouth, her mind dissecting everything she'd seen and heard.

Morton Anderson thought Bleddyn was a werewolf. He held ceremonies on the night of a full moon. There was really only one way to find out what she needed to know. She needed to talk to Morton Anderson.

Glancing at Bleddyn, she discovered he'd finished eating. He was relaxed in the corner, one arm draped along the top of the booth's back, staring at her with a strange expression on his face, an expression that was…tender.

Her muscles relaxed and she smiled, a feeling of warmth settling around her body. He was such a sexy man. Her mind drifted back to that afternoon when she stood with her cheek pressed against his soft chest hairs. His nipple had been so close. She'd had to stop herself from licking it.

"Do you want dessert?"

She blinked. "What?"

He smiled sensuously. "Do you want dessert? Penny's chocolate cheesecake is positively decadent."

She stared at him. *Not as decadent as your skin. I'd rather nibble on that.* A shiver danced down her spine. *Meredythe, get a hold of yourself*! "No thanks. I've had plenty, but please, order some for yourself if you want."

A smile tickled the corners of his lips. "What I want isn't on the menu."

Another shiver raced up Meredythe's spine as he flared his nostrils. His mouth and tongue on her body, sucking her nipples, nibbling down over her stomach, lapping her cunt. Her nipples tightened, sending a sharp stab of desire straight to her groin. How was he able to reduce her to a pile of quivering Jell-O with just a look? How was she ever going to get any work done? Work. She glanced down. Her open tablet lay before her. Morton Anderson's name leaped from the page.

Concentrate Meredythe. You're here to do a story, not be seduced by the sexiest man you've ever seen. "I need to interview him."

Bleddyn stretched his other arm along the back of the booth. His shirt pulled taut over his chest. "Who?"

Meredythe swallowed then wet her lips. "Morton Anderson."

The soft mist in his gray eyes turned to steel. His arms fell to his sides and he leaned forward. "I forbid you to go anywhere near him."

The seductive web he'd been weaving around her snapped. She stiffened. Her chin came up and her nostrils flared. Her voice was low and tight. "I *beg* your pardon!"

He growled his answer, low and dangerous. "You heard me, Meredythe. I forbid you to go near Morton Anderson. He's a dangerous man. You have no idea what could happen to you."

Shoving her tablet and pen into her purse, she grabbed it and pushed herself out of the booth. Tugging her purse strap over her shoulder, she glared down at him.

When he tried to push out of the booth, she planted her palm on his chest and shoved him back down.

"What gives *you* the right to dictate to me, Dr. Bleddyn Glyndwr?" she hissed through clenched teeth. "I am not your servant, wife or employee, and I don't need your permission to do anything. I am here in pursuit of a story and I have every right to interview whomever I damn well please, whenever I damn well please, whether you like it or not."

Spinning on her heel, she stomped out of the dining room.

"Fuck," Bleddyn muttered, shoving himself out of the booth and hurrying after her. He grabbed his coat—and Meredythe's—from the rack just inside the door and followed her out into the night.

Meredythe stomped down the street, muttering to herself.

"Forbids! He *forbids* me! Who the hell does he think he is, telling me what I can and can't do? Nobody tells me who I can and can't interview—nobody. And Dr. Bleddyn Glyndwr is not going to tell me how to do my job no matter how sexy he is."

She stopped and stamped her foot. "Shit, Meredythe. Is that all you can think about—his body? What's wrong with you? You've never let a man get to you before, and this one won't either. It doesn't matter how cute his ass is. He could be a murderer."

Yeah, her mind whispered insidiously, *and you're an international arms dealer.*

She jerked the strap of her purse higher on her shoulder and continued down the street, ignoring the festive Christmas lights shining in many of the storefronts. She glanced to her right and spied her reflection in a shining window. "Okay, so your gut tells you he had nothing to do with the murders. That still doesn't give him the right to tell you what to do."

A cold breeze whistled down the alley between two stores and she shivered. She'd forgotten her coat.

Turning, she took a step back toward the restaurant and came face-to-face with a woman wearing an old brown coat. Meredythe stepped back, involuntarily holding her breath and letting it out with relief when no overpowering odor reached her nose. She summoned a smile. "Can I help you?"

The woman stared at Meredythe for a moment, then said, "Come to us tomorrow. You will be a queen among women."

Meredythe made a frantic grab for the flap of her purse. Notes, she had to take notes. "What do you mean? Are you one of Mr. Anderson's followers? Do you believe you're a werewolf too?"

"One more night and all will be revealed," the woman repeated. Then she slipped into the alley and disappeared into the darkness.

Meredythe turned to follow her, shivering as another blast of cold air swirled around her.

"Meredythe, wait," Bleddyn called. "You forgot your coat and you're going the wrong way."

After one last glance down the alley—following an unknown person into a dark alley wasn't a very smart thing to do even if this was Smalltown, USA, and not nasty New York—she turned, planted her feet firmly and crossed her arms over her chest.

Bleddyn stopped before her and held out her coat.

"You forgot this."

She arched an eyebrow, clenching her teeth against their sudden urge to chatter and refusing to allow her body to shiver.

"Please, Meredythe, put your coat on before you get sick."

She dropped her purse to the sidewalk and grabbed her coat from his outstretched hand. Shrugging into it, she pulled her hood up over her head and yanked the zipper all the way to her chin. Bending over, she picked up her purse and hauled the strap onto her shoulder. Scowling, she pushed past Bleddyn and strode down the street.

When he grabbed her arm and pulling her to a halt, she shot an icy glare at him.

"Do. Not. Touch. Me."

Obviously biting off a curse, he shoved his hands in his pockets. "Please, Meredythe, I apologize."

Some of the stiffness left her posture.

"I had no right to tell you not to interview Anderson."

Meredythe relaxed more but remained wary.

Bleddyn shifted his weight as the wind whistled between them.

She didn't say anything.

"Look, Meredythe, I stay as far away from Anderson as I can, but that doesn't mean I don't know anything about him. Three times he's had animals removed from his farm because of neglect. He's suspected in a string of petty burglaries. His driving is so reckless, his license has been revoked. After the SPCA took away the last of his animals, he's threatened to shoot anyone who comes onto his property. Anderson is a dangerous man, Meredythe. There's no telling what he'll do. I don't want you getting hurt."

As Bleddyn talked, Meredythe inhaled the cold night air and looked up at the almost full moon. Bathed in its luminescent glow, she felt her anger drain away. Maybe she did overreact. She shook her head, fighting the sudden lethargic feeling invading her body. No, she didn't overreact. Bleddyn had no right to forbid her anything. But she should have stayed to listen to his explanation after she set him straight about the fact that who she interviewed during the course of her job was none of his business.

"Meredythe?"

She jerked her gaze away from the moon.

"What?"

His voice had become amused. "Do you want to stand here and stare at the moon all night?"

Jerking her purse strap, she stomped down the street.

"Let's get going. I'm sure the animals are wondering where we are. I know Methuselah will be pacing until I get back."

Bleddyn walked by her side silently. He'd be better off keeping his mouth shut. At least she was going back home with him. Once they were there, Methuselah and Shadow would erase what was left of her anger and any possible thoughts of leaving from her mind. Besides, the demon in his soul was hungry. If he allowed his anger to overcome his self-control…

Meredythe would never forgive what he'd do to her. She'd probably run screaming—if she were able.

* * * * *

After pulling the truck to a halt next to the garage, Bleddyn glanced over at Meredythe. She'd spent the entire ride back to the estate flipping through her tablet, scribbling more notes here and there and mumbling to herself.

"Meredythe, we're home."

"What? Oh. Do you need help with the groceries?"

"I can manage."

"Good. I'm going to go see Shadow for a few minutes. He's restless."

Shoving the tablet into her purse, she slid out of the truck and disappeared around the corner of the garage. A deep woof from Shadow told Bleddyn she'd reached her destination.

He got out and began gathering groceries. Leaning back against the truck, Bleddyn stared up at the moon and swallowed a deep breath of cold November air. Meredythe was safe.

The demon in his soul suddenly struck, fighting for dominance. Dropping the groceries, he braced his hands against the side of the truck and struggled to beat the darkness in his soul down with a powerful surge of his will. Gasping for breath, he leaned his forehead against the rim of the truck bed. He'd have to be careful tomorrow night. His control would have to be complete when he finally took Meredythe to his bed. The demon that rode his soul would not be gentle.

Pushing himself away from the truck, he picked up the groceries and glanced once in the direction Meredythe had disappeared. He turned toward the house. Shadow occupied all her attention.

"There now. Everything is fine," Meredythe crooned to Shadow as he stared at her through the chain link fence. "You go to sleep and I'll see you in the morning. I'm sure Methuselah is wondering where I am."

After a quick tail wag and low woof, Shadow disappeared into his kennel.

Meredythe stepped outside his enclosure and latched the gate. Throwing her purse over her shoulder, she shoved her hands into her pockets and trudged toward the back of the house. Soft light illuminated the kitchen windows and the light by the back door drove back the shadows of the night.

She sighed. When did walking into Bleddyn's house start to feel like coming home?

Chapter Twelve

The next morning, Meredythe unlatched the gate to Shadow's run and stepped inside. The wolf-dog stuck his head out of his kennel and growled.

"Not now, Shadow, okay?" she mumbled as she leaned back against the chain link fence. With a sigh, she slid down its length until she was sitting on the ground. Hugging her knees to her chest, she stared up into the clear, blue sky. A fluffy cloud drifted into her field of vision and she grimaced.

"What am I still doing here?"

Shadow stepped out of his kennel and sat on his haunches, ears pricked forward.

Glancing his way, she stated, "I'm a reporter, a damn good one. I go in, get my story and then get out—except this time. I've learned everything I can from Dr. Bleddyn Glyndwr, so why am I still living in his house? I should have left here days ago."

Shadow whined.

Meredythe broke eye contact and shifted as the cold seeped into the seat of her pants.

Shadow whined again.

Another glance in his direction. "The werewolf cult? Yeah, that's a good one. Right here under my nose the whole time. I should have been asking questions in town as soon as the roads were passable, so why didn't I? What is it about Bleddyn Glyndwr that keeps me here?"

Shadow rose to his feet.

Smiling, Meredythe crossed her legs and rested her elbows on her thighs. Cupping her chin in one hand, she continued, "But then I wouldn't have met you."

Shadow woofed and wagged his tail twice.

Ignoring her cold behind, she dropped her hands into her lap, leaned her head back against the fence and closed her eyes. It was time to leave. Her heart told her Bleddyn was not the killer. She'd pack up her stuff and go, stopping in town long enough to find out what she could about Morton Anderson although her gut told her he was too fixated on Bleddyn really being a werewolf to be the murderer either.

Bleddyn... Last night's conversation leaped into her mind. Biting her bottom lip, she fisted both hands. To think, he'd had the gall to tell her to stay away from a possible lead. Who did he think he was to tell her who she could and couldn't interview? Arrogant, egotistical...

When a cold nose touched her cheek, Meredythe jerked herself away from her musings and opened her eyes. Shadow stood before her, staring into her eyes. Then his tongue lolled out of his mouth. White teeth flashed.

Oh shit! What on earth possessed me to come into Shadow's run? And why did I take my eyes off him?

After one quick swipe around his muzzle, Shadow's tongue disappeared back into his mouth. Then wolf-dog sat down, ears pricked forward. A soft whine escaped his throat.

Slowly Meredythe relaxed and raised a hand to his neck. Another, more eager whine escaped as she began to stroke his soft fur. Sighing, he leaned into her hand.

"Oh Shadow," she murmured and threw both arms around his powerful shoulders.

Whining happily, the wolf-dog wiggled as close as he could.

Tears now streaming down her cheeks, Meredythe hugged him, laughing as he licked the moisture from her cheeks. Her back banged against the chain link fence when he flopped into her lap.

"Woof."

"I love you too, you silly boy," she said as she struggled under his weight. "Move over—you're squashing me."

With another happy woof, Shadow scrambled off her lap. Another swipe of his tongue had her wiping her face on the sleeve of her parka.

Meredythe pushed herself to her feet. Shadow stood before her, tail wagging.

"You're all right now, aren't you, boy? You'll be okay, won't you?"

Another low woof. He grinned a doggy grin.

She grinned back and stroked his head. "You wonderful, wonderful boy. I have to go tell Bleddyn. Is that all right with you?"

Shadow whined and leaned into her hands. His tail continued to wag.

"I'll be right back and give you the brushing of your life. How does that sound?"

"Woof."

After a few more quick strokes, Meredythe stepped out of Shadow's run. Then she sprinted to the house.

Bleddyn's sharp hearing registered the back door bang off the wall over the loud pulse of the hot water streaming over his head.

"Bleddyn!"

As he turned off the water, he heard Meredythe slide into the downstairs' hallway and skid to a stop before the open door of the study. Keri's questioning whine drifted out. She didn't know what had Meredythe so excited either.

He raked his wet hair off his face as he concentrated on Meredythe's thumping steps. Whatever she wanted must be important—she was leaping up the steps two at a time. Then she landed at the top of the stairs and dashed down the hall.

Frowning, Bleddyn wrapped a towel around his waist. Could something have happened to the wolves? He stepped through the door of the bathroom just as Meredythe shoved the door to his bedroom open and launched herself into the room.

"Bleddyn! You'll never guess—"

All thoughts of Shadow disappeared from Meredythe's mind as Bleddyn stepped out of the misty bathroom wearing nothing but a towel. A drop of water tumbled from his chin to his chest where it meandered obliquely across a well-formed pectoral muscle into dark, curly hair. Her gaze followed the droplet through his chest hair and down through the increasingly thin line of hair that plummeted over his flat stomach and disappeared beneath the towel. The obvious bulge against the front of the towel was impossible to miss.

She swallowed. "Oh my God."

Bleddyn combed the wet hair behind his ears with his fingers and smiled.

"Do you want something?"

Her gaze traveled slowly back up his body, stopping once again at his chest.

"Meredythe?"

She jerked her eyes to his face. Heat flooded her cheeks. "What?"

She watched as his hands dropped to the towel and tightened it.

"Do you want something?"

She licked her lips. "Umm. Yeah. I…"

He chuckled.

She shivered and jerked her thoughts back to the wolf-dog. "Shadow let me touch him. As a matter of fact, he crawled into my lap."

True joy lit Bleddyn's face as he strode across the room. Then a frown appeared on his face. "Why did you go into his run alone? How could you be sure he wouldn't attack?"

Her smile disappeared as she gritted her teeth. Why did he have to keep finding fault with whatever she did?

"Damn it, Bleddyn Glyndwr, why…"

The drop of water that slid down Bleddyn's neck snared her attention.

"Why what?"

Meredythe ignored his question. His voice faded as she inhaled deeply, and his sharp, piney scent assaulted her senses. Lifting her hand, she traced the droplet's moist trail down his shoulder to just above his nipple. Flexing her fingers, she caressed the hairs growing there.

"So soft," she murmured as she swirled her fingers deeper. "So soft—like Shadow."

A quick, indrawn breath escaped him.

She glanced up into his face. Fiery passion danced in the depths of his eyes.

"Meredythe?"

He lifted his hand and gently laced his fingers through the curls that had escaped from the sloppy French braid she'd hurried through that morning and slipped them back behind her ear. She shivered as he caressed her neck then slid his hand under the parka she still wore. Thumbing the pulsing beat on the side of her neck delicately, he leaned forward and kissed her.

A thousand pinpricks of desire exploded in Meredythe's body. Her nipples tingled with stabs of pleasure-pain as she surrendered to his kiss. At first soft and gentle, his lips teased then tantalized then tormented. With a moan, she leaned into him and slipped her tongue into his mouth. His groan melded with her sighs and his tongue tangled with hers, gliding and dancing together and apart as their kiss became more and more carnal. Throwing her arms around his waist, she pressed herself against him. The hard ridge of his cock that jutted against her thigh left no doubt of his desire.

Shivers raced up Meredythe's spine as he traced a delicate line up her neck then across her cheek to lace his fingers through her hair and cup the back of her head. His other hand tugged her parka from her shoulders. It slid from her body to pool at her feet.

With the bulky barrier gone, he caressed her buttocks then pressed her hips into his. His tongue began to dart in and out of her mouth to match the steady, rhythmic pressure he was applying to her hips. Moaning, she lifted her leg and wrapped it around his thigh, rubbing her aching cunt against his rigid erection.

Bleddyn was reeling. The scent of Meredythe's arousal surrounded him and his body clamored for fulfillment. When she wrapped her leg around his thigh and started to rub against him, he let go of his self-control. She wanted him as much as he wanted her.

Then the dark beast in his blood raged to life.

Mine! *Conquer*! *Mate*! *Now*!

A violent shudder racked his body and soul. This woman was his, his to take, to mount, to dominate. All he needed to do was rip her clothing from her body, force her to the floor, plunge his aching erection into the soft heat of her body and take her again and again and again until she knew she belonged to him.

Cupping her breast, he thumbed her nipple.

She leaned farther into his hand.

He squeezed her breast harder.

She shivered and moaned and ground her hips against him. "Bleddyn, please…" she murmured against his mouth.

Her scent surrounded him—her hot, compelling, take-me-and-fuck-me-until-I-can't-stand-upright scent.

Bleddyn lifted his head and looked down into her face.

Raw hunger leaped from her eyes.

Lowering his head, he captured her lips again and stabbed his tongue into her mouth. The beating of his heart surged, plunging passion and fury through his blood—passion for the woman in his arms, fury because he had not yet mounted her. His dark side was no longer willing to wait.

Mine! *Mount her*! *Now*!

He heard cloth rip.

Her teeth cut his lip.

The taste of his own blood brought Bleddyn back to his senses—somewhat. As the monster in his soul fought for dominance, fought to throw Meredythe down on the floor so he could mount her, so he could ram his cock into her, so he could declare to the world that she was his, Bleddyn struggled to regain control. He could not let evil touch Meredythe. And without the moon and its stabilizing strength, the sexual need and bloodlust pounding though his veins could tear her to pieces.

He would *not* allow that to happen!

Tearing his mouth from hers, he grasped her upper arms and shoved her away.

"I am *not* an animal!" he growled into her passion-fogged face. "I will wait for the moon. Only a few hours more."

Ruthlessly crushing the desire boiling in his blood, he dropped his hands from Meredythe's shoulders and stepped back.

Clenching his hands at his sides, he watched her stumble forward and brace a hand on a small table to catch her balance.

"Bleddyn?"

Her voice was low, compelling, confused. Her face was flushed. Her breath came in short gasps. She lifted one hand toward him.

His blood surged anew.

Take her!

Every muscle in his body screamed with anger and frustration as he turned away. "Leave me."

"What? But…" Her voice swam with confusion.

"Damn it, Meredythe, get out!"

Her muffled sob pierced his heart. Taking a deep breath, he stepped toward the bathroom. Another sob then quick steps toward the door. The doorknob rattled then the hinges creaked. Her footsteps echoed through the hall and down the stairs.

Bleddyn leaned his forehead against the wall. He had to wait for tonight. He had no choice. The power he absorbed from the moon would counter the violent impulses that surged through his bloodstream. Tonight… Why did she have to come up here now? How was he going to explain? Plaster showered to the floor as his fist slammed through the wall.

Meredythe stumbled through the lower hallway to the front door. Wrenching it open, she took two deep gulps of air. Then she rushed outside and ran down the steps. She shivered, as much from embarrassment and anger as from the cold. Her thoughts roiled.

Get out! *He told me to get out, after I threw myself at him.*

Fists clenched, teeth grinding, she raced around the house. Spotting Bleddyn's truck sitting in front of the garage, she hurried to it and jerked the door open. Shadow's questioning howl paused her, but then she saw the keys dangling from the ignition. Shadow would be fine for now. No way was she going back in that house for the keys to her own car.

Pulling herself up into the cab, she slid behind the wheel and turned the key. She stomped on the clutch, grinding the gears as she slammed the truck into reverse. Jerking the gearshift back to drive, she peeled down the driveway. For all she cared, Bleddyn Glyndwr could go to hell.

When she got to the main road, she headed into Winterbourne and drove right through it. Twenty minutes later, after driving aimlessly around on almost deserted country roads, she eased to a stop on a wide spot at the side of the road and slid the gearshift into park. Sighing, she crossed her arms over the wheel and dropped her head on them.

What the hell was going on? She and Bleddyn had been dancing around each other for weeks. He'd been interested—more than interested. Why had he rejected her?

"Damn it," she mumbled and pushed herself up. Sunlight bounced through the windshield and into her eyes.

A dark shape appeared in the corner of her eye. As she turned her head, the door was yanked open and she was pulled out of the truck. Before she could protest, a rank cloth was jammed into her face. Her eyes watered and she coughed. Then the foul-smelling concoction she breathed in overpowered her senses.

"Hurry," said the brown-robed man to his companion. "Tell the master I have a gift for him."

* * * * *

The door's slam still ringing in his ears, Bleddyn pulled on his jeans.

An angry yowl echoed around the room as Methuselah sprang through the door and began to stalk Bleddyn.

What did you do to her, Wolf? Why did she leave?

Bleddyn dropped into a crouch and snarled, "Go to hell, Cat."

The hiss that erupted from Methuselah's throat raised the hairs on Bleddyn's arms. Mist began to shimmer around him as he began to shift into wolf shape.

Stop this right now, both of you, snarled a sharp voice from the door.

Methuselah stopped, his tail lashing from side to side. *He's hurt Meredythe, Keri. You felt her. You know.*

Slowly, surrounded with dignity, Keri padded into the room and placed herself between Bleddyn and the furious cat.

What happened, Bleddyn?

Again Bleddyn struggled to conquer the dark entity that inhabited his soul. Once he had himself under control, he sank onto the corner of the bed.

"I refused her sexual advances."

Both Keri and Methuselah froze. Their exclamations were simultaneous.

What!

What?

Bleddyn locked gazes with Methuselah. "So you see, Cat. I didn't hurt her."

Methuselah sat down. His tail still lashed from side to side. *Perhaps not physically.*

Three steps had Keri in front of Bleddyn.

Why?

"Why what?"

Why did you refuse her?

His answer was delivered with a snarl. "Because the devil living inside me could have torn her to pieces. You know what I'm like when the bloodlust is on me. Without moonlight to counter the craving for violence…"

Blinking back tears, he turned his face from the wolf and stared out the window. "I will not allow myself to hurt her."

Keri licked his hand. *Bleddyn, you could no more hurt Meredythe than you could hurt me.*

He dropped his forehead against hers and threaded his fingers through the thick fur of her neck ruff. "Will you ever acknowledge the evil that lives in me?"

She sighed and licked his cheek. *I acknowledge the evil that seeks to conquer your soul, Bleddyn. None knows better than I how it got there. But* you *master it. It does not master you.*

Sitting up, he wiped his face with his hand. "It's getting harder and harder. I didn't want to take a chance, not with the full moon only hours away."

Keri sat back on her haunches and cocked her head to one side. *Put yourself in Meredythe's place. You rejected her.*

Bleddyn's lips twitched. "And she'll be mad as hell once she's thought everything through."

She may not come back.

Bleddyn stood up and grabbed the shirt he'd tossed onto the bed before he went into the shower. "She'll be back. She left that damn cat here."

Methuselah's angry hiss followed him out the door.

If he weren't your son, Keri…

The wolf trotted toward the door. *Calm yourself, Methuselah. Bleddyn's right. Meredythe won't leave here without you. She'll come back.*

Methuselah remained seated. Lifting a paw, he licked it twice, then began to groom his face. That stupid wolf had no idea how angry Meredythe could get. His plans for the evening just might not develop the way he expected.

Methuselah began to purr as he pictured the anger Meredythe would let loose on Bleddyn. Tonight would be very interesting.

Rising, he minced delicately across the room. Numerous mouse nests were scattered about the mansion's unoccupied rooms. The center of the wolf's bed would be the perfect place for the bodies.

* * * * *

"Hey, Bowers, are you ever going home?"

Jon straightened away from the microscope, pulled off his glasses, scrunched his eyes closed and pinched the top of his nose. After blinking, he rolled his neck and shoulders.

"I just want to finish this report."

Kim chuckled. "Trying to make some points with the boss, huh?"

Jon simply grinned.

Kim grinned back. "We busted our asses on this city alderman's case from the beginning and the work paid off. It's solved. Go home and rest. Better yet, give Meredythe a call and go out on the town. Celebrate. Thanks to us, there's another murderer behind bars."

Jon turned back toward his microscope. "She's not back yet."

Kim shrugged out of his lab coat. "What was that you mumbled?"

"Meredythe. She's not back yet."

Kim chuckled as he shrugged into his parka. "When that woman gets her teeth into a story, she doesn't let go. You sure you want to get involved with her? She'll always be running off after one story or another."

"Christ, Kim, I barely know her. Now you have us practically engaged."

"Yeah, but you'd like to get to know her a lot better. You're the one who keeps calling to see if she's back from upstate yet."

"Well, she's not back yet, and I want to finish this report. Go home. The sooner I finish this, the sooner *I'll* be able to go home."

Laughter followed Kim out the door.

After he heard the door slam, Jon made a few more notes then pulled the slide he'd been viewing from the microscope and put it away. Rising, he walked to his desk and unlocked the bottom drawer. Finally, he had the time and privacy to review the DNA test he'd completed on the hairs that had been found on that pimp's body. Now when Meredythe got back, he'd be able to give her some definitive information about whether the animal that had killed him was a wolf, a dog or a combination of the two.

Ten minutes later, Jon flopped down onto a stool and stared at the evidence laid out before him. No way was this possible. That first test by the lab hadn't been a mistake. He had the same results, and he knew he hadn't contaminated the sample. The DNA from those hairs came up wolf…and human.

No way could this be true, no way. It wasn't possible. But the evidence never lied.

"Jesus Christ. Meredythe is hunting a werewolf."

The stool toppled to the floor as he leaped toward the phone.

"Phonebook," he muttered as papers went flying. "Where's the damn phonebook? I have to call her paper."

He stopped and sank into his chair. "Who the hell is going to believe me? Nobody."

He looked back at the table that held his evidence. How was he going to contact Meredythe? She had to be warned.

Jon thought back to the dinners they'd shared. Meredythe had been very free with her praise for her boss—a smart, open-minded man who was willing to let her run with her ideas and feelings.

Jon rose and gathered up his evidence. "I'll go see this King guy now. The worst he can do is call me a lunatic and throw me out. But he'll know how to contact Meredythe. She told me she always checks in with him."

* * * * *

"This is a rather fantastic tale you tell, Mr. Bowers."

"You believe me?"

James King's eyebrow rose. "On one piece of evidence? I'm afraid I'll need more than that. Even if it is DNA, most scientists will be skeptical."

"But..."

King held up his hand. "I agree this is compelling information you have. But surely you don't expect complete belief on one DNA test?"

Jon sank into a chair. "I wouldn't believe it either if I hadn't done the test myself. But belief isn't the point. I'm worried about Meredythe. She could be in danger. Isn't there any way to contact her? She does have a cell phone, doesn't she?"

King reached his hand across the table. "I will call and pass on the information, Mr. Bowers. Meredythe is my best reporter. I don't want her hurt any more than you do."

Jon recognized a dismissal when he heard one. Rising, he shook King's hand. Picking up the results of the DNA test, he slid it into his briefcase.

"Thank you for at least hearing me out, Mr. King."

The older man smiled. "Any time, my boy. Any time."

James King's smile faded as the door closed behind Jon. Picking up his phone, he punched in a number, waiting impatiently for the connection.

"A tall, blond man wearing a brown overcoat just left my office carrying a leather briefcase. He's in forensics, so you'll probably be able to recognize him by his smell. You must get me that briefcase, tonight. He's got proof that Bleddyn's a werewolf."

After severing the connection, James sank into his chair. Damn, but things were getting complicated.

Jon trudged along the sidewalk toward his apartment. One more block and he'd be home. That subway ride seemed to get longer every day.

A gust of wind exploded out of an alley, staggering him. As he struggled to regain his balance, a dark figure grabbed his briefcase. Gripping it more tightly, Jon refused to let go. Damn muggers.

A pale face turned toward him. A smile appeared—a smile with fangs. Dark eyes bore into his.

"Release the case now."

Jon felt his fingers relax. He tensed his hand, but the compulsion had been laid. The briefcase slipped from his fingers. The dark figure disappeared back into the alley.

Swallowing twice, Jon leaned back against a mailbox. He had DNA that proved the existence of a werewolf and now a vampire had stolen it. Maybe he did belong in an insane asylum.

Chapter Thirteen

"She's waking up."

Concentrating on the strange voice, Meredythe crawled back toward consciousness.

"The master doesn't want her awake yet."

Just as her eyes fluttered open, a cloth was pressed over her nose and mouth. Meredythe sank back into unconsciousness. With the full moon shining through the small window, she began to dream.

The last, shrill scream of the air raid sirens faded away as Bleddyn scrambled through the rubble of Germany's second attack on London. Fires blazed out of control. So many had died in the first attack yesterday. So many more had died today. He pushed past dazed survivors. Meredythe hadn't been in the air raid shelter closest to her home. Where was she?

Screams and groans echoed through broken and blasted walls. When a gas line exploded and rubble rained down, he threw himself against all that remained of a house as the building across the street collapsed.

"That was too close," he mumbled as he pushed himself out of the debris. "I have to find Meredythe and get out of here."

Climbing the ruins of a crumbled wall, he swung his legs over and slid down the other side. As he pushed himself to his feet, the last house on the block collapsed.

A woman's scream bounced around the rubble.

"Meredythe!"

Tossing chunks of wood and plaster out of his way as if they were cardboard, Bleddyn sprinted through the wreckage. Dust settled around him when he skidded to a halt in front of what remained of the house where Meredythe lived with her aunt. A single, slender arm was visible amongst the charred ruins.

"No! Meredythe!"

Bleddyn tore into the debris around her, ignoring the gashes that ripped the skin from his hands. Muscles bulging, he heaved a massive chunk of stone and plaster over his shoulder. Another gas line exploded and he threw himself over Meredythe to protect her.

After the rubble settled, he shrugged a piece of burning wood from his shoulder and pushed the last of the debris from Meredythe. Her left leg was twisted at an odd angle. Three jagged ribs poked out of her right side.

Tears welled from Bleddyn's eyes and tumbled down his cheeks. "No, Meredythe, please. Don't die."

Blood trickled from the side of her mouth as her eyes fluttered open.

She moaned when he lifted her into his arms.

Another explosion.

Bleddyn jerked his head up and looked around. The fires were merging. Soon there would be no escape.

"She's dying, Bleddyn."

Meredythe moaned louder when Bleddyn spun around to face the dust-covered woman.

"Evelyn, you can save her, can't you?"

The woman's stern expression softened, but she shook her head. "No, I can't. She's hurt too badly."

His entire body drooped. "So it's the fire again."

"We must, if she's to survive."

Fire leaped onto the rubble behind Evelyn. Head bowed, Bleddyn gently laid Meredythe into the older woman's arms.

Evelyn staggered a bit under the younger woman's weight. With Bleddyn's help, she settled Meredythe and straightened. Turning, she stepped toward the fire. Bleddyn's hand on her arm stopped her.

"How long, Evelyn? How long must I wait this time?"

Evelyn's smile was gentle. "You know I cannot answer that, Bleddyn. We do not know when she'll be ready to be born again."

His entire body sagged. "I'm so tired, Evie. So very tired of fighting this demon."

A flicker of alarm appeared on her face. Before she could say anything, Meredythe coughed. Bright blood bubbled from between her lips.

"Bleddyn, I must take her into the fire before she dies. Be strong. She will come again."

Evelyn turned and faced the conflagration roaring toward her.

"*Tanau*! *Difannu*!"

Fire surrounded her and she disappeared into the inferno.

Something within the fire exploded, sending burning missiles into the air. Bleddyn ducked then leaped to one side. Ruthlessly crushing his despondency, he sprinted into a smoky alley, trying to outrun the horror he'd left behind him. He ignored the tears streaming down his cheeks. The smoke was irritating his eyes. The smoke was what that caused the tears, not the thought of the long, lonely years that stretched out ahead of him.

* * * * *

Fists clenched, Bleddyn paced his study, back and forth, back and forth.

"Where is she?"

Keri raised her head. *If you hadn't refused her earlier, she'd be in your bed right now.*

"Damn it, Mother…"

The shrill jangling of the phone assaulted his senses. He jerked it to his ear.

"Meredythe?"

"Bleddyn? This is Hank Gordon. One of my deputies found your truck out on Bear Hollow Road with the engine running. Any idea how it got there?"

Bleddyn stared at the phone in his hand. Bear Hollow Road? That was…

Keri leaped to her feet as Bleddyn's howl of anguish exploded from his throat. The phone receiver snapped in two. Morton Anderson's farm was out Bear Hollow Road.

Black mists swirled as Bleddyn ripped off his clothing and wrenched open the front door. A huge black wolf leaped down the steps and hurtled toward the woods.

* * * * *

The scents of rain, fresh pine and wood smoke tickled Meredythe's nose. Smooth but hard wood braced her back and cradled her buttocks. She kept her eyes closed. Better to let whoever dragged her from the truck think she was still senseless. She shifted and tensed her wrists slightly. They were bound to the arms of the chair. Damn! How was she going to get out of this one?

She let her chin drop to her chest, opened her eyes slowly and peered down at her lap. Her clothing was gone and she was wearing what looked like a long white slip. She curled her toes. Her feet were bare and cold.

Glancing out from beneath her lashes, she searched her surroundings for clues as to her whereabouts. Her vision blurred and a sense of déjà vu enveloped her. She blinked, trying to see through the mist that formed before her eyes.

Before her, head bowed and shoulders drooping, the old druid sagged against his staff. Still, his shoulders were tense and the knuckles of the hand were white. When he lifted his head and looked to the sky, Meredythe also glanced up.

A log in the fire burst. Meredythe started and blinked. The clouds that had been dipping and swirling in a black sky disappeared. Instead, a decrepit roof arched overhead. Bits of moonlight streamed through haphazard cracks and gaps.

Dropping her gaze, she glanced around. The walls were almost as dilapidated as the roof. A barn?

"So you're finally awake," said the brown-robed figure before her.

Meredythe focused her gaze on the man who had spoken—Morton Anderson, the man who thought Bleddyn was a werewolf. Even if she hadn't remembered his face, there was no way she would ever forget his stench.

Clenching her fists, she jerked against her bonds, opened her mouth to answer and gagged. Her mouth tasted like an open sewer.

"Helen," Anderson commanded, "water."

A brown-robed woman held a cup to Meredythe's mouth. She gulped a mouthful of water, swirled it around in her mouth then spit it at Anderson's feet.

He grinned. "You have spirit. Good. You will make a fine mate."

Meredythe glared at him. *Like hell*. "What are you talking about?"

He thrust his chin forward. "I have waited long enough for Bleddyn Glyndwr to accept his destiny. If he will not, I will assume his place."

Meredythe shifted and the wobbly chair creaked. This guy was a certifiable nutcase.

"What place?"

He straightened his lanky form, crossed his arms over his chest and said, "King of the werewolves."

Only the madness in his eyes kept Meredythe's laughter from erupting. King of the werewolves? Anderson needed to be locked up.

She shifted and the chair creaked again. The spindly arm wobbled. "And where do I fit into all of this?" she asked, carefully tensing and relaxing her wrist. The rope loosened.

"You will be my queen."

His queen? She shuddered mentally. Not even if hell froze over. The other arm of the chair loosened.

"Sorry, I'm not interested. I'm sure one of your followers," she nodded toward the group in brown robes milling about the sputtering fire in the middle of the floor, "would be far more worthy than I."

For the first time, anger appeared on Morton's face. "No! Bleddyn Glyndwr chose you. I will have what is his."

Meredythe froze.

Anderson's face contorted with hatred as he continued. "Bleddyn Glyndwr could have everything—power, wealth, fame—but he chooses to waste his time teaching people about wolves. Fool! He refuses to accept his destiny. So I will take his place. I will become a werewolf and take his power and his mate."

Meredythe shook her head. "I'm not Dr. Glyndwr's mate. I'm a reporter. I'm here to research a story."

Anderson glared at her then began to pace. "You lie. You are mated. You smell of him."

Smell of him? How could Anderson tell how she smelled considering his own stench? Meredythe chose her words carefully. "How are you going to do that? I mean, doesn't another werewolf have to bite you?"

A crafty expression appeared on his face. "That's what they want you to think, but I have researched carefully. It has taken years, but I have finally discovered the secret." He gestured to his followers. "Bring it here."

Two men eased into a broken-down stall and returned carrying a cage. They carried it to Anderson and set it down. Inside crouched an emaciated wolf.

"What have you done to him?" Meredythe snapped. "He looks starved."

Anderson shrugged. "It was necessary to control him."

Meredythe checked her anger. Wait until she told Bleddyn what this asshole had done to a wolf. "What are you going to do with him?"

Eyes glowing with madness, Anderson said, "I will drink a cup of his blood then pour the rest into open cuts on my chest. When our blood mingles, I will become a werewolf."

Meredythe shook her head. Anderson *was* nuts. "But what about being bitten by a werewolf?"

Spittle flew from Anderson's lips. "Lies, all lies. That's what those with the power want us to believe so we would not learn the secret of transformation. But I have learned—I, Morton Anderson. Tonight I shall fulfill my destiny. And you shall be my bride." He spun and gestured again to his followers. "Begin the ceremony. Now."

Over my dead body, Meredythe thought as she wiggled the left arm of the chair.

Two men began to pound on drums and the rest of Anderson's followers began to jump awkwardly about the fire. Again Meredythe's vision blurred. Brown robes transformed to white. A feral bonfire leaped toward a cloudy sky and the odor of wet pine wafted to her nostrils.

The wolf whined.

Meredythe shook her head. The small group of brown-robed people hopped around a pitiful fire.

The wolf whined again.

She jerked her gaze to the wolf. He crouched in his cage, his eyes locked on hers. He stared intently, as if he were trying to tell her something.

Meredythe blinked and shook her head. Whatever they'd used to drug her obviously hadn't worn off yet.

After Anderson stepped away from her, she wiggled and tugged and twisted her left arm harder. Nobody knew where she was, so nobody was going to help her. Besides, she was a strong, independent woman. She'd get herself out of this.

The wooden dowel pulled loose. Her eyes never left Anderson's back as she eased the rope off her wrist. Thanking all the powers she could think of that she was left-handed, she picked open the knots on her right wrist.

Holding her arms parallel to the ground as if they still rested on the chair's arms, she looked around for the door. There it was, on the far side of the barn. She shifted her gaze back to Anderson.

He was still standing with his back to her. A wooden table covered with a tattered, old quilt separated him from his gyrating followers. He chanted something indecipherable and lifted a butcher knife above his head.

Her gaze leaped to the wolf's cage. He was watching her intently.

Inching her butt forward slowly, she slid to the floor. Once there, she froze. No one noticed. Taking a deep breath, she rose to her hands and knees and crawled toward the cage, hoping the wolf wouldn't growl and alert Anderson.

Its gaze intent, the wolf remained silent.

"No one is ever going to believe this," Meredythe muttered as she reached the cage. Once there, she stretched out on her stomach and allowed herself a nasty grin. The door was tied shut with a piece of rope.

Again, she glanced toward Anderson. He was yelling gibberish now, raising the knife and then stabbing it over and over into a bowl of water. His followers continued to skip and hop around the slowly dying fire.

Bracing herself on her elbows, Meredythe picked at the knot securing the cage. She bit her lip when a fingernail ripped as the knot finally loosened. The rope fell free.

"Bitch! What are you doing?" Face red, eyes bulging, Anderson leaped toward her, knife gripped in his fist.

Meredythe rolled left, bunching her legs beneath her. Once her feet were under her, she straightened. One hard kick to the cage knocked the door open. The wolf staggered out. Weak as he was, he turned to face the charging Anderson.

Unintimidated, the enraged man hurtled forward. "Hell's bitch. I will drink your blood with the wolf's!"

The wolf leaped. His heart was willing, but the cruel treatment he'd received had weakened his legs. His leap fell short. Ignoring the teeth snapping at his wrist, Anderson plunged the knife into the wolf's abdomen.

"No!" screamed Meredythe. She hesitated.

A gurgling howl erupted from the wolf's throat.

She turned and sprinted toward the door she'd noted earlier.

"Get her," shrieked Anderson.

His followers scrambled after her.

One more step, she screamed to herself, *one more step.*

As she grasped the door's handle, a hand tangled itself in her long hair. She was yanked back. Someone wrapped his arms around her. The door creaked open an inch.

Anderson's voice rolled over her. "Now, bitch, you'll pay."

Meredythe stomped her heel on her captor's bare instep.

Bawling of pain, he released her. She stumbled then regained her balance. Her escape was only a few steps away.

As she reached for the latch, the door exploded inward and a black whirlwind blasted through the doorway. A rafter-shaking howl ricocheted off the walls. Meredythe froze and stared into the steel gaze of the huge, black wolf facing her.

Fangs flashed in his red mouth as he leaped. She screamed, but he landed past her at the feet of her pursuer. Shrieking, the man turned and tried to flee.

Instead, he tripped over the robe he wore and fell onto a stack of rotting boards. They teetered then crashed in all directions, slamming into boards that propped up part of the sagging back wall. The supports fell. A small section of the barn wall collapsed, pieces of old wood landing in the fire. With fresh, dry kindling, it roared to life, following the trail of old wood. The back wall burst into flame.

Anderson's followers screamed and scattered. One shoved Meredythe out of the way as he sprinted for the doorway. Smoke rose. Some escaped through the holes in the roof. Some floated about the rafters. The rest rolled back toward the floor. Coughing, Meredythe stepped toward the door. She stopped.

The injured wolf. She couldn't leave it. She had to try to save it. Spinning around, she searched for it through thickening gray smoke that dipped, parted and then swelled throughout the interior of the old barn.

She took a step away from the door. Where was that wolf?

Black mist swirled and Bleddyn stepped out of the billowing smoke—naked. A snarl twisted his face.

"Meredythe, get the hell out of here now!"

A black shadow appeared out of the smoke. Anderson lifted the knife above his head.

"Bleddyn, look out!"

"Now you will die, unworthy dog."

Spinning, Bleddyn grabbed Anderson's wrist and twisted it cruelly. The knife fell to the ground. The older man wrenched free and scrambled for the knife. Again black mist swirled. Snarling, the black wolf leaped.

Meredythe turned and fled through the door.

Twenty yards from the door she stopped. Which way was Winterbourne? She had to get away, away from *him*. Through a small line of evergreens, moonlight glinted off metal. Sprinting around the trees, Meredythe found a rust-spotted truck parked inside a ramshackle shed.

"The keys *will* be in it. The keys will be in it," she chanted. "It *will* start. It *will* start. Please let it start." Wrenching the door open, she crawled onto the cracked seat. A keychain dangled from the ignition.

Stomping one foot on the clutch and the other on the gas pedal, she turned the key. The engine coughed.

"Come on, baby."

She turned the key again and pumped the gas. The engine choked, then coughed, then sputtered to life. Shoving the gearshift into drive, Meredythe roared out of the shed, grinding gears as she went.

Fifteen minutes later, she careened up Bleddyn's driveway. Skidding to a stop in front of the house, she shoved the door open and leaped from the truck.

Bleddyn was here, in his house. He had to be. The smoke from the fire had gotten into her eyes and the tears had made her vision blurry. No way had she seen what she thought she'd seen. Bleddyn was not a werewolf. Werewolves did not exist.

Leaping up the steps, she pushed open the door. Keri met her, lips pulled back in an ugly snarl.

Meredythe skidded to a halt and yelled, "Bleddyn! Bleddyn, where are you?"

No answer.

"Bleddyn!"

Silence.

Her gaze returned to the wolf. "Keri, it's me, Meredythe. You know me." She held out her hand.

Saliva dripped from the wolf's mouth as her snarl deepened.

Meredythe backed away slowly. When her foot reached down for the first step, Keri gnashed her teeth and stepped toward her. Meredythe froze. She couldn't go forward, and she couldn't go back. Cold seeped into her feet and up her legs. Shivering, she tucked her hands into her armpits. Keri sank to her haunches. Ignoring the tears trickling down her cheeks, Meredythe stared at the wolf. All she could do was wait.

* * * * *

Bleddyn licked his jowls as he stepped away from Anderson's body. He sneezed. The smoke was getting thicker.

Brother?

Mist swirled as Bleddyn transformed to his human form. "Where are you?"

Here.

Kneeling by the wolf's side, Bleddyn gathered him into his arms.

The wolf yelped with pain. *No. My spirit will soon run free with the winds.*

Bleddyn laid his hand on the wolf's shoulder. "As you wish, Brother."

You must put me next to the man. They will believe I killed him.

Ignoring the fire that roared above him, Bleddyn bowed his head. Tears dropped onto the wolf's fur.

"Thank you."

Go to your mate. She has need of you.

Meredythe. Bleddyn's anger simmered. None of this would have happened if she hadn't run away.

The wolf's nose touched Bleddyn's hand. *Her presence gave me death with honor, Brother. She is worthy of you. Go now. Live free.*

Bleddyn stroked the wolf's fur once. "Go now, Brother. Die free." Lifting the wolf, he laid it gently next to Anderson's body.

The mist swirled once more and the black wolf leaped through burning timbers and out the door. As Winterbourne's fire truck roared toward the burning barn, Bleddyn disappeared into the woods.

* * * * *

Ears pricked forward, Keri whined and looked past Meredythe's shoulder.

Spinning around, Meredythe stared into the night. A wave of dizziness washed over her and her vision blurred. The full moon bathed the lawn, driveway and encircling forest with a pure, luminescent glow. A sudden movement drew her eyes to the edge of the lawn. A single triumphant howl echoed around the clearing as a large, black wolf leaped from between the trees and loped up the driveway. Gray and black mist swirled and another form materialized. Her shivering no longer caused by the cold, Meredythe trembled uncontrollably as a naked Bleddyn stalked toward her.

Slowly, deliberately, he trod toward the porch, the moon clearly illuminating his features. Thick, black tangles cascaded about his broad shoulders and down his back. Muscular arms relaxed at his sides as his long stride carried him toward her. Dark splotches of blood marred his shoulder, chest and chin.

When he reached the steps, she stepped back, then stepped back again and again until she was pressed against the wall. Her heart palpitating with fear, she still raised her chin defiantly as his gaze raked her shivering body.

Climbing the steps to the porch, he loomed over her.

She refused to lower her eyes. Trembling, she said, "That's blood."

His hand swept across his chest. His grin was feral. "Yes."

Only the brick wall behind her kept her shuddering body from collapsing. "You're not human."

"I'm as human as you are, with just a little extra added."

"What?" She tried to blink her tears away. "What do you want?"

"You."

Grabbing her around the waist, he threw her over his shoulder. Screaming, legs flailing wildly, she tried to wiggle out of his grasp. She pounded his naked back with her fists. She even grabbed a handful of hair and yanked it. He never broke stride. His left arm tightened around her thighs and the other smacked her right buttock. Once inside the front door, he kicked it shut and carried her up the stairs, Keri trotting silently behind them.

"Put me down!"

Her foot slammed into his stomach and she cursed at the pain that shot through her foot.

Then she yanked his hair so hard his head snapped back.

He snarled and slapped her behind again.

She shrieked as she pounded his back with her fists. "You son of a bitch! Put me down."

Keri growled.

Tail fluffed and claws extended, Methuselah careened out of Meredythe's bedroom and launched himself at Bleddyn.

Keri darted between them and Methuselah bounced off her with a yowl of anger.

No, Methuselah. The time has come.

Methuselah hissed and spat. *Not for rape.*

Ignoring both animals, Bleddyn kicked open the door to his bedroom, stalked in and kicked it shut behind him.

Stretching out in front of Bleddyn's door, Keri growled low in her throat. *He won't hurt her.*

Still hissing, Methuselah settled onto his haunches and flexed his paw. Long, sharp claws appeared. *If he does, I'll castrate him.*

"Damn it, you asshole, put me down!" Meredythe's open hand connected with Bleddyn's bare buttock. The crack echoed around the room.

Bleddyn heaved her off his shoulder. She landed flat on her back on his bed. He fell on her, pinning her beneath his body.

Fists swinging, she tried to wiggle out from underneath him. "Get off me, you…you…animal!"

Bleddyn tensed. Then he settled his hips on hers and stilled her flailing legs between his thighs. Capturing her pounding fists, he stretched them above her head and clamped his left hand around both her wrists.

His voice was harsh. "That didn't seem to bother you earlier."

"You weren't acting like an animal then," she hissed through clenched teeth. "Now let me go!" She heaved her hips, hoping to dislodge him.

He answered her hip thrust with one of his own. Her eyes widened when she realized the slip she wore was bunched at her hips. His cock bumped the inside of her bare thigh. He bared his teeth and ground his hips against hers again.

Meredythe stopped struggling. Bleddyn was staring down at her, his pupils dilated. Dark shadows danced across his face. Flecks of dried blood dotted his chin. Using his free hand, he grabbed the neck of her slip and ripped it from neckline to hem. He pawed her breast with his free hand. Burying his face in the side of her neck, he nipped her. His voice was low and hoarse.

"Mine. My mate. Now!"

Trembling, Meredythe tried to blink the tears from her eyes as his knees forced her thighs farther apart.

"Bleddyn, please."

He ignored both her struggles and her pleas. Another nudge from his knees spread her legs wider. The hard tip of his erection poked the inside of her thigh. Settling his hips on hers, he centered himself. Another nip, this time on her shoulder.

Heart fluttering, Meredythe gritted her teeth and turned her face away from his. She flexed her fingers, trying to free her hands, but his viselike grip remained locked around her wrists.

"Stop it, Bleddyn," she gasped, "now."

He growled at her.

Growled? What was she, an animal? Anger conquered the fear paralyzing her. She would not be raped! Her hands and feet were useless as weapons. There was only one thing left she could do. Opening her mouth wide, she bit Bleddyn on the fleshy part of his shoulder as hard as she could, hard enough to draw blood. Its coppery taste slid onto her tongue and she swallowed involuntarily. Her own blood seemed to boil.

Pain ripped through Bleddyn's shoulder and he jerked his face from Meredythe's neck. The dark entity that warred for control of his soul retreated. It had never been able to tolerate pain. He looked down into Meredythe's face, her anger, fear and revulsion registering in his mind. Cursing, he released her hands and rolled off her. What was he doing?

He lifted his head but made no attempt to stop her when she bolted from the bed and threw open the door. A snarling Keri met her. Slamming the door shut, she turned and braced herself against it. The fear and disgust on her face pierced Bleddyn's heart. What had he done?

Flopping back on the bed, he stared through the glass ceiling into the night sky. Light from the moon embraced him, calmed his turbulent thoughts, soothed his spirit. With a sigh, he pushed himself up, grimacing at the sudden pain in his shoulder.

He glanced down at it and froze. Blood seeped sluggishly from a matched set of teeth marks. He looked back to Meredythe.

"You bit me!"

Teeth bared, Meredythe snarled at him.

Bleddyn touched the wound then stared at the blood on his fingers. "You…bit *me*," he repeated. He looked back at Meredythe. Then he collapsed on the bed, laughing.

Grimacing at the coppery taste in her mouth, Meredythe licked the blood from her lips and glared at Bleddyn. Laughing. He was laughing. First he tried to rape her and now he was laughing. He had to be as crazy as Anderson.

A weapon. She had to find a weapon, fast. Her eyes locked on the fireplace. The poker. That would do.

She'd taken only two steps from the door when Bleddyn sat up. He'd managed to control his laughter, but he still had a stupid grin on his face.

"Meredythe."

She froze in midstep.

"I love you."

Chapter Fourteen

Meredythe gaped, her thoughts roiling. Here she was, stark naked, trapped in a room with a—she swallowed—a werewolf that had just tried to rape her. She'd bitten him until she drew blood and was seriously considering braining him with a poker, and he said he loved her! If he wasn't crazy, she was.

Meredythe shuddered. No, not crazy—dreaming. She was dreaming. She'd crashed during that snowstorm when she was driving to Winterbourne. She'd been in an accident. Right now she was lying in some hospital bed in a coma, dreaming all this. That was it. She was in a coma.

Bleddyn's grin became a warm smile. "You're not in a coma and you aren't dreaming."

She glanced at the fireplace and back to Bleddyn.

Could she get to the poker before he did? "You can read minds too?"

He shook his head. "You were talking out loud."

She glanced back at the poker.

He followed her gaze. "I can get there faster than you."

Before she could blink, he was standing in front of the fireplace. "I won't hurt you, Meredythe." He held the poker out to her. "You can have this if it will make you feel safer."

"Toss it over here."

The poker clanged to the floor at her feet.

Slowly, her eyes never leaving his face, she stooped and picked it up. He didn't move.

Gripping the poker with both hands, she rose and pointed it at Bleddyn. "Tell Keri to move away from the door."

Was that despair that briefly flashed across his face?

He shook his head. "She wouldn't listen to me."

The poker trembled as a lead weight settled in her stomach. She glanced around the room and then back past Bleddyn, scanning frantically for an escape route. He stood before the fireplace, arms folded across his chest, gloriously naked. Meredythe's breath caught in her throat.

Damn it, Meredythe! He just tried to rape you! her inner voice snapped. She shuddered at the memory.

"You really are a werewolf, aren't you?"

"Yes."

Her knees wobbled then unlocked and she was sitting on the floor. The poker gouged a dent in the hardwood floor. In the blink of an eye, Bleddyn was kneeling before her. She stabbed at him with the poker. "Get away from me."

He flinched when she poked his chest, but he didn't budge. "Please. I won't hurt you."

She jabbed the poker against his chest and braced it there. "Not hurt me! You just tried to rape me."

He wiped his face with his hand then finger combed his hair back off his forehead. "I-I wasn't myself."

"And just how am I supposed to tell the difference?"

After a deep sigh, he stared into her eyes. "While you've been here, have I ever hurt you? Did you ever think I wanted to hurt you? Did you ever fear for your safety?"

She licked her dry lips, wiping away the flecks of blood. Grimacing at the coppery taste, she dropped her gaze and shook her head. "No."

She kept the poker firm against his chest.

He leaned against its dull point. "Meredythe, please believe me. I could no sooner hurt you than I could hurt myself. I love you."

Her head snapped up. "Bullshit. You didn't even know me a month ago."

He smiled. "I've known you for over a thousand years."

Again she shook her head. He was lying. "Either you're certifiably crazy or you're the lousiest poet on the face of the earth."

"No, I'm just a werewolf."

Blood rushed through her veins and she shivered. He *would* have to remind her.

He stared into her eyes. "Meredythe, I do love you. I would never hurt you. You're safe with me."

She shivered again then lowered the poker. Her arm was getting tired anyway. Chewing her bottom lip, she glared at Bleddyn. There he was, a self-confessed werewolf kneeling naked on the floor in front of her, arms at his sides. And he said that he loved her. How could he do this to her!

Her chin itched. She wiped it with the back of her hand and gazed at the dried blood. Bleddyn's blood. She had really bitten him. Blood still welled sluggishly from her teeth marks on his shoulder. Her gaze wandered from his shoulder to his chest, then down his body. His stiff cock stood straight out. He wasn't circumcised. Damn, he was hot.

He was hot? Meredythe jerked her eyes back up to Bleddyn's face. His expression was amused.

"See anything you like?"

A full body flush warmed her. Anything she liked! He was a murderer, for God's sake. He killed people. How could she be attracted to him?

Her eyes widened at the thought. She did find him attractive. This morning she'd done her best to drag him into the nearest bed. She'd trusted him, believed everything he'd told her. And he'd lied to her.

"Damn you, Bleddyn Glyndwr!" She swung the poker. Eyes widening with shock, he recoiled slightly when she hit the fleshy part of his upper right arm, but he remained kneeling before her.

Shocked, Meredythe gaped at the poker in her hand then at Bleddyn. "How could you let me do that!"

He shrugged. "If that's what it takes for you to trust me, hit me again."

"Hit you again? Hit you again? What do you think I am?"

"Frightened—no, terrified. Of me."

Tears welled and she blinked. She *was* afraid. A wave of dizziness enveloped her. Shuddering, she dropped the poker and pulled her knees to her chest. Maybe *she* was the crazy person. Here she was, naked, sitting on a cold floor with the serial killer she'd been searching for not three feet away. And he was a werewolf.

Meredythe stared at the brown specks on Bleddyn's chest. "You killed Morton Anderson tonight, didn't you?"

He nodded. "He would have killed me—and you."

Meredythe sighed. Well, that was true, at least.

"You're the killer I'm trying to find, aren't you?"

"Yes."

The small bubble of hope tucked away in her heart burst. Bleddyn was a murderer. This man who was so gentle with his wolves and cared enough to try to save a dog anyone else would put down was a murderer. Even to her own ears, her voice sounded strained and foreign. "How? How could you just murder innocent people?"

His voice was dry. "They were far from innocent."

She shook her head. "That's not the point and you know it."

Bleddyn pushed himself to his feet and began to pace. "Damn it, Meredythe, it's not that simple."

She watched him pace, struggling to analyze him with the instincts she trusted the most, her reporter's instincts. *He paces like a wild animal locked in a cage.* She rubbed her itchy chin with the back of her hand then chewed the nail she'd broken freeing the wolf. Again she tasted his blood. "Enlighten me."

He raked his fingers through his hair again. "Would you believe me if I told you I was either defending myself or someone else each time?"

Her reporter's instincts blared a warning. She shook her head.

Again he sank to his knees before her. "Please, hear me out."

Why was she listening to him? Why didn't she get out of here? *Because there's a wolf with very sharp teeth outside the door.* She squirmed, trying to find a more comfortable position for her bare behind on the cold floor. What choice did she have? "I'm listening."

He rubbed his chin. "Most of the time, I'm no different from anyone else, except for being a little stronger, a little faster than the average person. However, there are times when the urge to hunt, to kill becomes almost impossible to deny."

She nodded then shook her head. What was that roaring in her ears? She shook her head again. Heat pulsed through her veins and anger surged. How could he sound so matter-of-fact? So nonchalant? He killed people! "Yeah. The full moon rolls around and you have to go eat somebody."

His nostrils flared and he bared his teeth. A shiver raced up Meredythe's spine and she wondered if she'd gone too far. Her hand dropped to the poker at her side. What made her say that? A good reporter never antagonized an informant.

Barely three feet from her, Bleddyn stiffened, clenching then unclenching his fists. After a long, shuddering breath, he continued, "I have never eaten anyone, nor do I ever plan to. Once a month, however, the urge to hunt, to enjoy the thrill of the hunt, becomes almost overpowering. It's almost impossible to control."

Her voice trembled. "But you can control it?"

He nodded slowly. "I have learned to, most of the time."

She dropped the poker and he relaxed.

"Then what happened in New York?" she asked.

"A friend developed a new medicine that was supposed to subdue the urges. Instead it shot my control to hell."

Meredythe tried to focus to what he was saying, but her concentration kept slipping. Something was interfering with her thoughts. She struggled to maintain a reporter's detached objectivity, but her emotions were rocking on a crazy roller coaster ride.

She struggled to ask a logical question, but her roiling emotions got the better of her. "So you went out to find someone to kill."

Anger blazed in his eyes. "Damn it, Meredythe! I am not a cold-blooded killer."

His anger inflamed Meredythe's already muddled emotions. Throwing her hair back over her shoulder, she rose to her knees, leaned toward him and jabbed her finger into his chest. "If you aren't a cold-blooded killer, then what are you?"

But Meredythe didn't hear what he said. The coppery taste of the blood she had swallowed remained on her tongue. Fiery warmth spread outward from her stomach until her entire body was tingling. She shook her head. What was happening to her?

Blinking, she stared at Bleddyn. Beneath her finger, his chest was firm. His skin was hot. Logic deserted her as her emotions whirled and heat surged through her veins. She had to touch him. Her palm replaced her stabbing finger.

He froze as her fingers swirled through his chest hair.

"So soft," she murmured. Her hand caressed his chest. "And so hard." She lifted her other hand, cautiously stroking the shoulder she had bitten. "I'm sorry." Dried blood flaked away and fresh welled.

Bleddyn covered her hand with his and lifted it to his mouth. He kissed the blood off her fingers. "I've had worse."

Leaning forward, he melded his lips to hers. His kiss was tender, searching. Lifting his head, he gazed down at her.

Meredythe licked her lips. Once again, the coppery taste of Bleddyn's blood caressed her tongue. Its warmth rolled down her throat. Her heart seemed to beat faster.

Bleddyn remained perfectly still, uncertain how she would react to his kiss. A few minutes ago she was ready to skewer him with the poker. His eyes were drawn to the leaping pulse in her neck as she closed her eyes and threw her head back. He shuddered as his cock jerked. He wanted to crush her to him and bury himself deep within her.

The darkness in his soul raised its head.

But the moon was at her apex, bathing them with her soothing luminescence. Closing his eyes, Bleddyn lifted his face and absorbed the moon's tender warmth, focusing on the strength she gave him. He placed Meredythe's palm against his heart and opened his eyes.

"Trust me."

She stared at him, eyes swimming with a combination of fear, curiosity, hope and was that…desire?

"Who are you?" she whispered. "What are you? Why should I trust you?"

"I'm the man who loves you."

She remained very still and Bleddyn could almost read her mind as he stared into her eyes. Did he really love her? Could she trust him? Would he hurt her?

"Damn it, Bleddyn Glyndwr," she growled, "you better not bite me."

Launching herself against his chest, she laced her fingers through the hair dangling about his shoulders, pulled his face to hers and kissed him, long, hot and hard.

Bleddyn answered her kiss, opening his mouth to her questing tongue, mating his to hers in a passionate dance. She moaned when his mouth left hers to trail nibbles down her neck. Lifting her in his arms, he stood and turned toward the bed. After another quick kiss, he said, "I promise not to bite—unless you want me to."

He dropped her on the bed and followed her down, nuzzling her ear as he cupped a firm breast. She stiffened.

He lifted his head.

"What?"

"There's something underneath me."

He rolled away, carrying her with him. Three groggy mice wiggled and squirmed amongst the folds of the bedspread.

Laughter burst from Meredythe's throat.

Bleddyn growled. "Methuselah. I'm going to strangle that damn cat."

As if sensing imminent danger, the mice staggered to their feet, scurried in three different directions across the bed, fell to the floor and disappeared.

Still giggling, Meredythe cupped Bleddyn's face with her hands. "Later," she said and kissed him.

He didn't need a second invitation.

Heat and passion thrummed through Meredythe's body, converging in her aching nipples and throbbing groin. She wanted him, wanted him more than she ever wanted anything in her life.

When he lifted his body from hers, she moaned a complaint.

"Patience, love."

He reclined on his side, bracing himself on his left arm. "You're so beautiful everywhere," he murmured. "But your breasts are especially lovely."

Leaning down, he kissed first one nipple then another. Rolling onto his stomach, he nipped her left nipple then sucked it gently into his mouth. Then he transferred his attention to her right nipple.

She arched into his mouth. "Oh God, yes."

Chuckling, he nipped her nipple as he slid his fingers between her legs. She was wet—very wet. Slipping his fingers between her glistening folds, he flicked the nub that swelled against his thumb. Her hips jerked and she dug her nails into his shoulders.

Raising his head, Bleddyn gazed into her face. "You like that, do you?"

She thrust her hips against his hand again. "More!"

He captured her mouth with a deep kiss as his fingers dipped and rolled and stroked. Her fingers danced up and down his spine as she stroked his back.

"Please."

"Not yet, love. Not yet."

His mouth left hers. Trailing kisses down her neck and shoulder, he paused and licked both rosy nipples. Then his lips and tongue continued wandering over her rib cage and abdomen, stopping momentarily to tease her navel.

He slipped a finger inside her.

She bucked against his hand. "Bleddyn!"

He chuckled. "Patience, love. I've waited hundreds of years. You can wait a few minutes." He inhaled deeply. "You smell of woman and passion. I must taste you."

Hundreds of years flashed through Meredythe's mind only to be erased by his *must taste you*. The sensations rippling through her body stymied all logical thought.

"Taste, oh God yes, Bleddyn. Taste me, please."

After another deep kiss, Bleddyn slid down her body and buried his face between her thighs. First he trailed soft kisses along the sensitive skin of her inner thigh, following them with delicate nibbles. Hot breath bathed her cunt as he blew gently. Then he lapped her moistness as if he were a wolf lapping water.

Arching against his mouth, Meredythe fisted her hands in the bedspread as he licked and suckled. He stabbed his tongue into her cunt, swirled it around, then sucked deeply.

"You taste better than honey. You're hot and sweet and ready for me."

Pressure built and pinpoints of pleasure stabbed her nipples as she writhed and bucked against his mouth. He pushed her thighs farther apart. His tongue swirled around her swollen clit and then his mouth closed around it, pushing her over the edge. Her body tensed and exploded into a million pieces.

When she finally returned to earth and opened her eyes, Bleddyn was lying next to her, smiling down at her.

Meredythe stretched and smiled in return. "I always thought that line about fireworks going off was an exaggeration."

His smile became smug.

She arched an eyebrow. "Conceited, are we?"

His smile was his answer.

"Jackass."

Before he could respond, Meredythe shimmied down the bed and captured his cock with her mouth.

Bleddyn jerked. As if a fist had been slammed into his stomach, all the air was knocked from his lungs.

Her busy mouth stopped exploring long enough for her to say, "That's for not telling me you were a werewolf."

She lapped his length. She sucked first one testicle then the other into her mouth. Then she nipped the base of his penis, hard.

His hips jerked off the bed. "Christ!"

"And that," she mumbled, licking the clear drops of liquid that seeped from the head of his penis, "was for even thinking about forcing me."

Meredythe pushed herself up onto her knees and began massaging his testicles with one hand while she circled the base of his erection with her thumb and forefinger. While her hand pumped up and down, she sucked the engorged purple head into her mouth, swirling her tongue from tip to base.

Digging his hands into the bedspread, Bleddyn concentrated on the moon as Meredythe's busy mouth pushed him closer and closer to a complete loss of control. That nip at the base of his cock had almost pushed him over the edge. Even the devil in his soul was powerless against the waves of pressure and pleasure building in his loins. Groaning through clenched teeth, he thrust himself deeper into her mouth.

When she practically swallowed him whole, he wrenched himself up, grabbed her under the arms and pulled her against his chest.

"You've proven your point," he growled, "but now I need to be inside you."

"Oh, yes," she moaned. "Deep. I want you deep."

He rolled her over and forced her hands and knees down onto the mattress. "Please, this first time, let me mount you." His fingers slipped between her thighs to tease and stroke.

Meredythe arched against his hand. "I don't give a damn! I need your cock inside me now!"

Growling with satisfaction, Bleddyn nuzzled her behind, kissing the rosy cheeks. Cupping her between the legs, he massaged her slick folds, pressing a finger into her as deeply as possible. He grew harder as he inhaled the rich musk of her arousal. Slipping a hand under her hips, he lifted her to his mouth to taste her passion again.

Meredythe shuddered and arched her back. After a final lap with his dexterous tongue, he rose and pushed a thigh between hers, the crinkly hairs teasing her tender skin. When he pressed his erection between her legs and rubbed back and forth against her slippery cunt, a momentary prick of logic stabbed her brain.

"Condom," she gasped.

His thumbs slipped between her legs and prodded them farther apart.

"Bleddyn!" she gasped again through the ripples of pleasure. She tried to pull out of his grasp. "Bleddyn!"

His hands tightened on her thighs. "What?" he snarled.

She shuddered when his thumbs pinched together on her most sensitive spot, but she still managed to gasp, "Condom!"

He froze then rolled away from her. A drawer was wrenched open and crashed to the floor. He was panting audibly as the bed dipped under his weight, and, for a moment, fear seeped into her brain. He was a werewolf! What if he changed…

Two warm hands grasped her hips. Strong thighs slid between hers and pushed them farther apart. A blunt hardness caressed her wetness once, twice. Meredythe shuddered as he repositioned her hips.

Bleddyn ached. The moon was at its zenith, her light flooding through the glass roof, filling him with warmth and power. Now he would finally have his mate. Now Meredythe would save him from the beast in his soul. With one hard thrust, he buried himself as deeply as he could.

She was so tight! With a moan that was half howl, he began to move, slowly at first, then faster. His gentle thrusts became harder as he sought to bury himself as deeply as he possibly could. With each thrust, her internal muscles tightened around him, gripping tightly.

She was so wet! Her moisture drenched both his thighs and hers. And her scent! Its rich, musky aroma alone was almost enough to make him lose control. Throwing back his head, Bleddyn opened his eyes wide and stared at the full moon. His thrusts became deeper, faster, more powerful. Encouraged by her moans, he finished each thrust by grinding his hips in a circular motion, first one way then the other.

Meredythe shoved her face into pillow wrapped in her arms and screamed with Bleddyn's first thrust. He was so hard, so thick, so good! When he pulled out and thrust again, she pushed back to meet him. Her passion flared higher and heat roared through her veins as his hands stroked and kneaded her back and buttocks. Groaning, she rubbed her aching nipples against the silk bedspread. She panted into the pillow as his hands stroked and kneaded her back and behind. When his thumb trailed her slick moisture into the cleft between her buttocks and pressed against her anus, she pushed back hard and reared up with a shriek of ecstasy. Still thrusting, Bleddyn arched over her back, cupped both breasts and squeezed her aching nipples.

Moaning with pleasure, Meredythe collapsed onto the pillow once more. Bleddyn clasped her hips once again to steady her. Then he bent over her back and trailed his tongue along her backbone. He kissed the back of her neck then lightly nipped her shoulder.

Burying his face in her neck, he groaned, "Now, love, now."

He slipped his hand around her waist, back between her thighs and rubbed her swollen nub.

"Oh God, yes!"

Throwing back her head, Meredythe ground her hips against Bleddyn as her internal muscles clasped his erection like a vise. He exploded with her and collapsed on her back. Meredythe sank onto the soft bedspread, Bleddyn still buried within her.

Slowly, Bleddyn's labored breathing eased. He slipped himself out of Meredythe and rolled off her back, pulling her with him after disposing of the condom and tucking her against his side. She snuggled closer.

Sighing with contentment, he gazed up at the moon. What he had just shared with Meredythe was like nothing he'd ever experienced before. She'd been wild and passionate in his arms. The goddess had truly blessed him.

She sighed against his chest. Gently, he pushed the hair away from her face. "I'm sorry."

She tilted her head and looked up. Her expression was puzzled. "Why?"

He caressed her cheek and lips with his thumb. "I was too…rough. Considering it was your first time, I should have been more careful. I'm sorry."

She pushed herself up. "First time? What are you talking about?"

"You were a virgin."

Obviously shocked, she stared then stated, "You have got to be kidding. It's the twenty-first century. I haven't been a virgin since college."

Bleddyn's stomach roiled as he stared at her. Not a virgin. That couldn't be true. She'd been so tight when he entered her. Pulling her into his arms, he rolled off the bed. The bedspread was rumpled but unstained. No blood.

He looked down at her. She snuggled against his chest and swirled her fingers into his chest hair.

His voice was a whisper. "What have you done?"

Meredythe stopped teasing his nipple and looked up. "What do you mean? I haven't done anything." She smiled. "Well, I did do a few things, but it seemed like you enjoyed them."

He dropped his arm from under her legs and set her on her feet. Grasping her upper arms, he stared into her face.

"Christ, Meredythe, you were supposed to be a virgin."

She stiffened. "I beg your pardon?"

Anger appeared on Bleddyn's face. "You had to be a virgin for me."

She jerked herself free of his hold. "Well, I beg your pardon!" she spat again. "If only I had known that the high and mighty Dr. Bleddyn Glyndwr planned to have sex with me someday, I would have saved myself for you. You fucking jackass. I didn't even know you existed until a month ago. What was I supposed to do, ignore other men?"

"Yes," he snarled. "You belong to me."

A deep flush rose to her face. "Like hell, shithead. I don't *belong* to any man, not now, not ever."

Fists clenched, Bleddyn took one step toward her. She didn't back away.

Lifting her chin, she challenged him. "What are you going to do? Turn into a werewolf and bite me?"

He stiffened. Slowly, he unclenched his fists. "You little fool. You've condemned me to a life of torment." Spinning away from her, he headed for the door.

She fisted her hands on her hips. "Life of torment? What the hell is that supposed to mean?"

He didn't answer. He jerked the door open to be met by Keri's questioning whine.

"Get out of my way, Mother."

Black and gray mists swirled and Bleddyn disappeared.

Chapter Fifteen

Meredythe gawked at Keri. "Mother. You're his *mother*?"

Keri looked back at Methuselah. *Why is everyone so surprised when they discover Bleddyn has a mother?*

Knees buckling, Meredythe sank onto the bed. Bleddyn's mother was a wolf—a talking wolf.

Methuselah trotted past Keri toward Meredythe. *No one can believe you're his mother because he's so recalcitrant and you're so pleasant.*

Meredythe jerked her attention to Methuselah. He could talk too? "You can talk too, Methuselah? You can both talk?"

Methuselah paused in midstride and looked back at Keri. *She shouldn't be able to hear us, should she? That isn't supposed to be a side effect of the ceremony, is it?*

Keri sat on her haunches. If it was possible for a wolf to look puzzled, she did. *I don't know. I didn't think it was.*

Methuselah sat and wrapped his furry tail around his forepaws. *Are there any precedents? Or could it be something unique about Meredythe herself?*

Precedents, no. Meredythe…I don't know. You've known her longer than I have. Have you ever noticed anything unusual about her?

Shocked, Meredythe's gaze swung back and forth between the wolf and cat. They were talking—really talking—about her as if she weren't even there.

"Hey. Animals. I'm right here. Precedents for what? What ceremony? Would somebody please tell me what the hell is going on!"

Keri rose to her feet. *We may as well take her to Rhys. He'll want to know why Bleddyn left too.*

Her emotions already roiling from Bleddyn's lovemaking and subsequent accusations of infidelity brought Meredythe's anger to a crest. "Stop talking about me as if I weren't here!"

Methuselah turned his green gaze toward her. *Put some clothes on, Meredythe. Rhys will be able to answer your questions better than either of us.*

She stomped her foot. "Who the hell is Rhys?"

The wolf stretched. *Just put some clothing on, dear. Unless you'd rather walk around naked? I'm sure Rhys won't mind.*

Throwing up her hands, Meredythe spun away from the animals and looked for something to wear. "I *have* to be dreaming. No way can all this really be happening." She grimaced at the torn slip lying on the floor. No way would she wear that even if it were in one piece. Glancing to her left, she spied a pair of Bleddyn's sweatpants and a t-shirt lying on a chair.

Put something on your feet, dear. The floors are cold, Keri added.

Muttering to herself about needing psychiatric help, Meredythe searched first one drawer then a second. She grabbed a pair of thick soaks and shoved her feet into them. Settling her hands on her hips, she glared at the cat and the wolf. "Now what?"

Fluffy tail lifted high, Methuselah sauntered toward the door. *This way.*

Grumbling under her breath, Meredythe followed him, Keri trailing along behind.

Once in the hallway, Methuselah turned left and headed into the darkness. His claws clicking against the hardwood floor was the only sound Meredythe heard.

Stumbling, she cursed under her breath. Great. Now she was being led off to who knows where, in the dark.

Keri bumped against Meredythe's side. *Put your hand on my shoulder. We'll be coming to a stairway soon and I don't want you to fall.*

Meredythe grabbed a handful of fur. "Stairway. Just where are we going? A crypt?"

Laughter tickled her mind and she faltered in surprise. Wolves could laugh?

Careful, we've reached the stairs.

Taking a deep breath, Meredythe slid her foot forward until she bumped a stone step. The stairway went up, not down.

"At least you aren't dragging me into someone's grave."

Again Keri's laughter echoed in her mind.

Slowly, they progressed upward.

"Doesn't anybody here believe in lights?" Meredythe grumbled as she stubbed her toe against a step. "I could go faster if I could see where I was going."

Beside her, the wolf climbed effortlessly. *Rhys likes to keep his presence here a secret.*

Meredythe shivered. The cold was seeping through the thick socks she was wearing. "Does Bleddyn know there's a strange man living in his house?"

Bleddyn knows about everything that goes on in his house. Watch your step. We're at the landing.

Two more steps and Meredythe was again walking on a wooden floor. Faint light glimmered through cracks in the door on the other side of the landing. Methuselah sat before it, his tail lashing back and forth.

He said to go away. He's busy.

A low growl rumbled in the wolf's throat. *Busy? I think not!*

Placing herself squarely in front of the door, the wolf opened her mouth and howled.

Meredythe clapped her hands over her ears as the howl echoed around the stone walls that encircled the landing.

Father, either you open this door right now or I will blow it down!

The door was jerked open and the bearded man she had met in her boss's office stood staring at Meredythe.

"If you must come in, come in," he rumbled. Then he turned and disappeared back into the room.

Meredythe gaped at the wolf. "Father? He's your father! But you're Bleddyn's mother."

That's right, dear. Rhys is Bleddyn's grandfather. What's so hard to understand about that?

Since she still had a handful of fur, Meredythe was dragged into the room.

Rhys was standing next to a table, staring at her. "Why are you here? Shouldn't you be downstairs with Bleddyn?"

Meredythe's brain was reeling. Bleddyn was a werewolf. Keri, a wolf, was his mother. Okay, that made sense, sort of. But a human was Keri's father, Bleddyn's grandfather. She sank into a beat-up leather chair. "I need a drink. No, I need a couple of drinks."

Methuselah jumped up into her lap and began to purr.

Keri stretched out on the rug before the fire. *Get her some of your special stock, Father. She needs it.*

Mumbling under his breath, Rhys removed a dusty bottle from a shelf and splashed some of the amber liquid into a glass. Stepping across the room, he handed it to Meredythe.

She gulped it down in one swallow. It burned all the way down then knocked the breath out of her.

"What—what was that?" she gasped as tears rolled down her cheeks.

"Four-hundred-year-old Scotch," Rhys answered. "Do you want some more?"

She dropped the glass to the floor. "No! That was enough."

"Good, now tell me why you are here instead of with Bleddyn." His tone was imperious.

She gritted her teeth. Arrogant, insufferable man. "Not that it's any of your business, but Bleddyn left."

A stunned expression appeared on Rhys' face. "Not here? But the full moon, the ceremony. He's been waiting centuries."

When her fists hit the arms of the chair, dust billowed. "What ceremony? Would someone please tell what the hell is going on!"

"Didn't Bleddyn explain—" began Rhys.

"Damn it! After mind-blowing sex, all Bleddyn did was bitch because I wasn't a virgin then turn into a wolf and run away."

Man, wolf and cat stared at her.

Meredythe snapped her mouth shut. That might have been more information than she wanted to share with a total stranger. There she went, letting her temper run away with her again.

Rhys sank onto a wooden stool. "You weren't a virgin? But that means the entire ceremony was useless."

Meredythe leaped to her feet, ignoring Methuselah's indignant yowl as he tumbled to the floor. In a few steps, she was standing in front of Rhys, trembling with anger. Jabbing her finger into his chest, she snarled, "Today I have been drugged, tied up, threatened by a nut with a knife, been caught in a fire, almost raped, accused of infidelity and then dragged up here by two animals who can talk in my head. If you don't tell me what is going on, I'll bite you too."

Keri's head snapped up.

She bit him. That explains that then.

Rhys had been shrinking away from her finger but he jerked upright at her threat.

"Bite me *too*? Did you bite Bleddyn?"

She paused in her tirade. "He was trying to rape me. What was I supposed to do?"

"Did you swallow any of his blood?"

Meredythe's stomach dropped. "Yes, a little, I think."

Rhys stared at her.

She swallowed. "What does that mean? Will I…am I going to turn into a werewolf too?"

Rhys indicated the chair she had vacated. "Sit down, Meredythe, and let me explain. First, you will not become a werewolf. But swallowing Bleddyn's blood has obviously brought some small changes to your physiology."

She stared at him. "Bleddyn's blood. That's why I can understand Keri and Methuselah, isn't it?"

"Undoubtedly."

"And I won't become a werewolf?"

"No."

"How can you be sure?"

"Swallowing a werewolf's blood will not transform a person into a werewolf."

Not bothering to hide her relief, Meredythe leaned back and closed her eyes. She opened them almost immediately. "But according to everything I've read, that's how werewolves are created."

Rhys rose and poured himself a drink. "Everything you've read is wrong."

She opened her mouth, but Rhys held up his hand. "Let me explain."

Meredythe sniffed. "It's about time somebody did."

"Approximately fourteen hundred years ago—"

"Fourteen hundred years!"

He sipped some Scotch. "Please, Meredythe, don't interrupt."

Methuselah jumped back into her lap.

Sighing, she stroked him. "Okay, start talking."

She continued to stroke the cat as Rhys explained how Bleddyn had waited almost fourteen hundred years for her, how Rhys had tried to bring them together four different times over the centuries only to be stymied time and time again. She shook her head as Rhys explained how he'd taken her dying body into fire to save her life so that she could be reborn sometime in the future.

When he finally finished, she shook her head in disbelief.

Easing Methuselah from her lap, she stood and began to pace, pondering everything Rhys had told her.

"No way," she finally said. "No way is this possible. Okay, Bleddyn is a werewolf. I saw him change with my own eyes, so I believe you. But having sex with a virgin—me—will stop him from being evil. Come on. And me, living in fire. No way. That's just not possible."

She paced to the fireplace and turned, sidestepping a bit so as not to step on Keri. Her foot came down on a stack of Rhys' books, which immediately toppled to the floor. One large tome landed on Keri's tail. With a howl, she leaped up, her shoulder catching Meredythe's hip which caused her to lose her balance. Throwing her hands out to brace her fall, Meredythe tumbled into the fireplace. The flames roared and rose to meet her.

A small corner of Meredythe's brain registered everything that was happening. As she fell forward, it seemed as if time slowed and she was standing outside her body, watching. She was going to be burned—badly.

As she watched, flames leaped toward her hands and arms. She managed to keep her legs out of the flames, landing on her knees on the lip of the fireplace. Her hands, however, landed among the burning logs.

"*Tanau*!" she cried.

The flames roared higher and embraced her upper body.

Jerking herself out of the fireplace, she knelt and stared at her hands. Flames danced along her arms and leaped from one hand to the other without burning her skin. She didn't even feel any heat.

"How…" She swallowed. "How do I make it stop?"

Rhys' voice was gentle. "Say *peidio*."

Meredythe swallowed then whispered, "*Peidio*."

The fire flashed then winked out. Still staring at her hands, Meredythe collapsed onto the floor.

"Here," Rhys said as he handed her another glass of Scotch.

She gulped then gulped again. Holding the now-empty glass up, she said, "More."

Instead Rhys grabbed her hand and pulled her to her feet. "I think you've had enough Scotch for now."

Meredythe shuddered, crossed her arms over her chest and rubbed her upper arms. She began to pace again, making sure she stayed well away from the fireplace. "Enough? I don't think so. I think I need to drink myself into a stupor."

She shook again, trying to come to grips with the fact she could juggle fire in her hands. She stopped in front of Rhys. "What was that I said when I fell into the fire?"

"*Tanau*. It's Welsh for fire. You must have stored the command in your subconscious one of times I saved your life. You were still conscious when those villagers tried to burn you as a witch."

Meredythe shuddered again. Burned as a witch! Raking her hands through her hair, she grimaced as her fingers tangled in a snarl. She needed a brush and a bath. Still another shiver ran down her spine. A bath! Closing her eyes, she shook her head. What she needed was to wake up from this nightmare.

Spinning away from Rhys, she started to pace again. She needed to get a hold of herself. Okay, she could juggle fire.

Lots of people, people like circus performers and...well, circus performers, could juggle fire. She wasn't so different from anybody else. She was still human, more human than Bleddyn. Wasn't she?

She stopped in front of Rhys again. "How did Bleddyn become a werewolf? How is it possible for you to be the father of a wolf and grandfather of a human—well, sort of human? Are you a werewolf too?"

"No, I'm a druid."

She stared at Rhys. A druid? She shook her head and tried to talk herself out of the hysteria growing in her mind. *Come on, Meredythe, get a hold of yourself. You can handle this. Think. Ask questions. Find out all the pertinent information.*

"What about Keri?"

I'm a wolf now dear, but once I was a woman.

Sinking into the leather chair, Meredythe glared from one to the other. "I think you better explain everything to me. Now."

"Let's see. Where to begin?"

Keri sighed. *Don't bother with the all the minute biological and physiological details, Father. Just explain what happened.*

Rhys frowned at the wolf, but settled himself on the stool. "Very well. Keri, my daughter, was once just as human as you and I. Right before she gave birth to Bleddyn, she was bitten by a wolf."

Meredythe frowned. "So, if a pregnant woman is bitten by a wolf, her child becomes a werewolf."

Rhys shook his head. "Please don't interrupt. Being bitten by a wolf doesn't turn anyone into a werewolf." He held up his hand when Meredythe would have interrupted again. "Just listen. After I finish, you may ask questions."

After Meredythe's nod, Rhys continued, "The wolf that bit Keri had been bitten by a vampire."

"Vampire," Meredythe squeaked.

Rhys ignored her. "As I'm sure you know, vampires need blood to survive." He waited for Meredythe's nod. "However, it doesn't have to be human blood. A vampire can survive quite nicely on the blood of any warm-blooded animal, which doesn't present any problems with herbivores. Carnivores, however…well, that's a different story."

Rhys paused and sipped his Scotch.

"Something in the physiology of carnivores reacts violently with a vampire's saliva. If the animal is able to escape the vampire before it drains too much blood and finds refuge from the sun, it changes subtly. Over a very short amount of time it becomes so sensitive to sunlight that it eventually dies. Few have the intelligence to hide away in a dark cave during the day."

Again Rhys sipped his Scotch.

"However, if one of these animals bites a human before it dies, that human becomes a werebeast."

"You mean there are more than werewolves?"

"Yes, though most carnivores still don't seem to have the intelligence to survive very long. Wolves, bears and cats do, and there was a wereboar once. Nasty beast until someone finally killed it."

"But why is Keri a wolf?"

An expression of deep sadness appeared on Rhys' face. "When the vamwolf bit her, Keri immediately went into labor. What with the trauma of birth and the effect of the vamwolf's bite… She was dying. The only way I could save her was to draw upon the wolf essence streaming through her blood and shift her shape permanently."

Meredythe turned her attention to Keri. "Did you know what he was doing?"

Of course, dear. I told him to do it. Becoming a wolf was the only way I was able to stay with my child. A child, I might add, who would, in all probability, be a werewolf. As a wolf myself, I'd be able to help him when the bloodlust finally rose.

"This..." Meredythe swallowed once. "This is all hard to believe. Why don't more people know about you?"

The wolf snorted before Rhys could answer. *And become laboratory experiments? No thank you.*

Leaning back, Meredythe tried to absorb everything she'd just learned. It was amazing. No one would believe it. She almost didn't believe it—almost. If she hadn't seen Bleddyn turn into a werewolf...

"Bleddyn said he was able to control himself most of the time, but he has problems when there is a full moon. What about all those myths about werewolves and the full moon?"

Rhys shook his head. "It's not the moon. As a matter of fact, the full moon gives him control over himself. The bloodlust, as he calls it, is what pushes him toward violence. It builds in him until it becomes unbearable. If he can stand under the light of a full moon, however, he can conquer the urge to kill."

"So the full moon doesn't turn him into a werewolf."

"No, he and any other werebeast can turn into a werewolf whether there's a full moon or a new moon. The bloodlust is what makes them dangerous. Those who choose not to control it don't survive very long. Those who do seek the full moon for her aid."

"Oh."

Methuselah purred in her lap. She stiffened.

"Is...is Methuselah a were...cat?"

Rhys shook his head. "No, he's a Familiar."

"Familiar?"

Rhys smiled. "Of course. Evelyn is a druidess—a very powerful witch, you know."

"Aunt Evie's *really* a witch?"

He nodded.

"After those idiots tried to burn you at the stake, we decided to have someone powerful enough to protect you raise you. You and Bleddyn would have been married approximately seventy years ago if Hitler hadn't decided to bomb London."

Meredythe shifted in her chair. Bleddyn again. Everything came back to Bleddyn. "What if I don't want to be Bleddyn's mate?"

Three sets of stares zeroed in on her.

"Well, if I understand everything you told me, it's not like anyone asked me in the first place."

"Now see here," began Rhys.

A loud pounding on the door interrupted him.

"Now what?" he snapped as he rose to his feet.

Before he could step toward the door, it burst open and a man clad completely in black lunged into the room.

"Rhys, King told me to bring this to you. Someone managed to get some of Bleddyn's DNA. Hopefully all of his notes and information are in this briefcase."

Rhys took the briefcase the stranger held out to him. "Thank you, Damian. I don't believe you've met Bleddyn's guest yet. Meredythe, this is Damian Winterbourne."

DNA, huh? She had to get to know this guy and find out where he got that briefcase. Meredythe rose and held out her hand. "It's nice to meet you, Mr. Winterbourne."

He turned to face her and she smiled. Definitely good-looking even if he was a little pale. And cold. His hand felt like ice. Of course, he did just come in from outside.

"My pleasure…" His voice trailed off as he stared at her.

"Is something wrong?" she asked as she tried to pull her hand free.

He swallowed once, twice. "You have a drop of blood on your chin."

As Meredythe watched, his canines lengthened and became prominent. His hand tightened on hers.

Methuselah hissed from the chair. Keri rose from before the fireplace, sauntered across the room and placed herself between them.

Damian, dear, you know how possessive Bleddyn is.

"Damn it, Damian," growled Rhys, "when was the last time you fed?"

Dropping her hand as if it burned, Damian stepped back.

Meredythe stumbled back to her chair. "You're a vampire."

His smile was wan. "Yes, I am." Turning to Rhys, he continued, "I haven't had anything to eat for the last thirty-six hours."

Rhys turned toward a low cabinet, admonishing the younger man as he did so. "Overconfident fool. You always push yourself too far. One of these days..." He turned back toward them holding a mug, which he handed to Damian. He waved his hand. "There, it's fresh. Now drink it before you fall over."

Meredythe watched Damian's Adam's apple bob up and down as he drank. Color appeared in his face.

"That... That was blood, wasn't it?"

Before she could answer, the door slammed open again and Bleddyn stalked into the room, naked. After sweeping the room with a quick glance, his gaze settled on Meredythe.

"Come with me now."

Her head snapped up. "I will not. And go put some clothes on. Didn't anyone ever tell you it's not polite to walk around naked?"

Bleddyn didn't say anything. He simply stepped across the room, grabbed Meredythe and threw her over his shoulder. Turning, he disappeared out the doorway, Meredythe's angry voice trailing after them.

"Put me down, you...you cretin. I'm not a side of beef!"

The sharp crack of a hand connecting with bare skin echoed back into the room.

Aghast, Damian turned to Rhys. "He didn't just hit her, did he? Bleddyn wouldn't hit Meredythe, would he?"

Keri's tongue lolled out and she grinned a wolfish grin.

No, Damian. Bleddyn wouldn't hit Meredythe. However, she has no such inhibitions.

Chapter Sixteen

"Damn it. Put me down."

Bleddyn kicked the door to his bedroom shut, walked across the room and dropped Meredythe on the bed. He fell down beside her.

"Oh no you don't. Not again." She rolled across the bed and off the other side. She scrambled across the floor and grabbed the poker from where it still lay.

A haunted expression on his face, Bleddyn flopped back against the pillows and closed his eyes. "You won't need that, Meredythe. I'm not going to attack you."

She stared at him a moment then crossed the room to the fireplace and set the poker back in its stand. "Why the caveman act?"

He didn't open his eyes. "What?"

She returned to the side of the bed. "Dragging me here."

"I need you."

She snorted. "Stupid way to show it. All you had to do was ask."

He didn't answer her. Instead he threw his arm over his eyes and turned his head away.

Meredythe cocked her head to the side and stared at him. His arm hid his face, but his body language conveyed his dejection.

"Is what Rhys told me true? You really believe you needed my virgin blood to save your soul?"

"Yes."

"How?"

He lowered his arm and stared at her. "How what?"

She shrugged. "How was it supposed to work?"

He sighed and covered his eyes again. "I don't know."

She cocked an eyebrow. "Then how do you know it would work?"

Sighing again, he dropped his arm and looked at her. "The werewolf side of me didn't emerge until I hit puberty. Two days after my first 'change', a druid seeress predicted that the lust for blood and violence would overcome me unless I found my true mate. Then under the light of the moon, with the blood of this pure and untainted woman, the demon of lust and carnage would be driven from my soul."

"How do you know I'm the right woman?"

Bleddyn's smile was weak. "Rhys cast a seeking spell. It led him to you. Besides, you wear a wolf head on your breast."

Involuntarily, Meredythe touched the mole on her left breast. There was a resemblance to the head of a howling wolf.

"Where did you go? Tonight, I mean."

"I ran. Running…calms me."

"You didn't kill anything."

He dropped his arm. "No, why?"

She hugged herself. "That bloodlust business."

He shook his head. "There was none. Sex satisfies the urge."

Stiffening, Meredythe opened her mouth. He cocked an eyebrow at her. She swallowed her retort. The sex *had* been fantastic. Instead she asked, "What are you going to do now?"

He shrugged. "I'll fight the beast as I always have." Then he sighed. "You, I will keep. I've waited for you too long, and I've come to love you in these last few weeks."

Flabbergasted, Meredythe gaped. Then she snapped her mouth shut. Breathing deeply, she struggled to control her temper. Closing her eyes, she shuddered then swallowed. How could any man be so damned egotistical?

"Keep me! What, like…like an eigthteenth-century mistress?" she asked in a low voice. "What about me? What about how I feel? Maybe I don't want to be kept! Maybe I'm a grown woman capable of making my own decisions. Maybe you should take your archaic ideas about love and shove them where the sun doesn't shine."

Spinning on her heel, she stomped across the room, jerked open the door and disappeared into the hallway, slamming the door closed behind her. Pieces of plaster trickled to the floor.

Bleddyn stared at the closed door. He probably could have handled that better, but… She'd soon realize that she loved him. She had to. Sighing, he closed his eyes. The beast in his soul was quiet and he was tired.

Stomping down the hall to the room she called her own, Meredythe wrenched the door open and launched herself toward the bed. Flopping on her stomach, she punched a pillow. Keep her! Here! Bullshit! She had a career and she was damn good at it. Now she was supposed to give it all up for a man she didn't even know existed two months ago. When hell froze over, maybe.

Rolling onto her back, she glared at the ceiling. "So why do I feel so guilty?"

Because you always feel like you should be able to fix everything.

Methuselah jumped onto the bed, sat down and began to wash his paw.

Meredythe glared at the cat. "Why didn't anybody bother to tell me—"

Tell you that you were destined to be the mate of a werewolf and save his soul from eternal damnation? Would you have believed any of us?

Glaring at the cat, she punched the pillow again. "Aunt Evie isn't even my aunt, is she?"

Methuselah started washing his other paw. *No.*

"So nice of her to lie to me."

Methuselah dropped his foot to the bed and stared directly at Meredythe. *Did the belief that she was your aunt hurt you in any way? She could not love you any more than she already does.*

Meredythe flopped over onto her stomach again. Damn cat. He was right. Aunt Evie was as good as or better than any mother ever could have been, and still was.

"So what do we do now?"

What do you mean?

"Bleddyn? What do we do about him?"

Methuselah stretched, extending each toe and claw separately. Then he stared directly into her eyes.

He's managed this long without you. He'll continue to manage. That's what you want to hear, isn't it? You have your own life to live. Your have own career with your own goals. You've always known exactly what you wanted out of life, so why are you worrying about Bleddyn Glyndwr? You've discovered your serial killer. You have the story you wanted, your ticket to recognition, fame, awards, right?

Settling down onto the other pillow, Methuselah tucked his paws under his chest, closed his eyes and began to purr.

Meredythe glared at the cat. "How can you be so unfeeling? You don't have to worry about wanting to kill people when the moon starts to get full."

He opened one eye. *Your point?*

She glared at him. "My point? You insensitive…cat! I can't write that story. They'd lock Bleddyn up and turn him into some kind of scientific experiment. I won't do that to him."

He closed his eye. *Why not? It's not as if you're in love with him.*

Muttering a curse about smartass cats, Meredythe shoved herself into a sitting position, crossed her legs, rested an elbow on her thigh and cupped her chin in her hand. Love Bleddyn? She barely knew him. Not that it mattered. She still wasn't going to write that story. As much as Bleddyn's attitude irritated her, she couldn't condemn him to the kind of life he'd lead if the scientific community found out about him.

Sighing, she shifted her chin to her other hand as she thought about what Bleddyn had told her. As for him thinking he loved her, well, she could understand how he felt. He honestly believed that she was the one to save him from himself, so to speak. After waiting that long for something only to lose it…

She cupped her chin in both hands. Okay, for the sake of argument, what if she was the one who would save Bleddyn? How would her being a virgin have helped him? What was so important about virgin blood? What if she had been a virgin without a hymen? Or one that broke sometime during childhood? That had been known to happen. What then? Besides, according to Bleddyn, the seeress said pure and untainted, not virgin.

She straightened and stared at the sleeping cat. She needed to know exactly what that seeress had said. Something was missing or misunderstood or mistranslated. She'd stake her reputation on it.

Scooting off the bed, she headed back to Bleddyn's room.

Bleddyn stared at the stars, brooding. None of them ever anticipated the possibility that Meredythe wouldn't be a virgin when he finally claimed her. If he ever got his hands on the man…

You'll what? asked Keri as she padded silently into the room. *Kill him*?

"Shut up, Mother."

I love you too.

He rolled onto his side and stared at her. "You know how important this was, how important it was for Meredythe to be a virgin."

Settling herself on her haunches, Keri stared at him. *No, I don't, as I've mentioned a number of times before. Evelyn also agrees with me.*

Bleddyn stiffened. "Did either of you know—"

No, Bleddyn. Neither of us had any idea. If you want my opinion, I doubt that Meredythe has had very many sexual partners. She's simply been too busy with her career.

"One or one hundred," he snarled. "What does it matter? The damage has been done."

With an attitude like that, it doesn't matter at all, now does it? When you stop feeling sorry for yourself and you're ready to listen to logic, we'll talk more. Rising to her feet, she trotted from the room.

Growling an unflattering curse about women in general, Bleddyn rolled over on his side and stared out the window.

"Bleddyn?"

He rolled over again. Meredythe stood in the doorway.

"What?"

She walked into the room. "There's a flaw in that seeress's prediction."

He snorted and rolled away from her.

"Damn it, Bleddyn, listen to me."

He kept his back to her. "Or what? You'll jab me with the poker? It's over by the fireplace, just where you left it."

The bed dipped. She grabbed his arm with both hands and rolled him over onto his back. "Would you stop being so pigheaded and just listen?"

"There's nothing to listen to. Unless you're here to tell me you've suddenly managed to become a virgin."

She gaped at him.

"No, I didn't think so."

"You asshole." Then she slapped his face.

Erupting from his supine position, he captured Meredythe's wrists, shoved her down on her back and rolled on top of her. She froze, her wide eyes tinted with fear.

His face only inches from hers, he growled, "Never, ever do that again."

She wiggled and tried to free her hands. "What are you going to do, bite me?"

Bleddyn stared down into her angry face. Pulling his lip back, he bared his teeth and snarled. She didn't flinch.

She's not afraid of me. For the first time since he'd discovered she wasn't a virgin, hope stirred in Bleddyn's heart. Over the centuries, almost every person who'd learned the truth about him had feared him. Meredythe didn't.

He smiled, remembering the sting from her slap. "Do you talk with your hands all the time?"

"Okay, I shouldn't have hit you. I'm sorry." She wiggled some more. "Let me go."

With the werewolf in his soul howling for a fast, hard mating, Bleddyn shook his head. She may not have been a virgin, but she was still his. "I don't think so." And he covered her mouth with his.

At first she stiffened with surprise, but his soft kisses and nibbles soon had her answering his kisses with her own. When he released her wrists, her hands fell to his shoulders and began to caress his upper arms.

His mouth left hers and trailed kisses down her neck while one hand slipped under her shirt and cupped her breast. She arched into his hand.

"Not fair," she gasped. "I can't...talk..."

"Good," he growled and ripped off her shirt.

Blood pounding in his ears, Bleddyn captured her lips again and sucked Meredythe's tongue into his mouth he yanked the sweatpants she was wearing down her thighs then slid his fingers between her legs.

She was so very, very wet.

Bleddyn groaned as his aching, rock-hard cock jerked once, then again. He needed to bury himself in her hot, wet cunt, but first, he wanted her to touch him.

Pulling his hand away from her thighs, Bleddyn captured one of Meredythe's hands and guided it to his erection, shuddering as she grasped it then danced her fingers first up and down its length, stroking down one side and up the other.

As he mated his tongue with hers, she gripped his cock and, slowly at first, then faster and faster, pumped it, her fingers squeezing then relaxing then squeezing harder again. Bleddyn groaned again into her mouth as she rubbed his first drops over the head of his cock. His balls tightened even more. The urge to explode built higher and higher.

"Easy, love. Not yet. I'll come too soon."

"Good," she hissed against his mouth. "About time you lost control."

Chuckling, Bleddyn slid his fingers into her wet slit. "You're the one who's going to lose control, love."

Meredythe moaned and spread her legs. Yes. This was what she wanted, what she needed. She stabbed her tongue into his mouth, mating it to his. When he slid first one finger then the second inside her, she sobbed and thrust her hips against his hand.

"More, please, harder."

She tilted her head back when his mouth left hers to trail kisses down her neck to her breasts. He sucked first one then the other nipple into his hot mouth as his fingers slid around and around her clit.

Moaning into his mouth, she thrust against his hand again.

He raised his head from her breast and stared into her face. "What do you want, Meredythe?"

She gripped his shoulders with both hands, straining against the fingers that swirled and danced between her thighs. "You," she sobbed. "Please, I need you inside me."

His breathing grew harsher. "Like this?" He thrust first one then two fingers into her.

A low, keening moan escaped from Meredythe's throat as she ground her cunt against his fingers, her internal muscles clutching at the slippery digits as he pumped them. The musty aroma of sex swirled and wafted around them, flooding Meredythe's senses. Her arousal spiraled.

He sucked her nipple into his mouth and slid a third finger inside.

Her stomach muscles clenched and her thighs shuddered. "Oh God, oh God, oh God."

He lifted his head from her breasts and looked into her eyes. "Now, love. Come for me now."

Meredythe shattered.

Before she stopped shuddering from her orgasm, Bleddyn sat up and settled back against the bed's headboard, pulling her onto his lap facing him. He had to be inside her. Now! "Put your legs around my waist, love."

Lifting her up, Bleddyn dropped her onto to his cock, thrusting into her as deeply as he could.

"By all the gods, you're tight," he groaned. He buried his face into her neck, gripped her ass and pulled her toward him as he began to pump.

"Ahh!" Threading her fingers through his chest hair, Meredythe pinched one of his nipples.

Hot lightning shot straight to his groin.

Balls burning, Bleddyn gritted his teeth. He didn't think his dick could get as hard and achy as it felt now. Still he fought against the pressure. He was going to keep burying himself into Meredythe as long as he possibly could, allowing her slick muscles to grasp, clench and squeeze him until she milked him of every drop of resistance. Only then would he allow himself his release.

Moaning, Meredythe arched her breasts toward Bleddyn's mouth as he impaled her on his cock. He was so very hot, so very, very hard. Her muscles stretched to accommodate his length then tightened to suck him farther inside.

Sitting on his thighs with her legs around his waist, she shuddered over and over as he stretched and filled her more than any other man ever had. She wiggled and he slid deeper. She caught his rhythm, pulling him deeper and deeper with each thrust.

He lifted his face from her neck, lowered his head, suckled a nipple then nipped it.

A bolt of electricity seemed to jolt from her nipple to her groin. He suckled again and twisted his hips.

Meredythe gyrated her hips and strained against him, pulling his cock even deeper. She felt hot—so damn hot! Pressure built. Throwing back her head, she screamed as another orgasm ripped through her.

Beneath her, Bleddyn stopped fighting. He slammed his cock into Meredythe one final time as his cum erupted from his balls and surged up through his cock. Her muscles tightened and grasped and sucked until he was wrung dry.

"Fuck. That was… Fuck."

Her chuckle as she collapsed onto his chest conveyed her triumphant agreement.

* * * * *

Meredythe awoke alone. Squinting her eyes against the sunlight streaming in the huge window, she contemplated the previous night. Both times she tried to talk about the seeress's ambiguous prediction he'd started kissing her and…

She smiled. When it came to sidetracking her, Bleddyn was very, very good.

Sitting up, she scooted from the bed and headed for the bathroom. A hot shower would help put her thoughts in order.

Twenty minutes later, she walked out of the bedroom to find Methuselah comfortably ensconced on Bleddyn's bed.

Is your story finished?

Meredythe glanced toward Bleddyn's desk. Her briefcase with all of her information stood next to the computer—her ticket to fame.

"Oh hell, I can always write another story," she muttered. Stomping across the room, she grabbed the case and set it on the desk. After tapping in the combination, she wrenched the lid open and stared at the contents. After another muttered curse, she grabbed everything, carried it to the fireplace and threw the folders, papers and CDs on the still-smoldering coals.

Concentrating on the material, she said, "*Tanau*." Flames burst among the material, and she watched as the paper burned to ashes and the disks melted.

When nothing remained but ash, she turned toward the door. Forefeet propped up on the headboard of the bed, Methuselah watched her.

"What?"

The cat stared at her.

"You didn't expect me to let him be used as a scientific experiment, did you?"

When he didn't answer, she sniffed and headed for the door.

Smirking, Methuselah jumped off the bed and followed her out the door.

After a quick stop in her room for a fresh shirt and jeans, Meredythe headed downstairs and made her way to the kitchen. Pushing the door open, she walked in to the sight of Damian Winterbourne drinking a thick red liquid from a goblet.

She swallowed. "Is that…"

"V8," he filled in with a grin. "I always did like vegetables."

She headed for the coffeepot. "Where is everybody?"

Damian smiled. "Bleddyn is out with his wolves. He said you should go out to Shadow. He's been upset ever since you left yesterday and didn't go back."

Meredythe gulped her coffee. Shadow! The last thing she wanted to do was worry him. She set her mug in the sink and hurried out the back door, only stopping long enough to slip her feet into boots and throw a coat around her shoulders.

The wolf-dog was waiting at his gate for her. *You said you'd come back.*

She slipped the latch and stepped in, not thinking twice about being able to hear him talk. "I'm so sorry, Shadow. It's just that Bleddyn made me so angry."

I will challenge him if you want.

"Challenge him? No! I'm not angry anymore."

He sat back on his haunches. *You have chosen him for your mate?*

She leaned back against the fence. "My mate? No!"

You have mated with him. The wolves told me. Therefore, he is your mate.

She shook her head. "No, it doesn't work like that with people."

Why?

"Come on, I'll get your breakfast," she said as she stepped back toward his kennel. "Do you have enough straw? Are you warm enough?" She stuck her head in his kennel.

"Bleddyn, you can't just shrug this off."

Meredythe glanced around. Where was Rhys' voice coming from?

"And what should I do—go to New York and lend credence to what this fool says?"

Her gaze zeroed in on the back wall, a wall shared with the shed where Bleddyn kept the wolves' food. She crawled into the kennel and leaned against the wall.

"What's he going to do, Rhys, publish his findings in a medical journal? He'd be laughed out of the profession."

"But he has proof, Bleddyn. DNA. Yes, most in the medical community will laugh at him. But some will listen. They'll study and research more. Eventually they'll come to you."

The frustration in Bleddyn's voice was unmistakable. "What do you want me to do—kill him?"

Covering her mouth with both hands, Meredythe waited.

"Of course not, but—"

"But nothing, Rhys. This Jon Bowers undoubtedly has his material backed up in at least fourteen different places. All I can do is ride this out. Now if you'll excuse me, I have to feed the wolves."

Dropping her hands, Meredythe slid to the straw-covered floor of the kennel. Jon Bowers. The black hairs from the pimp's body. He said he was going to run another DNA test to see if it was a wolf or dog.

"Oh my God. Jon knows about Bleddyn." She looked up at Shadow. "I have to do something. I have to talk to him."

Are you leaving again?

She pushed herself to her hands and knees and crawled toward the entrance. "I have to, Shadow. If I don't, Bleddyn could be in danger. If people find out he is a werewolf, that werewolves really exist…" She glanced up at him. "Well, bad things will happen."

He followed her. *You must take me with you.*

Once outside, she rose to her feet and looked back at the wolf-dog. "I can't do that, Shadow."

He leaned against her thigh. *Then you must take Bleddyn.*

"Yeah, as if he'd ever listen to me," she answered, not caring if Shadow understood sarcasm or not.

Then I must go with you. There is danger.

She headed for the gate. "Shadow, I said no."

Then I will tell Bleddyn what you are planning to do. He will not allow you to leave.

Turning, Meredythe stared at Shadow. He was sitting on his haunches, his tongue lolling out.

"I don't have a choice, do I?"

No.

Sighing, Meredythe turned back toward the gate. Animals were running her life now. "Come on then. We have to leave now, before Bleddyn has a chance to stop us."

Stepping out of the kennel, Meredythe looked around. Bleddyn was outside, back in the enclosure with his wolves. Her car was in the center garage. Bleddyn said he left the keys in the ignition. With a little luck, she'd be gone before he knew it.

She made it to the garage without being seen. Opening the back door, she motioned Shadow in. "Stay down. If someone sees me, I'll tell them I'm just driving into Winterbourne to the shops."

Trying to be as quiet as possible, she lifted the garage door, cringing at the grating noise. As soon as the door was up, she hopped into the car, backed it out and turned toward the driveway. Bleddyn was striding out of the wolf enclosure toward her.

Rolling down the window, she shouted, "I'm going into town. Be back soon." She stepped on the gas and roared down the driveway.

Standing at the top of the driveway, Bleddyn watched as Meredythe's car disappeared. She had said something about visiting the shops when he'd taken her to dinner. Turning, he headed into the house.

Damian was sitting at the table reading the paper. Bleddyn cocked an eyebrow. "Comfortable?"

Looking over the top of the paper, Damian grinned a toothy grin. "Quite."

"Why is Meredythe going to town?"

"How should I know? She's your woman, not mine."

* * * * *

A tired Meredythe pulled into her parking garage late that afternoon. She should have been home hours earlier, but a nasty traffic accident then a quick stop at a pet store for a leash and collar had kept her on the road much longer than she'd planned.

Pushing her tired body out of the car, she opened the back door and Shadow jumped out.

"Hold still, Shadow," she said as he growled. "And you have to wear the collar and leash while we're in the city. Two blocks and we'll be home."

With a sigh of relief, Meredythe rounded the corner to her street. She'd go see Jon tomorrow. First she'd find out what he knew. Then she'd figure out how to keep him from publishing the information.

Shadow's growl brought her out of her musings. Three police cars and an ambulance were parked in front of her building. She paused at the edge of the small crowd, searching for a familiar face.

"Mrs. Scandelli, what's going on?"

"Meredythe? Meredythe! You're all right. Officer, look, here she is. She's not dead."

A policeman turned toward them. "Meredythe Welsh?"

"Yes."

"Come with me, please." He started to reach for her arm but stopped when Shadow growled.

"Ah, follow me." Pushing his way through the small crowd, he led her through the door of her apartment building, muttering a blasphemy under his breath when he discovered the elevator was out of order.

Meredythe ignored his grumbling. "What's going on, Officer?"

"There's been a break-in."

She sprinted up the stairwell, Shadow at her side. When she reached the third floor landing, she shoved the door open and dashed into the hallway.

A policeman stood just outside her open door. Yellow crime scene tape was plastered across the entrance.

The officer stepped to intercept her. "I'm sorry, miss. You'll have to go another way."

"But that's my apartment. I'm Meredythe Welsh."

Eyeing Shadow dubiously, he stepped back. "You better brace yourself."

Ducking under the police tape, Meredythe stepped into her apartment. Neck hairs bristling, Shadow followed, a low growl rumbling in his throat.

There is danger here. I have never smelled this smell before, but it is evil.

Meredythe stood in the middle of her living room and stared at the chaos that had once been her apartment. Every piece of furniture was broken, shattered pieces scattered from living room to kitchen. Dirt from uprooted plants was mounded next to glass shards from picture frames. CDs were embedded in the walls. Her refrigerator was shoved partway through the wall separating the living room and bedroom.

Dazed, she turned in a slow circle, her mind blank. Shadow was plastered against her thigh.

"Meredythe?"

She turned toward the voice. Jon Bowers waved his hand in front of her face.

She blinked then shook her head. "Jon? What happened? Who did this? Why are you here?"

"One of your neighbors called the police. Your door was open, and well, you see what the place looks like. You hadn't been seen in awhile and the first officer on the scene found blood in the bathroom."

She focused on him. "Blood? Whose?"

"We thought it was yours."

"Excuse me, miss," interrupted another officer, "your neighbors haven't seen you around for a while. Where have you been?"

"Upstate," she answered. Closing her eyes, she took a couple of deep breaths. Then she opened her eyes and continued in a stronger voice, "I'm a reporter. I was working on a story."

"Do you have any idea who could have done this? Do you have any enemies that you know of?"

She shook her head. "No, no one." She looked around again. "I don't understand. Who could hate me this much?"

Chapter Seventeen

Four and a half hours later, Meredythe stood in the middle of a hotel room and stared at the walls. The police had questioned her for close to three hours about who might have trashed her apartment and what, if anything, was missing. Thank goodness Jon had been there to vouch for her identity. She'd left Winterbourne on the spur of the moment without her purse and had no identification on her.

After the police left, Jon had remained. But before he'd had a chance to ask any questions, there'd been a knock on the door. James King had sent a car and driver to take her to a hotel. Jon had insisted on accompanying her.

Now he held a cup. "Here, drink this."

Shivering, she hugged herself. "What is it?"

"Coffee. Room service sent a pot up. They also sent enough food for an army." Jon looked around the luxurious suite. "Nice to have a boss with this much pull."

Ignoring the sarcasm in his voice, Meredythe accepted the coffee and gulped. Who trashed her apartment? And why?

Jon waved his hand in front of her face.

"What? The suite," she answered, her mind still on the break-in. "He keeps it for out-of-town guests."

Shadow trotted out of the bedroom and plastered himself to her side with a growl.

Jon stepped back.

"Is that the werewolf you went looking for?"

Wrenching her mind away from her dark thoughts, Meredythe concentrated on Jon fully for the first time since she'd returned to the city.

Werewolf? Shadow? He had to be out of his mind. Then she shook herself mentally and prodded her tired brain. Jon had done DNA tests. He was why she'd come back to New York. But Shadow? "Are you nuts? This is one of the wolf-dogs your friend Frank had at Columbia University."

He crossed his arms over his chest and said, "So where's the werewolf?"

Meredythe gripped the cup tighter. He knew there was a werewolf. Damian had stolen his briefcase, but had Jon backed up any of the information? She had to find out. She closed her eyes and jogged her mind again. She had to think!

Her hand drifted to Shadow's head. "What are you talking about?"

He scowled. "Forget the innocent act. I did the second DNA test myself. Then I did a third one because I didn't believe what I was seeing. DNA doesn't lie. Werewolves exist, and I know you know it."

"Jon..."

He shook his head. "Don't try to deny it. I won't believe you. I may have once, but that was before my briefcase was stolen right after I showed your boss my evidence. And look at how your apartment was trashed. No normal human being could do that amount of damage. What the hell is going on, Meredythe?"

She sank onto the sofa.

Shadow lay down at her feet, his gaze locked on Jon. *He is angry and he wants you for himself.*

Sighing, Meredythe closed her eyes. Why had she allowed Jon to come with her? Why hadn't she told him she'd see him in the morning? If only she weren't so tired that her brain wasn't functioning clearly. These last forty-eight hours had been hell.

Bleddyn Glyndwr, a man she'd found very attractive, was a werewolf—and a murderer. Even so, she'd given in to her body's urges and slept with him. Next she'd discovered she could walk in and out of fire without being hurt. Then a maniac had destroyed her apartment, and now Jon was acting like a jealous lover.

She opened her eyes and focused on his guarded expression. His body was stiff. He'd dropped his arms to his sides, hands clenched into fists. Surely she hadn't encouraged him that much, had she? She'd only gone out with him twice.

Sighing, she blinked. Damn, but she was tired. If only she could just go to sleep. But first she had to find out what Jon knew and whether or not Bleddyn was in danger.

Relaxing her stiff body, she leaned back, grabbed a pillow and cradled it against her chest. "I didn't believe it myself, Jon, but I did find a werewolf."

He interrupted before she could continue. "He's the murderer, isn't he?"

Think, Meredythe, think. She shook her head. "It's not like that, Jon."

His eyebrows rose and he took a step forward.

Shadow growled.

He stopped but said, "Not like what? Murder is murder. Did he kill that guy in the park or not?"

Again she shook her head. "You have to understand, there's a compulsion. Usually he can control it, but he'd taken a new kind of medicine. And the people who died were all bad! He's not really a murderer."

Shock and outrage colored Jon's features. "Not a murderer! What would you call him?"

"He was protecting the girl, damn it," she snapped. Then she took a deep breath and grabbed hold of her temper. "Jon, he's a good man who's done good things. I won't ruin his life because he accidentally killed a jerk who was beating a girl."

"Accidentally killed? What's wrong with..." He stopped and stared at her intently. A look of comprehension appeared, the anger drained from his face and his shoulders drooped. In a hollow voice, he said, "You've fallen in love with him, haven't you?"

Meredythe froze. Love! Bleddyn? Sure he was sexy and great in bed. But love? She didn't love Bleddyn, did she? "I..." She swallowed.

He held up his hand. "Don't say anything else. It's perfectly obvious. I'm not dense."

"Jon..."

"I guess I'd better get going. I'll see you." Turning, he walked toward the door.

Clasping the pillow tighter, she blurted, "Jon, do you have any more evidence?"

He froze. His laughter was bitter. "I should probably leave you hanging, but I won't. No, everything I had was in that briefcase. Pretty stupid of me, wasn't it?" He grabbed the doorknob then looked back over his shoulder. "Tell me, was that guy who stole it really a vampire or was he just dressed to scare me?"

Meredythe swallowed. How was she supposed to answer that question?

His lips quirked into a sardonic smile. "Never mind. If you found a werewolf, I guess there can be vampires too."

Meredythe stared at the closed door then sighed. She'd think about everything in the morning. Dropping the pillow, she heaved herself to her feet. "Come on, Shadow. Let's get some sleep."

* * * * *

Meredythe pushed the scrambled eggs room service had delivered around on the plate. Setting the fork down, she picked up a muffin and broke off a little piece and nibbled. Sighing, she continued to break off pieces of muffin and drop them to her plate. She'd gotten little sleep last night, tossing and turning as the truth of Jon's words kept rolling around her mind. She loved Bleddyn. Now what was she going to do?

Shadow lifted his head from his breakfast. *Someone comes.*

Seconds later, there was a knock on the door. Pushing herself out of her chair, she stumbled to the door and looked out the peephole. With a sob, she jerked the door open.

"Aunt Evie," she cried as she launched herself into the older woman's arms, "how could you do this to me?"

Evelyn hugged her niece close. "There, there, Meredythe. Everything will be fine." Grasping Meredythe's upper arms, Evelyn disengaged herself and stepped back. "Perhaps it would be better if we went into your room instead of providing entertainment for whoever comes into the hallway?"

The slight trace of amusement in Evelyn's voice brought a weak smile to Meredythe's face and she stepped back into the room. Evelyn followed and closed the door. Looking about the room, she spied the wolf-dog.

"So you're Shadow. How do you do?"

He sat back on his haunches and licked his jowls.

After shrugging out of her coat and dropping it over the back of a chair, she bustled across the room and poured herself a cup of coffee. Settling herself in a comfortable chair, she looked expectantly at her niece.

Meredythe followed her aunt and dropped onto the sofa, slumping against the cushions. "I'm in love with Bleddyn Glyndwr," she mumbled.

Evelyn sipped her coffee. "Is that such a bad thing?"

Blinking, Meredythe sniffed and fingered a tear from her cheek. "Of course it's a bad thing. He's a werewolf."

Evelyn cocked her head to the side. "And what does that have to do with the price of tea in China?"

"Damn it, Aunt Evie," Meredythe snapped as she shoved herself up and began to pace. "He's not completely human. He's not normal. He *kills* people."

"Only if he doesn't have any other choice. He's not a bad man, Meredythe. Rather he's a very good man suffering from a rare disease, you might say. Is it fair to hold that against him?"

Meredythe stopped pacing and stared at her aunt. "How can you defend him?"

Evelyn set her cup down, rose and clasped her niece's hands tightly. "Meredythe, I know Bleddyn almost as well as I know you. He's always been a kind, compassionate man who hates what happens to him. He's been searching for a cure for hundreds of years. Nothing has ever worked."

Tugging her hands free, Meredythe fisted them on her hips. "So he relied on my virgin blood. Well, I have news for you, Aunt Evie—I wasn't a virgin."

Smiling, Evelyn sat back down and continued to sip her coffee. "I was pretty sure you weren't. However, since you never mentioned having sex with anyone, I decided not to pursue the subject."

"But," Meredythe swallowed, "if you thought I wasn't a virgin, why didn't you..."

"Tell Rhys or Bleddyn?" Evelyn finished. "I didn't tell them because your life before you met Bleddyn is your business, not theirs. Besides, I don't believe your virginity is important. I think there's a different meaning to 'pure and untainted'."

"What?"

Evelyn smiled and shrugged. "I'm afraid I haven't figured that out yet." Setting her now-empty cup on the table, she continued, "What are you going to do now?"

Biting her lip, Meredythe spun away from her aunt and paced across the room. When she reached the window, she turned and paced back. "I don't know. I don't want to love Bleddyn. All it does is complicate my life. The fact that he's a werewolf aside, I have a good job with a great future. Why should I give that up for him?"

Her aunt cocked an eyebrow. "Who said you have to?"

"Aunt Evie, he's a werewolf."

"Again, what does that have to do with the price of tea in China?"

"You aren't any help." Spinning away, Meredythe strode to the fireplace then turned. "*Tanau*," she said and fire blossomed from her fingertips. She glared at her aunt. "Did you know I could do this?"

"No," Evelyn said with a warm smile, "but I'm not surprised."

"Why?"

She shrugged. "Spending as much time in fire as you have was bound to have an effect."

Meredythe smothered the flames and crossed her arms over her chest. "Then how come I can burn my hand on a hot pan?"

"That's just heat, not fire."

Throwing her hands into the air, Meredythe stomped back across the room and flung herself onto the sofa. "Is there anything you don't know?"

Evelyn laughed. "Of course, dear, many things." Then, leaning forward, she continued, "Meredythe, the only logical thing to do right now is talk to Bleddyn. You two have to sort things out, and you can't do that if you're here in New York and he's in Winterbourne."

"I wanted to talk to him, Aunt Evie, but then I heard Rhys and him talking about Jon having DNA proving Bleddyn was a werewolf and I had to come and find out what Jon knew."

Evelyn smiled. "And why was that?"

Sighing, Meredythe grimaced and muttered, "Because I care about what happens to him."

Evelyn leaned back. "That should explain things far more clearly than I can. Trust your feelings, Meredythe. They've never been wrong before."

Meredythe raked her fingers through her hair and rose. She smiled and said, "You're right as usual. Let me take a shower and put on some clean clothes. I did manage to find some that weren't ripped." She cocked her head to the side. "Do you have any idea who trashed my apartment?"

Evelyn frowned. "I would imagine it was Slade."

"Slade?"

Her frown deepened. "Didn't Bleddyn or Rhys warn you about him?"

"No."

"Men! It's a wonder the world still exists at all." Rising, she grasped Meredythe's hands again. "Slade is another shapeshifter and an enemy of Bleddyn's. He wants you for himself because he believes your blood will make him invincible."

Meredythe swallowed. "How much of my blood?"

"All of it, I imagine." Evelyn continued in an irritated tone, "I can't believe they didn't warn you."

"I didn't exactly give them a chance. I left pretty abruptly. I don't even have my purse with me."

Evelyn snorted. "You were there how long? Plenty of time to warn you." She dropped Meredythe's hands. "Well, no use dwelling on it now. Go get cleaned up. Then you and I will return to Bleddyn's estate together. You'll be safe from Slade there."

When Meredythe didn't move, Evelyn shooed her toward the bathroom. "Go on. The sooner we get everything settled, the sooner I can calm Methuselah. He's not very happy with you right now, you know."

Chuckling, Meredythe headed for the shower. Methuselah was undoubtedly expressing his displeasure by leaving mouse bodies all over Bleddyn's house.

After Evelyn heard water running, she turned to Shadow. "We shouldn't have any problems getting to the estate, but if we do…"

The wolf-dog grinned a toothy grin. *I will protect her with my life.*

* * * * *

Late that afternoon, Evelyn shifted in her seat and sighed. "I'm glad we're finally here. I hate long car rides."

In the backseat, Shadow whined in agreement.

Meredythe grinned. "You're the one who insisted on detouring to your house."

"I needed an overnight bag."

"You didn't have to agree to a late lunch."

"I couldn't hurt Mary Francis' feelings, Meredythe. Staying for lunch didn't delay us that long."

Meredythe glanced in the rearview mirror. "No, but we'd have gotten here before dark if we hadn't stayed."

Evelyn shifted again. "I'll still be glad when we get there. I shouldn't have had that second cup of tea."

"I offered to stop, but you insisted on driving straight through," Meredythe said with another grin. "Don't worry, the driveway is right around here somewhere."

A relieved expression appeared on Evelyn's face. "Thank goodness."

"Here it is. A few more turns and we'll be there. Don't mind the gargoyles," Meredythe added with a grin.

Rounding the first turn into Bleddyn's long driveway, Meredythe glanced over at her aunt then back to the road.

Gasping, she slammed on the brakes. Even so, the car plowed into the tree that lay across the drive.

As the car shuddered to an abrupt halt, both airbags deployed. Evelyn screamed and Shadow yelped as he was thrown against the back of the front seat. A tire exploded.

Punching and shoving the airbag out of her way, Meredythe reached for her aunt. "Aunt Evie, are you okay?"

A moan answered her.

"Shadow?"

I'm stuck back here, but I don't think I'm hurt anywhere.

Releasing her seat belt, she said, "I'm going to get out and go around to Aunt Evie's side."

She pulled the door handle. Nothing. "Come on, damn it." She pulled the handle again and shoved her shoulder against the door. Groaning, it opened about three inches. Thrusting with both hands, she managed to shove it open wide enough to squeeze out.

Once out, she hurried around to passenger side. Grabbing the door, she wrenched it open. "Aunt Evie, are you okay?"

To her left, a large mass emerged from the growing twilight. A triumphant growl and Shadow's frenzied howling were all she heard before something clipped the side of her head and she lost consciousness.

* * * * *

Jon Bowers closed his eyes and pinched the top of his nose. Why he'd come to the lab last night instead of going home, he wasn't sure. But he wanted to check out the blood sample he'd gotten from Meredythe's apartment. If that blood did come from the werewolf, maybe he'd be able to convince her she was in danger.

Rolling his shoulders to relieve the stiffness, he returned to the information before him. Grabbing a magnifying glass, he examined it carefully. Frowning, he rubbed his eyes then looked again. This DNA wasn't exactly the same as the other werewolf sample he'd examined. Something was different.

Giving his wheeled chair a push, he rolled over to his computer. Tapping a few keys, he waited for the information to pop up. When it did, he froze and stared. Impossible.

The chair spun away and bounced off a table as he leaped to his feet. Lurching to his desk, he grabbed the phone and punched in the number for Meredythe's hotel.

"Meredythe Welsh, please. Suite 1406."

Drumming his fingers, he waited.

"What do you mean she checked out? When? This morning?" He looked at his watch. Five o'clock. "Fuck!"

Dropping the phone, he shoved the papers and folders on his desk out of his way. "Damn it, where did I put that phone number?" Looking around his small office, he spotted the wastepaper can. Grabbing it, he upended it, dumped everything on the floor and started rummaging through the trash.

"Ah, here it is."

Grabbing the phone, he punched in the number. "Mr. King, please. This is Jon Bowers."

James King was staring out his window when his secretary buzzed him. "There's a Jon Bowers on the phone for you."

For a moment, he was tempted no to accept the call, but if Bowers had kept some DNA evidence… "Put him through."

"Mr. King, Meredythe is in danger. The blood samples I retrieved from her apartment last night are a mixture of human and bear. I tried to reach her, but she's checked out of her hotel room."

James sighed. More evidence for Damian to steal. "Thank you, Mr. Bowers, but Meredythe is fine. She's with her aunt. Please don't worry about her. Thank you for calling."

Ignoring the voice sputtering on the other end of the line, he gently placed the phone back in its cradle. Something would probably have to be done about Jon Bowers.

Even though they were sure Slade was the one who'd vandalized Meredythe's apartment, it wouldn't hurt to call Bleddyn. He picked up the phone and punched in the number.

"Bleddyn," he began when the connection was made, "have Meredythe and Evelyn arrived yet?"

"No. Evelyn called saying they were stopping for lunch. I expect them any time now. Why?"

James shifted nervously. "It's probably nothing, but Jon Bowers just contacted me. He knows the blood in Meredythe's apartment is from Slade."

Bleddyn shivered as the phone fell from his hand. Ever since Meredythe had left yesterday, he'd been uneasy. None of them knew exactly where Slade was.

Outside, the wolves began to howl.

Heaving a table out of the way, Bleddyn leaped across the den to the doorway and headed out the hall and into the kitchen. He was barely halfway to the back door when Damian wrenched it open.

"Something has happened. The wolves are frantic."

Damian stumbled back as Bleddyn pushed past and leaped out into the darkening twilight. He sprinted toward the wolf enclosure, tearing his clothing off as he ran. Damian kept pace at his side.

"What is it?"

Evil has come, howled the one-eyed wolf from the enclosure. *He has taken your mate.*

"Slade. He's close. How could I have missed him?" Bleddyn growled.

A faint howl drifted up the driveway. Both men slid to an abrupt halt.

"That's Shadow," Bleddyn snarled. He reached down and wrenched off his boots and socks.

"I'll go," Damian said. "I'm faster." With those words he was gone, nothing more than a ripple of air signifying his passing.

Finally naked, Bleddyn concentrated. Dark mist swirled and the huge, gray-eyed wolf lunged toward the driveway.

* * * * *

"Evelyn, Evelyn, are you all right?"

She forced her eyes open. Her voice was weak. "Damian, is that you? What happened?"

He wrenched the door completely off the car and gently lifted her out. "You were in an accident. Where's Meredythe?"

But Evelyn was unconscious again.

Shadow whined.

Damian shifted Evelyn to one arm and jerked the back door from the car. Shadow wiggled out and shot off into the darkness.

Bleddyn's wolf form hurtled over the downed tree and landed on the hood of the car. He leaped to the ground and stared intently at Damian.

"Shadow went that way."

Bleddyn followed.

Yowling wildly, Methuselah leaped out of the darkness and landed on Damian's shoulder, claws digging deep. *Take her to the tower. Rhys is waiting.*

Air shifted as Damian complied.

* * * * *

The scents of fresh pine and wood smoke tickled Meredythe's nose. Hard, craggy wood scraped her back and rough, scratchy rope abraded wrists that were tied above her head. She kept her eyes closed. Better to let whoever dragged her from her aunt's side think she was still senseless.

She let her chin drop to her chest, opened her eyes slowly and peered out from beneath her lashes.

Before her, a small fire burned. A superior feeling of satisfaction caused her to smile. Whoever had kidnapped her this time didn't know about what she could do with fire.

A shadow appeared at her left so she closed her eyes. A large hand grabbed her chin and yanked her head up. A rough voice said, "So you're awake, wolf's bitch."

She opened her eyes and stared into her captor's face. He was a huge man with wild hair and a bushy beard. Triumph gleamed from close-set, reddish-brown eyes. Her gaze left his face. He was naked. His chest, stomach, arms and legs were covered with a mat of dark hair. She kept her gaze away from his groin. She had no interest in what hung there.

"You're Slade," she said in a level voice, wondering how quickly his hairy face would catch fire. "What do you want with me?"

His teeth were large and white. "Your blood."

She kept her tone even. "In case you're too dense to figure it out, I'm not a virgin."

Dropping his hand from her chin, he threw back his head and roared with laughter. When his laughter finally diminished first to chuckles then to an evil smile, he said, "You think I would mount a skinny, sickly woman such as you? Ha! I have a woman, a strong woman with big breasts and wide hips, a woman who does not tear in half at my first thrust. You are nothing to me. But your blood, that I will have. Then I will be invincible."

Meredythe shook her head. "You honestly believe that?"

His humor disappeared, and he scowled at the obvious scorn in her voice. "The druid seeress foresaw that your blood would grant immortality."

She tried to move her wrists, but they were tied too tightly. "You're already immortal."

"I can be killed. Your blood will prevent that."

"What a crock. Are you normally this gullible?"

His slap slammed her head back against the tree. Stars danced before her eyes as she struggled to retain consciousness.

Slade grunted and turned away.

Breathing deeply, Meredythe remained perfectly still, willing the pain to lessen. She would remain conscious. She couldn't call fire if she couldn't concentrate. Bleddyn would come and she would help him.

An enraged howl rolled out of the trees. Throwing back his head, Slade answered with a roar of his own. The air around him roiled sluggishly and he transformed into a huge, black bear.

A streak of brown darted from beneath the trees and leaped toward the huge bear standing on its hind legs.

"Shadow! No!" She ignored the pain that exploded anew in her head.

At the last minute, the wolf-dog feinted to the left. Leaping past the bear's sweeping foreleg, he tore a long gash in its hind leg. The bear roared with pain. Turning far more quickly than seemed possible, Slade lashed out at Shadow's darting figure. The dog yelped as one claw slashed his ribs. Spinning away, Shadow feinted right then left again.

He didn't fool Slade this time. The bear met his charge with a bone-shattering slap of his huge paw. Howling with pain, Shadow flew across the clearing and slammed into a tree. He dropped to the ground and lay silent.

Slade lumbered to the body, transformed back into a man, grabbed Shadow by a leg and threw him toward the fire. "This is not the wolf. Where is he?"

Meredythe struggled to control the pain throbbing in her head. She tried to concentrate on fire, but the pain kept interfering. "You son of a bitch," she screamed. "I'll kill you myself."

"That won't be necessary, Meredythe," Bleddyn said calmly as he walked out of the forest. "I'll do it."

Slade grinned. "I will keep you alive long enough to watch your bitch die, wolf."

Bleddyn ignored him and concentrated on Meredythe. "Are you all right?"

Clenching her teeth, she nodded. "Except for one hell of a headache."

Slade shifted to his bear form and exploded into a lumbering run. In an instant, Bleddyn was the black wolf, jumping to the right as the bear barreled past him, leaping in enough to leave a long, bloody tear on its hairy shoulder. Roaring with anger, Slade rose on his hind legs and whirled, his huge paw with its razor-sharp claws reaching for Bleddyn. The wolf dove low under the swipe and ripped a chunk of skin and fur from the bear's stomach and leaped away. Again Slade roared, more with anger than pain.

Tears trickling down her cheeks, Meredythe struggled to concentrate, trying to form a clear picture of fire in her mind. Finally the image held. "*Tanau*!"

Flames burst from her fingers and ran up her arms. The rope tying her wrists together disintegrated to black ash. Dropping her arms, she held them before her. "Now you, asshole, fight this." Pointing both hands at the bear, she screamed, "*Tanau*!"

Nothing happened.

As the bear and wolf continued their battle, Meredythe stared at the fire enveloping her hands and arms. Why didn't that freaking bear catch fire?

Frustration racked her body. "Damn it, what good is carrying fire around if I can't send it anywhere?" Pulling her arm back, she threw it forward. The fire still danced around her fingers.

"Oh shit." Reaching down, she grabbed a stick. It burst into flame. Awareness dawned and she grinned. She couldn't throw fire, but she could throw things that were *on* fire.

Holding the stick like a spear, she took a few steps forward and launched it at the bear's back. He howled with rage when the fiery missile connected, but it bounced off him and fell harmlessly to the ground.

Noting the still burning stick, Bleddyn jumped to his left. Slade spun to follow him and stepped squarely on it.

Howling, he reared to his hind feet, momentarily off guard. Recognizing the opening, Bleddyn leaped straight into the bear's grasp, his sharp teeth and powerful jaws tearing at Slade's throat.

Roaring in pain and desperation, Slade raked Bleddyn's body with his deadly claws. Bleddyn shuddered but kept his jaws locked around the bear's jugular. Slade fell to the ground, thrashing and rolling. Bleddyn dug his blunt hind claws into Slade's belly. Finally, after one especially violent roll, the bear loosened Bleddyn's hold. The wolf bounced to the ground with a painful yelp and lay still.

Blood streaming from his neck, Slade rose over Bleddyn, jaws wide.

Leaping forward, Meredythe grabbed a handful of black hair and screamed, "*Tanau*!" Fire exploded from the hunk of fur she held and spread rapidly up his back. Bellowing with pain, Slade whirled to face his new attacker, his swiping claws catching Meredythe's arm as she scrambled away. She grabbed a dry branch and fire surged down its length. Pointing it at the bear, Meredythe stumbled backward.

The bear's shoulders continued burning while blood streamed from his ripped jugular. He was weakening rapidly. But the rage in his eyes told Meredythe he still had enough strength to slap the branch from her hand and tear her to pieces. She threw the branch at his face, turned to run and tripped over a rock. Screaming, she threw her still burning hands over the back of her neck.

Nothing happened.

Clawing at the dirt, she leaped to her feet, turned to face Slade and froze. Damian Winterbourne stood two feet from the burning bear, his dark, hypnotic gaze locked on Slade. The fiery air shimmered and Slade returned to his human form. Then, with a final, painful roar, he collapsed. The nauseating stench of burned flesh permeated the clearing.

Extinguishing the flames on her hands, Meredythe darted to Bleddyn's side. He too had reverted to human form, a form covered with blood. She pulled his head into her lap. "Damn it, Bleddyn Glyndwr, if you die on me now, I'll strangle you."

After Meredythe settled Bleddyn's head on her lap, he opened his eyes, his smile a grimace of pain. "Meredythe," he whispered, "you're safe now. That's all that matters. And I-I will finally…be free…of the monster in…my soul." His eyes closed.

"No! You are not going to die. You can't," Meredythe sobbed. "Damn it, I love you."

His eyes fluttered opened and he smiled weakly. When she moved slightly, he gasped with pain. Blood began to trickle from his mouth.

Meredythe jerked her eyes around the clearing. She would not let Bleddyn die! There had to be a way. Damian watched her, commiseration and sadness on his face. Her eyes locked on the fire Slade had built.

"Throw more wood on that fire, Damian."

He opened his mouth.

"Now, damn it. I don't have time to argue."

Shrugging, Damian darted around the clearing, heaving branches and chunks of deadwood on the dying flames. Soon a massive bonfire leaped toward the sky. The waning but still almost full moon drifted from behind a cloud and luminous white light bathed the clearing.

Rising to her knees, Meredythe hooked her hands under Bleddyn's armpits and began to drag him toward the fire. The blood from the cut on her arm smearing against cuts on Bleddyn's back. She looked back over her shoulder and glared at Damian. "He's heavy. Help me."

"Meredythe, are you sure about this?"

"Do you have a better idea? If Rhys could save me like this, then I should be able to save Bleddyn."

Damian grabbed Bleddyn's feet and helped her carry Bleddyn to the fire. "I can't let the fire touch me," he said.

Meredythe glanced at him, her expression softening momentarily. "Just help me get him there."

When she felt the fire's heat against her back, she straightened. "*Tanau,*" she said and stepped back into the flames.

Damian heaved with all of his strength, dropping Bleddyn's feet before the flames reached his hands. Stepping back, he stared at the fire. Shadowy figures seemed to leap and dance in its center. A low whine drew his attention. Back broken, hind legs dragging behind him, Shadow struggled toward the fire.

Stepping to the wolf-dog's side, Damian lifted him effortlessly and strode toward the flames.

"Meredythe," he called. "Shadow is dying."

Flames melted away from a slender arm. It motioned toward the fire. Taking a deep breath, Damian heaved the wolf-dog into the flames.

He watched as the flames roared higher. "I just hope she caught him."

* * * * *

Two hours later, Keri led Rhys, Evelyn and Methuselah into the clearing. Bleddyn's wolves followed silently behind them. They followed Keri up to the bonfire and placed themselves at evenly spaced intervals around it.

Rhys helped Evelyn to settle onto a log then turned to Damian and asked, "What happened?"

"Bleddyn ripped out Slade's throat while Meredythe set him on fire."

Rhys started. "Meredythe?"

The vampire nodded. "Bleddyn's ribs were broken, some of them probably pierced his lungs. He was dying so Meredythe dragged him into the fire. They're still there, I think. Oh, I tossed Shadow in too."

Rhys' eyes bugged out. "You 'tossed' Shadow in? She has to be touching him for him to live."

Damian shrugged. "I think she caught him. He'd have dragged himself in without my help and burned before he got to her."

"Calm down, Rhys. Everything will be all right," Evelyn murmured.

Methuselah jumped into her lap, his rumbling purr filling the clearing as she stroked him.

In the darkness just before dawn, the bonfire suddenly winked out. In the middle of the charred pile of wood sat Meredythe, Bleddyn's head on one thigh, Shadow's on the other. Her face streaked with exhaustion, she looked up and smiled tiredly.

"Why didn't you tell me how hard it was to keep a fire burning?"

Evelyn blinked as Shadow staggered to his feet then shook himself. His tongue lolled out and he wiped it across Meredythe's face. Then he jumped out of the fire's debris. Immediately, Bleddyn's wolves surrounded him. After mutual sniffing and tail wagging, they bounded off into the forest.

After Shadow disappeared, Meredythe's gaze returned to Bleddyn. He was smiling up at her.

"Did you mean it?"

"What, that I'd strangle you if you died? Yes."

He chuckled, grabbed a long, dangling curl and pulled her mouth down to his.

Rhys scrambled through the bonfire's ashes. "Meredythe, are you all right? Is Bleddyn…"

With a disappointed sigh, Meredythe lifted her mouth from Bleddyn's. He released the fiery curl he'd twined through his fingers and smiled. Then he rose to his feet.

"I feel fine." He smiled at Meredythe again. "Although I don't remember anything after Slade burst into flames."

Meredythe cocked an eyebrow and held out her hand. As he pulled her to her feet, she said, "I was just supposed to let him crush you? What good is playing with fire if I can't use it for anything?"

"The wound in his throat was fatal. You didn't have to put yourself in danger."

"Too bad." She crossed her arms over her chest, the torn sleeve of her shirt dangling from her shoulder.

Frowning, Bleddyn traced a finger down her arm. "You were cut. I remember your arm bleeding."

She shrugged. "The fire healed it, just like it healed all of your injuries."

Bleddyn stared at her a moment then froze. His eyes became unfocused.

Meredythe grabbed his arm. "Bleddyn? Bleddyn, what's wrong." She looked from Rhys to Evelyn. Rhys looked puzzled, but Evelyn was grinning triumphantly.

Her attention was yanked back to Bleddyn when he pulled her into his arms and kissed her, deeply, wildly, passionately.

She was completely lost in his kiss when he stopped, and would have collapsed if he hadn't been holding her.

His voice danced with joy. "It's gone."

She blinked, trying to bring her fired emotions under control. "What's gone?"

He kissed her again. "That hellish darkness that fought me for my soul. It's gone."

Passion dueled with logic. "What? How?"

"Your blood, dear," Evelyn answered. "The blood from your cut mixed with Bleddyn's. Then when you took him into the fire, the flames flowed into his bloodstream with your blood, burning away the darkness."

Emotions now under control, Meredythe leaned back in Bleddyn's arms and glared at him. "You still owe me an apology about all that virgin nonsense—a big one."

He grinned. "I'm sorry."

"I'm sorry! That's all?" She struggled to free herself.

Bleddyn pulled her into a tight hug and whispered in her ear, "I'll take you to dinner tonight. Then when we get home I'll show you all the different ways a werewolf can make love."

Meredythe crossed her arms over her chest. "Okay, that's a start."

"Now that everybody is fine, I'll be going," interrupted Damian, nodding his head in an eastward direction.

Meredythe turned to Damian, her reporter's curiosity beginning to stir. "It's true then that vampires can't be out in the sun? Are all those legends about garlic, holy water and all that stuff true too?"

Damian smiled. "I don't have time to answer your questions now, but feel free to visit me anytime. I'll tell you everything you want to know." He turned away.

She scrambled after him. "Wait, where do you live?"

He glanced at Bleddyn and shook his head. "The east tower. Bleddyn bought Winterbourne from me." Then he was gone.

Spinning around, Meredythe glared at Bleddyn. "What else is there about you I don't know?"

Grinning, he held up his hands. "Nothing. I promise."

She raked his naked body with her irate gaze. "Wouldn't you be more comfortable with some clothes on?" She rubbed her arms. "It's cold out here."

Methuselah twined between her legs. *He's part canine. That makes him too dimwitted to know any better.*

She picked up the cat and cuddled him in her arms. "Thuse is nice and furry. Holding him will warm you up."

Both Bleddyn and the cat growled.

Chuckling, Rhys said, "Come along, children. It's time to go home."

Why an electronic book?

We live in the Information Age—an exciting time in the history of human civilization, in which technology rules supreme and continues to progress in leaps and bounds every minute of every day. For a multitude of reasons, more and more avid literary fans are opting to purchase e-books instead of paper books. The question from those not yet initiated into the world of electronic reading is simply: *Why?*

1. ***Price.*** An electronic title at Ellora's Cave Publishing and Cerridwen Press runs anywhere from 40% to 75% less than the cover price of the exact same title in paperback format. Why? Basic mathematics and cost. It is less expensive to publish an e-book (no paper and printing, no warehousing and shipping) than it is to publish a paperback, so the savings are passed along to the consumer.
2. ***Space.*** Running out of room in your house for your books? That is one worry you will never have with electronic books. For a low one-time cost, you can purchase a handheld device specifically designed for e-reading. Many e-readers have large, convenient screens for viewing. Better yet, hundreds of titles can be stored within your new library—on a single microchip. There are a variety of e-readers from different manufacturers. You can also read e-books on your PC or laptop computer. (Please note that Ellora's Cave does not endorse any specific brands.

You can check our websites at www.ellorascave.com or www.cerridwenpress.com for information we make available to new consumers.)

3. ***Mobility.*** Because your new e-library consists of only a microchip within a small, easily transportable e-reader, your entire cache of books can be taken with you wherever you go.
4. ***Personal Viewing Preferences.*** Are the words you are currently reading too small? Too large? Too... ANNOYING? Paperback books cannot be modified according to personal preferences, but e-books can.
5. ***Instant Gratification.*** Is it the middle of the night and all the bookstores near you are closed? Are you tired of waiting days, sometimes weeks, for bookstores to ship the novels you bought? Ellora's Cave Publishing sells instantaneous downloads twenty-four hours a day, seven days a week, every day of the year. Our webstore is never closed. Our e-book delivery system is 100% automated, meaning your order is filled as soon as you pay for it.

Those are a few of the top reasons why electronic books are replacing paperbacks for many avid readers.

As always, Ellora's Cave and Cerridwen Press welcome your questions and comments. We invite you to email us at Comments@ellorascave.com or write to us directly at Ellora's Cave Publishing Inc., 1056 Home Avenue, Akron, OH 44310-3502.

Cerridwen, the Celtic Goddess of wisdom, was the muse who brought inspiration to storytellers and those in the creative arts. Cerridwen Press encompasses the best and most innovative stories in all genres of today's fiction. Visit our site and discover the newest titles by talented authors who still get inspired - much like the ancient storytellers did, once upon a time.

Cerridwen Press

www.cerridwenpress.com

Discover for yourself why readers can't get enough of the multiple award-winning publisher Ellora's Cave.

Whether you prefer e-books or paperbacks, be sure to visit EC on the web at www.ellorascave.com for an erotic reading experience that will leave you breathless.

LaVergne, TN USA
11 January 2011
212024LV00002B/94/P

9 781419 957390